National Acclaim for

THE RISE OF THE STASHI EMPIRE

Self Published

Second Edition © 2017 by Del Simpers III

Paperback ISBN: 978-1973352310

This book is dedicated to anyone who has ever lost hope or hit a tough spot in their life. Keep fighting. Some of our greatest work comes at our darkest hour. It's only in a game winning buzzer beater when mere seconds before the winners were losing. Always keep hope alive, no matter what. It's all we have.

—Del Simpers III

Table of Contents

Chapter 1 1

Chapter 2 5

Chapter 3 7

Chapter 4 9

Chapter 5 11

Chapter 6 14

Chapter 7 17

Chapter 8 20

Chapter 9 24

Chapter 10 26

Chapter 11 29

Chapter 12 31

Chapter 13 33

Chapter 14 34

Chapter 15 36

Chapter 16 39

Chapter 17 42

Chapter 18 47

Chapter 19 50

Chapter 20 53

Chapter 21 58

Chapter 22 61

Chapter 23 66

Chapter 24 70

Chapter 25 74

Chapter 26 77

Chapter 27 79

Chapter 28 83

Chapter 29 85

Chapter 30 88

Chapter 31 92

Chapter 32 94

Chapter 33 96

Chapter 34 99

Chapter 35 102

Chapter 36 106

Chapter 37..108
Chapter 38..111
Chapter 39..114
Chapter 40..117
Chapter 41..122
Chapter 42..125
Chapter 43..130
Chapter 44..133
Chapter 45..138
Chapter 46..143
Chapter 47..149
Chapter 48..152
Chapter 49..158
Chapter 50..161
Chapter 51..168
Chapter 52..174
Chapter 53..179
Chapter 54..183
Chapter 55..190
Chapter 56..197
Chapter 57..206
Chapter 58..214
Chapter 59..217
Chapter 60..224
Chapter 61..231
Chapter 62..238
Chapter 63..243
Chapter 64..250
Chapter 65..254
Chapter 66..257
Chapter 67..265
Chapter 68..272
Chapter 69..274
Chapter 70..280
Chapter 71..282
Chapter 72..285
Chapter 73..288

Chapter 74..293
Chapter 75..298
Chapter 76..303
Chapter 77..309
Chapter 78..313
Chapter 79..318
Chapter 80..322
Chapter 81..327
Chapter 82..330
Chapter 83..334
Chapter 84..337
Chapter 85..341
Chapter 86..343
Chapter 87..347
Chapter 88..351
Chapter 89..356
Chapter 90..358
Chapter 91..361
Chapter 92..362
Chapter 93..367
Chapter 94..371
Chapter 95..373
Chapter 96..374
Chapter 97..376
Chapter 98..377
Chapter 99..380
Chapter 100..383
Chapter 101..388
Chapter 102..392
Chapter 103..395
Chapter 104..398
Chapter 105..400
Chapter 106..405
Chapter 107..408
Chapter 108..411
Chapter 109..413
Chapter 110..416
Chapter 111..419

Some people can solely entertain themselves, but by doing so, they'll barely survive. That is why God created a system where you must share with the rest of the world. His gifts must be transferred into joy for others which in turn sparks creativity, happiness, and innovation. Share unconditionally.

THE

RISE

OF

THE

STA$HI

EMPIRE

Del Simpers III

Brace yourself for the story of a lifetime....

Chapter 1

"WHERE THE *HELL* IS THE CASH AND THE STASH AT?"

As the masked men pointed a gun in my face, I trembled. "*Who are these guys?*" I thought to myself. I had never seen them before in my life, but it had to be someone close to me who knew my business.

"I'll ask you one more time…" said the masked man slowly. The bandit cocked the hammer back on the gun calmly. "Where is the cash and the stash?" I was petrified but quiet. I wasn't going to surrender everything that easily. I clenched my teeth.

"Oh, we got a tough guy here." The second bandit hit me over the head with the pistol handle. I fell to my knees.

Ruff! Ruff!

Lucky me. I had just put my dog Champ in his cage before I had answered the door. He would always get stir crazy whenever I smoked weed. He would've given these guys a run for their money. One bandit is tearing up my living room and kitchen rummaging through everything. The other one has his pistol aimed at me.

"Nothing in here." The bandit picks me up, drags me into the bedroom, and drops me on the ground, feet away from my mattress. "You better hope to God there's money in here or we're going to kill you!"

"Screw you!"

Crunch!

The bandit kicks me in my face. Hard. I think that crunch was the sound of my nose breaking. They start tearing up my bedroom. Pulling out cabinets, knocking down pictures, and then they lift up my mattress. Nooo. I think to myself. I could feel the blood trickling down my face from that gun blow to the head. Their eyes lit up.

"Bingo!" They let out a low hum of astonishment. "You really keep all of this under the mattress?" one of them questioned. Everything I had worked so hard for was about to be taken by Tweedle Dum and Tweedle Dumber. The bandits start grabbing the pillows on the bed and taking them out of their cases.

I can see them smiling devilishly through their ski masks. I hate thieves with a passion. You lazy bastards. You need to put your own work in! I'm thinking this while I'm watching them stuff my pillowcases with my money.

"Y'all are SCUM!" I yelled. The bandits looked at me. The one on the left side of the bed walks over to me again. I'm trying to muster up enough energy to grab his weapon.

"Shut up!" He pulls out his gun and points it at me. I reach out to try to grab it.

Ruff! RUFF!

Champ is barking nonstop. He can smell the danger. He pulled the weapon back and kicked me back down. I knew that I was playing a dangerous game since they had no other use for me. I tried to scramble to get back up. I wasn't going out like a chump. He took two steps back. I could see the animosity in his eyes. He raised the gun. I ducked my head.

Bang!

I wake up on my back, staring at the spinning ceiling fan, in a puddle of blood. I feel lightheaded. My whole body aches. My vision is fuzzy. It's dark except for the dim moonlight shining through the window. My head is throbbing every other second. I can feel my brain swelling up against my skull. I breathe slow and deep. I just want to be still. Blood is everywhere. I can taste it, bitter and metallic. I can feel it. I can smell it. It wasn't until I felt my hand run along the floor that I realize how much blood I've lost. Most of my body was soaked in the warm, red fluid. I'm feeling a combination of being lightheaded and numb. I'm so disoriented mentally that I need to concentrate just to regain my coordination. "Daamn!" I thought to myself. I have to get help quick, or else I am going to die in this puddle. My hands start trembling, and my teeth start chattering. I am getting colder and colder. I have to get to my phone. I try to remember where was the last place I had it before this whole incident took place—oh yeah, the coffee table. I was watching TV in there when I heard the knock at the door.

Arrrrrhhhhhh!

I grunted heavily as I try to ignore the sharp pain throbbing throughout my body. I roll over on my stomach. All I feel is warm soggy carpet through my palms and fingers. I clench my hands into a fist and start to army crawl on my forearms. Now I'm so lightheaded that I feel sloppy drunk. I've lost all feeling in my legs. I feel tears rolling down my face as I am crawling. I don't think it's from the pain either. I think it's from the fact that I can never have anything without someone taking it away from me.

I stopped crawling. Hell, maybe I should just die right here? Maybe this is how it was supposed to end? Maybe this is how I want it to end? I mean, if I clock out now I won't have to put up with this crooked world's nonsense anymore. No more suffering, no more threats, and no more loneliness. The more I think about it, the more I start fading out of consciousness. Take me now Lord. I think I'm ready.

Then I thought about my mom. She would have no one left, no one to go to church with, no one to spend Christmas with. She'd cry her heart out once she found out about this. She would never truly be happy for the rest of her life. She would just grow old, miserable, and bitter. I couldn't do that to her.

Snap out of it Randy! Fight! Fight for life! To hell with them! They're going to have to try harder to kill off this spirit.

"Arrrrrggghhhhh!" I yell again. I pull my head up and focus on my destination. Come on Randy! You're almost there!

Right elbow down. Left elbow down. My heart feels like it's about to beat out of my chest. Right elbow down. Left elbow down. There's only one thing keeping me alive right now—adrenaline.

The coffee table is getting closer. Only a little more to go. Right elbow down. Left elbow down. I squirm in between the couch and Lazy Boy chair. I reach out my hand and grab the phone. I start fading out again. Focus Randy! *Focus*!

I look at the phone. I push the buttons as quickly as I can, but everything seems like it's in slow motion. "Nine...one...one....talk" I put the phone on speaker, and put my head down. A woman's voice talks slowly on the phone.

"Nine one one. What's your emergency?"

I mumbled gruffly with the last energy I had left in my body.

"Ughhh eighteen... Ugh...fifty-two Creekway Court... ambulance... noooow!"

"Sir, what did you say?" The sound of her voice gradually faded to mute. My breathing began to slow, and I closed my eyes.

That's when my vision turned bright white.

Chapter 2

It's black. I hear noises. Where am I? What happened?

I died. I had to have died.

I called the ambulance, and they didn't make it. That was the last thing I remember before I faded out. Well, I had fun being Randy Stashi. I had gone from the slow to the fast life quicker than a zero to sixty acceleration time. Honestly, I really wanted to live just a little bit longer. There were still a couple more places I wanted to see, people I wanted to party with, and women that I still wanted to bone.

Maybe I'm not in heaven though. I mean, my first thoughts were sex that I wished I had.

Is this heaven or hell? Heaven should be bright and fun, like a reunion, shouldn't it?

I hear my mom's voice low in the background. It sounded like sad mumbles. Why am I hearing my mom in heaven? I hear beeping in the background. Maybe I'm not in heaven. Maybe I'm alive.

I try opening my eyes. I hear the beeping getting louder. Then there was light.

I hear my mom's voice getting louder. Even with the lights, everything is blurry. I hear screams as fuzzy silhouettes stand over me. As my vision adjusts, I see my mom on the right of me, mouth wide open. On the left side is the nurse. Her back is turned while she adjusts the machines.

"ARGHHHHHHHHHH!" My mom let out a high-pitched, shrill scream. Yep. That's the confirmation right there.

I'm alive. I feel horrible, but at least I'm alive. I can feel my blood start to rush, as I am overwhelmed with joy. The swelling on my face must've made my smile look more painful than peaceful. It was probably a smile that only a mother could love. I made it!

"THANK YOU, GOD! THANK YOU, GOD! HALLELUJAH! YOU ARE THE POWERFUL, THE MERCIFUL!"

My mom's yells could wake up the dead.

My vision is blurry and still keeps fading in and out.

Do my arms still work?

I slowly raise my left hand. While it's raised, I wave it back and forth like a president waves.

Check.

I slowly raise my right hand. Repeat. Check.

"What are you doing?" questioned my mom with a stern gaze. I tuned her out mentally and focused back on the task at hand.

I try to lift my left leg a few inches. I can only bend my knee. Whoa, what's going on?

I try to lift my right leg. It doesn't move at all. I can feel my face get hot. I start to panic. I try again—nothing.

I began to cry.

My world began to fade back to black.

Chapter 3

I awoke in darkness. Phew. What a dream that was!

I'm glad I'm in my warm bed, at my comfortable apartment, with my dog Champ.

As I reach for the alarm clock on my nightstand to discover what time it is, I feel an awkward cold metal railing. That's odd, I don't have a railing next to my bed. Where am I?

The sad epiphany slowly sets in like devastating news always does. This isn't my bed, and that wasn't a dream. This is real. This is a real-life nightmare. I tried to remember all the details leading to this point. I was watching TV, then a knock, then the guns, pain, and blood, and now I'm here. The scariest part of it all was the darkness. The more I remembered, the more my astonishment grew. I couldn't believe I was still here, breathing—and alive.

Suddenly, I feel a panic surge throughout my body. It takes my breath away, and I can feel my chest caving in. I feel helpless and confined like I am trapped between the bed railings. The walls seem like they are slowly coming closer and closer to my bed. I am trying to breathe, but all I am doing is choking on spit.

I think I'm having a panic attack. I squirm to the edge of the bed to get on my feet.

I *need air*!

I push myself off the bed and onto my feet. I can hear the tubes snatch out of my body. The disconnection must've triggered the alarm. I continue to pull the remaining cords from my body as I dismount the bed.

I fell down to the ground like a Slinky. I can't feel my legs. I just lay there, motionless, discouraged, beaten.

I hear the door open.

"I need help in here! NOW!" the nurse yells. She has spotted my limp body outstretched across the tiled linoleum floor. I hear her rushing over to me, and moving my body. I feel her cold, old wrinkly hands grasp around my neck. "Help! Hurry!" she reiterated. My whole life had turned upside down within

7

mere minutes. Just when I thought it was getting better, it had taken a sharp turn. More quick footsteps entered the room. "He's unconscious, but he's still breathing!" I hear them yell.

But I wish I wasn't conscious. I wish I wasn't breathing.

Chapter 4

I will never be the same again. That's not what the doctor said exactly but, it might as well be what she said.

I can't believe this right now.

I was trying to earn enough for a better life, and I'm worse off than when I started. At least when I was broke as hell, I could walk by myself. Now, it seems like I have to depend on everybody for anything.

"NUUUUURRRRSSEEE!"

My appetite had been nonexistent. Loss of a limb sensation and depression can really take the excitement out of eating. For some reason today though, I'm starving.

"NUUUUURRRRR—!"

The door opens before I can finish my yell.

The nurse is a small framed woman a little over five feet. She looked in her mid-fifties with some wrinkles around her eyes. Her bright red curly hair reminded me of Carrot Top. Maybe that's why I call her in here so much. I always loved Carrot Top.

"Yesssss? What's going on?" she asked. By the way she drug out the yes, I could tell she was aggravated.

"Edna, I'm hungry." She gives me a blank stare in disbelief.

"Randy, you just told me you didn't want your lunch today when I brought it in here an hour ago...."

"I know, I wasn't hungry then, but just now, my stomach sang an off-key song to me." She smiled at me while checking my vitals. You can tell she's biting her tongue. I was a little bit obnoxious before all of this, but this incident just made it worse. Much worse.

"I will be back with your lunch, Mr. Stashi." She turned her back toward me and began walking to the door. Before she reaches the door, she turns around swiftly. "Is there anything else?" I think of all the things I could ask for; money, legs, another shot at life.

"Can you bring an extra applesauce?" That was the only request I knew she could deliver.

"Sure." She exits the room, and I am left back in this cold silence. Of all the things I could ask for, the thought of applesauce was my only joy. I begin to cry again.

Why God? Why?

Chapter 5

"You know Randy, time heals all wounds." I usually hate hearing the philosophical quote, but the way my mom said it, it was comforting.

"Yeah, Mommy, except for this wound." I pointed to my leg with a serious face.

"Don't say that Randy; if God brought Jesus back, surely it is nothing to bring back your leg." Sigh.... I let out a deep breath. As much as I wanted to believe her, I couldn't. The sooner I accept this fate, the less my disappointment will be. "Besides, the doctor said he's seen rare cases where rehabilitation has restored feeling in the limbs..." Mom said.

"KEYWORDS, MOM. RARE. Are ay are eee. You know what that means? Not frickin' me!" I yelled. I feel my blood rushing as I get angry laying in the bed.

"DON'T FEED ME THAT BULL!" My mom looked startled by my reaction. Her face droops down, and I see her eyes watering up.

"Don't talk to me like that, Randy.... I'm your mother!" I see her trying to hide her emotions behind reprimanding me. My mom has a caring, tender heart. Sometimes, I forget how gentle I have to be with her. I hate seeing her hurt in any way because she doesn't deserve it no matter what it is. I reached out my arms to hug her.

"I'm sorry, Mommy. This is just very *hard* for me right now." She picks up her head and reaches her hands behind my back to hug me. She grabs and holds me firmly. I start to feel her warm tears running down the side of my face. This is not what my intentions were. It's ironic how you risk everything to buy your mom the finer things so she can be happy. Then when it backfires, she ends up having to buy *you* things just to stay alive.

I've never been much of a crier before. I always thought that was for the weak, but this month has been a never-ending tear jerker.

"The doctor said you start rehabilitation next week," she told me.

"Rehabilitation?... For what? I thought I would be going home next week. I wanna go home. Please don't make me stay here." The mere thought of staying any longer than next week had me contemplating suicide. Why didn't

11

they just kill me then? Why? Now I'm forced to wake up every day in this hell. I wish I were in heaven right now. At least I could use both of my legs.

"We're going home, baby. I will help you move your stuff out of your apartment—"

"WHAAAAAT?" I yelled. My mom looked startled and in shock by my reaction.

"I mean umm, that's not necessary, Mom. Tracy can take care of me. I'll be fine."

"Tracy has her own life son, her own priorities. She's not your caretaker. What's going to happen if y'all get into a fight?" she asked.

"We don't fight, Mom, and we're in love."

"You don't even have a job, much less a way of getting one.... Who's going to pay the rent, the lights, your groceries? I don't have enough for my house and your apartment, baby."

My mom was always the voice of reason. She could talk sense into the most ignorant person alive, by speaking slowly and staring into their eyes. Today, however, I'm more ignorant than the most ignorant person alive.

"Tracy makes enough money for us, Mommy. We'll be okay..." I reassured her. It wasn't that I didn't like staying with my mom, but I had already moved out once and for good. I swore up and down, time after time again that I would never live under that roof again. To take a step back would be an embarrassing confirmation of failure. Take a step back? Even if I remotely wanted to, my foolish pride wouldn't let me.

"I'm going to have a talk with Tracy, Randy."

"No, you aren't, Mommy!"

"You need a *mother*, not some fly-by-night floozie Susie! I was put on this earth to mold you and care for you. I need to do my job. Look at yourself, baby.... I let you move from under my roof, and look at you now. You were nearly killed over only *God* knows what!"

Sigh. My mom could be a real migraine sometimes. I didn't want to argue with her, but I couldn't go back to her house. That would set me back mentally. I am already set back physically. How do I play this one? Think quickly, Randy!

I know, act unconscious. I look at my mom then I slowly close my eyelids and roll my head back.

"RANDY? RANDY?" I could hear my mom yelling at me.

"I KNOW YOU HEAR ME, RANDY! DON'T PLAY DEAD WITH ME!"

I just started thinking happy thoughts, like life before this fiasco. I can slowly hear her voice get quieter and quieter. My world starts to go dim.

Nighty night.

Chapter 6

I wake up groggy being pushed in a wheelchair down a bright hospital hallway. The ammonia smell is so pungent my nostrils begin to flare. I breathe deep while I turn around to see who's pushing me. I nearly choke on the air from the strong ammonia. I think to myself this stuff could get you high. I breathe deeper.

It's my nurse, Edna, who is pushing me. She smiles while I look back.

A feeling of warmth, comfort, and security overwhelm me. I had grown to love Edna. No matter how pissy I was toward her, she was always cheerful and kind spirited toward me. I didn't mean to treat her bad, but this incident really had me in a bad mood twenty-four seven. Her attitude could really heal someone, probably anyone—just not me right now.

"Where are we going, Edna?"

I hear Edna chuckle behind me at my question.

"You're going home, Randy."

"What? Wait! What?"

"You heard me. It's time to go home, sweetheart." I put my hands on the wheels to stop the wheelchair suddenly. Edna trips over herself by how suddenly the chair stops. I feel her bump into the back of me and the chair tilts over. I topple onto the floor, *hard*. I should've rethought that plan of action.

"Sorry, Sorry!" I hear Edna apologize as she picks the wheelchair up. The ground is hard and cold. I feel the bare parts of my skin touching the cold linoleum through the hospital gown.

"Sorry, sorry Randy.... I'm so sorry." She wraps her arms around my midsection and starts to lift me up in the wheelchair.

"What do you mean, I'm going home?" I questioned Edna with a stern gaze. I wasn't too fond of hospitals, but I was nowhere near ready to accept the reality of my new life and living conditions.

"Randy...you're leaving this hospital. There's nothing else we can do for you here. We have to let nature run its course and let your body heal naturally. I'm going to miss you, and I wish you the best."

I clenched my teeth. I wasn't in the mood for Edna's sappiness. Plus, it was all fake gibberish anyway. Edna has thousands of patients a month, you think she really is going to give a damn about me once I am more than ten feet out of this building?

"Who's picking me up?" I asked while I repositioned my body in the wheelchair.

Edna gets behind me and begins to push again.

"Take a guess." she instructed.

A pleasant thought made me break out into a warm smile. Maybe it was Tracy waiting for me. Yeah. She would be the one to nurse me back to health. She would hug me, hold me, and kiss me. Then possibly on the way back to my house, I could get some sloppy, wet fellatio. Oh, oh yeeeah. Then she would cook my favorite meal and give me a back massage until I faded into a deep sleep. She would cater to my every need, spoon feed me hot soup while she'd be dressed up in a seductive nurse outfit with fishnet stockings. I chuckled at my imagination. If she was my nurse, I might never want to get better.

"I don't know who, Edna...." I answered innocently.

"Well, I'm not going to ruin the surprise for you," she replied with glee.

Her answer made me suspect that Tracy was coming to pick me up even more. Edna knew I loved her to death by the way I would refuse medication and naps whenever she was coming to visit me.

We took the elevator to the lobby. I was silent for most of the ride. This was the first time I had been out of my hospital room in what seemed like eons. It's always fascinating to see people in the midst of their hustle and bustle. With everyone focused on their own priorities and obligations, who has the time to care about little 'ole me? Tracy would. She was the world to me, and I knew I meant the world to her too. I felt it in my heart. She would be the one to be there for me. Our love was too strong. Plus, we had already talked about it at the hospital.

We rode through the hallways, past the gift shop and restaurant, to the front entrance. I slowly scanned my line of vision from left to right. No one familiar in sight.

15

"Where is she?" I asked Edna while twisting my body to look at her.

"She probably went to get the car," she mumbled while gazing through the parking lot. Not even ten seconds later, an older model blue Taurus pulled up. I knew exactly who owned this car. All of the energy in my body deflated within the blink of an eye. She parked in front of my wheelchair and got out.

"You ready to come home, sweetie?"

The worst had come true. It was my mother. Damn. Damn. Damn! I could feel my freedom and independence draining from my body, as I soaked up the thought of living back at home again. A queasy feeling suddenly interrupted my thought process, and my stomach turned over into knots. A sour taste formed in the back of my throat. My face started to scrunch up in pain. Everything started moving in slow motion, and I began to feel lightheaded and dizzy. My body reacted the only way it knew how to this disgusting news.

I leaned over the wheelchair railing and began to throw up.

Chapter 7

I spent an excruciating amount of time thinking and reflecting while I was on bedrest. There were a lot of regrets, a lot of shoulda, woulda, coulda. Every day seemed easier, but it was still a long shot from the life I was living. I made my way into the kitchen.

"How are you feeling, soldier?"

My mother was the only person in the world who could make me feel like a champion when I was losing.

"Better." I could've given a longer answer, but I was still bitter and embarrassed at having to need my mother's help again. Just when I was starting to become completely independent with my girlfriend, everything was taken from me.

"Can you feel your leg yet? The doctor said your injury isn't permanent so every day your recovery should progress." I stared into my mother's eyes blankly after she finished her hypothetical nonsense.

"I can't feel a thing!" The crystal ball the doctor must've been reading from wasn't working. My mother cut me a look that I'll never forget. She looked surprised and sad at the same time. I know she hated my brashness, but she could also hear the frustration in my voice.

"I know you feel helpless baby, but you're going to have to change your attitude."

"What attitude, *Mom*? I'm back to being shackled up under my mom's roof, my girlfriend left me, and I can't feel my effin legs." It's crazy how a downward spiral can be summed up in one short sentence. How quickly months of work can be taken in minutes.

"I know it feels like your world is over, but you're only twenty years old. You have your whole life in front of you. What was your plan? Break the law until you got rich, and live happily ever after with your girlfriend?" I know she was being sarcastic, but it did sound like a foolish fairy tale. I just looked at her in silence. I had no response to that last statement. The truth had taken my breath away.

"Not get rich, mom, just support myself until I found a better way."

"Now look at you…" she snapped cutting me off, "I have to support you again!"

"Mom, this is only temporary until I get back on my…" I couldn't even complete the sentence. The pun was unintentional. My mother could see the sadness and discomfort in my face as my voice trailed off. She lowers her voice back to a soft, soothing whisper.

"All I am saying is this…. You need a plan, son. You're young. You have energy. You should use that to your advantage. If your leg heals tomorrow, what would you do?"

"If my leg healed tomorrow, then I would move out," I said coldly. I hated living back under my mother's roof. Every second here was torture. I could see the disappointment in her face by my answer. She knew I was only here because of my circumstances.

"Moving out won't solve anything. You still need a job with income and a plan for your career. You're growing up, Stashi. What do you want to accomplish in life?" I stared at her blankly. That was a great question that did not have an answer. My quest for independence had ended exactly where it had started—my mom's house. Even though I was living on my own, I had no real goals except to get as much money as possible and live independently. The highlights of my day included smoking the finest weed that I could get my hands on, and blowing my girlfriend's back out. I always thought that a better opportunity would present itself when the time was right, so I never felt the pressure to step up my hustle. Now, with the addition of these traumatic events, I had a couple of new challenges to overcome. I wanted to walk again.

"I want to walk again." I let my last thought be the answer to her question.

"You've already walked before. Therefore, you can't accomplish that again. And what if you don't regain control of your leg, baby? Are you just going to give up on other gifts that you might have?" She shrugged her shoulders.

"I have no dreams, Mom. All I ever wanted to do is have my own things and be filthy rich."

"Being filthy rich is a dream, son. Being independent is a dream, son. Those are dreams that don't require walking." She smiled as she said that last line, and I realized that she was right. I have to start focusing on what I have to do. I could still be rich because I am still alive. I'm still above ground. That

18

epiphany made me smirk.

"You're right, Mommy. I love you."

"I love you too. Now eat your food before it gets cold," she instructed.

I tasted it.

The food was already ice cold.

Chapter 8

Ring… Ring… Ring… Click. "Hi! You've reached the voicemail box of Tracy Reynolds, I'm not in right now so please leave a message or text me. Buh bye." Beep. Click.

Man, what a snake! I had shared everything that I possibly could with her, and now look where I am. I can't even get her to reply to a text. Everyone wants to ride when the car is running, but catch a flat, and they vanish. There's not a feeling worse in the world than the feeling of being betrayed.

This whole time we were wining and dining, smoking and poking, I thought we were in love, but she was just joking. I initially thought our feelings were mutual. However, as the days progressed and I pondered it more, maybe she was just in love with what I had to offer her. It wasn't until I was alone, moping around my mom's house, that I felt played like a sucker. She came to the hospital a handful of times but went MIA right after that. Maybe I wasn't even in love. Maybe I was just infatuated with the fact that I had a stunning girl who was actually into me. I mean, she had dark curly hair, big juicy tiddies, and a fat round behind that would demand anyone's attention. All of my guy friends were jealous of us, and I think that motivated me to keep her. I mean, we had only been together for two years, but *two* years is a long time when you're only twenty. That's like a tenth of your life. Now, I can't even get a Facebook like from her. She played me like a fiddle and left me behind like an orphan.

"*Mom!*" I waited for her to answer from upstairs. Before I moved out the upstairs room was mine, but due to these recent events, we had traded rooms. "MOOOM!" This time I dragged her name out a little bit longer in the annoying tone that she hated.

"WHAT?" she answered back in an aggravated tone.

"Has Tracy called the house?" I texted her my home phone number because sometimes my cell phone reception liked to play games.

"I haven't heard the phone ring, sweetie."

"Is the ringer on?"

"Hold on…" Ten long seconds of silence pass as I'm guessing she's scrolling through the missed calls.

"…Yes, baby. She called twice."

I could feel a sigh of relief rush over my entire body. I smiled from ear to ear. She still loved me.

"Did she leave a message?"

"No."

"Okay, thanks, Mommy."

I reached over for my phone on the dresser and unlocked it. Hmm… Should I call or text her? I was so used to playing macho slash nonchalant around her that I didn't know how to express my true feelings. I had already called her once today, so I decided not to overkill it, and text her.

"Hey, big head, wya? -XOXO"

I always called her big head for two reasons. Reason number one, was because her forehead did protrude out slightly. Reason number two was to humble her slightly. Sometimes, these dudes pumped her head up so much it might explode. Yes, she was gorgeous, but appearance isn't everything. Spoiling her with compliments will only develop a high siddity complex. Even though I hadn't seen her since the hospital, Tracy knew what I was over here going through. I had to move my things out of my apartment by myself and was left to recover, by myself. As I waited anxiously for her text response, I started thinking about my injuries. What if she didn't want to date me anymore because of my new ailment? What if my manhood isn't up for the job? What if she doesn't want to take care of me at all? The more time that passed awaiting her response, the more insecure I got. Maybe she just wasn't that into me.

Five minutes passed. Then twenty minutes passed. After thirty minutes passed, I was tired of waiting. I reached over for my phone to text her again. I could feel my anger starting to surge after the disappointment of her not responding in a timely fashion. I'm about to let her have a piece of my mind. I began texting rapidly.

"I…Can't…Frickin'…Believe…You…Stupid…"

Knock! Knock!… Ding dong!

I looked in the direction of the front door, alarmed.

Dun dun dun!

I could hear my mother stomping down the stairs. Whoever was at the door had me temporarily distracted. Maybe it was someone for me, I hoped. This place had me wishing for visitors like I was incarcerated.

"Who is it?" No answer. I made my way to my bedroom door to open it. I've got to learn how to get better at moving around in this wheelchair.

"Who *isss* it?" my mother asked again louder.

Ding dong!

The mystery person at the door wasn't playing by the rules. My mom looked slowly through the peephole. Then she turned deliberately and smiled at me.

"It's Tracy," she whispered. My head jerked up. "Should I let her in?" she asked quietly. She kind of knew that we weren't on the best of terms.

"Tracy?" I said shocked. Never would've imagined her out of all the people. Hell, I was just about to cuss her out via text message. Her? Here? Now? I was startled yet excited at the same time. I didn't even have to answer my mom's question. She could tell by my facial expression that I wanted to see her. She turned around and clicked both the deadbolts clockwise. She pulls the doorknob, and the door seemed to creak open in slow motion. Bright blinding sunlight pierced through the doorway. There she was, my baby, glowing brightly with a smile with the aura of an angel. She was wearing a sexy pastel-colored sundress and smiling radiantly with a card and roses in her hand.

"RANDYYYYY!"

She ran up and hugged me while trying to fight back tears.

"Baby, I'm so glad you are finally out of the hospital. I've been worried so dearly about you that all I've been doing is praying that you have a speedy recovery. I stopped visiting you because I hated seeing you in so much pain. I'm just happy you're recovering so well. They said surviving an attack like the one you did was nothing short of a miracle. DON'T YOU EVER SCARE ME LIKE THAT AGAIN! DO YOU HEAR ME RANDY? NEVER AGAIN."

I could hear my mom marching back up the stairs in the background. Judging by the stomps, I don't think that she was too fond of Tracy being over. Oh well, she'll have to.

"I'll let you two be alone," she announced as she reached the top of the stairs. We were still hugging each other tightly, and I could feel her wet tears start to run down my face.

"I thought you left me, baby," she whispered in my ear. I was still astonished by her surprising house visit.

"Let's go to my room."

It's crazy how five minutes ago I hated this girl, I mean, absolutely loathed her. I hated every second and dollar that I'd spent with that disloyal and ungrateful bum. Now that she was here, hugging and crying on me, I felt like I couldn't live life without her.

"Come this way."

She got behind my wheelchair, wheeled me into my room, and closed the door behind us.

"How do you feel, baby?"

"Terrible," I answered without hesitation.

"How does this feel?" She grabbed my hand and placed it on her booty. She knew I loved her rump.

"I'm starting to feel a little better, I guess...."

"Oh really?... Only a *little*, huh?"

I was lying. I could feel my manhood growing hard as steel in my pants, and my heartbeat began to thump faster. It was officially time to rekindle the flame.

Chapter 9

I pinched her behind.

"Aaah!" She reacted playfully, but too loud.

"Shh… Keep it down! My mom's in the other room." I pulled her hair more. She closed her mouth completely, and her moans became muffled. I laid on my back and watched her ride me slowly. Her soft plump cheeks felt like pillows bouncing on my thighs. I wrapped her long black curly hair around my hand and pulled harder.

"Go faster, I'm almost there."

My breaths started becoming irregular and fast paced, as I felt the pressure growing in my balls.

"I'm…about…to…" I could feel my voice getting higher pitched. She hurriedly slid off my stick, turned around, and put it in her mouth. She sucked it back and forth while staring at me directly in my eyes with anticipation.

Nom. Nom. Nom.

The combination of that sucking sound plus her eyes staring into my eyes was too much. I could feel a numbing tingling sensation, the pressure of exploding my juices all in her juicy mouth.

"Aaaaaah" she moaned as she felt her mouth fill up with my thick frothy nut.

"Mmm…mmmmm…mmmm…" I groaned in ecstasy. She slowly removed her mouth from my shiny head and pursed her lips, so she didn't spill a drop.

"Don't spill it…. Swallow it…. Swal-low it!"

She closed her eyes, leaned her head back, and gulped. She opened her eyes slowly, looked at me and smiled.

"You missed some." There was still some of my milk on the corner of her mouth. I pushed it with my thumb onto her tongue. She wrapped her lips around my thumb and slowly sucked it, while I pulled it out leisurely. We were always pushing the envelope of nastiness.

Mopp!

My thumb made a suction sound when I pulled it out of her mouth.

"All gone," she announced.

"Aahhhh…" I exhaled. My entire body relaxed as I laid my head back on the wet pillow and closed my eyes. I could feel my sweat on the sheet under me. The last moments of our sexcapade replayed in my head.

What a nasty little freak she was, I thought to myself. I loved her so much because she gave me something irreplaceable—confidence. For the first time in a long time, it felt like everything was going to be all right.

Chapter 10

I felt her hand run across my stomach as she laid her head on my chest. I could feel her soft cheeks on my nipple. Damn, I realized that I really loved this girl. My breaths got slower and slower, and I felt myself drifting into a light sleep. Soon enough we were both knocked out.

Knock! Knock!

It must be my mom knocking. I loved how she respected my privacy. I got into my wheelchair and wheeled myself slowly to my bedroom door. I unlocked the doorknob and twisted it. I opened the door slowly and was greeted with the barrel of a gun.

"WE'RE BACK!! WHERE'S THE CASH AND THE...?"

"AHHHHHH!" I woke up sweating, gasping for air, with my heart racing. I looked around realizing it was just a nightmare. Thank God it was only a nightmare. I looked to my left. Tracy was no longer on my chest but curled up sleeping softly. What a beauty she was.

vvv. vvv. vvv.

I heard a vibration coming from across the room. Must've been Tracy's phone because I had my ringer on.

vvv. vvvvv. vvvv.

Then the vibrating stopped after ten seconds. I turned my head over to go back to sleep. Hopefully, no more nightmares. Just when I closed my eyes, I heard the vibration again.

vv. vvvv. vvvv.

Now that I think about it, that's pretty odd. Tracy loved showing off her favorite song by her ringtone, so why was her phone on vibrate all of a sudden? I couldn't think of an answer, so I made my way to her phone. Without waking her, I sat up and crawled to the edge of the bed. I reached for her purse and grabbed her phone out of it while it was still lit. The number calling was saved as the letter D. Who was D? I had to pick it up now. I hit accept but didn't say a word. I waited for whoever was calling to say something as I breathed heavily into the phone.

"Hey baby, you busy?" the mysterious caller asked in a gruff voice.

"Baby?" I repeated disgustedly with a sour face. "Who is this?"

"This is Montrell. Put Tracy on the phone, man."

"Naw bro, this is her boyfriend. She's sleeping."

"Boyfriend? Ha ha ha!" I could hear him laughing at me. My blood began to rush as I felt I was being toyed with. I remained quiet and let him speak.

"You sure you're her boyfriend? She's been at my house the past couple of days getting the snot banged out of her," he said scoffing.

"Yeah, right." I shrugged him off before I started thinking about what he said.

"Ha ha ha!" His laughter was piercing my eardrums as I clenched my teeth. The way he was carrying on, there had to be some truth to it.

"Is this Ralphy?" he asked. Wow, homeboy already knew of me.

"No, it's Randy." I corrected him in a menacing tone. "Randy Stashi."

"Well, whatever your name is, tell her to come over tonight. I got someone to cover my shift so we can go out again." I could feel myself exhaling slowly, letting the gravity of the situation sink in. I hung up the phone. There had to be some truth to what he was saying because I hadn't heard from her all week. The deceit, the treachery, the nerve of this chick. I started shaking her.

"Wake Up!" I shook her harder. "I said *wake up!*" She slowly awoke looking disgruntled.

"What? What?"

She could tell I was irritated. I passed her the phone, so she could look at it. She looked at it, looked bewildered, then looked at me.

"Montrell called!"

As I said it, she glared at me with nothing but fire and fury in her eyes.

"Why are you going through my phone?" she shot back. No denial of Montrell there.

"Awww…" I felt my heart fall to the ground as I realized I had been played for a fool.

"I didn't think you were going to recover so quickly.…"

"So, you went out, and forgot all about me, that freakin' quick?" She wasn't making any sense. She looked at me, then looked down and bit her lip. I could tell she was embarrassed. She knew she was in the wrong and was trying to figure out how to react.

"I've got to go, Randy!"

She rose from the bed and started picking her clothes up frantically off the ground. I was still in a state of shock, as I watched her get dressed.

"You have nothing else to say but 'I've got to go?' You ungrateful, unfaithful, disloyal…*HO!*"

"DON'T CALL ME THAT, RANDY!" she thundered while wagging her finger at me.

"ARRRGHH!" Now, I was furious. My mind sat there racing with a million questions, but I sat there speechless. Tracy was the light at the end of the tunnel that gave me hope and kept me thinking positively. Now I found out that was all a lie. She grabbed her belongings and headed for the door. She opened it slowly and turned around.

"I loved you, and I never meant to hurt you, Randy."

"Shuut Uppp LIAR!" I exclaimed vehemently. She gave me a cold stare after the vulgarity resonated in the air. Then she exited, slamming the door loudly behind her.

Whaaap!

I sat there for a couple of moments in silence. I felt empty, alone, betrayed, and hurt, all at once. She told me she loved me, and I really believed her. The only good thing I had going for me just walked out the door.

Sitting there all alone in silence helped me realize one thing…

My life sucks.

Chapter 11

"Honey…your food is getting cold."

The recent events of my break-up and nearly fatal injury threw me into a cold depression. I sat there motionless with a blank stare. My mom had the TV turned to The Window. She always watched The Window. It was a daytime hot gossip show, hosted by a wealthy sexy older woman named Porsha Gottfrey, who interviewed all of the globe's socialites. I disliked most talk shows because they were biased and had petty topics. However, her beauty and charm kept her on top. Porsha always had the who's who of the world while retaining a jam-packed audience. She had the highest ratings of all the talk show hosts, but as a male, most of the topics weren't catered to me. Which, in my eyes, is what made the show interesting and boring at the same time. I didn't really mind though, Porsha was so damn gorgeous, I could watch her all day long.

"I'm not hungry."

"You need to eat, honey. How else do you expect your body to heal without proper nourishment?"

I stirred my fork carelessly into the mashed potatoes.

"Well, have you thought about going back to the university? Your acceptance letters are still valid for another two years."

"Go to school and do what, Mom? Spend thousands of dollars going into debt learning subjects that I will never see again in life. Yeah, I thought about it, Mom, long and hard." It was more like quick and easy.

"You know what? I have a great idea, Mom. How about I mysteriously disappear like my low life dad did, and live happily ever after?"

My mom glared at me. I could see her eyes beginning to fill with water. Her mouth began to quiver, and I realized I had just taken it way too far.

"I didn't mean that, Mom."

Her fork clanked on the plate, and her seat grated against the floor as she pushed her chair away from the table. She stomped up the stairs noisily but didn't say a word. I knew I had just cut her—cut her deep. Great job, Randy, I thought to myself. Piss off everyone who is trying to help you get better. That

29

comment about my dad was a low blow. My personal misery was starting to make others miserable. I shoved a forkful of cold mashed potatoes into my mouth. They were so buttery and creamy that I had to close my eyes to savor every morsel.

"Mmm…"

I washed it down with a cold glass of water. Even though staying at my mom's house sometimes felt like hell, her cooking was straight out of heaven.

Dun… dun…dun…

She came back down the stairs five minutes later with red eyes and an old dusty forest green shoebox. She moved my plate out of the way and replaced it with the dusty shoebox.

"What's this?" I asked anxiously. My mom was always good at surprises.

"Open it!"

I opened it and gasped for breath.

"Wooooow" I was startled. No way in hell. My eyes couldn't believe what they were witnessing. Even though I had never seen him before, I knew who it was. After all these years, I could finally connect a face to my misery.

"No way…"

Chapter 12

I couldn't believe what was actually in front of me. It was an old, dusty box of all my dad's memories; pictures, envelopes, notepads, and even an old VHS tape. I picked up a picture and dusted it off. It was one of him and Mommy posing at a theme park. You can tell it was old by how high their pants were. My dad had put two fingers for bunny ears behind my mom's head. There was an unexplainable peace and calmness that poured over my body as I looked at their eyes in that picture. I was mesmerized.

"Your dad didn't disappear. He was killed." My mother's voice trembled as the words left her mouth. I glanced away at the picture to make full eye contact with her. Now, she had my full undivided attention.

"Killed?" I repeated it as if I didn't understand.

"Yes. He was killed before he even knew I was pregnant with you." I scrunched my face trying to process my mom's new stunning revelations.

"I don't know, how, when, or where but it was no accident. He was on to something—something big—something enlightening and they took him out." Her words lingered in the air. *Took him out.* What does she mean took him out? My attention focused back on the pictures. I flipped through them slowly, examining every detail. I had seen my dad maybe only twice in my life. I never cared to see him or what he looked like because I thought he had never cared to see me. Now that I knew the story, it was different. Now I cared.

"What was Dad's full name?" I asked. It felt weird even saying the word— Dad. I knew his first name was Ernest, and obviously, his last name was Stashi (because of my last name), but I didn't know his middle name.

She spoke softly and slowly pronouncing each syllable clearly and crisply

"Ernest… Stashi… Mla…Den…Ka…"

"Mladenka?" The last name threw me off. "Wait! Stashi wasn't his last name?"

"Noooo, sweetie. I gave you his middle name instead to protect you."

"Protect me?" I didn't even know I was in danger but Thank God I was, Stashi sounded way better than Mladenka.

"Yes, protect you from whoever put a stop to your dad."

"Mladenka is such a unique name. I did it to keep you out of harm's way."

I scrunched my eyebrows in confusion. My brain was still trying to comprehend everything that had been revealed to me in these last few minutes. Why did she switch my name? Is she just being overly paranoid, or was I really in grave danger like my father supposedly was?

I started to get dizzy. This was too much to comprehend all at once. I didn't even know what the truth was anymore. Sometimes things sound so unbelievable that they're actually believable.

Chapter 13

"He was the right-hand man to Steward Milde, who had also mysteriously disappeared." This was starting to sound unreal.

"What were they doing?" I asked. My mother smiled and nodded her head.

"Changing people's lives for the better."

"How?"

"You have to watch the tape, honey."

"I pulled the tape out and blew the light layer of dust that had collected on it. I marveled at it in awe. This tape had to be of dire importance if it had cost two people their lives. If this tape was the sole reason why I had never met my father, I knew it had to have something really important on there. Honestly, I was anxious, yet afraid at the same time. I could feel my stomach turn over in my belly as I got lightheaded.

"Do you even have a VCR, still?"

Chapter 14

We gathered around the television to watch the last memoir of my dad and his partner. The screen was fuzzy with sporadic static lines, but you could still see the picture and make out the sound. There was a gray-haired man with a nice pin-striped suit speaking eloquently into a microphone. He was obviously the host of the presentation and sitting behind him looking stern was my dad. I was still in awe at the sight of him. Our noses and chins were almost identical.

"And you know these people when you see them. It's raining, my dog died, I hate my job. They give off a contagious destructive energy that they want you to soak up. Pretty soon, you will be saying how much you hate the weather, how your job sucks or your pet will fall ill...."

"This is why I always ask you to change your attitude, son. Listen." My mom adlibbed.

"Winners don't win by luck, they win by focus, positivity, and their ability to visualize the finish line, which brings us to the subject of money. Do you know how much money the world has? Trillion, quadrillion...? Who knows? It doesn't matter. What matters is that we live in a world of abundance. There's no ceiling on how much a person can have. Just because someone has money doesn't mean that they're happy. There are no rules in this game of life—well, except for one—the rule of reciprocity. What's the rule of reciprocity, you ask? Well, it's not an actual stated rule, but an implied rule rather, a rule that is a mandatory guideline of all business and politics. If you scratch my back, I feel obligated to scratch your back, in some way, shape, form or fashion. Nothing is free. Whether it is a reciprocal gesture or money, I will feel the need to give back the energy that you spent on me. How many people here knows someone that goes to the same restaurant religiously?"

The hands shoot up slowly and sparsely throughout the crowd. Stewart raises his hand up as well.

"There're a million different restaurants, but this particular person only eats at this one because of the energy that the restaurant gives them. It makes them feel better about life. People will spend their last dollar if they feel the energy is worth it."

"This is some powerful stuff right here, honey," my mom noted to me in a volume barely above a whisper. I could see my dad on the TV nodding in agreement behind the speaker while he clicked the presentation slides. "Pay attention. It will change your life."

My eyes became glued to the TV again as I dissected everything the speaker was saying. You can be filthy rich, but first, you need to prioritize servicing the world. Once you find a way to please the world, the world will start pleasing you.

The information was like a breath of fresh air. I suddenly became overwhelmed with motivation and excitement while soaking up the words coming from the television. My purpose in life was beginning to dawn on me.

"How many people know about the principles that they were taught?" I asked my mom, still intrigued that this was my actual biological father on TV.

"Not very many, Son. Their show was always to a closed audience. This tape was actually your father's copy that he used to practice and perfect. They were trying to revolutionize the world before they were stopped cold in their tracks."

Before I saw this video, all I wanted to do was become filthy rich. Ironically, my father's whole mission in life was to open people's minds so that they could become filthy rich as well. I thought I had deviated from my own path, but I didn't. I was actually right on course to pick up where my father left off. My only hope was that it wouldn't cost me what it allegedly cost him. But maybe that's just speculation. Maybe I'm being overly paranoid.

Chapter 15

For the first time since my world was turned upside down, I had totally forgotten about my leg injury, staying under my mother's roof again, and my sorry excuse for a (now ex-)girlfriend, Tracy. I now had become immersed in the principles and doctrines of my father and his partner. I wanted to learn every meticulous detail about their beliefs. This had to be some eye-opening and very dangerous material if it had supposedly cost them their lives.

"You can't reap positive rewards with a negative mind." I wrote down everything important on the tape and then provided an example of it in the real world.

"Randy! Are you ready for your therapy appointment?" My mother interrupted my train of thought.

Damn! I forgot that was today. About twice a week I had to go to rehab to improve my leg injury. The medical staff told me my legs were slightly improving. It really sounded like a load of baloney to me just to keep me coming back spending money because I really couldn't feel a difference.

"Awww, do I have to?" I asked her honestly. I didn't even care. I thought it was a waste of time. I was trying to weasel my way out of today's meeting by any means necessary.

"How do you expect to walk again if you don't do what is required?" she asked in a matter-of-fact voice.

She was right. She was almost always right. Damn, I hated it when she was right.

"Change your attitude, and you'll reach—"

"A new altitude." I finished up the statement for her, unamusingly. We started speaking the same language. All of her little catch phrases could be traced back to that videotape. I finally understood her. I put away my tablet and pen and began to change into my workout clothes.

***

"All right Randy on three; one…two…"

The nurse was pretty cute. She had short red hair, looked like she could be in her late twenties. Her name was Chelsea. She had a sexy light voice and smelled delicious like sweet roses. Wishfully thinking if rehab came with a sponge bath, I would've probably tried to move in here. Yes, I sure would.

"Three!"

"Awrrrright…" I grunted as I pushed down on the wheelchair, and leaned on my left leg. I felt the nurse pull the wheelchair from under me.

"Okay Randy, just a couple of steps," she instructed as I grabbed onto the railing as I struggled to keep my balance. I closed my eyes as I felt the excruciating pain surge through my leg like a thousand daggers piercing my leg.

"I can't. I CAN'T!" The unbearable pain put me into submission.

"Yes, you can," she assured me.

I tried to shift my focus to something pleasant but I couldn't. The stinging sensation hurt too much. I toppled over and fell onto the cold blue padded mat.

"SHIIIIT!" I tried to voice my frustrations in the politest way possible, but the intense pain contorted my excitement.

"Up, up, up…" I could feel the nurse's arm wrap around my midsection.

"Grab onto the rail." I grappled with the railing and heaved myself up. I felt the wheelchair slowly come under me, and I gently eased back into it. I felt embarrassed and ashamed at my inability to complete the task.

"You almost did it, Randy!" Deep down, I knew she was lying, but Chelsea always had a way to make me feel better. It was probably just her smile combined with her flowery perfume that made me weak.

"I almost had it…" I replied, knowing damn well that I was nowhere close.

"You had it until you cussed.…"

"Sorry for the S word." I really wasn't sorry, but I simply apologized out of respect. I could hear her let off a slight chuckle.

"Not the S word, Randy, the C word, you should never say the word can't." I glanced away from her shamefully. I felt defeated both mentally and physically, but she was right. I had to convince myself to overcome this grueling disability. However, today was not the day.

"I'm ready to go home."

"Let's try one more time, Randy," she said sweetly.

I tuned her out.

"No. I'm ready to go home!"

Chapter 16

I had always been a hustler. I remember as a kid dragging Mom's lawnmower door to door, to see who needs their yard trimmed. At band camp, I would take soda orders during the daytime, and deliver them at night. I took advantage of the limited selection from the high-priced soda machine by offering more variety at twenty-five cents cheaper. At school, I had my custom CD hustle. People would make a list of their favorite songs, and I would burn it on a CD for them. My mind was always thinking outside the box about how to solve a challenge. I hadn't thought of anything creative in these recent years hustle-wise though because I didn't need to. Selling drugs had allowed me to become indolent because the drugs sold themselves. People already had their habits and addictions. If they didn't get it from me, they would get it from somewhere else. There was no way to monopolize or innovate. My only duty was to serve and protect, the latter of which I had failed. Selling dope works out for alot of people. It's a necessity that will never go away. Most of it needs to be legalized anyway. I can only speak from my perspective and it's just something that didn't work out for me. Everyone's different.

The tape of Milde and my father had consumed all of my time ever since my mother introduced me to it. To me, it was utterly fascinating. I had compiled notes and examples of all the information I found insightful. Surprisingly, it had turned into a pretty lengthy literary work. My notes were scribble scrabble, all over the place. This was going to take immense revision to make any of this readable. I had my work cut out for me.

"What was Dad like?" The man I used to hate had now become the sole interest of my curiosity. My mom's eyes rolled back into her head as she had a mental flashback contemplating my answer.

"He was witty. Also very soft spoken, and…meticulous. He had an answer for everything." She gave staccato responses as she remembered a mental picture of him. My dad had now morphed into a mythical urban legend. He was almost like a modern-day superhero.

"Who do you think killed him?"

My mother's facial expression changed from glee to grave at my question.

"I wish I knew baby." I could hear the dissatisfaction and anguish in my mother's voice.

"It had to be someone or some group with power and connections. The facts surrounding his death make no sense. Almost like, like a...*cover up!*"

I let the eerie silence resonate in the room. I could feel my stomach turn as I thought about my pops being murdered mysteriously. All of the fatherless holidays and birthdays that stung me were possibly due to someone else's greed and jealousy. When I thought about all of it, I kind of wanted to avenge his death. If any of this was true, then I definitely wanted revenge.

"I've been working on something, Mommy." She scrunched her eyebrows in confusion. I pulled out the journal that was wedged into my wheelchair's back pocket and placed it slowly onto the table within inches of her plate. The pages were ruffled around the edges with colorful sticky notes throughout. I doodled some scratch artwork on the front cover. It almost looked engraved because of how I carved the pencil lead into the cover.

"The Stashi Life..." My mother read the front cover carefully with scrunched eyebrows unsure of whether she wanted to proceed. "What is this?" As she asked, she turned the spiral counter-clockwise until it was perfectly aligned with her line of vision.

"It's Dad and Steward's teachings, Mom. Everything important that they said, written down, with real-life examples." I could hear her gasp as she flipped slowly through the pages.

"Oh my God!" She had a horrified expression as she put her hand over her mouth. This was not the reaction that I had hoped for, not at all. I didn't know if she was happy or sad about what I had done.

"Why did you do this?"

"To carry on his legacy, their teachings have kept me positive and optimistic through my hardships. These notes can help other people who have lost hope like me." She was only halfway paying attention to what I was saying but still focused on flipping through the spiral. "I want to publish it Mom, so the world can—"

"No. The HELL you aren't!" She cut me off sharply before I could finish my statement. She closed the book then glared at me menacingly. You could feel the wrath in her stare and the tension tight as a tight rope. I knew that look in her eyes. She was on the verge of exploding. "The world needs to hear this!" I pleaded.

"HELL NO! I'M NOT LOSING ANOTHER LOVED ONE! NO WAY!" I felt the sorrow and fear in her pitch. The events surrounding my father's mysterious murder had scarred her for life. We locked eyes as I sank back down into my wheelchair, disappointed and defeated. Then I began to feel the rebel start to awaken in me. *Eff that.* I couldn't let my father's words die on those pages. I had to figure out a way for him to live on, and this was it. This was how I was going to honor my father and his message. All I was doing was making a little motivational journal. No harm, no foul. And even if there was a mysterious group of people that covered up my father's death, they wouldn't kill me for doing something positive, right? I mean, that was decades ago. Times have changed, freedoms have changed. Maybe "they've" changed too. Or maybe I just need to quit being a paranoid little psycho worried about invisible people that probably don't even exist. With that thought, I suddenly pushed all of my mom's grim premonitions to the back of my head and focused back onto the journal sitting on the table. Are you going to do this or not, Randy? The question kept echoing loudly inside my head. My mom snapped me out of my daze. Without warning, she grabbed the journal and stomped up the stairs. *Baaam!* Her door slammed with a force that shook the house. *Damn!* I needed to get that journal back, ASAP. It was too important to me, and more importantly, to my father's legacy, to have it collecting cobwebs in a dusty shoebox. I began to obsess over how I could get that notebook back into my hands. I looked up slowly at the stairs.

They looked like mountains.

Chapter 17

It's funny how when someone tells you not to do something, you want to do it even more. I don't know if it's the thrill of disobedience or the satisfaction of finding out for yourself. Either way, I know I was motivated more than ever to complete my journal. I made my mom a promise that I would only use it for personal benefit. That was the only way she allowed me to have my spiral back. If I had known the outcome of her reaction, I definitely would've never shown it to her in the first place. Note to self, sometimes you can't even tell your *own* family your business. In other news, I had gained full feeling back in my left leg. It had always been at half strength, so this was just an indicator of good things coming.

"Raaaaaandyyyy! Chazz is on the phone!" She shouted from the top of the stairs. My mother interrupted my train of thought with that announcement.

"Okay!" I yelled through my closed bedroom door. I wheeled myself over to the house phone sitting on my nightstand dresser.

His call was surprising but not out of character. Chazz was my old childhood friend from middle school. He was a couple of inches taller than I was and was slightly heavier. He had a blatant, obnoxious humor that was only funny in doses. We learned a lot about growing up through each other. From playing school sports to driving, and even losing our virginities. Whoever learned a tip or tidbit about life first had a responsibility to share the experience with the other. We knew every juicy detail about each other's lives until high school graduation when we parted ways. I had moved out of my mom's house, got intimately involved with my (now) ex-girlfriend Tracy, and started hustling. He, however, took a different route after high school. He got accepted into an elite business school halfway across the country. We messaged each other a couple of times during the year on social media, but it wasn't anything worth remembering. His random phone call just now had caught me off guard. I picked up the phone and anxiously covered the talking piece.

"I got it, Mom!" I yelled loudly so she could hang up her phone. House phones were something foreign to me.

"Okay!" she responded as I heard her line click off.

"Hellooo…" I said slowly in a deep voice.

"Hell-oo!" he said mockingly in an even deeper voice. I let off a chuckle as he made fun of my tone.

"Whaddup chump?"

He greeted me in his usual manner. If you didn't know the extent of our relationship, then you would've thought that there was a vendetta between us. I laughed even louder. It was soothing to hear the voice of my old friend.

"I just wanted to make sure you were home before I slid through." I was taken aback by his respectfulness. Usually, he just popped up like the annoying neighbor on a sitcom.

"Yeah, I'm here just chillin' in the cut…"

"Good, because I'm *at the door!*"

Ding dong. Click up. I heard the doorbell, and the phone hang simultaneously. I usually hated when he did this because I would be undressed, or napping, (or taking a comfortable dump), but since I was bored out of my mind right now, I gratefully welcomed his presence.

"I got it!" I hollered to the top of the stairs to call off my mom. I wheeled myself to the front door and unlocked it. I pushed myself back a couple of feet so I could open the door inward. There he was, standing on the front doorstep, smiling from ear to ear. He was wearing a crisp polo tee and looked noticeably slimmer. He turned his face up a little, adjusting to seeing me in a wheelchair. It was the first time that we had seen each other since the incident.

"Whaddup *bit*—" He didn't even get a chance to complete the word when something suddenly caught his eye in the background.

"*Ohhh!* Hi, Miss Stashi!" *Chazz* said in a lighter gentlemanly tone, trying to cover up his initial greeting. He could turn his respectful politician's voice on like a light switch.

"Hey, Chazz!" my mom greeted from the top of the stairs. My mom had always liked Chazz. She held him in high regards because I never got into trouble when I hung out with him.

"How's college going for you?"

My mom wanted me to get back into school desperately, and she wasted no opportunities to remind me. Dun…dun…dunn… She clomped back down the stairs.

"It's hard and stressful…but it's fun!"

My mom gave him a hug as he finished answering her question. She pulled back from him.

"You look like you've lost some weight."

"I've been running more and staying away from the potato chips. Health is wealth."

"Helf is welf…" I said mockingly in a high-pitched girl voice. They both looked at me slowly.

"Be nice; Chazz is right," my mom scolded.

"*You* need to be nice, and quit lying to fat boy."

I said it sternly while looking into her eyes. She didn't look amused. I didn't want to trigger a lecture, so I quickly backed down.

"I'm just joking, Mom."

"He's always mean to me, Ms. Stashi. I've grown used to it by now." As raunchy and vulgar as my friend's mouth was, he always knew how to play an angel. What was even funnier is that after all these years, my mother had never even caught him once, not one time in one of his moments of indecency.

"How are your parents doing?" questioned my mom.

"They're doing great! They just got back from a church mission trip."

"They're always getting back from somewhere. You tell them I said hi, *okay*? And to take me with them one of these days."

"I sure will when I see them tonight," Chazz answered.

"Hey Mommy, we'd love to chit-chat with you, but we have some major catching up to do." My mom's smile disappeared into a grin.

"I won't hold y'all up. You hungry?"

"Maybe in a little while, Mom," I said, getting irritated by her endless barrage of questions.

"Yes ma'am," replied Chazz.

I rolled my eyes and started pivoting my wheelchair toward my bedroom door.

"I'll fix you boys something good," she murmured while heading toward the kitchen. Chazz and I went into my room and closed the door behind us. Our manly discussions weren't meant to be heard by sensitive motherly ears. Since we had grown apart, he was definitely living a more interesting and intriguing lifestyle than I was. I was envious of his travels and adventures, but also happy for him at the same time. He had really transformed into a social butterfly since we had first met in middle school.

"You look like shit!" he observed.

"Your breath smells like shit!" I always had a quick, witty remark up my sleeve for his insulting compliments. We could've gone back and forth for days with the vulgar slander, but he just sat on my bed quietly looking around as if he was surrendering.

"You look as if you haven't had some punani in about a decade, bro."

That's when I realized he wasn't surrendering; he was just reloading.

"Ha ha ha...." I tried to laugh it off. Honestly, my dry spell had felt like a century. "You're right; you're right." I agreed.

"You trippin'. At my school, the females outnumber males nine to one. They'll screw the brains out of you just because they're bored. Bad chicks too. Not like the struggle mutts you're used to."

"Ha ha, don't make me bring up Carolyn."

"Ooohh," he formed his mouth into the shape of a circle as he recalled his past lover. He always argued in her defense that she had a great personality. It had to be something because she was hideous.

"Speaking of exes, on Facebook, I seen your girl, Tracy, got married to some lame, tall dude. That was pretty quick man. What happened?" There was still a disgusting feeling that formed in my gut when I thought about her unfaithfulness. I didn't want to dig that up right now.

"We both moved on," I said half-lying. She had moved on, but I was still stuck at the Heartbreak Hotel.

"I guess you weren't hitting it right. I betcha that marriage won't last long though," Chazz added. He could sense my sensitivity to the subject when he glanced at me.

"Plus, the college girls make Tracy look like a troll."

"Ha ha ha ha ha!" We both laughed hard.

"I sure hope so," I replied optimistically.

Irony is a very funny thing. For months, I had rejected and resisted my mother's pleas for me to enroll back into school for fear of the worse. I didn't want to go through all the hoops, hurdles, and hassles of school again. Until one day, I hear from a trusted source about the social life there, and in the blink of an eye, I'm sold. Maybe my mom was right. Maybe Chazz was a positive influence on me after all. That ratio was all I needed to hear to get onboard the ship.

"Did you say *nine* to *one?*"

Chapter 18

The more I thought about school, the more it made sense. I could finally be under my own roof again. I would be surrounded by fine females in my age group, which would actually be kind of healthy for me considering my last break up. Not to mention it would give me an opportunity to meet new people, that might help me attain my goal of becoming affluent. I didn't know how yet, but I did know according to recent studies, college graduates did acquire higher paying jobs. I didn't want just a job though; I wanted a passionate career, a lifestyle. Maybe this was a step in the right direction. Nine to one, nueve to uno, the conversation from my old pal's recent visit kept replaying in my head. My mom wanted me to go to school. I wanted to get that journal published. That's the absolute least I could do for my father. To do so, I knew that I would have to go against her will, unless... The idea lightbulb flicked on above my head. Unless I could use going to school as leverage to getting this journal published. It was worth a shot. If my mom desperately wanted me out of the house, then she would oblige. I could win on both fronts without needing to act against her will. I started to prepare for my argument. If I had some convincing points as well as rebuttals readily available, I might be able to have my cake and eat it too. Just like that, I had made up my mind. The debate to determine my future would commence at dinnertime.

***

"NO FREAKING WAY!" my mother screamed at the top of her lungs. Welp, this isn't going as planned, I thought to myself.

"ARE YOU CRAZY?"

I was totally unprepared for her spazzed out reaction.

"Crazy for wanting to go to school and better myself!?" I shot back. I was playing ignorant. I know the dilemma wasn't enrolling in school, but rather, the journal that I had unintentionally centered my life around.

"No. School is fine and dandy, Randy. I'm talking about that damn journal."

I sighed heavily. Don't give up Randy, I thought to myself.

"That journal is the only thing I have going for me right now. I have to carry on Dad's legacy."

"That journal is what got your father killed!"

No one was eating anymore. What had started out with a lovely dinner of pot roast, had transformed into a no holds barred shouting match. We sat on opposite ends of the table, arms folded not breaking eye contact with each other. I could see a tear slowly rolling down the side of her nose.

"You don't *know* why he was killed, Mom, or who did it," I stated calmly.

"For all we know, it could have been aliens." She shook her head no. She wasn't buying my objections.

"We can't live our lives in fear, Mom. I know you're scared, but we can't let it control us."

"I'm not going to lose you like I lost your father."

"Mom, you already almost lost me! LOOK AT ME!" I wheeled the chair back and did a 360-degree spin in front of her.

"LOOK AT ME!" I shouted again even louder this time. I could feel the anger beginning to boil in me when I thought about my current physical state.

"I can't walk! I can't WALK!" I shouted in disdain. I could feel my blood pumping faster as the rage grew in my head. My eyes began to fill with water. The thought of never being able to walk again made me shed a tear.

"Are you really going to let Dad die completely?" I looked at her glumly. "If you let me publish that book, Mommy, I'll fulfill your wishes and go to school." She continued to gaze at me, speechless. She could tell that this was something I really wanted to happen. She could also tell that I wasn't backing down.

"You don't even have any family or relatives close to your school in case you need help." She was finally starting to let up.

"Yes, I do. Chazz will be there…"

"Chazz is graduating next year, honey. He won't be there for much longer." Geez, Louise, she had a hurdle to throw in front of me every time.

"He's going to get his masters, so he'll be there for another three years

Mom. I know I *can* make this work." Can was a word of confidence and empowerment. She shook her head no again, but this time she grimaced slowly.

"Please, Mommy. I won't let you down."

Her frown broke out into a wide smile. Gawd, I loved it when my mother smiled. It just made you feel warm inside. I guess she was finally going to grant me my wish.

"You can publish that book under one condition."

"What's the condition?" I asked eagerly.

"You don't *mention* your *father's* name *anywhere* in that book. an…eee…where!"

"Fair enough." I answered her so quick, it sounded unbelievable.

"Okay, Mom. I understand." I replied solemnly.

She didn't say a word after that. She just stared at me. It was the look of hope. The silence made everything serious and uncomfortable. She looked down at her plate and began cutting.

"So, when did you want to start school?" She smiled vibrantly as she asked.

I smiled back at her, satisfied with our negotiations.

"ASAP!"

Chapter 19

Five percent of life is about obstacles. Everyone has had something misfortunate happen to them or an event that doesn't go "according to plan." Most of the time the circumstances are beyond our control. In my scenario, it would be me growing up fatherless or that uneventful night when I lost my limbs, which brings up the other percentage. The remaining ninety-five percent of life is how you *react* to those obstacles. I have wanted to quit so many times since my downward spiral but have kept on pushing. To quit would be the equivalent of dying. Surprisingly, the only thing that has kept me pushing forward through all of this, was writing this journal. My father and his partner had created a master of a doctrine. The ideology and their principles could motivate a procrastinator into an initiator. I was living proof. I had turned from a hopeless handicap into an avid writer and future college student. I've learned not to to let the physical interfere with the mental or spiritual. This literary work that I had devoted my life to had actually served as a catalyst to get me back on the right track. It was something that I had grown quite proud of. If you apply the instructions they gave, it could change your life, and ultimately the world. I still don't know for a fact, if this was the *real* reason why they were murdered. They could've made a deal with or owed the wrong people. It could've been purely coincidental that both of them mysteriously passed away. The possibilities were endless. My mother could just be paranoid about the whole issue altogether. For some reason, she did always seem to be on edge with her emotions running high. Either way, I took heed of her warning whether she was bluffing or not, partly because I had made a deal with her, and mostly because I wasn't trying to find out.

"RANDY!" a shrill, high-pitched voice came from the top of the stairs that broke me completely out of my train of thought.

"WHAT?" is what slipped out. I knew I was going to pay for that reply.

"DON'T YOU DARE WHAT ME!" she snapped back right on cue.

"MA'AM," I responded in a respectful tone.

"ARE YOU READY?"

"READY FOR WHAT?" I was completely clueless to what she was referring.

"For your last rehab appointment, sweetie; we're running late!"

"I don't want to go." I sounded like an eight-year-old begging for a sick day from school.

"I'm taking you in ten minutes!"

Welp. I guess this topic wasn't up for negotiation.

***

"How have you been, Mr. Stashi?"

I was prepared to play dead at my mom's house to avoid the appointment altogether. The game changer was how beautiful my nurse Chelsea was. I couldn't leave town without saying goodbye one last time.

"I'm doing all right, just staying strong." As I said it, I pushed my sleeve back and flexed my bicep.

"Ha ha," she let off a cute chuckle. I loved the way she flirted with me.

"Naw really, *look at this!*" I wanted to unbuckle my pants and let her have it, especially since this would be our last time seeing each other. This would be the perfect farewell. Ahhhh, only in my fantasy. Instead, I bent over in my wheelchair and started untying my tennis shoe. I pulled it off, and then slowly peeled off my sock.

"Watch!" I was bubbling over with excitement at my newfound trick. She stared at my foot anxiously yet confused, as to why I demanded her attention. First, I concentrated on my big toe. I pushed it forward then curled it back. At that exact second, her eyes lit up with excitement as she covered her mouth with both of her hands. She let off a quiet gasp and raised her eyebrows in shock.

"I can feel my toes, Chelsea. I can feel my toes again!"

"Yes, yes!" She couldn't contain her joy any longer as she exclaimed her emotions.

"You did it, *Randy!*" She jumped up and down as she leaned in to hug me. I became smothered in curly red hair that reeked of flowery Herbal Essence.

That distinct smell became synonymous with this whole rehabilitation experience. I felt her supple, soft breast against my chest as we wrapped our arms around each other and rocked from side to side. I felt comfortable, appreciated, and accepted it all at once. Honestly, I didn't want to let go. I could feel her heart beat rapidly on my chest.

"I'm proud of you, Randy." She said it softer due to the proximity of my ear.

Most of the time, doctors and nurses went through the motions with their patients. They had seen everything under the sun, so nothing was shocking. However, today, at this moment, it was different. It was genuine. I could feel her happiness for me. We stopped hugging, and she leaned back upright.

"I knew you could do it."

I smiled from ear to ear with glee. I could feel my left leg again, toes and all. I guess miracles do happen. I had stayed optimistic and was starting to see the results. My father's teachings were beginning to make a positive impact on my life.

"How is your other leg?" she asked inquisitively. I stopped smiling at the thought.

Life was good, but it wasn't perfect.

Chapter 20

She could see the melancholy expression on my face. She knew the answer, without even getting an answer. She could feel my mood transition and quickly became embarrassed by her follow-up question.

"Don't worry, sweetie."

I stared at the ground. I could taste my saliva becoming bitter. In one instant, my emotions had turned from blissful joy into dismal anger. It was amazing how energy could be transformed and transferred in a split second.

"The feeling should come back *soon*, Randy. Look what happened to your other leg," she said reassuringly.

"Soon?" It sounded like lies. Recovery speed and time had no rules or guarantees. My ailment could be healed in five minutes or it could take a lifetime. There was no way to tell. My only hopes were that soon actually meant *soon* and not later or never. I looked into her eyes with a smug expression on my face. The reality of the situation was harsh. I might never be able to walk one hundred percent again. I turned my head toward the window, bright with sunlight. She looked at me, then at the window. By my response, she could tell that I wasn't buying her BS. There was nothing else to say. There was nothing else that could be said.

"Excuse me for a couple of minutes, Randy."

I nodded yes slowly while attempting to think about something else. She turned around and began walking toward the door. Her round butt cheeks jiggled with each step in her loosely fitted nurse's outfit. Usually, watching her walk away excited me. However, today I wasn't in the mood. Cheer up, Randy, I thought to myself. At least you're still alive. That thought alone was humbling, and a true testament to what I had survived. I still had my mother and would be attending college shortly. Nine to one. I smiled. At those odds, I knew there was even a shot at love for the handicapped man. You have to stay positive at all times, Randy. My conscience had become my motivational coach, which was actually just repeated excerpts and affirmations from my father's memoir. Just then the door creaked back open. Chelsea reappeared with a folder in her hand. Her usual smile had returned, as she walked briskly toward me. Maybe she was smiling because this was our last meeting. Maybe she was smiling because of the contents of that folder. Or maybe she was smiling because all of this time she had a huge secret crush on me that she couldn't wait another second to reveal, but since it was my last day, she was going to rip off my clothes and make love to passionately. The last one was a long shot but either way, I was about to find out shortly.

"What's that?" I asked eagerly.

"Ha ha, impatient, aren't we?" Judging by her laugh, I knew she had something to lighten up my spirits.

"I'm only impatient if it's good news. If it's bad news, I can wait an eternity." That was the truth.

"Ding ding, it's a little of both."

"It's either bad news or good news. It can't be both...."

"Well, it's good news. Unfortunately though, you'll have to wait; luckily for you though, it won't be an eternity."

"Hmm... I have no clue of what you're talking about, so spill the beans already." She took a deep breath then exhaled.

"Okay, here's the deal Randy. We have a doctor, no not a doctor, more like a specialist in the foot field."

"A podiatrist?" I clarified.

"Exactly, but more like a former podiatrist. He no longer deals with patients directly—"

"Then how can he help me...?" I cut her off.

"Gosh, let me finish Randy."

I could sense her starting to become irritated. I nodded my head.

"Okay...."

"Anyways, this doctor no longer deals with patients directly. Instead, he's been working on a device that will ultimately cure them."

"What kind of device?"

"This kind of device...."

She opened the manila folder and inside contained a thin brochure. On the cover, it had a black bulky wheelchair in a trashcan. At the bottom of the cover, it said in bright gold letters 'Welcome To The Future.' I grabbed the thin brochure from out of the folder and marveled at the cover. Maybe there was hope for me after all. Chelsea continued the explanation while I was staring at it.

"A brilliant doctor in this field has been researching and conducting experiments on how to make the handicapped walk again, and he has come up with something revolutionary!" I turned the page and was astonished by what I saw. It looked like a man wearing a futuristic foot cast, but it was floating in midair. It looked cool on the page but unrealistic in real life.

"Dr. Tracz calls it the Floatfoot 3000."

"Who? Huh?" Chelsea had officially lost me. She laughed at my confusion.

"The Floatfoot 3000. It's a device designed by a bioengineer named Dr. Tracz to help amputees or people with a loss of leg sensation to walk again—or simulate walking rather. It's something from the future, designed just for people like you, Randy."

I began to bubble over with joy and excitement.

"Well, how does it work!" I asked anxiously.

"Basically, you clamp it on the end of your leg, set the height with the dial, and it hovers above the ground. It's actually quite a phenomenon, Randy. With the device, it can balance and stabilize your foot upright while you move. It eliminates the use of a cane, stroller, and a wheelchair. It was designed so those who want to be mobile again, can be. It's going to be like your accident never happened!"

"Woooooow..." a low exhale of breath was all that came out. I was in a state of utter shock. I started thinking about running again, playing basketball, going up a flight of stairs. This device would change my world.

"How much does this gadget cost? I needed it yesterday!"

"It's going to cost a pretty penny. They're projecting it around eighteen to twenty grand."

"Wow, that's the price of a nice car."

"Yeah, but unlike a car, you only need one of these for life. And that's just a guesstimate. It could be much cheaper." She did have a good point. That price was kind of steep to stomach right now. I wasn't working nor hustling, plus I was about to enroll in college, which was the antonym for cheap.

"Do ya'll have payment plans?" I asked seriously.

"Ha ha," the nurse laughed at my question; I don't know if it was because twenty grand wasn't much to her or she was taken aback by my anxiousness.

"I'm sure when it is released they will."

"Wait, wait. This hasn't been released yet?"

"Not yet, Randy. Dr. Tracz is almost complete with a working prototype."

I exhaled slowly, pushing air through my teeth. The reality of this invention not being readily available disappointed me.

"When will it be released to the public? I need one *baaad*, Chelsea." She could hear the desperation in my voice.

"Dr. Tracz has it slated for release in three years. His contact info is at the bottom of the page if you want to be put on the waiting list.

"Three years?" I yelled with disgust. "*Three years?*"

She scrunched her face up. She knew three years was not the same time frame I had in mind.

"I appreciate your optimism, Chelsea, but I have one question for you. Just a little itty bitty one. *Why in the world* would you show me something that won't be available for another three years?" She had gotten me all hyped up for nothing—empty promises.

"Help is on the way, Mr. Stashi. People are working around the clock to aid your circumstances." Wow again. While I never actually read the Bible, I did always remember the verses my mom would scold me with growing up. I think it was time to share a good one with Chelsea. I looked my nurse dead in her retinas.

"Now Chelsea, I'm going to share a verse out of Proverbs that my mom always shared with me. Listen up now"

She leaned back and crossed her arms, but still stared at me intently. I continued with my spiel.

"Don't brag about tomorrow since you don't know what the day will bring...."

She didn't say anything. An eerie stillness filled the room.

I looked back down at the brochure hopelessly. According to me, our rehab session had officially ended. I began to wheel myself toward the exit. What a let down.

Chapter 21

Life can be very funny sometimes. It's crazy how some things you swear up and down you'll never do, you end up doing. I'll never forget my friend, Aerol. He was the most active in D.A.R.E. (Drug Awareness Resistance Education) when we were in the fifth grade. He had the t-shirts, the activity books, and even the rebuttals memorized. By the time we hit ninth grade he reeked permanently of ganja, and was numbed out on painkillers—every day, no later than fourth period. The same thing happened to our high school president, Amy. Her mom was a Math teacher at the same school, so she was always proactive in the school activities. She had a sweet innocent look and always carried herself in a professional manner. Whether it was fundraisers or school dances, she was a role model figurehead you either idolized or envied. Fast forward to two years after graduation, she moved to a rural town and became a porn star. Not saying I'm not a fan, but I never saw it coming.

Now it was my turn. I had always been a rebel against the institution and have denounced the expensive college structure countless times, and now here I am all packed up and starting school in less than a week. I really felt like a sucker for going back on my word because a person should never do that. Even Scarface said it. All I have in this world is my nuts and my word, and I don't break 'em *for no one*. All in all, though, I think you begin working on your plan, and somewhere along the way, you find out God's plan for you. Either way, I was happy to be pursuing higher learning, but I was more excited to be living on my own again. Back to meeting new people, back to the parties, and back to the women. I felt like I was being brought back to life. My left leg had completely healed finally, so now I had a choice whenever I went out—a wheelchair if I felt lazy, or crutches if I wanted to be more mobile. Crutches came in the clutch too, because I was starting to gain weight from sitting around all day. I thought I would be ecstatic, but it actually felt bittersweet. I had a renewed love for my mom while staying here and I would miss our enlightening conversations, her cooking, and seeing her daily. I knew she was sad too because she insisted I do everything with her these past couple of days. Today was no exception. She had to run errands and made it mandatory that I accompany her. I tried to weasel my way out of it, but I found myself, no less than fifteen minutes later, riding shotgun.

"So…where are we going?" I asked impatiently.

"I need some shoes." she declared. When she said errands, initially, I thought it was to go pay some bills or something quick and painless like that. However, when she is shopping for clothes, it's an entirely different experience. She has very picky tastes, so at the bare minimum, it could take hours, and hours…*and hours*. I went with her once and became, tired, starved, and began hallucinating. It was not a pleasant experience. I swore up and down that I would never accompany her during this tedious process again. As I stated before, there's your plan, and then there's God's plan. So here I was about to be drug into the black hole of department stores. Luckily, today was my last day home, so there is somewhat of a time limit.

"Aww *Mom*! *Shoes*?" I had to question her motives as well as disapprove her plan.

"It couldn't wait until I left?" I reasoned.

"I wanted to wait until you left but today is the only day they're on sale! For Christ's sakes, they're sixty percent off!" Oh, good answer. My mom was always a deal hunter, and as much as I wanted to argue with her, what she said made perfect sense.

"How long is this going to take?"

"Only a couple of hours."

"Are you serious, Mom? You can't be serious right now."

"*Damn*, Randy! It's not going to take that long!"

I exhaled a sigh of frustration.

"Argh… Wake me up when we get there!" I said surrendering my hopes of an enjoyable afternoon.

"I will baby. I'm not going to leave you in the car. It's hot outside," she said in a protective tone. I looked out the passenger side window, leaned my head back, and closed my eyes. After twenty minutes, I was knocked out like a baby, snoring and drooling on myself. I only woke up because I felt the car come to a complete halt.

"We're here!" I could hear the jingle of her purse straps as she grabbed it from the backseat off the floor.

"Randy, WAKE UP. We're here!"

I slowly opened my eyes dreading what I was about to see, probably a crowded mall parking lot, or worse the local coffee shop where the lines stretch out the door. Instead, I opened my eyes to a fifteen-foot green jalapeno pepper on top of the building. I could feel the adrenaline start to rush through my body as I became excited.

"You tricked me!" I yelled at my mom when I realized where we were. She looked at me giggling. We were at my favorite restaurant in the world. My mom always knew how to put a smile on my face.

"Peppers!" I yelled as I anxiously stumbled out of the car, fumbling to get my crutches out of the backseat. I almost fell on the pavement.

Quite frankly, I loved Peppers.

Chapter 22

The room was filled with an aroma of sizzling fajitas, body fragrances, and smoky barbecue. I had loved Peppers ever since I was a kid. I had worked there all throughout high school for play money. I called it play money because I had no bills or obligations. I could do whatever I wanted to with the income. Truth be told though, the only reason that I worked there was for the half-priced food (that was with the employee discount). Yes, it was that good. I ended up staying there though because of my co-workers. Everyone was older than I was, so I loved listening to their experiences, humor, and advice. I learned about smoothing my game, the city's hot spots, and how to party from here. No one cared I was underage because we all worked together. I was granted access to college parties that I normally wouldn't have had. The fun memories of this place made me nostalgic. I think that is why I loved eating there, not so much the food, but reminiscing the experiences that molded me.

"Can we start off with the boneless buffalo wings please?" I asked the waitress impatiently. She wrinkled her face at first, then smoothed it out with a smile. I guess it could be perceived as rude by barking orders at her before she even introduced herself.

"Sounds good. And what would ya'll like to drink?" She had a sweet voice, with blonde hair and blue eyes. That sounds like the description of a beautiful date but a horrible server, one who doesn't get tips off of service but looks. Hopefully, I was wrong.

"Water for me," my mother said while perusing the menu. She had her reading glasses on the edge of her nose while she was flipping through the laminated pages carefully.

"Water for me too," I added. I was never too fond of sodas. All of that carbonation made me either burp or fart. Beverages that makes your body react like that surely can't be too healthy. Liquor to me, however, was an exception.

"Coming right up…and if you need anything, my name is Ashley." She smiled as she said it while looking at me in the eyes. Most people would've thought maybe she liked me. I, on the other hand, knew she was flirting for that tip. She began to turn around and walk away when I hollered at her. Her tight pants made her butt pop out.

61

"Can you add an El Nino margarita to that—no salt, extra sugar?"

I could feel my mother's eyes staring at me when I lowered the menu. She was still getting used to the fact that I could drink legally.

"Randy!" she said sternly. I could tell she didn't approve.

"It's a toast, Mommy. I'm going to school." I smiled at her with longing eyes as if I was pleading with her then returned my focus back to our server, Ashley.

"Thank you," I said to our waitress. She nodded as confirmation.

"Coming right up!"

I could taste the sweet combination of sugar, orange juice, and tequila already.

I deserved a victory drink for one of my legs healing. Accomplishments take the time to be realized. We ate our appetizers and drank our drinks. By the time the entrees got there, I was feeling good. I could feel the warm liquor flowing through my body. My mom was throwing last-minute advice and tips throughout our conversation as guidance for the future. I was only halfway listening as I was chomping through my meal.

"So, how's your book coming, Son? What chapter are you on?"

"I'm done," I replied modestly.

"Done as in you're not writing it anymore?"

"No. Done as in it is complete, finished, finito. And let me tell you it's actually pretty good." My mom looked at me with a startled expression.

"You completed it and didn't even tell me? You dirty dog…"

"Why would I tell you? You know what it's all about."

"Aww Randy, I still would like to read it."

"I'll make you a copy, Mom, it's not a big deal."

"This is your very first literary work and might be your last if you don't intend on writing another. It is a *very big deal.*" Well, when she put it in those exact terms, I guess it was kind of a big deal.

"Where's the original if you're going to make me a copy?"

"I sent it to an agent, a book agent."

"A book agent? Why would you do a thing like that?"

"I want them to publish it, Mommy. She's going to shop it around to different companies and see if anyone likes it."

"What if no one likes it?"

"I like it."

"You know what I mean, What if no one else likes it?"

"She sends it back, no harm, no foul."

"And what if someone does like it?"

"Then they'll publish some copies and see if it will sell."

"You think they'll like it?" she asked.

"I hope so," I said uncertainly. "I put a lot of time into it."

My mom slowly broke out into a smile. I could tell she was proud of me.

"So…what did you end up naming the book?"

"The Stashi Life."

"The Stashi…Life…" She said it slowly, sounding out each word as if she didn't understand, as if I was speaking in a different language.

"The Stashi Life," I confirmed.

"The Stashi Life," she repeated again, this time faster as if she was getting accustomed to the name. "It has a nice ring to it." She nodded her head in acceptance. She always knew the right thing to say.

"Wait until you read it. It's *eye-opening*!"

She gazed at me deeply and then blinked twice. Her expression had changed. I could tell she was thinking about Dad.

"Did you keep our promise?"

"What promise?" I began to think. The margarita had put me in a forgetful mood. It seemed like the volume of the restaurant music quieted as she became serious. There was a grave expression on her face.

"The promise that we made that night at dinner; when you said you wouldn't put his name in that book. You didn't mention him, did you?" By now she had her arms crossed, leaning back while waiting on my answer.

"Ohh…that promise…." I was in a playful mood. I loved pulling my mom's leg.

"Randy, I'm not messing around. I'm serious as hell right now. Now I'm going to ask you one more time. Is Ernest Mladenka or Stewart Milde's name anywhere in that book? And don't lie to me!" I could tell that fun time was officially over. This subject always struck a nerve with her. My dad was always a very emotional issue.

"No, Mom, I didn't. I didn't put their name anywhere in there. You happy?"

She put her hand over her heart, closed her eyes, and breathed a sigh of relief. She can be so overly dramatic sometimes. Or maybe she wasn't overreacting. Maybe there was an imminent threat that I was oblivious to. Whatever the case was, I intended to reread the book. I totally forgot if his name was in there or not. At worst, I would have to re-edit and resubmit the book and begin the whole process over again, which I did not want to do. Or I could leave it alone, ignore my mom's paranoia and pray for the best. I didn't want to be disobedient, but I also didn't want to plagiarize my dad's teachings. Decisions, decisions. This would have to be decided at a later time. Critical decisions should not be made while inebriated.

"Would you like dessert, Mom?" She patted her stomach and closed her eyes halfway.

"No. I'm full, honey. You can get some if you like."

"I was full as a tick. One more bite and I was liable to puke. I glanced over in our waitress' direction while she was conversing with the bartender. I scribbled my hand in the air as if I was writing on an invisible notepad.

"Check, please!"

There's nothing like spending time with family. Even though I really did cherish this evening, I couldn't wait for tomorrow.

Chapter 23

Does time really fly when you're having fun? Einstein theorized it as time relativity. Time moves relative to what you are doing. It's funny how the DJ finally hits a hot streak playing only the best songs and then the lights come on and the club is closed. Or how when you are in jail, time seems to go backward.

Today was no different. It was the first day of class, and the teacher's monotonous tone combined with a demanding syllabus made time freeze. The semester just started, and it felt like I was already behind. Being out of school, and not having to challenge my brain definitely put me out of the loop. The only thing that really kept my attention were the females. My oh my, this class had some hotties. There's one in the front right with jet black hair, juicy lips, and a risqué tattoo on her neck. Then there's another one sitting behind me with plump titties, green eyes, and a tongue ring. I turned around to ask her for a pen, but the idiot next to me slid me one before she could even respond.

While they looked good, they had nothing on the girl two rows in front of me. OH, MY GAWD! She looked straight out of heaven. She had pearly white teeth, hazel eyes, smooth skin, and smelled like caramel. She walked past my desk smelling delicious. She was a little slimmer than what I was used to, but her posterior made up for it. As a matter of fact, that's probably what happened. All of her fat was used to shape that robust posterior. A product of great genetics. Her booty jiggled like gelatin every time she took a step in that black mini skirt. Left, right. Left, right. She walked in slow motion. Her bright lime green shirt already commanded attention. She was so fine, it was intimidating. I mean, I started making up excuses my damn self of why I didn't have a shot with her. A thousand dudes must holler at her daily. I know she has to have a man. She's so fine, she has to have a bad attitude. We never even spoke, but I started making outlandish assumptions to save myself the embarrassment of getting rejected. Randy, think positive; you got this. Man oh man, I'd lick that chick from head to toe like a human popsicle. I mean I would beat the brakes off that voluptuous…

"Mr. Stashi, when is our test again?"

Caught. Fantasizing about these beautiful ladies had left me daydreaming. The professor could tell I was not listening to his lecture and called me out. Physically, I was in class; mentally I was in a different world.

"Oh yeah, the test is on the umm…" I grabbed my syllabus and flipped through it rapidly in search of the assignment calendar.

"We have to study first so umm…" I stalled trying to buy some more time. Where was the damn test date listed?

"Umm," my professor said mocking me. He was a young guy, probably in his early thirties, wearing a maroon polo. just showing off to flex his newly appointed authority.

"Umm umm… Who would like to help Mr. Stashi out since he can't remember what I *just* said 60 seconds ago?" Wow. This professor was cutthroat. About five hands shot in the air. I felt like an idiot. He looked around and pointed his finger at a hand. Just my luck, he picked the goddess that I was just dreaming about. He had looked at the seating chart before he addressed my newfound crush. I wondered how her voice sounded.

"Missus Dorr."

"Next Friday, Professor Pine…."

"Yes, next Friday. Glad to see someone was paying attention." He glanced at me sternly, then back at the rest of the class.

"Chapters one, two, and three…"

"Ughhhh." You could hear the class let off a sigh of disgust.

"And if no one has any more questions, then class is dismissed." He quickly scanned the room to see if anyone's hand was raised. The sounds of closing binders and zipping backpacks filled the room.

"Well then, have a great weekend! Mister Stashi, see me after class." I could feel my colleagues stare at me with raised eyebrows and O-shaped mouths. As the class slowly emptied out, the pretty girl with the last name Dorr walked past me. She gave me a sympathetic look as our eyes met. I wanted to respond verbally, but all that came out was me looking confused shrugging my shoulders. Damn, I wanted to talk to her and introduce myself, but instead, I had this meet and greet with the professor. I was already starting off on the wrong foot. Man, not to mention it was only the first day. I grabbed my bookbag, and my crutches and began hobbling to the front of the room. I could already feel it. It was going to be a long semester.

"Heeey, Professor Pine…" I said it as cheerful and clueless as possible.

"Mr. Stashi…what are your expectations for class?"

Ooooh. Good question. I really had no expectations. I learned when you expect something most of the time you are sorely disappointed. Honestly, I just wanted to pass. I had been out of school for so long, that I felt like an A was out of my league.

"I just want to pass.…"

"You just want to get by?" My answer didn't seem to impress him. Great job, Randy.

"Getting a B would be nice, I mean," I quickly followed up

"Well, let me warn you a B or even passing is a hard task to do, if you're not taking notes or paying attention to the lecture."

"I'm sorry, I got distracted," I said truthfully. I was finding out that women can get you into a lot of trouble.

"You're going to have to focus in here or else I will be seeing you next semester. Do you understand?" That was a scary threat. At least he was giving me the heads up.

"I understand sir." Part of me wanted to say "understand these nuts," but I chose to exercise self-control.

"If you don't mind me asking, what happened to your leg?" He looked down, then back up, curious and concerned.

"Car accident." I learned to use that response because I hated people all in my business.

"Sorry to hear that," he said sympathetically. "Well, I hope it gets better for you."

"Thanks."

"We'll that's all I wanted to say to you, Mr. Stashi. Please heed my warning, and take this class seriously. Remember, test next Friday."

"I will.…"

I turned around and strode away toward the exit. What a prick, I thought to myself. I hobbled outside of the classroom slightly ashamed, more so irritated. I started my long journey toward the on-campus apartments. One thing about being handicapped is it's just a tad bit tougher getting to the next destination. I began thinking about my shrewd new professor and how this semester was actually going to be a challenge. Then, fifteen feet away, a lime green shirt caught my attention. I gasped. It was the girl with the last name Dorr from class. She was walking toward me slowly. My heart began to race as my eyebrows raised. Now she was ten feet away. This was the golden, magical, once in a lifetime opportunity. I felt myself getting nervous. My mind started to go blank. She was now five feet away. I had no clue of what to say, but I had to say *something*. Think quickly, Randy.

Think *quickly*!

Chapter 24

"Hey, kiwi!"

"Kiwi? Huh?" She looked confused and insulted simultaneously. Smooth move, Randy. Hurry. Clean it up.

"Uhmm…kiwi, the fruit. I was referring to your shirt." She looked down at her shirt as if she forgot what she was wearing.

"Oh," she said finally understanding. She let off a smile.

"I like bright colors."

"You must love attention…."

"Doesn't everybody?"

"Depends on your childhood."

"No, it doesn't."

"Look at Michael Jackson"

"What about Michael Jackson?"

"Everybody loved him, billions of fans, rough childhood…."

"But I had a great childhood."

"You might be the exception to the rule, but I highly doubt it."

"Why?"

"Life's a balance. You either get loved early, or you search for it later."

I looked deep into her eyes when I said it. I tried to be as smooth as possible while balancing on the crutches. As long as I didn't fall, I'd be all right.

"I've never heard that before. Are you a psychology major?"

"Naw, business administration. I'm taking the necessary electives though so I can still change it. I'm bad at commitment."

"Really. Me too." I was confused about her "Me too." Either she was studying the same major or she couldn't keep a man. Now that was a gift and a curse if it was the latter. That means she's a freak, but at the same time, it also meant she would cheat. Tracy's infidelity still haunted me. Maybe I was thinking about this too deep.

"I'm a business administration major," she announced. Ha. Joke's on me. My thought process had jumped the gun maybe a tad.

"Wait. Aren't you in Professor Pine's class with me at 11:00am?"

"Yeah, I think so." I tried to downplay that I had seen her before. Of course I remembered this girl. She almost made me have a wet dream in class.

"Yeah, you're the guy that wasn't paying attention earlier." Well, that's just great. She remembers me not because of my looks or attire but as the class idiot that everyone laughs at. Next class period I had to redeem myself.

"And you're the girl that likes kissing the teacher's hairy ass!" I quickly shot back. She giggled at my slick retort.

"Whatever.... So, what's your name?"

"Randy." I stuck out my right hand to shake hers.

"Randy Stashi. And what's yours?"

"Chloe. Chloe Dorr." I could smell her sweet caramel perfume invade my nostrils. I could feel the smooth skin on her palm during our handshake. I didn't want to let go.

"Dude, are you going to let go of my hand?" What seemed like fractions of a second to me, could've easily been longer, much longer.

"Sorry."

"Well, it was nice meeting you, Randy." She looked slightly offended, and maybe that's why she became dismissive.

"Nice meeting you too…Chloe"

I had trouble recalling her name because I was dumbfounded by her beauty. Her nipples poked through her shirt.

"You going to be ready for the test on Friday?" I asked.

"I don't know. I heard Pine's test can be pretty tough."

"I heard that too. We should probably study together if you don't have a study buddy." She paused before answering. She must be thinking of some BS to tell me.

"Can't say that I do. I usually study by myself." Game time.

"You know teamwork makes the dream work. I definitely might need your help studying."

"What kind of grades do you make?" she asked cautiously.

"B's" Truth be told, the last time that I had made a B on something was when our school let us play at recess. So technically I didn't lie to her.

"Oh okay. Well, just call me when you want to study. You got a phone or a pen?"

I hurried and fumbled through my pockets trying to retrieve my cell phone. I took it off phone lock and opened the keypad screen.

"What is it?"

"832 blah blah blah" I called it so she could have my number stored. I heard her phone ring in her purse. I hung up.

"That's me. Lock me in, beautiful, I mean Chloe." I was already slipping up. Never admit feelings. That' a sure way to crash and burn. She blushed.

"I sure will."

We both started moving away from each other then faced our own directions.

Wow. Like wow. I felt like I had won something. I just got the number and a study date from the most gorgeous chick in our class. Getting her number put me on an instant natural high. I was on cloud nine without any weed. After ten minutes of hopping along, I finally had my dorm room in sight when all of a sudden, I heard a deep voice bellow behind me.

"Yo skippy, what you doing hollering at my girl?"

I really wasn't up for fighting on one leg, but I wasn't going to tolerate disrespect—not here, not now, not ever. I could feel my body tense up. I turned around slowly to see who it was while mentally preparing myself to fight. I gasped for air quickly. I whispered under my breath.

"Awww man! This guy again…"

Chapter 25

My fists were clenched while my crutch rested under my right shoulder.

"YO' BASTARD! I'm talking to YOU!" He yelled it softer this time as he was approaching closer. If I didn't recognize the tone, I should've known who it was by their vulgarity and obnoxiousness.

A slow grin broke over the aggressor's face. "Chazz! I should've known it was you cornball!" It was refreshing to see my old friend again. We exchanged a couple of text messages but hadn't hung out since I got there.

"I knew it was you as soon as I seen you hopping along like an offbeat rabbit. You've never had any rhythm." He jumped up and down on one foot with his tongue out like he was tired. There's always a window of time which you shouldn't joke about someone's misery. It's still a new and sensitive subject that arouses painful emotions. Apparently, Chazz thought that window had passed.

"You know why ugly people are so loud?" I asked rhetorically without giving him a chance to answer. "Because it's the only way that they can get people's attention! Ha ha!" I laughed at my own joke, partly to hype it up, mostly because it was the truth. Ugly people really are the loudest.

"Ha ha," he laughed in a mockingly high tone.

"I get chicks, unlike you, desert dick."

"Not like the one I just got.... Oooh Lawdy!" Thinking about my classmate in the lime green shirt.

"You talking about Chloe? I saw you talking to her." Aww man, he already knew her name. I hate when you try to romance a girl like a gentleman just to find out later that she's been gangbanged by the football team.

"You know her?"

"Yeah. We used to do some *thangs* last semester."

He held one hand outward palm down and moved the other hand back and forth like he was slapping her cheeks during doggy style. Maan, it's supposed to be nine to one, and supposedly we're messing with the same girl. My previous exuberance from getting her number disappeared into a state of disbelief.

"You serious?" I examined his face to see if he would flinch or blink. A sure telltale sign that he was lying. He nodded his head slowly, with his eyes half-closed and a smirk on his face.

"I'm just playing." He broke out into a laugh. I really couldn't tell if he was joking or just trying to crush my pride. "Or am I?"

"Whatever...." I shrugged it off nonchalantly.

"You get her number?" he asked.

"Maybe...but we're in the same class, so it's nothing major."

"That's the best way to do it, my brother. The 'I want to study slash not really, I'm just trying to see if we have chemistry.' And they love that!" As silly as he sounded there was actually a hint of genius to it.

"Ha ha. Anyways, anything exciting happening this weekend?"

"There's a whooole lot going down.... They're having the pajama juice jam at Club Mode, and then there's the paint party at Chubby's."

"Sounds interesting. You trying to roll together? I don't drive out here." Campus rules didn't allow freshmen to have cars.

"We could do that, but don't get too messed up because I am not babysitting you."

"I know you aren't talking to me after that one party at Sophia Thomas' house. You were running down the street in your underwear pissing on the neighbor's lawn."

"I already told you, somebody spiked the punch that night. It wasn't my fault," Chazz reasoned. Even if the punch was spiked that night, everyone drank it, and he was the only one who took it past the extreme.

"We should probably take the shuttle or a cab," I said reminiscing about that unforgettable night's shenanigans.

"That'll work for me. You never have gas money anyway." The bad part about having a crony who knows your tendencies is that they always love to use it against you. Couldn't argue with him about my previous hardships though.

"Bet," I said confirming our itinerary.

"You ever had Professor Pine?"

"Yeah. He can be a real thorn, and his tests are nearly impossible."

"You pass?"

"Barely. I had to stay in his office like it was my second home that whole semester. I think he got so annoyed with me he passed me so he would never have to deal with me again. Whatever his reasoning was, it worked for me."

"Awww…" I breathed a sigh of frustration. I wasn't enthusiastic about hearing my professor's test difficulty. I wasn't a good test taker, and the "scenery" made it hard to focus. Chazz could suddenly sense my anguish.

"Don't stress bro. This weekend is going to be *epic!* I guarantee it!" Chazz reassured. I couldn't wait. I had only been in class a week, and I was already ready to jump ship. There was something about authority that made me cringe.

Chapter 26

"Yo, pass the blunt!"

I looked over at Chazz's hand, and his index finger was tapping against his thumb like crab pinchers. I slowly inhaled the blunt. I could feel the thick billows of smoke seeping down into my lungs. Then I felt the blood rush to my head and a relaxing sensation take over my body. I closed my eyes and exhaled slowly. A light fog of smoke lingered in the air. This was some grade A weed. I looked back over at Chazz, opening my eyes only halfway. I passed it back to him. I was high as a kite.

"This is some good kush, ain't it?" Chazz asked. I smiled and nodded my head slowly in agreement. I was definitely functioning incredibly slowly. "Dang man, why do you always have to *drool* on the blunt!" His face scrunched up in disdain. He lit the lighter and waved it under the mouthpiece end of the cigar to dry it. I sucked my teeth. He always had something to complain about. Right now was no different.

"You ready to hit the party? The shuttle leaves at eleven…" I asked changing the subject.

"Yeah. Let's get ready to ride!"

Bus stops on the weekend turned into campus activity shuttles. I guess they figured out students couldn't pay tuition if they died in a DUI. Made sense. I didn't feel like using crutches, so I got in my wheelchair. I could feel the warmth from the Hennessey and cranberry flowing in my blood. I was starting to feel great and ready to party. We made our way down the street.

"Maan, am I really going to have to wheel you around all night?" he said pushing me from behind.

"Damn, am I going to have to put up with your nagging all night?" I fired back. "You've got to change your attitude playa. Attitude determines altitude."

"You know I'm just messing with you.…" He chuckled softly. One thing about liquor is it sure does make your thoughts come out easier.

"I like that motto though; where'd you get it from?"

I could've easily made up some bs, like a motivational infomercial or a church sermon, but the truth sometimes is easier and effortless.

"My dad."

"Whose dad?"

"My dad," I repeated.

"You mean like your mom's got a new boyfriend or someone that you call Dad."

"My mom never had a boyfriend, at least to my knowledge."

"I thought you never met your dad like he left you before you were born."

"I mean, I thought he left too, but that's not the case."

"Then what is *the* case?"

"He was killed, mysteriously, according to my mom."

"Whoa whoa! Back up! What did you just say?"

"You're not going to believe this…"

"I probably won't, but I still want to hear it."

And just as I was about to delve into my family's secret history; our bus pulled up.

Chapter 27

"NO FREAKING WAY!"

Chazz was still in disbelief about the story of my father. I really didn't like telling people my business because they always find a way to use it against you. It's like a tool they use to their advantage in an argument or a secret weakness they like to expose to boost their self-esteem. I remember when I told Chazz about my first middle school crush. When my plan of love and seduction failed, he ridiculed me for months. Whenever Tiffany (my crush) walked by he would start singing *Never Gonna Get It* by En Vogue.

This time was different though. My father's fatal incident had altered my entire life. In fact, I felt obligated to tell my best friend just because I finally had an explanation for all of the years of my family's hardships. Just him even listening to these outlandish events was therapeutic. His advice and his opinions were futile because at this point nothing could be changed.

"How do you know all of this is the truth?" We were waiting in line outside of Club Mode. Everyone was dressed up. Button downs and slacks were the popular choices of most of the male patrons waiting in line. Ladies were in tight fitting dresses with their hair styled. Initially, I thought their dress code was a little too demanding to be a college party, but now I saw why. The women here looked stunning!

"I wouldn't have believed it either unless I had seen the tape with my own eyes. He was there sitting down behind his partner, Stewart Milde. It's real bro. Too real."

"Hmm… What were they discussing?"

"Transferring energy. It's complex; from thoughts to passion to monetary gain. It has nothing to do with the physical; only the mental and spiritual."

We inched closer and closer to the entrance. This line was packed tonight!

"I've got to see this. It sounds priceless. Do you have the tape?"

"Nope. It's back at home. If I even tried to take that tape out of my mom's house, she would kill me her damn self. No bull."

"Dayum!" He turned his head in disappointment.

"I've got something better for you though, homie."

"I'm listening."

"I wrote a book about it. I analyzed and explained the core values and fundamentals of this lifestyle. It's groundbreaking and life-changing!"

"Do you have the book?"

"Nope, my book agent is still shopping it around to different publishers."

"ID fellas…."

We were next in line as the bouncer requested to verify our credentials. I pulled mine out of my wallet while leaning to the left side of the wheelchair. Chazz pulled his out too. We paid the cover and moseyed on inside.

"So how long has your quote unquote book agent been shopping it around for?"

"A couple of months now. She had the preliminary version a while ago though. Hopefully, somebody will pick it up."

"Well, if that's the case, don't get your hopes up, playboy. It sounds like a pipe dream."

"Well hell, everyone should have a pipe dream. If your goals seem reasonable or feasible, then they aren't big enough."

"Oooh," he nodded, acknowledging the profundity of the statement.

"That's in the book too," I said in a matter-of-fact tone. I looked at his face. The previous statement (which was taken straight from my dad's videotape) was still enlightening and compelling information after all of these decades. I continued looking around. People were dancing and talking, bartenders pouring drinks and the DJ's yelling birthday shout outs on the microphone. I had once become bored with redundant nightlife in the past, but tonight is different. Tonight, the club is pumped all the way up. There were beautiful women *everywhere*. I couldn't focus.

"Whoo. Time to turn up!" Chazz observed while absorbing the energy as well.

"Let's go get a drink!" he suggested. We made our way to the bar, and Chazz ordered four Jaeger bombs. The bartender was a green-eyed blonde haired bombshell. That's one observation about college towns. All of the girls were beautiful. Chazz passed me two Jaeger bombs.

"Let's toast!" He paused momentarily as if he was thinking carefully about what to celebrate. I could tell he was still zooted from that weed we smoked earlier.

"To Stashi for coming to college!" We clanked our glasses and gulped the fiery concoction. It was rough, hot, and bitter.

"Ugh" I groaned. I looked back at him, and he held up the other shot glass in his hand.

"For the next one, I want to congratulate you on your book. Even if no one picks it up because it's boring and it sucks, at least you completed it!" He chuckled. Funny how I never thought this book would be an accomplishment. I wrote it so nonchalantly, and it was mainly my father's words. That's why it felt effortless. Nonetheless, no one had shown any interest in my recollection. So, it felt good to receive praise. We clanked glasses one more time, and I rocked my head back to take another shot.

"Thanks," I said slowly.

"Let's party." We mingled; we flirted; we danced. Within no time Chazz transformed into his smoother alter ego and started putting game on a tall curly-haired chick. She had an athletic build like she played volleyball. I had stumbled across a smaller, thin red-haired chick with frizzy hair. She had freckles and a sweet smile. One of the perks of being in a wheelchair was the lap dances. Usually, this would only happen at the strip club. Since I was unable to dance, this was the next best thing, which was actually a better thing. It was hard not getting hard while her salacious body was grinding on me. Chazz and his girl linked back up with us. We talked, joked, and made fun of each other's dancing. Our flirtatious teasing kept them entertained for the remainder of the club. We were perfect wingmen for each other because we knew how to play off each other. Right before the club ended, we caught a cab on the way home.

Everyone was drunk in the cab anticipating after-the-club activities. I was excited. Usually, on a night like this, I would be confined to watching Netflix and naughty websites in my room at my mom's house. I began to smile. I can truly say, I was content with my decision to go out. We ended our cab ride reaching our destination at my house. The girls got out first while we fished our money out to pay for the cab. Chazz looked over at me and smiled with a drunk, disoriented grin. He curled his hand up in a fist to touch knuckles with me, indicating that it was about to go down. I bumped knuckles with him lightly. I couldn't be too obvious.

"I've got to keep it real with you, Randy. Just because you confided in me with your secrets about your fam, I have a secret to tell *you*." I squinted my eyes at him. I didn't know what to expect. Usually, when someone wants to tell you a secret, they're trying to unload their stress on you. Quite frankly, I wasn't in the mood to hear anything unnerving. I was tipsy and feeling good. We had the girls. The deal was almost sealed. I stared at him blankly, yet eagerly, not knowing what to expect. He whispered, so the girls were out of earshot of our cab convo.

"To be real, I never banged Chloe Dorr. I wanted to, but never did…" Chazz admitted slowly.

"Ha ha ha. You dirty bastard," I chuckled. "I should've known."

Chapter 28

"Some of ya'll did pathetic on my test!"

Professor Pine was a very blunt individual, so blunt and insulting, you questioned if he got a kick out of it. Maybe he wanted everyone to fail. You would have to retake the class, which meant more money for the university and ultimately more money for his salary.

"If you did poorly, remember you have two options. Option number one is to tighten up, immerse yourself in the subject, and take every assignment, quiz, test, and lecture period serious from this moment on. I've seen some students change their habits, bounce back, and pass the class. FYI, I've only seen a *very* selected few that were able to turn it around. Option number two is to just withdraw. Come back when you're more mature and ready to succeed. There's nothing wrong with returning at a later date. When I call your name, raise your hand.

"Bosh...Baxter... Derricks..." He paused after each name to allow time to reach the student and placed their test face down on their desk.

"Dorr...." I was eager to see what my crush had received. We studied hard together before the test. Amid the studying, we had gotten sidetracked. We shared goals, passions, and previous relationships. She revealed a lot of her past, and I reciprocated. We touched each other in a friendly manner. I didn't make a move because everything was going too smoothly. More importantly, I really needed a study partner for this nearly impossible class. I didn't want to mess up a good thing, at least not yet. Professor Pine passed back Chloe's paper face down. She turned it over with hesitation. She looked back at me and smiled. She mouthed ninety-one to me in silence. Wow. So, she was stunning and smart. Nine points away from perfection. Not only that but she seemed unbothered by my disability. I finally felt regular again.

"Stashi!" I snapped out of my daydream and raised my hand. He waddled toward me and laid my paper face down. "Not bad!" Professor said with a smirk. I smiled at him and hastily turned my paper over. Seventy-eight. I really was expecting an A because my study partner received one, but I wasn't going to whine about it. Seventy-eight is passing. Chloe turned back around at me and pointed at my paper.

"What did you get?"

"Seventy-eight."

She put her thumb up indicating a good job. At that moment, I realized that I had to keep studying with her. I *wanted* to continue studying with her. They say that you should always train with someone better than yourself. Not to mention, her beautiful face and plump posterior were encouraging bonuses. For the first time since I got to school, I felt accepted. Like I belonged.

Like I could really succeed here. This was just the start.

Chapter 29

Two years later…

The blazing sun slowly crept through the blinds. I tried to ignore it, but the gaps were too big. There's always a point in the morning where you're in a sleeping dilemma. You can either hop out of bed and start your day off to a roaring start or you can simply close your eyes and forget you were awake. I chose the latter. Class began later today, and I intended to enjoy every second of my rest until then.

Vvvv. Vvvv.

I tried to tune out the noise.

Vvvv. Vvvvv.

My phone was vibrating on the dresser. Sheesh! Who could it be this early? It's way too early for this nonsense, man! Some people have no respect for others. I stretched out my arm and grabbed the buzzing phone. Surprise, surprise. The word 'mommy' flashed across the screen. Not now. Anytime, but not now. I knew she meant the best, but right now I was incoherent. I put the phone back down and rolled over. I felt the fan on the ceiling circulating a cool downward breeze on me.

Vvvv. Vvvv.

The delayed vibration meant my mother either left a text message or voicemail. I reached over to grab the sheets and quilt. Chloe was hogging them all while snoring lightly on her side. I pulled them toward me gently, attempting not to wake her up, partly because I wanted to go back to sleep, mostly because I really wanted her to complete her sleep. Whenever she woke up prematurely, her grumpy side surfaced. No matter how attractive she is on the exterior, a bad attitude can transform anyone's beauty. She looked so adorable and peaceful sleeping that it was fascinating. What once started off as study sessions for a nearly impossible class, had now blossomed into a passionate, romantic relationship. To say the least, I was very grateful.

My life was gradually becoming splendid. I used to feel depressed and deprived staying at my mom's house, forcing myself to watch comedies to stay upbeat. Now, I wake up with a gorgeous girlfriend in my own apartment, one day closer to finishing school. I changed my thoughts into optimistic ones, and my life had ameliorated. I pulled the sheets closer to me. I could see her curvaceous body underneath the sheets. She was sleeping in the fetal position with her back facing me. Her Chinese tattoo meaning carpe diem sat right above her pink thong on her lower back. Her butt cheeks that protruded outside the satin fabric looked like two soft round bouncy balls. Enough was enough. I was getting aroused. I could feel my dick growing firmer. Did we have enough time to pleasure ourselves before class? I ignored the voicemail notification and looked at the clock on my phone. One hour and three minutes before class started. Perfect. I opened my nightstand drawer and felt around for a condom. Nothing! Just torn, empty wrappers. Kinda made sense; we had been busier than jackrabbits lately. I quietly opened the drawer under it and felt around again. A thick book, probably my Bible, a bottle of lotion, and a thin piece of paper. I pulled out and glanced at the paper. It was the pamphlet advertisement for the Floatfoot 3000 by Dr. Tracz. I had grown so used to maneuvering on one foot, I had forgotten all about his upcoming invention. It just might have been released already, thinking about how old this ad was. I hadn't spoken to my old nurse, Chelsea, since my last treatment when we parted ways on less than friendly terms. I could feel myself suddenly getting excited. Maybe I would finally be healed of my disability, never having to worry about crutches, wheelchairs, or ramps again. I totally became sidetracked and eagerly called the number on the bottom of the pamphlet. A recorded female operator's voice came on, "We're sorry, but the number or code you have dialed is incorrect. Please hang up and try the number again. Goodbye!" Wrong number. Damn. I dialed the old clinic's number that I still had stored on my phone. I had recently changed numbers, but luckily, I still had the same contacts saved. Ring... Ring... Ri— "Thank you for calling the Cleaver Rehabilitation Center. This is Dorothy speaking. How may I help you?"

"Umm... Hi.... Is Chelsea available?" I whispered.

"Hold on one second."

The standby music was pleasantly relaxing. They had one of my favorites playing, The Lacrimosa by Mozart. The phone clicked back over, but it was Dorothy's voice.

"I'm sorry. She's with a patient right now. Would you like her to call you when she's done?"

"Yes, please," I left my contact information and told her to mark it as urgent.

I hung up the phone and looked back over at my damsel. She changed sleeping positions, and casually looked in my direction. The phone call must've woke her. She was now smiling at me with a seductive look in her eye. I put the pamphlet back in the dresser and felt a foil plastic crinkle. Yes! One last condom left. Hallelujah. I held it in front of Chloe's face.

"What time is it?" she asked mischievously. I leaned in next to her. I kissed her on the lips slowly then shoved my tongue into her mouth.

"It's time for a quickie…" I whispered in her ear. I moved my fingers down her breast, past her abs, past her belly button, past her soft patch of pubic hair, and into her moist, sweet spot. She let off a soft moan when I inserted my fingers. She was already dripping wet. I was hard as a rock. Wow. Our love was so comforting and simple. It was crazy how being with her made me take my mind off everything. She made me forget about all of my troubles.

At least all of the troubles that I knew about…

Chapter 30

"You're late…" my professor bellowed after observing my tardiness. Our morning quickie took longer than expected, but it was well worth it. Love will make you disregard a lot of things.

"Traffic…" I said meekly while shrugging my shoulders. It was a lame excuse, but the only one I could think of at the spur of the moment.

"You *need* to manage your time better, Mr. Stashi…" I sat down at the back of the class.

"Anyways, like I was saying before I was rudely interrupted, we are trying something new this year."

I was entering the last phase of my matriculation through college. I was excited that graduation was coming closer. I had grown tired of the tedious test taking, studying, and the daily commute, not to mention the inflated expenses. Every class needed a textbook plus some wanted an online registration. Ughh! Point blank, school was expensive. I had received a partial scholarship early on, but that ran out after the first year. I asked my mom for money from time to time but stopped because I hated feeling dependent. It was a pride issue, but I hated seeing my mom dip into her savings. She hadn't worked in a while, so I kept my borrowing to a minimum. Luckily, I had Chloe. She worked as a waitress at the local bar. Her tip money came in handy; it helped keep the landlord away and the lights on. I don't know what she loved about me, but we were solid. Not only that but she was smart enough to help me with my papers. Math always came easy to me, but English is something that I struggled with immensely. To capitalize we worked as a team. Anytime she needed help with numbers I would handle it and vice versa. I would like to say that I was independent, but that was a lie. We were a solid team.

"The school is experimenting with a new integration of curriculum. For your new year-long assignment, you will be grouping up with students from different majors."

"Awww…" The class expressed its blunt disapproval in unison.

"Wait wait before y'all jump off a cliff. Listen to the assignment. It's simple; build a city from scratch." By now the class was at attention.

"Awwwwwww!" More boos from the audience. Where was the Sandman when you needed him?

"I don't care about yall's whining, pissin', and moaning. This is college. Grow up! Believe me, life is going to get way harder than this. Anyways… before I was rudely interrupted, you will be in a group with other upperclassmen in different majors. Business majors will be grouped with a civil engineer and an architect major. You will be graded on how functional your city is. I would advise you to meet pretty frequently to accomplish the city's planning. Your job as the business major is to find the financials and budgets for everything. Major buildings, neighborhoods, sewage lines, need to be included as well. You will also need to create an attraction that encourages your city's tourism. You will need to find out how much your city will cost, and how much it will generate over the next five years. Similar data from other cities will need to be gathered to ensure accuracy. I will have instructions on our section's website next week."

Gasps. Utter silence. This was big. The intricacies of the instructions made it an intimidating assignment for everyone, especially for me. I hated group projects with a passion.

"What if my other group members are slacking?" some nerdy dressed kid in the front asked.

"No worries. Everyone is judged on their corresponding part. It is entirely possible that you could earn an A and your group members fail. To take the pressure off, we will have bi-weekly deadlines to ensure gradual progression."

This new project sucked bad. Like really bad. Just when I thought I could coast through these last semesters, I was quickly reminded of the uphill battle ahead of me.

"I'll let ya'll soak that in. If no other questions, then class…is… dismissed…."

The sound of backpacks zipping and chairs sliding on the floor filled the room. Whoo! You could see the gloom on my colleagues' faces. We had a very daunting task ahead of us. I suddenly needed to smoke one. I hobbled out of the room on my crutches. I had one text and two missed calls. The text was something sweet from Chloe. The two calls were from my mom and Chelsea. I decided to call Chelsea back first. Maybe she had some good news that would brighten my day.

Ring... Ring... Ring...

"Thank you for calling the Cleaver Rehabilitation Center. This is Chelsea speaking...."

"Hey Chelsea, it's Randy Stashi.... How have you been?" You could hear her smile through the phone.

"Heeeey, Mister Stashi, happy Thursday! Been doing wonderful.... How are you feeling?"

"I'm okay for the most part. I'm still dealing with the leg injury. Still, have no feeling in it...."

"Awww... I'm sorry to hear that. Are you coming back in for treatment?"

"I'm afraid not Chelsea. I'm still hundreds of miles away in college."

"Oh.... Well, I'm glad to hear you're finishing school. Good for you."

"Thank you. It's hard staying focused."

"I know. I've been there. So, Randy, if you aren't coming back, how can I help you?"

"Well, I called you because I wanted to hear the progress on the Floatfoot 3000. It was supposed to be released this year, but when I called the number, it said it was disconnected. What's the word on it?"

Silence. There was nothing but silence on the other end of the phone.

"Ooooh.... I really hate to inform you Randy, but that project was *scrapped.*"

"Scrapped?" I repeated in disbelief and disgust. The word made me nauseous.

"Yes, Randy, scrapped. The doctor who was in charge, Dr. Tracz, was unable to finish the project due to lack of research funding. He went through a nasty divorce that stripped him of all of his savings. He became distraught and shut down the project. I'm sorry to inform you Randy, but there is no such thing coming out. At least not for a while."

I wanted to punch something. Destroy something—anything. I could feel myself getting angry.

"Well, thanks for nothing Chelsea," I said glumly. I clicked the phone off before she could even respond.

I felt my heart drop toward the ground. I felt mad, disappointed, and discouraged simultaneously.

"NOOOOOOOOOOO!"

And just like that...there was my only hope, my only chance. Gone.

Dammit!

Chapter 31

"What's wrong, baby?"

I looked blankly at the spaghetti Chloe had cooked me for dinner. She was an all right cook at best, but I'll admit this was one of her better meals. I played in it with my fork. The news from my old nurse caused me to lose my appetite. I was trying to conceal it from Chloe, but I couldn't. I was too distraught. Within minutes she was questioning the source of my misery.

"Nothing's wrong babe...."

"Is it the spaghetti? I made it with the crispy sausage just the way you like it." I always applauded Chloe's efforts. She always did her best to make sure I was happy. At some moments, she reminded me of my mother, vaguely. It was very comforting.

"No. It's not the spaghetti. I love the way you make it sweetheart."

"Then what's bothering you? Is it school?"

I quickly had flashbacks to our new daunting cross-major assignment. I had completely forgotten about that nonsense until she had brought it up. It made me fret even more.

"Don't worry about it..." I said in a somewhat depressing tone. I forced a forkful of spaghetti in my mouth to avoid conversation. I had figured out a genius strategy. I wouldn't have to talk if my mouth was full of food. That's just not good etiquette.

Vvvv. Vvvv.

My phone vibrated in my pocket. I took it out to see who was calling. Should have known—Mom. It was her third time today. I silenced the phone and put it face down on the table. I made a mental note to return her call after dinner.

"Who is that?" Chloe asked curiously. It's funny how women always suspect it's some mysterious lover on the side whenever you ignore a phone call. Only a clown would cheat on a girl like Chloe. She was a Godsend. She did way too much for me to even think about another woman.

"My mom..." I admitted.

"Pick it up."

"We're eating...."

"Just pick it up and tell her we're eating. Something could be wrong." She glared at me with a polite smile. Gosh, I hated the voice of reason. I picked up the phone, face stuffed with a mouthful of noodles.

"Hey, Mom!"

"Randy! Where have you been? I've been calling you all day!"

"I was in class earlier when you called. Now I'm eating. Can I call you right back?"

"I could've been dying, or it could've been an emergency!"

"Sorry, Mom..." I apologized guiltily.

"I've got a question for you, Son, and I need you to be very VERY honest with me. Did you use your father's name anywhere in that book that you wrote?" I couldn't believe she was still kicking this dead horse.

"No mom. Why?" There was a brief pause as she absorbed my response.

"Well, I'll find out shortly," she resolved.

"How mom?" She had lost me.

"I just ordered a copy."

"From where?" I became perplexed by her line of questioning. More importantly, how could she get a copy of my sacred treasure. I thought it was with my agent, in trusted hands. I started to become flustered.

"You can get it from anywhere, sweetie. Your book is on the New York Times Bestseller List!"

My fork fell out of my hand and clanked on the plate. My brain was having a hard time registering what she had just said.

"Quit playing, Mommy! I'm not in the mood...."

Chapter 32

"Your literary agent Dana said she's been trying to get in touch with you for months; why haven't you answered her?" All of this was coming out of left field.

"She must not have my new number. Remember, I changed it," I explained.

"Ohhhhh…" the epiphany hit her.

"What about your email?"

"I only check my school email."

"You're going to have to handle business more professionally, Son; you need to give her a call to thank her."

"Thank her? For what?"

"Randy, you have checks here for big sums of money."

I could feel my body tense up.

"What kind of sums?"

"One for thirty, another for sixty-three, and another for one hundred and fourteen."

I quickly added it up in my head. Two hundred and uh. Two hundred and seven. It wasn't much, but an extra two hundred and seven dollars was better than nothing. My phone bill and light bill were coming up.

"Can you deposit that two hundred and seven dollars into my account Mom; I appreciate it."

"Ha ha ha!" Her laughter was like more cackling. Maybe she was going to charge me for past back rent, for when I stayed there. It wasn't much, but if she needed it, she could have it.

"Randy…" she continued, "it's not two hundred seven dollars. It's two hundred seven *thousand* dollars!"

Suddenly, everything started moving fast. It became a struggle to breathe.

"Huh?" I said meekly. I began to blink rapidly. The phone fell from my hand. I could feel myself getting lightheaded as my heart started jolting my whole body with every beat. My vision began to fade to black. At this precise second, I could only hope for two things.

Number one, I hope I wasn't being pranked.

Number two, I hope I wasn't having a heart attack.

Chapter 33

It's unbelievable how God works sometimes. Your luck can change in a heartbeat. One second you're full of energy rationing out Ramen noodles with your girlfriend, saving for textbooks. The next second you're blacked out on the floor gasping for dear life at the mere thought that you might have hit it big. Life can turn around at any moment. That's why you have to keep the faith. After being briefly unconscious, I eventually started to awake on the floor, but not without scaring Chloe half to death. I slowly rotate my head. I can't hear anything. Splash. I'm soaking wet and laying in a puddle of water. Clap! Something forced my head to turn quickly. I looked up slowly and sluggishly. I could barely feel it, but Chloe was slapping me in the face repeatedly. She finally stopped hitting me and looked me in my eyes.

"Thank God you're alive! Paramedics are on their way!"

"Call them off, babe.... I'm okay...really." I said slowly regaining consciousness.

"What happened? What the hell did your mom say?" she questioned frantically.

"I can't remember." That was a lie. I remember exactly what happened, phone call—great news—lights out.

"You should call your mom back, so she thinks you didn't die. You just scared the life out of both of us!"

"I will...right after I shower."

Chloe called off the EMS. I took a cold shower while contemplating what my mom just revealed. The cold water had me thinking clearly again. Don't get too excited, Randy. It could all be fake, maybe a scam or maybe it was real. Maybe my father and his partner were modern-day prophets cut short. Maybe the last memoirs of their work really were monumental. I put all of my energy and effort into it when I was at my lowest. I lost my girl. I lost my leg, but I didn't lose hope. It had actually inspired me to overcome my handicap and focus on other aspects of my life.

Now I was in a little dilemma. Should I tell Chloe? I don't know yet. I first had to verify if the events were true or not. Our love was never about finances, and I wanted to keep it that way. I hopped out of the shower and got dressed.

I phoned my mom out of earshot of Chloe. I needed to get in touch with my booking agent, Dana, immediately. My mom gave me her contact information. I gave her my account info and instructed her to deposit those checks when the bank opened. I rang Dana, but only reached her voicemail. Tsk. Tsk. I guess I would have to wait for an official confirmation in the morning. By the time I was finished conversing on the phone and researching on the computer, Chloe was in the bed asleep or lying down rather. I eased into the bed attempting not to wake her, but it's impossible to wake someone who's not asleep. She curled up next to me within seconds and began rubbing my chest. She always knew my sweet spots.

"Baby, are you okay?"

"Now, I am. I got some bad news earlier.…"

"What happened?"

"My grandma gave me two hundred and seven dollars as a graduation present." She sucked her teeth. I don't know if she was buying my story or not. I had to keep it going.

"Really? Only two hundred and seven dollars?"

"Yeah. It was all in change she had been saving for me. They found it in her house."

"Who found it?"

"Whoever discovered her body. They found her dead in her bedroom earlier this week."

"Ohhh.…" She became silent.

"Yeah, it's a touchy subject babe…" I said sadly.

"Were ya'll close?"

"Close enough that I don't want to talk about it."

I felt bad about lying to Chloe, but I had no choice. I didn't know if what my mom had told me was the actual truth. I would find out the exact details in the morning. Until then, gotta stick to the sad granny story. I had to hype it up to something traumatic too, since I went a little overboard when I fainted.

"Goodnight, babe."

"Goodnight Randy…. Sorry about your grandma," she mumbled. "Tomorrow will be a better day for you, I promise." She kissed me goodnight on the cheek.

"I sure hope so…. I suuure hope so."

Chapter 34

"We finally made it, babe!" I kissed Chloe on the cheek. I hugged her close and spun her around so fast that her legs lifted off the ground.

"Ha ha!" She laughed in my ear and held me close. We were tired but excited. We had been counting money and smoking good weed all night. It was all twenties, but luckily, we had a money counter. The bright emerald bricks of greenbacks radiated from on top of the dresser. I couldn't believe the overnight success of my book.

It felt like a fairy tale.

Knock! Knock!

We looked at each other immediately in silence, and then looked in the direction of the front door. It's amazing how an unexpected knock at the door can disrupt the whole mood. I walked to the door slowly and looked through the peephole. Wow. Talk about a surprise. It couldn't be who I thought I saw. No way. It was so outrageous I had to confirm it.

"Who is it?" I turned and looked back at Chloe with shrugged shoulders. This was about to get ugly.

"It's Tracy…" the quiet, sweet voice from behind the door answered. My worst suspicions had been confirmed. Luckily, her voice was low enough where Chloe couldn't hear.

"Umm…I'm busy…" I yelled out politely.

"Who is it?" Chloe lip-synced to me in confusion.

"It's them *damn* Jehovah's Witnesses again! They're relentless!" I exaggerated with facial expressions. I was hoping she would buy it and, retreat back to the room. Because if she didn't, all hell was about to break loose.

"Tell them to go away," Chloe insisted. Without a second's hesitation, I turned back to the door.

"We don't want any! We're on the *non*-solicitation list!"

Chloe turned her back to walk away, satisfied with my rejection.

"Randy, quit playing! OPEN THE DOOR!" Tracy screamed through the door.

Chloe stopped cold in her tracks. She turned 180 degrees and began walking back toward me. She was at full attention now with a scowl on her face.

"Open the door, NOW RANDY!" Chloe demanded shrilly. I shook my head no. Not a chance. I had to defuse the situation not detonate it. I was motionless, standing my ground.

"OH! PEN! THE *DAMN* DOOR! RANDY!" Now my girlfriend's curiosity and animosity were apparent. I didn't have a choice anymore. I had to do it. I twisted the deadbolt and proceeded to open the door.

There she was....

The nostalgia came over me the instant I laid eyes on her. All my old feelings of love returned and I could feel myself starting to melt. She smiled back at me coyly. It felt like the first time we met all over again.

"We ended so abruptly Stashi-poo, I just wanted to know one thing...." She licked her lips after she spoke. Damn, she knew how to get me going.

"OWWW!" I yelled. A sharp pinch interrupted our stare down and made me drop one of my crutches. I almost fell but luckily caught my balance. How embarrassing. I looked back. Chloe was not amused.

"Whaaat?" I hollered. I realized that I would have to conceal my emotions from my new girlfriend before I didn't have a girlfriend. As I returned my attention to Tracy in our doorway, I saw a devilish grin appear across her face. She snapped her fingers, and instantaneously a masked man jumped out from the blind spot to the right of the door. I saw the flicker of the sunlight reflecting from the metal of the gun he was slowly raising. It stopped when it was at my eye level. Fuuuhhh. I was staring down the dark barrel, just feeling helpless. Hopefully, he was just a robber and not a killer. Hopefully.

"WHERE THE *HELL* IS THE CASH AND THE STASH AT? You punk MOTHER-!"

Bang!

Gasps.

I panted heavily while sitting up on my bed. My heart was racing. My body and face were covered in sweat. I was breathing like I had an asthma attack. I looked over at Chloe sleeping undisturbed. It's crazy how she could sleep undisturbed while I'm being tortured and tormented in my sleep less than three feet away. It's even crazier how it happened so many years ago, but I'm still being haunted by that same traumatic experience, still recovering from the same crippling injuries. At least I'm still alive. I laid my head back down on my pillow relieved that it was only a dream. I looked upward at the ceiling fan in an attempt to let the spinning blades hypnotize me back to sleep. It was early in the morning. The sun was beginning to creep through the blinds. I closed my eyes and fell back into a light sleep.

Vvvv. Vvvv.

I looked toward the dresser. My phone was ringing. It was a weird number that I didn't recognize. I silenced it and put it back on the dresser. It was too early to deal with bill collectors. I started to close my eyes again.

Vvvv. Vvvv.

Again? Same number too. It must be something important. Click.

"Yo!" I greeted groggily, "Who is this?"

"Morning big shot! It's Dana!"

My body began to surge with excitement. It was just the woman I wanted to talk to.

Chapter 35

"You went incognito on me, Randy. I thought I would have to spend all of this money by myself."

"Ha ha," I chuckled, but there wasn't a damn thing funny about it due to my present financial state. I was hurting.

"No really. I've called you infinitely, wrote you emails, and even tried to message you via Facebook. Is everything all right?"

At first, I'll admit, I thought her efforts were lazy in her "supposed" attempts to contact me, but now, after hearing her explanation, I could understand her frustration. I had cut myself off from the past world, in an effort to solely focus on school and my relationship, and it came with benefits as well as consequences.

"I changed my number. I got hacked so now I use the school's email for correspondence, and I hate social media because there's no privacy."

"Ohhh..." she said understandably. She paused to let everything register.

"Well, from now on we'll make sure that we never get out of touch, no matter what. Promise?"

"I promise," I said in a low voice.

"Swear to me...."

"I swear...." I was going to snap if she asked me again.

"Okay, soooo here's the rundown. You wrote a book, the critics read your book...and umm..."

"Get to it!"

"Randy, the critics LOVED your book. They're calling it a divine masterpiece! A modern-day must own!"

"Wow!" I was genuinely shocked at the occurrence of events. My mom had alerted me initially, but I hadn't actually believed the news until Dana had confirmed it.

"You must be living under a rock or on a remote island, aren't you?"

"...Or on a college campus, where they make us study for these things called exams."

"Real cute. Anyway, your book is on every reputable book list from New York City to Los Angeles. What irks me is how could you not have seen this?"

"Ironically, I don't read very much," I muttered.

"Ha ha. I guess good authors don't have time to read. I'm sorry, I meant bestselling authors!"

"You've got to be kidding me!" Reality still hadn't set in yet.

"I don't have enough time to be pulling your leg, Randy," she rationalized. "This is *real*. Did you get the checks that I had sent you or should I cancel and reissue new ones?" I guess my mom wasn't joking. Those checks were authentic. Jackpot! I began to bubble up with giddiness.

"No, you don't have to cancel them, but in the future, you can mail them to my new address."

"Just text me the info, and this is my cell phone number too. Soooo...what are you doing with your life right now?"

"I'm a couple of semesters away from graduating college. Why?"

"Awww..." You could hear the disappointment in her voice as if she wanted another answer.

"I don't know how you want to balance this, but the publisher has big plans for you—a tour to be exact. They need you to be on the road, doing book signings and store appearances to boost sales. Randy, you really have an opportunity ahead of you to be a multimillionaire. Your path is etched in stone if you accept it. It's going to be hard to balance college and a nationwide promotional tour if you know what I'm getting at." I knew exactly what she was hinting at. She wanted me to drop out.

"You want me to quit school?"

"Mmm… Don't think of it as quitting. You can always return. Think of it as merely postponing." The way she said it made it sound fishy.

"I'm so close though. Will there be an opportunity like this after I graduate?"

"Possibly, maybe, but I can't guarantee it though. Randy, listen to me. You have to strike when the iron is hot! That book you wrote, "The Stashi Life," that's hot!"

"My mom wants me to finish school...."

"But what do *you* want? This is your life. With the new money you'll be making, you can buy your mom anything she wants." Even though this was all coming out of left field, she did have a valid point. I was in a substantial amount of school debt, not to mention eating noodles more often than I'd like to admit. Everyone grows accustomed to failure, but it was the actual success that was intimidating.

"I have to think about it, Dana. I don't like to rush life decisions."

"Well, think about it if you like, but remember the clock is ticking. You have fans now. People are ready to embrace and love you, and I just don't want you to miss the boat."

"I don't want to miss the boat either," I honestly pleaded, "but I have other obligations Dana. Just give me some time. I never heard your opinion though. What did you think about the book?" I asked. I was eager to hear her criticism.

"Honestly, I couldn't put it down. The facts and examples you used were sheer brilliance. Some of your points are genius and instrumental in empowering your own attitude and self-confidence." Hearing her spew out praise for my book made me feel proud. I finally created something that was life-changing and well received by an audience. For that brief moment, I forgot about all of my shortcomings and obstacles. I was bewildered by my own achievements.

"Thank you for everything, Dana. I know that you busted your tail to get my work in the right hands and I'm perpetually grateful."

"You're so welcome, Mr. Stashi."

"We'll talk soon. I'll let you know my decision when I'm done pondering."

"Sounds awesome! Let's stay in touch, okay?"

"Cool."

"Oh yeah, I got a quick question for you before we part ways."

"Ask away...."

"Who is Stewart Milde and Ernest Mladenka?"

"Huh?" But I knew I heard her correctly. I could feel a pang of uneasiness develop in the center of my stomach. Suddenly, my spit tasted sour. I began to feel very sick. The epiphany of my mistake had hit me like a brick. I forgot to omit the names of my father and his accomplice in my book. Wow! How could I miss that? *Aww Maan*! Now, thousands of people all across the country had that book, and it was way too late to revise. Damn. *DAMN*! This couldn't be good. This could not be good. Hopefully, I was just overreacting.

Chapter 36

"You know why the earth is always moving?"

Dylan was a sharp dude, slightly older than I was but not by much. I had already grown tiresome of our major project finale, and surprisingly, it had nothing to do with the people I was grouped with. More so, I hated group projects in general. There was always a scheduling conflict and always a difference of opinion. There were leaders as well as slackers. People who really cared and people who could care less. I was still trying to figure out where I stood on the subject.

"That's a good question. Why is the earth always moving?" Mariam asked. I hadn't the slightest clue either. Mariam was another group member, but more like the group planner. She was a very pretty person who would throw pissy fits at the group's tardiness and day to day activities. One of her strong points was that she was very organized, a necessity for any success. I hated any species of micro manager. However, it kept us on track, so I was grateful.

"Because if you stay still, you will get left behind." Dylan snickered at his own joke. It would have possibly been funny if his laugh wasn't so damn annoying. No matter how corny he came across though, the punchline was actually good advice. You have to keep moving, just to stay still.

"Ohhh…" I said blandly but understandingly. "So where are we on this project? I'm getting tired of working on it quite frankly." I mean we were progressing but nowhere near the finish line.

"Me too…" replied Mariam. "I'm ready to say, I'm done with this!" Looking into her eyes, I couldn't tell if she was joking or serious. Dylan let off a loud sigh of frustration.

"We can't quit, y'all! We're almost done of this forever! We've worked diligently and persevered this far. My parents have sunk a lot of money into my education and to turn away now would be a complete waste, and hinder my graduation date. To be perfectly honest, they'd kill me. How much time do we have left before we graduate?"

"Some of us have less than a year," I answered dryly, speaking about me in particular. The energy in my tone made it seem like we were discussing a lifetime.

"Exactly. A year from now all of this will be behind us, and we'll never have to speak or see each other ever again. I'm tired of all of this BS just as much as y'all are. Believe me."

Ever since I became aware of my book revenues, my perspective on school had changed. I felt as though it wasn't mandatory because I had accomplished more than my colleagues could ever dream of achieving. The more that I thought about Dana's proposal and this nonsense assignment, the closer I was to quitting altogether.

"To quit now would mean to accept failure, to settle for mediocrity. You know, there is nothing more shameful to yourself than spending the rest of your life wallowing in self-pity simply because you forfeited when the going got tough. We were all brought here together by fate, and we have an opportunity slash obligation to fulfill our destiny. We *need* each other, y'all! I need y'all! I can't do this project by myself...." He sounded helpless and desperate. I could feel his ambition and frustration to get this done. It was touching. I would've left at the drop of a hat, especially since the discovery of my new finances, but the more I thought about it, Dylan was right. To turn away after coming so far would be a complete waste of everything I worked so hard for up until now. I only had less than a year left. After that, I could do whatever I desired.

"You're right, Dylan!" Mariam glanced at him with her eyes half open peering through her glasses. The other group members, Evelyn and Quincy, nodded their head in agreement. Truth be told, the financial aspect of it was no longer an issue. I had enough money to fund scholarships for the entire class, but that was a secret, one that I would keep to myself. I wasn't ready to be treated differently, not just yet at least. Even though I wanted to quit this assignment bad, I couldn't sabotage the group. We had come so far. Plus, they didn't deserve that. It was a perfect example of how someone could quit and crush another person's dream, just like how Dr. Tracz had crushed my hopes by scrapping his floaty thing-a-ma-jig. That was everything I had my heart set on.

"Well, let's quit playing around and get this done!" Even though I was trying, it was still extremely hard to be gung-ho about the project when Dana's proposition was still fresh on my mind. I really could be somewhere else. Like on a tropical island. Sipping mojitos.

Chapter 37

I still remember how empty I felt when I heard the news that Dr. Tracz had shut down Project Hoverfoot. I felt misled and betrayed because I was shown something that would never come to fruition. That was then; this is now.

Ring... Ring...

"Hello, and thank you for calling the Cleaver Rehabilitation Center. This is Chelsea speaking. How may I help you?"

"Hey Chelsea, it's your favorite patient here...."

"Oh, James...."

Maybe I gave myself too much credit sometimes.

"Nooooo.... Chelsea, your next favorite patient."

"Oh, Ronald, how are you today?" Come to think of it, it had been a couple of years since she had seen me, so she was probably thinking of her more recent patients.

"No Chelsea...from a couple of years ago."

"I'm really not too good with the games, sir."

"Think back. I'm muscular with sexy eyes. You used to have a crush on me."

"Ohhh...." You could hear her pause as she finally solved the riddle.

"I know who this is.... It's Tristan McDowell, how have you been?"

"Damn Chelsea. It's Randy! Randy Stashi!"

"Oh, hey Randy, I was just about to name you next."

"Sure, you were," I said unamused. Sometimes it's best not to know the truth. It can be a real pride killer.

"Sooo, how can I help you today, Mr. Stashi?"

"I need a number from you Chelsea, an important one...the number for

Doctor Tracz."

"Ohhh…I see.…" There was a long pause before she continued. "Well, like I told you before, he's out of the picture. Plus, I'm not authorized to give patients doctors' numbers." That wasn't the answer I was looking for.

"I understand all of that Chelsea, but you see, today I'm operating under different circumstances. I'm not calling as a patient, but as an inquiring business partner who needs him back in the picture. I desperately need his help."

"Okay, Mister Stashi, I understand, but I'm still not authorized to give you his personal number. I'm sorry, but rules are rules." Well, since she officially wanted to play hardball, it was time to drag her on a guilt trip.

"Aren't you a nurse?"

"Umm…yeaaah."

"Well, didn't you choose this profession to help people?"

"Yes, but—"

"But nothing Chelsea. Where has your compassion gone? I came to you in my time of desperate need, with the will to be healed. I've shelled out thousands of dollars to your clinic with the hope to make a full recovery, which, might I add, didn't happen. I'm still ailing from the same handicap that I have been suffering from for years, waking up with the same traumatic injury. You are healthy as an Olympic athlete, claiming to be a healer to all. How can you be a healer when you are harboring the one tidbit of information that I desperately need, the one missing piece of the puzzle that could cure me? How Chelsea? How?" I could hear her inhale and exhale deeply through the earpiece.

"You definitely know how to make someone feel bad," she murmured.

"I appreciate your empathy."

"Hang on for one second."

"Gladly." I could hear her flipping through pages rapidly.

"You didn't get this number from me. Okay?"

"Get what from who?" I confirmed.

"You got a pen handy?"

"Yes," I jotted down the number.

"Now this is his cell number, Randy. I don't know if it's the same, but I'm advising you to please call during a respectable hour."

"Agreed. Do you have any other contact information for Dr. Tracz?"

"Just his house number, but I wouldn't use it."

"Why not?"

"He just got cleaned out in his divorce. I highly doubt that he's still living there."

"Give it to me anyways, just in case." Old information was better than no information. At least in my eyes, it was. I now had all the leads I needed to find him.

"Thank you from the bottom of my heart, Chelsea!"

"Don't mention it. It's the least I could do."

"I owe you big time!"

"Don't mention it at all, actually. Please don't mention my name or where you got this information, or I could be in big trouble for this—for real."

"You're worrying about the wrong thing, sweetheart. It was great talking to you again."

"Likewise, take care of yourself, okay?"

"You're not here, so I really don't have a choice."

Click.

Chapter 38

Finding Doctor Tracz was much, much harder than I had anticipated. It reminded me of when I was little playing Where's Waldo. It was a puzzle book from the nineties, where you had a bird's eye view of a place with millions of people and attractions and in the midst of it all was a skinny man in peppermint stripes, smiling happily with circular bifocals on. It was all fun and games as a kid when it was in a colorful book. Now that I'm older, and have no helicopter to give me a bird's eye view, quite frankly, it's not that much fun.

Difficult wasn't the word though. It was more like damn near impossible finding this man. The only reason it was damn near impossible instead of just plain impossible is because I was both hard-headed and determined. That's a deadly combination. I had to keep hope alive, no matter how slim the chance was. I had tried his cell phone, but it always went unanswered. There was no way to even verify if this was still his cell phone number, but I kept calling. When a voice finally answered a week later it was an older woman who sounded aggravated and only spoke Spanish. I didn't know the language, but I *knew* the tone. Her aggravation was either fueled by my relentless calling or the fact that maybe I wasn't the first one calling for Dr. Tracz. If I had to guess, it would have to be more for the former than the latter. I called his house number with the same hopes but with even quicker rejection. It was the annoying crescendo of phone beeps followed by the automated female operator's voice.

"We're sorry, but the number you've reached is no longer in service."

Damn, my only chance at getting with my shaman was gone. I had heard a lot about terrible divorces from greedy spouses who weren't the breadwinners of the household. I never realized how devastating they could be until now. Dr. Tracz had become a mere memory, a myth, a ghost. I put myself in his shoes. If the love of my life walked out on me, then I would probably discard or sell everything. That's when it hit me. I remembered Chelsea gave me his house number, but I had lost the paper. My lightbulb had officially clicked on. If I was going to sell everything we shared to downsize, my home would be one of the first items to go. If I was selling my house, it would be on the real estate market listed by a realtor. If a broker is selling it, then they have to have up to date contact info to correspond with the owner. Bingo. I looked up the online phone directory to anyone who had the last name Tracz with a matching house telephone number.

After thirty minutes of searching, I found one.

It had to be him. I then subscribed to the mailing list site that discloses addresses for the purpose of sending advertisements via mail. I was always curious about how coupons in the mail always knew and appealed to my preferences. It turns out, they didn't. They just relentlessly stuffed your mailbox with the hopes that you would bite the bait. Persistence is an amazing thing.

After finding his address, I cross-checked it on the housing market of homes available for sale. I really should've become a lawyer or detective the way I was searching for him. I felt like I was a bounty hunter or U.S. marshal. Proud to say that all of my younger days of playing the game Clue were finally paying off! Eureka! The property was being sold for a whopping $750,000 by a lady named Lucy Scheznik. I phoned her immediately for updated contact information on Dr. Tracz.

"I understand what you're saying Mister umm…"

"Mister Stashi," I said flatly.

"Yes, Mr. Stashi, I understand that you desperately need his help, but unfortunately, I am unauthorized to give you his contact information. It's against the law."

"What law? You can't be serious right now! I am one of his ex-patients that still needs his assistance. Do you even know what I had to go through just to get your number?"

"Check the real estate website?" she said coyly.

"No, Miss Scheznik. I had to jump through hoops of fire just to find you. Now I am finally at the last door, and you want to act like a total prick and guard it! This is ridiculous! I need his help!" My frustration was beginning to surface in the form of anger.

"Honestly, I do not care about your problems. Everyone has problems. However, if you want to discuss buying this house then we can talk business." By that answer, I could tell that I had rubbed her the wrong way. A couple more rambunctious outbursts and I would surely be talking to the dial tone.

"What kind of indecent, selfish human being are you? I don't care about your problems. Is this the attitude that you have while selling houses? If it is, then I'm inclined to believe that you really don't sell much because that's the wrong view to have in business." I could hear a quiet pause on the phone. I had her hooked. I couldn't let up on her now.

"Just to let you know, I am the class president (not really) of one of the most prestigious business universities on this side of the hemisphere. Pretty soon my colleagues and I will be graduating. Who knows? Some of us, might get good jobs, make families, and you guessed it Ms. Rude & Prude, buy houses. Your name could easily be shared among the thousands of future echelons of the white-collar business class that would ensure you endless clientele and hefty commissions, or you could do it your way. The selfish way."

If you couldn't tell, I was boiling mad now. Being mad is never good because it lowers your IQ, scientists say thirty points. I had completely forgotten about the original purpose of my phone call and became entangled into showing this realtor how detrimental selfishness could be.

"I can see why you don't sell much because you lack the fundamental people skills required to—"

"You know what, Mr. Stashi?" She cut me off before I could finish handing it to her.

"I guess the best I could do for you is leave a message for Doctor Tracz. What would you like it to say?"

"Tell him this is Randy, Randy Stashi. I'm interested in financing the Floatfoot until the project has reached completion." I could hear her scribbling furiously.

"Is that all?"

"Yes. Please tell him ASAP. Oh, and one more thing."

"What is it?"

"Make sure you become his future buying agent."

"Why?" she asked cluelessly.

"Because after this deal goes through, he'll probably be in the market for a bigger house."

She chuckled. I didn't.

Chapter 39

"I don't understand why they're so anal about giving extra sauce. Are they really going to lose their job or die for giving me one more friggin' sauce for my chicken nuggets?" These people acted like they were guarding Fort Knox. Chloe shook her head in disgust. I didn't know if she was shaking her head in agreement with my point of view or in disgrace of my stinginess. I looked at her tray. She only took a couple of skimpy bites from her food. I didn't know if it was because of lack of hunger or her disappointment in my restaurant choice—maybe even both. Right now, I was clueless. On a side note though, she looked glamorous. She was wearing a silky purple glittery dress, with the inside curve of her supple breasts protruding out. One look at her could make any person, male or female, lose their train of thought. I told her to dress up because we were going out and, my oh my, did she not disappoint, which is probably the reason why she had become so tight-lipped when we popped into the local fast food restaurant. Everyone loves a good surprise. On the contrary, everyone despises a bad one. So far, our dinner had been awkwardly quiet. I didn't know the exact reason, but I could tell Chloe wasn't happy—at all. I knew she was about to blow up. I just didn't know when.

"Why would you make me get all dressed up and fancy, with not just any kind but the expensive perfume on, to take me to this fast food restaurant?" I was bothered by her ungratefulness but also wanted to laugh at her honesty.

"Babe, I've been eating here since I was a kid. You don't like it here? I've been so busy with so school, that I thought we could use some *us* time."

"I can't believe you! I took an hour and a half to get ready, for *chicken nuggets?*" I guess my charm wasn't working.

This is exactly how people lose their spouses. They struggle financially and try to make the best experiences out of what they have for their partner. Then someone else comes out of nowhere and entices them with affection and luxuries they could only dream of. They figure they deserve better, drop their spouse, and hop on the money train to a seemingly better lifestyle. This was the road that I seemed like I was on, but my story was slightly different. There was a method to my madness. I still hadn't told her about my book acclaim or revenue, and surprisingly, she hadn't found out. I still needed to test the authenticity of our relationship. It's easy to love someone when they're rich. There are so many gold diggers out there that I knew once word got out, love for me would be hard to decipher. I didn't want to do it, but I had to test Chloe to make sure what we had was genuine before things got complicated. One of the most memorable fairy tales of growing up to me was the princess and the pea. Just in case you don't know the story, it went a little something like this. The prince was looking for a wife. He invited all of the potential candidates a chance to sleep in his castle. They all came for marriage and royalty, but before he picked his bride, they had to sleep in the guest room. Now, this was the tricky part. The bed in the guestroom had a single pea under the mattress. A regular woman could sleep there and not notice a thing. However, a real potential princess would notice discomfort and spend the whole night restless and miserable. He would interrogate them the following morning at breakfast. Most of them would brag about how comfortable they rested, eager to show that they were ready to sleep in the castle permanently because they couldn't feel the pea. It wasn't until a particular woman griped about the harsh sleeping conditions. She had to call for the workers to stack multiple mattresses up to the ceiling to lay comfortably and she still slept miserably. When she revealed this to the prince in the morning, he knew he had found the one. This was my princess and the pea story. Here I was, with six figures in the bank, and still taking my girlfriend to the cheapest place in town.

"What can't you believe?" I wanted specifics.

"That out of all places in the world, you made me dress up to come *here?* I can smell him!" She jerked her head backward to point out the guy sitting three tables adjacent to us. He looked homeless. He had a lot of dirty clothes on with his plastic bags of belongings sprawled out across the table. Even three table away you could smell the pungent combination of rancid feet and stinging mustiness. It was a pitiful sight, but seeing him makes you appreciate your own life a little more.

"Baby, stop it. You don't like it here?" I looked deeply into her eyes. This was the moment I had been waiting for, the turning point in our relationship, the test that would define if we would continue life together or if I would need to drop her like a sack of potatoes.

"No! It's not that I don't like it here. I mean c'mon. I go through the drive-through for a quick lunch or breakfast, or even after the club munchies."

"Then what's so different about now? You're eating with the man of your dreams."

"What's different is…I don't like feeling tricked or played. It's like you toyed with me tonight. You said we were going out, get razzle-dazzled up. So, what do I do? Umm, exactly what you say, which might I add, took a lot of time and effort. And of all the places this city has to offer we come to this shack!" I didn't like how she was taking our date.

"But baby, I love you. If all I can afford is this shack, would you still want to be with me?"

"Hell naw. I wouldn't want to be with you! And you know why, right? Because that would mean you have lost your drive, your determination, and your ambition. That would mean you've become comfortable with mediocrity. There're a million other guys that I could date that have two working arms and two working legs, and don't need wheelchairs or crutches. Don't be so shallow minded. I love you because no matter what your obstacles are, you overcome them. Money doesn't mean anything to me. I mean c'mon, we met studying for those impossible computer exams. You have the heart of a champion, the smile of a leader, and the humor of a comedian. You really make me happy, Randy. But I don't like being tricked, lied to, or deceived. And that's what you did to me tonight. That's why I'm so ticked off with you right now. I spent so much of my time getting dressed up to go to a place that limits the sauces you get. Ughhh! We could've watched Netflix and chilled at the house instead of coming here!" Wow. Now, I felt bad. I felt ashamed for even questioning our love. I never knew what she liked about me until now, until I forced her to put all of her inhibitions on front street. I gazed in her eyes speechlessly. I could feel my heart pump harder and louder. Suddenly, all of our surroundings became silent. It was at this precise moment that I fell truly in love with this beautiful girl that was sitting across from me pissed off, this girl named Chloe Dorr. I became overwhelmed with this fascination of her. I wanted her to be in my life forever. I always wanted to see her smile. I wanted to take her on this journey with me. She had passed my improvised test with flying colors.

"You silly little airhead!" I said squinting as if I was displeased. "Let's get out of here. This is just the beginning of our date." She smiled at me, grabbed her purse, then grabbed my hand as we made our way to the exit.

Chapter 40

Jesus saves. For some odd reason, that phrase always stuck with me. I remember being young in church with my mom reading these shirts at a church barbecue. I imagined Jesus like Superman or Batman with a cape and tights on, rescuing people from evil villains and dangerous criminals. As I grew up, I realized that my original depiction was slightly off. He saved people in different ways, most importantly from eternal damnation. I realized that while we were nowhere close to having Jesus' powers and habits, people could still save people, not in the sense of saving them eternally or their spirit, but from their own self-destruction. At some point, everyone needs someone to lean on.

I had imagined Dr. Tracz as an Einstein-esque gray white-haired professor talking in accents and broken English. I was very afraid I wouldn't be able to communicate on an intellectual level because he was a genius' genius compared to me. I just had the important part—the cash. He was an innovative revolutionary that the whole world had been waiting on while I was just an undergrad student, who happened to hit the jackpot with my father's memoirs. These weren't my ideas originally, but I had revised them slightly and to appeal to a younger generation. I thought that if he were here today, he would've wanted me to carry on his legacy. These principles were eye-opening to anyone who hasn't heard it before.

When I called Dr. Tracz, however, he sounded very, very different than what I expected. I guess he was much older, probably in his mid-fifties or early sixties. I thought we were going to have a quiet meeting over the webcam. However, when I explained my future plans, he insisted I meet him in person. Thank goodness his new location was in a city only three hours away. I needed a ride there and back and didn't want Chloe to take me.

It wasn't that she wasn't capable. I just didn't want to involve her in my business matters. Never mix business and pleasure—ever. So, I resorted to calling my lifelong friend, the one person I could always count on, Chazz. I convinced him by offering a couple of incentives on the trip. Gas and a free hotel room were all he needed to hear to oblige. He described it as a mini-vacation. His words exactly were "I always need something pretty in another city." During the three-hour excursion, we caught up on each other's life. Chazz was actively pursuing employment at a prestigious accounting firm, so his time left in the college town was fleeting. He had already graduated so there wasn't much left for him to do out here. When you're in such a small college town, by the time you spent four years there, you damn near knew everybody and everybody's business. I didn't want to bore him with my book accolades, but I did let him know the reason for our trip. That was to see the good doctor.

We had our original meeting scheduled at Tootsies at 5:00pm. We pulled up around 5:20pm. I knew it wouldn't be a good first impression being tardy with a potential business partner, especially when I still needed to convince him to join this operation. Even though it was unavoidable and unpredictable when we ran into a hellacious traffic jam on the interstate, it was still no excuse. We pulled up to Tootsies antsy to get out. I pulled my crutches from out the back. I was expecting a Hooters-like establishment. You know, cute girls, skimpy clothes, hot wings. I initially told Chazz to drop me off, but after I thought about it, it was better for him to come in for at least the first couple of minutes. I didn't know what to expect.

"I don't see what the big deal is anyway," he murmured as we exited the vehicle.

"There is no big deal...." Not yet anyway, I thought. "It's just personal playa. Do I accompany you when you get an STD test?" He chuckled and nodded his head in agreement. "See? Plus, it's not a big deal anyway. I'm just asking him what happened with his invention he was working on. If he can heal me or help me become more mobile, then it was all worth it." We entered the establishment, and it was nothing like I expected. There was a strong thick haze of pungent cigarette smoke that lingered in the air. Flashing disco and strobe lights bounced on every wall. The back wall was full of mirrors that added a nice touch and the illusion of more space. A big man sitting on a stool asked for our IDs before we took our third step. I'm guessing he was supposed to be outside because if we were underage, we shouldn't have been seeing what we were seeing. MY jaw dropped as I exchanged glances with Chazz. He was in awe just like I was.

"Umm, excuse me, sir, what kind of establishment is this?" I asked the bouncer curiously. He examined my ID even closer, suspecting it was either fake, I was underage, or an undercover. After careful scrutiny, he finally answered my question.

"What does it look like to you?" I grabbed my ID back and proceeded. Man, oh man. There were naked tiddies *everywhere*, tiddies shaking, bouncing, and jiggling in every which direction. My eyes lit up like a kid in a candy store.

What kind of business meeting was this? I mean I wasn't complaining, but it definitely caught me off guard. It was like a fantasy with all of the different types of women here, all different complexions, all different colors of hair. Two were dancing on the pole, and a handful of others were spread out giving other patrons lap dances. The bartender locked eyes with me as I walked past her.

"Any drinks, gentlemen?" she said slowly, and seductively in our direction.

"No thank you," I answered at her smiling. It was so easy to say yes, so, hard to say no, but I had business matters to conduct. Always had to remember to never mix business and pleasure.

"I'm staying" Chazz declared. I guess that was his way of announcing his separation from me in the strip club.

"Have you seen an older guy by himself?" I asked the bartender, wondering if she had seen Dr. Tracz. At first, she shrugged her shoulders at my vague question, and then she pointed to a nearby corner.

"Thank you," I replied.

"I'll have a Hennessey and cranberry." Chazz wasted no time getting to it. It didn't surprise me because I already knew his tendencies. I pivoted around on my crutches.

"Take it easy, homie. You still have to drive," I scolded him. I hated sounding like Papa Bear, but only the smart live long.

"Ten-four, Dad!" he answered. He never missed an opportunity to showcase his obnoxiousness. I proceeded slowly to the corner where the bartender had pointed. There were three patrons who I had eliminated mentally because they didn't look old enough. The fourth guy couldn't have been Dr. Tracz because he was enjoying himself a little too much. He was having his own personal bachelor party. There was a thick Asian girl bent over in a black thong bouncing slowly to the beat. The guy she was entertaining was slapping her left cheek with one hand while stuffing dollar bills in her crack. The table next to him was filled with empty glasses. There was no one else in this corner of the room but him. There was no way this could be the mastermind I was looking for, no way.

"Shake it for daddy, baby!" he yelled with glee. "Yeaaaah!" This dude was

119

having the time of his life. He even went as far as biting her butt cheek.

"Dr. Tracz?" I assumed, hoping that was very, very wrong. Suddenly, the older man looked back at me instantly shocked by the fact that someone knew his name. He looked like a guilty kid caught red-handed with his hand in the cookie jar or, in this case, his hand caught in the butt crack of some Asian stripper. He slowly removed his hand while squinting at me, alarmed, but still in confusion as to who I was or how 1 knew him. Hopefully, he hadn't gotten so drunk that he forgot about me.

"Dr. Tracz, it's me…Randy!" He glanced down at his watch.

"Simone we'll finish this later." The bare-chested woman flashed a dirty look at me before leaning in to hug Dr. Tracz.

"Don't keep me waiting doctor," she said slowly. She pecked him on the cheek and left.

"You're thirty minutes *late*! So far, not a stellar first impression. I had already dismissed you mentally and started the party. You see, time is money, Mr. Stashi!" His quick change of attitude had taken me by surprise. I could now feel his animosity toward me as he glared at me menacingly.

"Sa sa sorry…" I stammered, "There was a fatal traffic accident that had me at a complete halt for—"

"Blah blah blah…."

I began to grow irritated.

"Look, I wouldn't drive three hours away if I thought this wasn't important."

"You would've been on time if you thought this was important!" he retorted. At that moment, I realized the importance of punctuality. I could never, nor would ever, be late again. I was already starting off on the wrong foot with the person who was my last hope. Not good. He stared at me for what seemed like a decade before opening his mouth.

"Have a seat." I plopped down in the chair right next to him. "Before we get started, what's that stuff on your nose?" I brushed my nose clueless of the possible boogers I had hanging out. I should've checked myself out in a mirror before I got out of the car.

"It looks like a powder substance on your nose. Do you have *cocaine* on you?" he asked me disgustedly. He stared at me menacingly as if my answer was a dealmaker or deal breaker. No one likes to do business with a druggie, I figured.

"Umm no…" I answered confidently. I had never done the drug a day in my life. He squinted at me again reading my face to see if I was blinking or flinching, aka lying.

"Damn!" He threw his hands up in the air. "Well, did you at least bring some weed!?" His line of questioning totally took me by surprise.

"Umm nooo…" I answered uncertainly.

"Well, *how* are we supposed to have fun?" he howled at his own joke while slapping me hard on the back, "especially with all of this beautiful kitty cat running around here?"

Wow.

Just wow.

It took a second to comprehend what exactly was happening. Talk about the surprise of the century. Is this the man who I was actually destined to do business with? Was this the man sent to heal me? This is the man that I was supposed to *trust* my money with? I wanted to be right, but it was beginning to look like I was wrong.

Very, very wrong.

Chapter 41

So, we spent the weekend in and out of restaurants and various strip clubs all over town. I originally objected alleging that it was unnecessary, but Dr. Tracz insisted, plus paid the tab. He appreciated my genuine interest and inspiration to reboot the Floatfoot project. When we got down to the nitty-gritty, he had estimated he was about four months away from a completed prototype when he shut it down. That was good news as well as bad news. It sounded hopeful because once funded we were so close. Only four months away meant we would be witnessing a viable solution, damn near a miracle this year. It was bad news because it raised a lot of questions as to why Dr. Tracz couldn't finish this project on his own. Was he in debt? Did he lack motivation? I had to find out what happened to prevent failure again. There had to be a reasonable explanation for his shortcomings. On the second night, somehow, Chazz and I ended up at his house smoking a gracious amount of strong weed. After all the tough guy antics, he was finally starting to let his guard down. He finally started revealing who the real Dr. Tracz was.

"You think I'm crazy, don't you?" He looked at me with his eyes halfway open and bloodshot. I hated discussing important things with people under the influence because when they sober up, they don't remember anything that was said. That's great if they unknowingly divulged lucrative secrets. It's horrible when they agree to fulfill obligations.

"I don't think you're crazy; I think sporadic is more fitting, but maybe you are crazy. I think all geniuses have a little cuckoo in them to challenge new or proven principles."

"I'll take some of that as a compliment; I'll ignore the insulting part because I'm not cuckoo, Randy."

"Chazz, can you excuse us?" I expected him to be following our conversation intensely, hanging on to every word spoken. However, it was the complete opposite. He was knocked out on the couch, snoring and drooling. Good weed does it to him every time. I turned back toward Dr. Tracz.

"Anyways, like I was saying, you are a little cuckoo. Every minute with you is a surprise. I don't know if this is a special occasion or just a typical weekend for you. Quite frankly, it kind of scares me."

"What are you scared of?"

"You taking my money and spending it on blow and hookers while not completing this project, that's what I'm afraid of. I mean, this ain't chump change we're talking about here, Dr. Tracz!"

When I said that, he lowered his head. I could tell that I had struck a nerve and he became slightly embarrassed of our squanderous escapades.

"I'm sorry for this weekend's shenanigans—really. I just wanted to relieve some stress and take the edge off of this potential deal. This is a lot of pressure on me."

"What pressure? You have something that I want—damn—something that the whole world wants. Don't you want to help people?"

"I do, Randy. I mean, I really do, but I'm still recovering."

"Recovering from what?" I was frightened of his next answer. I didn't know what he was about to say. Some people's problems are better left buried. I didn't want to open Pandora's Box and be unable to close it.

"FROM THAT *WITCH?*" he said with anger, but it looked like he was beginning to tear up. It was all starting to make sense.

"What witch?" I asked for clarification. We were finally starting to get somewhere.

"My wife, well, ex-wife—she took everything, all of the furnishings, appliances, the cars, the kids, the dog, everything except the house. I can't even afford the taxes on it anymore. That's why I'm selling it." Now, I had *finally* understood why we had been surrounded by naked girls, alcohol, and drugs all weekend. He was still coping with his divorce.

"How did she get everything? Isn't it supposed to be split fifty-fifty."

"It should have been, but she started accusing me of infidelity due to my long hours."

"Were you having an affair?" This man had a very intriguing life, and I really wanted to give him the benefit of the doubt.

"Not really. A couple of dates here and there but show those pictures to a judge, and that's all it took. No remorse for the working man. She turned ruthless and greedy and left me with nothing. ABSOLUTELY NOTHING!"

By now he was in tears, sobbing like a kid. Wow. Now it all made sense. He was still distraught over his traumatic divorce. It was probably why he stopped working, probably why he felt like everything was meaningless, probably why the invention never came to fruition. I walked over to him and hugged him.

"I'm a loser, Randy. You hear me? A grouchy sixty-three-year-old loser, a nervous wreck with nothing!"

"No, you're not," I said rubbing his back. "You're a winner, the sixty-three-year-old genius, who invented the Floatfoot and is about to change this world for the better. That's the Dr. Tracz I know." He pushed away from me to scan my face.

"You think so, my boy?"

Things are never what they seem. I remember I was nervous with anticipation the whole road trip arriving here. I had a meeting with a man who had all the answers, and I was afraid of saying the wrong thing. Now as we stood here with him crying on my shoulder, I realized nobody has all the answers. Yes, some people are better off than others are, but we all need each other. At some point in life, everyone falls down and hits a low point. That's when you need someone to help pick you up and put you back on the right track, someone to rescue you. Chazz kind of rescued me from my mother's house. It wasn't until this precise moment that I realized I was here to rescue Dr. Tracz, to get him back on the right path, to save him from self-destruction.

"I know so, Dr. Tracz. We have an obligation to the world. Let's fulfill the destiny that God has intended us to accomplish." I extended my hand while I looked at him dead in his pupils. He squeezed my hand firmly. I could feel his pain. Suddenly, I felt reassured about him. I felt like we had united for more reasons than just this little invention.

I felt like this was fate. Our fate.

Chapter 42

Life was finally coming together. After my successful meeting with Dr. Tracz, I was now the majority owner of Stashi Inventions Inc. I assumed the majority of the ownership simply because I had financed the rest of the operation. I was exuberant, to say the least, to be an initiator in the revival of a dead invention. I was the sole reason it was coming back to life. At some point in time, I remember how much I hated my life, watching an endless amount of Netflix to stay entertained. Now my life had taken a full 180-degree turn. I was beginning to have too much on my plate balancing school, my book, and my new entrepreneurial endeavor with Dr. Tracz, not to mention my love life. Luckily, Chloe was understanding because my agenda put her on the back burner many times. She still had no clue of my book success, but she suspected something good happened income-wise because we weren't eating Ramen noodles every other night for dinner anymore. I was making a lot of people proud that were in my corner, mainly, because I was mere months away from accomplishing my most intimidating task yet, earning my bachelor's degree. Our group was finally clicking for our senior project, and we were almost finished. What started out as an uncomfortably annoying group assignment, had blossomed into a beautiful, cohesive team. Everyone brought something to the table; Dylan, Mariam, Quincy, and Evelyn. It was a daunting and cumbersome task building a city from scratch. It took hellacious planning, patience, and thoroughness, but we unfolded and attacked all of the intricacies head on. Pretty soon, there was no objective too challenging that we couldn't solve as a team.

"What are the main pitfalls of a city?" Quincy asked. Quincy was a deep thinker, really, a shot-out pothead that would go so far out the box, you would sometimes question his sanity.

"In what regard?" asked Evelyn. We had grown in the habit of questioning the relevance of Quincy's abstract thoughts. He was always on a random tangent.

"Like pitfalls... Why do some cities thrive and others look like ghost towns?"

"Ohhh," chimed in Dylan. "Economy is a major factor...."

"Tourism holds a lot of weight too."

"I said pitfalls, y'all, not the good things, the bad stuff," Quincy clarified.

"Crime. I don't like cities that aren't safe," said Evelyn.

"That's a good one," I confirmed.

"Umm poverty...homeless people."

"How?" Quincy asked.

"I hate going to cities where everyone has a cardboard sign with their hand out."

"Yeah. That can be very annoying," said Mariam.

"It's annoying, but remember, God loves a cheerful giver," replied Dylan.

"True, true," I nodded my head feeling slightly guilty.

"Even though that's true, it doesn't hurt the city. Even though they don't generate or contribute any goods or services, they spend money back on the city's goods and services," Quincy responded. He was going somewhere with this. I just didn't know where.

"What about taxes?"

"What about them?"

"Wouldn't you think citizens would be better off if they weren't getting robbed for thirty percent of their paycheck?" Quincy had everyone's attention now.

"I mean, if people had more disposable income, wouldn't they be able to spend more with other business, boosting the economy instead of forking it over to politicians who squander it on expensive campaigns and lobbying in fancy cars and first-class flights?"

"Ooohh ooohh." There was a low hum of epiphany from us.

"That's a good point," Evelyn noted.

"Hell yeah, that's a good point. I mean there's property taxes, sales taxes, business taxes, license taxes, you name it, and there's probably a tax on it!"

"But you forget, Quincy, that those same taxes fund construction, police, fire departments, and schools."

"True true, but how much do you think that actually costs?" Construction can be privatized. Policemen are underpaid, so they're clearly not receiving their cut, and schools have alumni, boosters, and tuition. I don't think taxes can be entirely abolished, but they can be lowered significantly."

"How much is significantly?" I asked curiously.

"Way lower than thirty percent. I'm not sure exactly, but I know that the system must be reworked substantially to utilize every tax dollar effectively. It's not fair for certain appointed officials to be dining luxuriously on the city's tax dollar. It's just not right, you know?"

"I feel you Q," I answered, "but what does that have to do with anything?"

"We should implement it in our city. The strategy alone will influence the professor to give us an A."

"I need an A…," said Mariam, "…especially after that horrible accounting grade from last semester."

"Not trying to be nosy, but what did you get in accounting?" asked Dylan.

"I got a B."

"*Awww,*" we all scoffed at her in unison, surprised by her goody two shoe answer.

"What y'all? I'm trying to get into law school. Every grade is important."

I sighed with envy. I was just satisfied to pass the class. That's all I needed.

VVV. Vvvvv.

Just then, I felt my phone vibrating in my pocket. I looked down at it.

It was my mother.

"Excuse me y'all," I said as I politely left group table. Before all of this, I would've probably hit the silent button and called her back at a later time. But ever since she found out her only son's book had hit the country's bestseller list, we had grown closer. I don't know if it was because she was extra proud of me or just missed me. Our conversations were more informative and cheerful. The admiration and the payoff had made her exceptionally proud of me. I took her calls more frequently just because I never knew what surprise news she was going to alert me with. For a long time I used to think of her advice as nagging. I guess I was growing up because I started to take heed of all of her warnings. She was no longer just my mother but more like my unofficial secretary keeping me informed from the home front. I knew she had always believed in me, but her jovial tone was always the undeniable confirmation.

Vvvvv. Vvvv.

"Hey, Mom!"

"Don't hey Mom me! Where are you at?" My smile quickly faded into a frown. I regretted picking up the phone almost instantly.

"I'm in a group meeting. Why? What's up? You all right?"

"No, I'm not all right, Randy."

There's nothing worse than hearing discomfort in your mom's voice. It was a very unpleasant feeling.

"Why aren't you all right?"

"I just read your book, Randy...."

I felt offended. Of all people, I would've expected a different reaction from my mommy. I was perplexed by her unexpected response.

"You didn't like it?"

"I actually loved it. It was very well put together and thought provoking. I just didn't like one part of it."

"Which part?"

"The part where you put your father's name in it. I asked you nicely not to do so, so why in the *world* would you do that against my wishes, *Randy? Damn Son!*"

My mother rarely cussed, so when she did it was almost like a dagger stabbing my ear. She protected the deep dark secret of my father's identity for decades, and I hope I didn't jeopardize that no matter how paranoid I think she was being. I could tell by her angry and frightened state that this really struck a cord with her.

I couldn't have foreseen in a million years how much danger and chaos that that name could still stir up.

Chapter 43

"Calm down, *Mom*!"

"No! Don't calm down *Mom* me, *Randy*! I only had one request. One freakin' request! That's *all* I asked! And you lied to me!"

The ripple effect. I've learned through a movie I saw once (The Butterfly Effect) all about the ripple effect. It's the principle that when a pond is completely still if you throw a rock in it, it will cause massive ripples in the water. No matter how small the rock is, it will cause huge ripples in the water that get bigger and bigger the farther they go. No matter how small the rock is, it will cause disruptions that can be seen for feet, yards, or even miles. It also relates to life. No matter how small you think the lie or action is, the reaction will always disrupt things unforeseen. I hadn't even begun to grasp the full extent of this aftershock. This was only the beginning of the ripple.

"You have to take your father's name out of that book immediately!"

"Why Mom? He's dead! D. E. A. D! He at least deserves some credit for this! I didn't make up these principles on my own. He taught them to me."

"Do you want to end up like your father, *dead*?"

"Quit bringing him up Mom, I know he's dead. He wasn't there for my birthdays, my football games, or prom. That videotape was the only memoir, the only visual, the only time I've ever heard his voice! I wrote that book to continue his legacy, to complete his mission, not to tear it down!"

"Well, you're tearing it down, Randy. You're going to tear what's left of this family down. Putting his name anywhere is striking a match in a gasoline flood."

"Awww, gimme a break. You don't even *know* how he died, Mom."

"In a car crash. I told you already."

"You know how many random car crashes happen, how many hit and runs, how many drunk driving accidents happen?"

"It was no accident. It was on purpose!"

"Then who killed him, Mom? Since you're the lead detective on the case, why are there no suspects?"

"They killed him."

"Who is *they*!? You sound *insane* right now!"

"I'm not crazy. Don't you ever call me that again! You hear me? Everyone used to call me that, and I refuse to hear it from my own *damn* son! Looky here, he didn't just die by accident, and whoever killed him has power—*lots* of *power*, so much power that the investigation was closed, and no traces, hints, or clues were recovered. Can't you see? It was all a cover up!"

"Huuuuuuuuuuuh!" I let out an exhale of grief. I could hear my mom sniffling on the other end of the phone. I could tell that this shouting match was beginning to take a toll on her. I had struck a nerve. Twenty some odd years later, this was still a very, very sensitive subject. I hated being the cause of my mom's anguish. She always did her best to make me happy, so it wasn't fair to return the favor in that manner. Hearing her cry made me cringe.

"Look, I'm sorry, Mom. I know I went against your wishes, but what would you like me to do now? It's on every reputable booklist in the country and slated for global and internet release next month."

"I want you to take his name out of your book."

"It's a little late for that, mommy."

"It's never too late. Call your publisher and tell them that there is a mistake in the book that needs to be revised."

"Why? It's not that big of a deal."

"It is that big of a deal, to protect you, to protect me, to protect what's left of this family."

"I'll see about it, Mommy."

"If you don't want to do it for yourself, then at least do it for me—please."

"I'll talk to them about it. Is there anything else? I've got to get back to this group meeting."

"Not really. What kind of group meeting is it?"

"It's a big project. We're building a city from scratch."

"Sounds like fun, I'll let you get back to work, baby. I love you."

"Fun isn't quite the word I would use to describe it, but I love you too." Click. I hung up the phone. It's funny how a conversation can take you a million miles from where you are physically. I had momentarily completely forgotten that I was even in a group project meeting. I walked back over to where the rest of the group members sat.

"You done, Randy?" Mariam asked sarcastically. I could feel their frustration glaring at me through the stern looks that they gave me.

"Sorry y'all, urgent phone call from my mom." I sat back down. "Where are we?"

"Well, you're going to be in charge of the finances for the political and judicial system," Quincy said.

"Cool."

"We need everything done by this Friday," Dylan emphasized.

"Cool."

"Well, call me if anyone has any questions. We're getting down to the nitty-gritty, and we need everybody to come through in the clutch." Dylan stated.

"See y'all later," Mariam added.

We all zipped up our backpacks, briefcases, and purses, and adjourned the meeting. I waved goodbye and began hopping on my crutches back to the parking garage.

Vvvvv. vvvv.

I felt a quick vibration in my pocket, meaning it was a text. It was from the one person I had begun waiting to talk to—Dana. It read, 'Hey, hot stuff! Can you hurry up and graduate already? The publisher is ready for you to go on a nationwide tour. The world is ready to start living the Stashi life!'

Now, what kind of sense did it make to revise a book receiving so much critical acclaim?

Not too much sense to me.

Chapter 44

'Don't call me. Don't text me. Just come home! We need to talk face to *FACE!*'

I had just gotten done working out at the local gym and was recuperating in the locker room when this text message popped up on my phone. It was from Chloe. I knew it couldn't be good, simply because she used not one, not two, but three exclamation marks at the end of the text. It couldn't be too off the wall though because she knew exactly where I was. It would've been nothing to confront me in this gym where I always am. So, I chalked it up to being one of three things. One: she thinks she's pregnant, which could be possibly true since we had been having rough steamy sex almost every day. Possibility number two was she suspected me of cheating, which wasn't even true in the least sense. I mean, I flirted from time to time with some of my classmates and when I hit the club, but I knew my limitations. If anything it was really just practice to me to keep my game sharp. Nothing worth mentioning so I knew it couldn't be that. The third possibility was the one that I had dreaded the most—my private journal. It wasn't anything too revealing, but I didn't want her to find it. I had a variety of secrets in there that I wanted to remain secret. I was so shaken up by my father's mysterious death that I didn't want to leave the world without a part of me being left behind. In there, I had details of prior sexcapades, experiences with drugs, and mental fornication with some of my celebrity crushes. It would be hard to defend some of the raunchiness on those pages because it was the uncensored truth from my perspective, all real. I was excited to get done working out and head home until I read my girlfriend's text message. Now, I was in the car driving as slowly as possible, stopping at yellow lights, and taking the long way to get home. I knew that I was about to be in a combustible situation and honestly, I didn't feel like dealing with it today. I had a plan though. One thing I learned about being in a relationship is you had to out "ante" your partner. That's what keeps the fire alive and the love strong. If she dresses stunning, then I have to be dressed to kill. If she cooked dinner one night, then the next evening I would turn into a sous chef. If she wanted to be mad, then hell; I would be furious. This was the perfect game plan for tonight. I didn't feel like getting angry, but I had no choice. I didn't even have a reason. But as I drove home, one started to formulate inside my head. Within an instant, I began to realize how sour my day was going. I hadn't finished my portion of the group assignment. I couldn't go on tour yet because of school, and there was a big chance the offer would no longer be on the table when I finally graduated. Not only that, but I lost big time in fantasy football this past weekend to some unpredictable conditions. Arrghhhh!

I pulled up into the apartment parking lot suddenly raging mad. If I was madder than Chloe, she would have no choice but to instantly back off of whatever nonsense she would be griping about. I opened the front door anxiously, and yelled out "Chloe!" To my surprise, the house smelled like sweet smelling perfume, the kind that I knew she loved. The room was dim and lit up with candles everywhere. I smelled a strong scent of garlic and herbs, which meant she was preparing one of my favorite dishes of T-bone steak and potatoes. I looked down at the floor, and it was sprinkled with rose petals. The trail led from the front door to the bedroom. I was in shock. All of my imitation rage subsided, and I began to smile. I was confused but in a good way. Then, the bedroom door opened. Low and behold, it was Chloe. She was looking so sexy and seductive, wearing a matching hot pink bra and thong outfit. Her hair was wet like she had just gotten out of the shower. She was dressed in a white bathrobe that was open in the front. You could see her pointy nipples poking through the satin bra. She smiled at me while biting her lip. God, I hated how I couldn't resist when she did that. It made my heart race, my blood pump, and my little friend hard.

"Time for your bubble bath, big daddy."

Mmmm... I loved being treated like royalty, but before I would commence with the festivities, I needed some answers. She had to have either messed up, or she wanted something *really* bad.

"Umm... What are you up to, woman? This seems like a setup." I had watched bait car too many times to play Boo Boo the fool. Chances are, if it's a nice car, with keys in it, then there's probably a task force watching not too far away.

"It's no setup, baby. It's what you deserve. You've been working so...so... hard...on your school project, and rehabilitating your leg that I thought I would cater to you tonight." It sounded good, almost too good to be true. I was still suspicious of her abnormal behavior. She walked toward me and hugged me. She smelled amazing, like fresh, sweet smelling conditioner and expensive perfume. She kissed me slowly while throwing my crutches to the side. She put my arm around her neck and helped me hobble to the bedroom.

She pushed me onto the bed and then undressed me slowly. She undid my pants and took out my boner, which was as hard as a lead pipe right now. She spit on it and then put it in her warm, wet mouth. All I could feel was her moist, soft tongue going up and down my shaft, up and down, up and down. Then she wrapped her lips around it firmly. "Ah" was all that I could mumble. The pleasure was overwhelming. I was in complete ecstasy. She started moaning louder while sucking it faster and faster. "Please bust in my mouth, daddy!" she begged in between slobs.

"Don't stop!" I could suddenly feel a tingling sensation take over my body as I became numb. "Ahhhh!" I groaned as my toes curled. My dick began to have spasms as I squirted quick shots of my warm load in her mouth. She smiled and giggled when I released all of my tension. Then I heard her slosh around my man milk from cheek to cheek before gulping it down. Amazing! She was playing no games tonight. Her kinkiness was a turn on, but also kind of frightening how good it was at the same time. She really did satisfy me.

"Now it's bath time." She grabbed my hand and walked me into the bathroom one hop at a time. She situated me in the tub and, afterward, began to brush her teeth into the sink. "Don't soak for too long, Papi. Dinner's almost ready." She left the bathroom, while I sat there in the hot bubbles. What in the *HELL* was going on? Chloe was treating me like a king without an explanation. Even though I was enjoying the hospitality, I knew better. Something was up. I eventually got out of the tub, got dressed, and made my way to the dining room table. There were two steaming plates filled with juicy steaks, creamy buttered mashed potatoes, biscuits, and green beans. She sat down on one end while I sat on the opposite side of the candlelit table. Some slow R&B was playing in the background. It felt like I was in a movie. I didn't know what I did to deserve this, but whatever it was I needed to keep doing it. This felt too good. As much as I didn't want it to end, I had to get to the bottom of this. She blessed the food, and I took my first bite of the steaming steak—medium well, just how I liked it. As soon as I sunk my teeth into it, all I could taste was tender juiciness, seasoned to perfection. This was the straw that broke the camel's back. Enough was enough. I needed an answer—now.

"Baby, I love the setup, and the dinner is fabulous, almost too incredible. It makes me raise an eyebrow like why are you doing this? I mean, what is all of this about?"

"What's this all about?" she repeated defensively. "Wow, Randy. I can't do something nice for my loving boyfriend?"

"Don't lie to me, woman! This steak taste too damn good! You ain't never cooked a steak this good before! What's up?" She looked at me deep into my eyes. She could tell I wasn't buying her bull. She looked down at the table as she started explaining.

"Well, I was at the computer today..."

"And..."

"I googled your name, babe..."

"And..."

"And I got a question for you." Google could find anything relevant in society. I didn't know if she had run a background check on me, or maybe looked up my embarrassingly low credit score. Either way, I felt like it was a trust issue to violate my privacy by snooping around on the internet.

"Well, go ahead, ask away. I really don't appreciate you invading my privacy like that."

"I'm sorry, babe. I really didn't mean to, honestly. But is your real name Randy Stashi or is Randy just a nickname?"

"Umm..." I was bewildered by her dumb line of questioning. "You know Randy Stashi is my full government name babe. Quit playing."

"Are you sure?"

"One hundred percent sure."

"That's what I thought. That means someone else has your same name or you're responsible for the latest New York Times bestselling book, The Stashi Life."

That's when it hit me like a brick. I smiled and looked into her eyes. I suddenly had an epiphany of why I was being treated like a sultan.

"Umm... No...."

She looked at me slowly and then focused back to the food on her fork.

"You know baby, you're really going to have to get better at lying, especially if you're going to be famous!"

Cover—completely—blown.

Chapter 45

"They say those who laugh last, think slowly, but I know for a fact that this is not a class of slow thinkers, so this should not be our last laugh! Our journey shall be filled with any laughs and joyful moments long after this as we press on to greater achievements! You've done it! Congratulations colleagues! Yeaaaahh" Loud applause roared from the crowd, as we stood up.

"When we call your name, please come across the stage and receive your diploma...." Here I stood among a graduating class of about 600 students. We had finally completed our year-long laborious group project of building a city from scratch. In the end, there were a lot of disputes and arguments, but as a group, we got it done. What was most impressive was the amount of detail that we had put into it. It didn't require the minute in-depth logic, but our efforts solidified our grade as an A.

"Kallub Smith."

Applause. So here I was slowly making way to the stage about to officially become a college graduate. It still hadn't hit me yet, the actual magnitude of this occasion. I think that's how most major life events are. It doesn't hit you until after the fact, like when you get the news that someone dies. It doesn't hit you until weeks later when their phone is dead, they don't make an update on their Facebook page, or you don't see their car driving around anymore. I was feeling absolutely and positively nothing right now. I was in a room full of thousands of people. Alumni, family, and faculty, all shouting, whistling, and clapping as loudly as humanly possible.

"Neil Patterson."

Applause. They were calling the names slower and slower as I got closer. I was in an oversized cap and gown that stopped at my ankles. It was humorous to me, at least how we were all dressed. People had different patches, sashes, and pins. You could tell what classification a person was by what they were wearing.

"Samantha Pierre!" the announcer's voice boomed. Applause. Some people had big hats or different colored sashes. It all looked kind of silly to me, like we were all in a real-life game of wizards and warlocks. The professors looked like sorcerers and magicians, while we looked like wizards in training with the lack of gaudy paraphernalia. I started making my way up the stage

138

steps as they got closer in the alphabet to my name. I was very careful walking with my crutches. My mom and Chloe were somewhere in the crowd. I had spotted them during the dean's commencement speech earlier somewhere in the crowd. It felt good having people who loved you there being supportive. Chloe had graduated a semester earlier, due to her previous high school credits being transferred to college courses. My mom had driven nearly twelve hours by herself to witness the event. I never got too excited about group honors, but I was happy for them to be there. It was almost my turn to walk across the stage.

"Jason Rubio"

Applause. The only thing I was thinking was don't trip. Don't you dare trip. I had decided to walk across with my crutches instead of my wheelchair at the last minute.

"Randy Stashi!"

Applause. My turn. I felt kind of nervous. I swayed across the stage while smiling fervently. I shook the dean's hand, grabbed the diploma, and posed for the photographer. Click. The flash blinded me for a couple of seconds, and I made my way back to my seat. I was done, completely finito. Even though I don't know what the future holds, I felt accomplished because I had completed something. We were dismissed shortly thereafter, and we congregated in front of the auditorium. Looking back on it, college was a blast, a lot of parties, a lot of drinking, all types of drugs, and an incredible amount of sex. I met my girlfriend, cool colleagues, and attained my degree. From this point on, on paper, I was certified in the art of business administration (with a bachelor's degree). My mind could now be freed and applied to bigger things that I had my heart set on. After the ceremony was over, I linked up with Chloe and my mom outside for some quick photos on their smartphone.

"Congratulations, sweetie."

"Thanks, Mom. I appreciate it."

"Where do you want to go out to eat?"

"It doesn't matter. I'm in the mood for hot wings."

She hugged me tightly, and we continued with the small talk. I was looking around for my other colleagues while she was talking when suddenly, someone pinched my backside. I turned around startled. It was Chloe.

"Hey, lady!"

"Hey, handsome!" I pecked her on the cheek while holding her close. I looked over my shoulder and saw my mom looking confused.

"Sorry for being rude. This is the girl I've told you about so many times mom, Chloe. And Chloe, this is my mom Ms. Stashi." Chloe extended her hand, but my mom reached out with both arms for a hug.

"Awww... I've heard so much about you, Chloe."

"I hope they were all good things." She cocked her head as she said it.

"More good than bad. Thanks for taking care of my son for me."

"It's more like he takes care of me. Ha ha ha." They both laughed and looked at me.

"I don't tell her too many bad things about you, babe." Just then I felt a tap on my shoulder. I looked over. It was a middle-aged man with glasses and a pin-striped suit. Who was this? He didn't look familiar. I had no idea who he was or why he wanted my attention.

"Can I help you?"

"Sorry for interrupting y'all...."

"You're good. What's up?"

"I have a quick question for you."

"Go ahead."

"Please forgive me if I've made a mistake, but are you Randy Stashi?" I didn't like where this was going.

"Depends on who's asking." I could see my mom and Chloe looking confused in my peripheral vision.

"I'm just asking, I know you probably get this a lot but are you the author of the book, The Stashi Life?" He caught me totally off guard with his question. A wave of relief came over me. I just smiled while I thought of something witty to say.

"Ha ha. I knew it. Hot damn, I knew it! That book has changed my life man! What an honor it is to finally meet you in person!" He squeezed my hand so hard with excitement that I thought he was going to break it.

"Honey, come here! I told you it was him!" I proceeded to meet his wife and his daughter who happened to be in my graduating class. "Can I get your autograph?" He shoved the graduation itinerary and a pen into my chest space. Wow. I was in a complete state of shock that someone thought so highly of the book. My first fan, and my first autograph that I was aware of.

"Who do you want me to make it out to?"

"Michael Wayne and family."

"To…Michael…Wayne… Keep living the Stashi life so you can get the most out of life!"

"Wow. They aren't going to believe this. He gave me another hug and shook my hand again before he walked off. My mom walked up afterward. She had observed everything from a distance.

"Who was that, honey?"

"Just a fan." I smiled at her while readjusting my crutches.

"A fan?"

"Hey, hot shot!" It was a familiar voice yelling from my side. I was trying to pinpoint who it was, but my mind drew a blank. I turned to the right and saw a lady in a black dress with short hair and a pearl necklace.

"Congratulations on graduating, Mr. Stashi!" Once she spoke again, I realized where I had heard that voice before. We had talked on the phone many times, although we had never met in person.

"It's me, Dana."

"Heeeeyyyyy Dana!" I hugged her so tight that I ended up dropping my crutches.

"Whoa!" She exhaled.

"I'm happy to see you."

"Not as happy as I am to see you."

"What are you doing here?" I questioned anxiously.

"What kind of book agent would I be if I didn't show up to see my top client accomplish a major milestone in his life?"

"A pretty selfish one, I guess."

"I know." She smiled.

"Well, I'm glad you came. I really am."

"And I'm glad that you've finally finished this chapter in your life. No pun intended. Ha…" she giggled at her own joke. It was goofy, but it did make me feel at ease.

"Me too. It definitely was a challenging one."

"I bet. Are you ready to embark on the next exciting chapter of your life?"

"And which chapter is that?"

"The one where we make you a household name silly goose, your nationwide book tour!"

Ahhhh. It sounded glorious, but truth be told I didn't know if I would be able to handle the publicity. I hoped I wasn't scared of success. It was only a few moments ago that I had signed my very first autograph. While it did feel remarkable, at the same time, it kind of creeped me out that a stranger can know every detail about you and your life. I realized that your privacy is no longer your privacy. This was the crossroads where I had to decide if I would cross the line. This could possibly be the turning point, the big break, where my life could change forever.

Decisions. Decisions.

Chapter 46

Never say never, not unless you're saying can't in the same sentence. In that case, it only works because it's a double negative. Never and can't have to be added to the forbidden vocabulary list because no one ever knows their limitations. So, check this out. Here I was, little 'ole me, backstage at the hottest talk show on daytime television, The Window. It was hosted by the world-renowned television personality, Porsha Gottfrey. Right now, I'm in the midst of it all. I am backstage receiving last-minute instructions from the stagehands. It still doesn't feel real yet. The importance and magnitude of this whole ordeal hasn't even begun to set in yet.

"Okay, you'll be on in about five minutes. Do you remember the guidelines?" The stagehand was wearing a plaid flannel shirt, faded denim jeans, and headphones with a microphone attached to it. He had a soft feminine voice that stood out immediately when he spoke because it didn't seem to match his appearance.

"Yes, I remember the guidelines.… Read the teleprompter if the red light is flashing."

"What else?"

"Wait until the applause button dims before you begin speaking."

"And last thing."

"No profanity unless we're on break."

"No, no! Not even when we're on break. People are always watching."

"Got it."

"Good. Now stand in this area right here, and I'll direct you where to walk. You nervous, Randy?" My hands were trembling. My forehead began to sweat, and my spit began to taste bitter. I took a deep gulp.

"Me? Nervous…? No way!" Lies. I had to hype myself up to mask my anxiety. Biggest daytime talk show according to the ratings, nationwide television audience, millions of reruns. The sheer monstrosity of those numbers began to make me dizzy. I wanted to faint. Focus Randy, focus!

"Good. You'll be on in four minutes and counting." Momentarily, I had spaced out and totally forgotten about the stagehand standing right in front of me. I came back to reality and gave him the thumbs up. I turned around to scope the one person who could build me up instantly. I spotted him humoring some beautiful girls in tight dresses on a couch. "Heeeeey!" I motioned him to come toward me quickly. He looked annoyed but still excused himself and strode to where I was standing. He was wearing a blue long-sleeve button-down with a red polka dot bowtie. I didn't know why he chose that ridiculous outfit, but it would suffice. Nerds never seem to dress well because they're too preoccupied with matters other than fashion. This person and his tendencies were no different.

"Sorry for interrupting you."

"You're not sorry first of all, and I'm definitely working on something for you, so you don't have to go home and jack off by your damn self, Randy!"

"Don't forget what we're here for, Dr. Tracz. Business first, pleasure optional. Do you remember what they said?"

"Yeah, no profanity, blah, blah, blah." He pulled a flask from inside his pocket. He then unscrewed the cap and started gulping it down.

"Hey, Doc—!" I reached for the flask so he would stop chugging it immediately. I snatched it out of his hand and began to scold him. You could smell his whiskey breath from where I was standing.

"We've worked way too hard for you not to take this seriously, Dr. Tracz!"

"Ninety seconds!" the stagehand yelled. I could feel my heart pump faster and my eyes widen. I was still overcoming my stage fright. Awww, screw it! I turned my back to Dr. Tracz and began chugging everything in his flask. I could feel the gasoline-like burn go down my throat.

"That's the spirit my boy!" he cheered. I wiped my mouth with the back of my hand slowly as I passed the empty flask back to Dr. Tracz. "Feel better?"

"Not yet?" I noted, knowing that it was bound to kick in momentarily. He shook the empty flask realizing there was none left.

"Well, you better start feeling indebted because you drank all of it, you greedy bastard." I smiled widely with satisfaction.

"Welcome back from the break. It's The Window with Porsha Gottfrey!"

The applause peaked and then faded. "I have a special treat for y'all today. Our next guest is a breakthrough author on the rise with a masterpiece that is adored by the masses. His book, *The Stashi Life* is on every bestseller list and bookshelf in the country. It talks about mind control and transferring energy spiritually. He has recently accomplished his bachelor's degree in business administration and is an inventor slash entrepreneur in his latest endeavor Stashi Labs, which is dedicated to aiding the handicapped and physically challenged. Not to mention ladies, he's pretty cute. Can we please give a warm Window welcome to Raaaaaaaaandy Staaaaaaaaaaashi!"

"Go!" The stagehand motioned for me to walk on stage. After that flattering introduction, I couldn't help but smile. This was the moment that I had been waiting for. This was what I had worked so hard for. Showtime. I walked out on my crutches slowly and deliberately. The spotlights hit me with blinding lights and extra heat. It was an audience of about 150 people clapping and looking excited. I continued over to Porsha and gave her a hug and a kiss on the cheek. She smelled like sweet cinnamon.

"Pleasure to meet you," she whispered to me inaudible to the audience.

"The real pleasure is all mine," I mouthed back.

She outstretched her arms as a gesture to have a seat. I sat down and leaned my crutches on the chair. By this time, the applause light had dimmed, and the clapping and cheering dissipated.

"My oh my! What a pleasure it is to finally meet you, Mr. Stashi."

"Pleasure to be on the show. And thank you for the superhero-like introduction. It made me blush." The crowd chuckled quietly.

"Ha ha, yes. Your resume is quite impressive, to say the least. You've been quite the busy bee. So, tell us about your latest project that's been stirring up all the excitement throughout the country. Tell us about The Staaa-shi Life."

"Whoooooo !" Cheers and applause from the crowd ensued as she magnified the book cover on the big screen behind us. Then people started standing up, one by one. I became overwhelmed with joy and astonishment that this book had garnered so much appreciation and attention. I smiled and waved as I waited for the noise to die down. I looked back at Porsha. I had completely lost my whole train of thought.

"What was the question, again?" She laughed.

"Well, alot of people need no introduction to your piece of work, but for those who don't know, tell us about your book, The Stashi Life."

"Oh yeah, well first off I want to thank everyone that got a copy. I'm only here because of you. And for those who don't know, it's a book that I wrote while I was living at my mom's house rehabilitating."

"Rehabilitating?"

"Yes, rehabilitating my legs. I got at least one still kicking." I patted my left leg and heard a mixed reaction of chuckling and gasps from the crowd. Porsha gave me a concerned but curious look at my awkward answer. It was the way she scrunched her eyebrows.

"Aww. What happened Randy?"

I paused for a moment unsure if I should reveal what had transpired. I'll just keep it short.

"I was robbed and shot at point blank range. Basically, I was caught up in the wrong things, and the wrong people found out. I thought I was dead."

"Awwwwwwwwwww…" I could hear sympathetic moans coming from the crowd. Their empathy was relieving. No matter how much time had passed since that incident, I still remembered that painful experience like it was yesterday. I still remembered lying in a puddle of my own blood thinking that I was dead, thinking of how much my mom was going to cry when she heard the dreadful news that her only son was killed.

"So, then what happened?" Porsha asked.

"Well, I was on bedrest for quite some time, so I started reading and researching principles about energy and thought transformation, and realized that this was an interesting subject that could help a lot of people. I was mad Porsha. No, I was furious, at myself, at the people who shot me, at my girlfriend who just up and left me, at a lot of things. So, I thought to myself, What if I channel this anger and frustration into something positive that could be utilized for the greater good? Then voila! That became the motivation for this book." Loud applause filled the room after I gave that answer. Porsha was clapping with surprised raised eyebrows.

"I love it, Randy! One part of the book that was really eye-opening for me was the visual communication. It's going to sound far fetched ladies, but follow me through this process. He defines it as you look someone in their eyes and think mentally about what you are trying to say to them. They can understand and respond without a word being said. It's almost like mind reading. It is a deeper level of communication because you are making a connection through concentration. Now that's deep, Randy." Quick applause filled the room.

"That's a great way of explaining it, Porsha. It is deep because when we as people connect on a deeper level, less has to be said and more can be understood. If I feel like we have a connection, I'll break my back and fly to the moon for you—not because you want it, but because helping you helps fulfill my life's purpose. You succeeding means we succeeded." Applause. I smiled and nodded while rubbing my hands. They were understanding.

"I have a quick question for you. Where did you come up with this?" I looked over at her, not knowing how to answer.

"I came up with these ideas from the teachings of my…" I was about to give credit where credit was due not even thinking, but luckily, I caught myself. My mom begged me time and time again never to mention my father or Stewart Mild's name. To do so would be a blatant and deliberate betrayal. This conversation would bring her to tears every time, so I dropped the whole issue and maintained my promise. I stopped in mid-sentence. My response lingered in the air.

"…I came up with these teachings and principles from my research on the internet and various motivational speakers." Ahhh, it sounded lame, but it would have to suffice. I spotted my mom; she was in the front row nodding yes.

"It's a great read y'all. You're going to have to pick this one up. It'll change your life, mindset, and goals forever!"

"Thanks, Porsha."

"Now, we have to get the juiciness.…"

"Uh oh," I always hated being put on the spot. Quiet laughter.

"Are you married, single, got a girlfriend?"

"Oooh, I am currently in a relationship with my girlfriend. Hey babe, I'm on TV…" I waved and stared directly at the camera. The audience let out an "Awwww." I didn't know if they were expressing sentiment to me waving at my girlfriend, or just genuinely disappointed that I wasn't single. "She loves your show by the way."

"If that's the case, you should've invited her."

"She had to work. Someone's got to pay the bills."

"Ha ha," the crowd erupted.

"That's crazy that you didn't bring anyone to the show with you." I pointed to her.

"I did. There goes my mommy…. Wave, Mom."

She waved bashfully, my mom was always the shy type.

"Oh…so, now I see where you get your good looks from," Porsha complimented.

"Everyone says that we have the same nose and dimples."

"Almost identical, Mr. Stashi. Ha ha," Porsha chuckled. "Well, when we come back, Randy has something exciting and new that the world has never seen. I can't wait, and I know you can't wait either, so don't touch that dial!" You're watching the best show on daytime television, The Window!" Ahh, Relief. Part one of this episode for us was over. The applause light came on. Now I began to ponder about part two. We were now mere moments away from shocking the world, with something that's never been seen before. This was years and years in the making. It was so much money invested just to get to this point. Hopefully, everything would go smoothly. Hopefully, Dr. Tracz wouldn't mess this moment up for us!

Chapter 47

Being a kid and being an adult are classified on opposite ends of the spectrum, but they really aren't opposite, more like parallels. As a kid, you play outside in a playground; as an adult, that evolves into partying at the local club or a concert. As a kid, you have to do chores so you can get an allowance. As an adult, you have to work to get a paycheck. Fridays as a kid were very memorable, to me at least, because at school, that was show and tell day. Some Fridays I dreaded because I had nothing new and exciting to share with the class. Other Fridays I was ecstatic because I had a new Teenage Mutant Ninja Turtle action figure or a souvenir from some odd place we had traveled. Now, as an adult, I was sitting in front of hundreds of people on the hottest talk show on daytime television, The Window, about to unveil and demonstrate my latest discovery. I hadn't done it in decades, but I felt like it was show and tell all over again, except this time, it was professional adult show and tell.

"So how are you liking the show so far?"

"It still feels unreal; my mom watches this show all the time!"

"That's funny because it feels unreal to me that you're here right now. Your book was recommended to me by our reader's club a long time ago. I read it and fell in love with the insights and perspectives. We've been trying to get in touch with you to be a guest on our show and it seems like forever. Your publisher always gave us an excuse. So I assumed our show didn't suit your taste, but here you are...the man, the myth, the legend; sitting right next to me."

I guess Dana really wasn't lying. The whole time I was blowing her and the tour off while I was in school, there were people who were really requesting my presence. They wanted to see me. They wanted to hear me. They wanted to meet me. It felt good to be needed.

"I am so so grateful for this opportunity Porsha. You just don't know. I do apologize for keeping you waiting for so long. I was just kind of nervous about this whole ordeal. One minute you're at your mom's house, bored watching Netflix, and the next minute you're on The Window talking to the world-renowned, Porsha Gottfrey. It's mind-blowing how quick your life can change."

"Yes, it is." she agreed. She then leaned in toward me, placed her hand on my knee and smiled at me.

"You don't have to be nervous...."

We made deep eye contact and held it for a long, long time. Realistically, it couldn't have been more than five seconds, but it felt like an eternity. I didn't know if she was making a pass at me or if this was standard guest protocol. Either way, I had to keep my composure. I have a loving girlfriend that's probably watching this, and this was strictly business. I was here to promote, not picnic, not even if she was sexy, not even if she was the host of the hottest daytime talk show on TV. Not even if she could change my life forever.

"We'll be back on in thirty seconds," said the stagehand.

"Do you need any water?" Porsha asked slowly. I was still in a deep trance gazing into her eyes. I nodded my head up and down. She looked away and motioned the other stagehand.

"Water please!" she yelled, then pointed at me. The stagehand walked over hurriedly with a small bottle of water in her hand. She twisted the cap off and passed it to me. I gulped it down instantly. Now, this is what I call service! I was only a guest on the show, but I was being treated like a king. Any wish was at my command. If I wanted something, all I had to do was snap my fingers, or wiggle my nose! I passed the bottle back to the stagehand, and she walked away quickly.

"Ten seconds!" the stagehand yelled.

"Get ready," Porsha said to me.

"Everyone start clapping in...five...four...three...two...ONE!"

You could hear the volume of the applause gradually increase from the claque. Porsha smiled as the applause died down.

"And we're back to The Window, giving you a different view of the world. I'm your host, Porsha Gottfrey, and we're here today with bestselling author Randy Stashi. How are you feeling?"

"Good, mixed with some nervousness, and sprinkled with stressed!"

"Ha ha. That's all right," she said to me before looking toward the audience. "The reason why he's nervous is because he is unveiling his latest invention! Right here! Right now, on The Window!" Cheers of excitement roared from the crowd. I felt a huge surge of energy tingle throughout my body. This was the moment we were waiting for. This was the moment that was years in the making.

"Let's give a warm Window welcome to Mr. Stashi's partner, Doc-taa Traahkz!" She had pronounced it wrong. It's like trays. The c was silent. I think it was European. I couldn't blame her, it looks different than it sounds on paper. I glanced over to the right, not knowing what to expect. Dr. Tracz came out in typical Dr. Tracz fashion. You would've thought he was the headlining fighter about to get in the boxing ring or a NBA star making a spectacle with a flashy pre-game ritual. He jogged slowly up to the front row and gave everyone high fives. He then did a little shimmy walk that could've passed for an end zone dance. After that, he came to give Porsha a hug while slowly moving his hand down her back onto her buttocks. Porsha frowned vaguely after feeling Dr. Tracz's hands move into the no-fly zone. Then he gave her a slight peck on the cheek. You could tell she was partly startled, and partly resisting his womanizing tactics. He took a seat on the chair and continued to blow kisses to the audience in every direction. If Dr. Tracz hadn't been so successful in medicine, he would've definitely blossomed in Hollywood.

"Welcome to the show, Dr. Tracz. Am I saying that right?"

"Not quite Porsha, but you can call me whatever you…like. I love this show!" You could hear laughter from the claque.

"What an exuberant intro you gave us. You're quite a showman!"

"I'm a teenage college frat boy trapped in an old doctor's body." Everyone began laughing again, this time, even Porsha.

"That's pretty funny, I'm sure you keep your wife at home thoroughly entertained." You could tell that last statement struck a nerve with him because his facial expression changed.

"No wife, Porsha. In fact, I'm recently divorced and alone. I'm just looking for a special someone to fill that void in my life." He sounded sad and looked even sadder.

"Awww…" The whimpers from the crowd added to the drama. I had to hand it to Dr. Tracz. He sure did know how to play on people's emotions, especially women's.

151

"You hear that ladies? He's single and ready to mingle!"

"Ooooh…" some ladies in the audience cooed at him.

"Now, let's get to the nitty-gritty. I want to see the surprise you have waiting for us."

"Rowr! Easy tiger," said the doctor.

He motioned the stagehand to come to the stage. She was holding our prized possession, our baby. It glowed as the newness emitted a radiance. She placed it on the table in front of us. It had silver parts that shimmered in the light. Bold gold letters were on the back of it. It looked like an expensive, luxurious toy designed for only the affluent.

"What is this?" Porsha curiously questioned. I began to answer her in my deep movie trailer voice.

"Ladies and gentlemen, today I'm bringing you something that is going to change lives dramatically and revolutionize the world as we know it. The first groundbreaking invention from Stashi Labs… Behold! The Hoverfoot 3000!"

It was only at that moment that I had realized the gravity of what we had accomplished. Our wrath of genius had finally been unleashed to the world. And it felt awesome.

This was probably the last time I would ever need crutches or a wheelchair again EVER!' I quietly thought to myself.

Chapter 48

"A-ha! We did it, my boy!"

Dr. Tracz was dancing around like the old grandpa when Charlie found out he had the golden ticket. He ran up and hugged me tightly, lifting me off the ground while spinning me in circles. I felt like a hero backstage. Our new invention had finally been revealed, and I had thrown my crutches away in the garbage can on national television. We were now regarded differently, as genius inventors who had crafted a miracle that would heal the world.

"Yes, we did!" I shouted back at Dr. Tracz, hugging him. It had been a long journey up to this point, but we had finally completed the mission. Everyone was giving us handshakes and high fives backstage. Celebratory praises for our invention were everywhere. It felt like we had just won a presidential election. I knew that I had to contain my excitement to maintain some level of professionalism, but I just couldn't. I felt like an eight-year-old at sunrise on Christmas morning.

"Baby, you did it! Hallelujah!" I could detect my mom's voice anywhere. I turned around to see her face. She had a smile, Kleenex in her hand, and tears rolling down her cheeks. If she frowned, she could've been mistaken for weeping, but her smile indicated that they were tears of joy. My foot floated inches above the ground as I walked toward her. Her eyes were fixated on my right leg. Then she slowly looked back up to my face. She couldn't believe what she was witnessing. Muah! Muah! Muah! She gave me big kisses on the cheek while she held me tightly.

"You know you're one of a kind, Randy. I knew you were special!" There's nothing more valuable or heart-warming than hearing a parent's praise. It feels like their approval can compel you to fly or save the world. I suddenly didn't feel human anymore. I felt immortal. I knew I was human, however, because I still couldn't feel my leg. I also felt supernatural because I realized that anything I wanted to accomplish, I could—anything. There were no boundaries or limitations. We had just shocked the whole wide world on the most popular daytime television talk show on television, The Window. My heart was beating as loud as a drum, and I couldn't stop smiling. I felt high, but this wasn't like a temporary drug high. It was a high on life high, a high that was indescribable and undeniable. I knew that I would have a hard time calming down for quite a while. I finished up the conversation with my mom finding out her evening plans as well as her plane departure itinerary. I confirmed a dinner date with her as soon as my schedule calmed down. I waved goodbye to her and then I felt a hand on my shoulder. He spoke in a low grave tone.

"Stashi, my boy, thanks for bringing me back to life! I would've probably killed myself by now overdosing on the drugs, party life, or coping with that nasty divorce if you didn't rescue me. Thanks for believing in me!" I turned around and looked at Dr. Tracz. His eyes were red and watery.

"I couldn't have pulled this off without you. You were the light at the end of my tunnel. Now, I no longer have to be restrained by crutches and wheelchairs. I can walk again freely, Dr. Tracz, something that I thought I would never be able to do again in this lifetime. I didn't rescue you. *You* rescued *me!*" I hugged him again with a tight grip. Emotions were running at an all-time high backstage, a lot of tears and a lot of smiles. It kind of reminded me of a scene from a trashy talk show when they finally find out who the kid's father is, and they end up having a group hug slash emotional family pow wow backstage.

"I want to introduce you to some people, Randy, come this way." I followed him without hesitation. I was eager to find out who else I would meet today. I felt like I had hit the lottery or just been elected for something important.

"You're going to love the surprise that I have waiting for you!" The word surprise always got me excited. I loved surprises. Only the good kind though. As we walked up, I noticed three sexy, scantily dressed women focused on me. One was popping her bubble gum, the other was licking her lips, and the last one was fluttering her eyes at me. All three of them were staring at me like a piece of meat. All three of them looked good enough to be award winning pornstars.

"This is Tina, Tanya, and Teresa. Say hi ladies to the mastermind who orchestrated all of this...Mr. Stashi!" They all came over to me at once and started rubbing my hands, chest, and arms.

"Hi, Mr. Stashi!"

"Umm... Hi, ladies!" This seemed too good to be true.

"We've heard so much about you, and we're big, big fans of your book," Tanya said seductively. I could feel my dick slowly turning into steel. I could get used to this life of fame. I already liked the perks.

"I'm glad you liked it!" They smelled like sweet vanilla and fruit. It was intoxicating.

"Ooooh! Can I play with your Floatfoot?" Tina whispered into my ear as she started rubbing the front of my pants.

"Whoa! Whoa!" I took a step backward. As much as I wanted to have fun with these hookers or groupies, I remembered my beloved girlfriend at home. She stuck with me through thick and thin before any of this happened. Having fun with these girls would be no way to repay her loyalty.

"Dr. Tracz, what's going on?"

"What do you mean Randy? It's time to party. Ayee!" It took every ounce of self-discipline in my body to resist Dr. Tracz's offer with these bombshells.

"I'm going to have to catch up with y'all later. I've got some things to handle."

"Aww…c'mon Randy, don't be such a party pooper!"

"Yeah, Randy…. You don't like us?" Tina grabbed my hand and put it on her plump booty. It felt so good, so soft, like a pillow. I couldn't help it. I squeezed it just to feel how juicy it was. Then I came to my senses. What am I doing? Whatever it is, let it go. It's not worth it.

"I really do like y'all. It's not that. I just have some other things to handle. Imma link with you later, Dr. Tracz."

"Awww," the ladies groaned in unison.

"Welp, call me when you're ready kiddo. Ladies, it's time to hop on the love train. Choo choo!" He signaled his arm like he was pulling the horn like a train conductor. I had to hand it to Dr. Tracz. Wherever he went, he had a beautiful damsel right there next to him if not two or three. He definitely still had some smooth pimpin' in his blood. His post-marriage life was something similar to the likes of Hugh Hefner. I don't know what he took for his perpetual sex drive, but by him being a doctor, I know he had access to the best pills money could buy.

"Great show, Stashi!" I was so deep into my thoughts about the show, and the backstage groupies, that I had forgot where I was for a second. I turned around. To my surprise, it was Porsha. She looked like an A-list actress in person.

"Thanks again for allowing me to be here. This was nothing short of a dream come true."

"Likewise..." She looked stunning. It was amazing how on a TV screen someone can look like an untouchable, bigger than life celebrity who you will never share the same oxygen with. Now that we were backstage minus the bright hot lights and audience, she seemed like a regular down to earth person, just like anyone else, someone who felt real, someone who had flaws. Someone who was normal.

"Where's your next stop?" she asked.

"Excuse me?" I was confused about what she was getting at.

"You're on a book tour, correct? Don't you have another destination after this?"

"Ohhh, I mean yeah. I have to check my email again, but it is somewhere not too far, hopefully; between me and you, I hate traveling."

"I know exactly what you mean. By the time you get comfortable, wah-wah, it's time to pack up and leave again."

"Ha ha... Basically, but I really can't be mad at anyone but myself. This is what I signed up for."

"Gotta take care of business, so business can take care of you."

"Never heard of that one before."

"Well, if you're not leaving today I'd really like to learn more about your new endeavors and some more background information on your book. It really helps guide me positively in my daily routine if that's okay with you. If you need to leave; I understand."

RED ALERT! RED ALERT! PANIC! Mayday! Code blue! Nine one one! I'm about to faint. No, you aren't, Randy. Get a grip on yourself. Did I just get asked out by the hottest host on television, who's rich, popular, and drop dead gorgeous? Am I dreaming? Don't faint, Randy. Keep it together, please. I had to try my hardest to restrain from fainting or acting like a Powerball lottery winner.

"Umm, I think my plane leaves tomorrow afternoon, so I'm kind of stuck here until then." Her smile brightened at my response.

"Sounds like you'll be bored until then."

"I hope not."

"Well, write down your number, and I'll give you my card. We can meet up around sevenish at the Downtown Palm Tree Plaza." She handed me two of her cards. I wrote my number down on one and kept the other for myself. I passed her the one with my number, and she winked as she slipped it into her purse.

"Well, I know you've had a long day, so I'll let you go, Mr. Stashi. Thanks again for coming and I'll be seeing you soon."

"I can scratch this off my bucket list now, Ms. Gottfrey."

"Hehe, don't scratch anything off just yet, Randy." She fluttered her eyes at me slowly while she said my name. I didn't know if this was sexual tension, flirting, or she was just extra friendly. I hugged her and began to walk toward the exit slowly.

"Remember, Stashi, this is strictly business," I heard her call out behind my back. "I want to help you promote your book." I turned to face her while walking backward.

"Understood," I replied with my thumbs up in the air. I didn't know if that was her true intention or just a code phrase to disguise her intent. Either way, she was a great person to have in my corner, especially with me embarking on a new level. Either way, she wasn't the typical run of the mill college girl; she was a renowned talk show luminary. Either way, it was hard to contain my excitement. Of all the people in the world, I just got asked out by the one and only Porsha Gottfrey. This was epic. I had to tell someone, anyone—well, almost anyone.

Anyone, except for Chloe.

Chapter 49

Decisions, decisions. Life is all about decisions and their consequences. Sometimes, you should've made a left instead of going right. Some people are resilient while others never bounce back. The resilient ones can make a bad decision, face horrible consequences, learn from them, and still have the willpower to make it back on top. Others make bad decisions, and rather than learn from them, they blame others or spite themselves. They never really understand the cause and effect principle, and as a result, they crumble. Making good decisions always puts you in a better place while making bad decisions forces you to become a better person. I like to think of myself as the former rather than the latter. I was doing something that I had no business being involved in and almost died. Yeah, at some point, living at my mom's house almost became suicidal especially when I reminisced back to before the incident, but I eventually overcame and progressed. I made a bad decision, paid for it, but crafted an invention to correct it, which as a spillover benefit could be used by the masses. I was the chosen one. Without me and my handicap, there was a chance that the Hoverfoot would've never seen the light of day. I had to suffer and sacrifice so others wouldn't need to suffer and sacrifice. I turned my selfishness to selflessness. I turned bad into beautiful and now I was bathing in a five-star hotel suite on one of the top floors in the heart of downtown, compliments of The Window. God is good.

I hopped out of the shower and dried off. I looked at the clock next to my nightstand—5:55pm. Good timing, but I was still undecided about what I was going to do for the remainder of my evening. Basically, I had three options. I could sightsee the town alone while showcasing the brand new Hoverfoot prototype. I had money, so there were no limitations on what I could do in the city tonight. Option number two was to hang out with Dr. Tracz and those three hot chicks. We would probably take turns banging them, drinking, and doing drugs all night long. My final option was to rendezvous with the one and only Porsha Gottfrey and see what she had in store for me. She might even help me fuel my already successful business or she could just be using that as a deceptive ploy to get intimate. Either way, I had no way of finding out unless I took that chance. Once again, decisions, decisions. As I started getting ready, I could see my phone blinking red, which indicated that I had some missed notifications, one missed call and three new text messages. The first text was from Dr. Tracz asking me when I was dropping by. His room was a couple of doors down from mine. He informed me to bring condoms and rolling papers if I was coming by. He had grown into a good and responsible friend. For one, he wanted to share his women and his weed, and two, he wanted to practice safe sex. It was an enticing offer. Maybe if I was single, but I wasn't. However, if I needed a victory toke to calm down my jitters, then I would pay him a visit later. The call and text were from Chloe. I hadn't talked to her since right before the show, so I know she was calling for an update. Since I missed her call, she typically sent me a text message to transcribe what the call was about. I checked my voicemails every other day, so she never bothered leaving one, claiming it was obsolete. I had to tighten up on this if I was trying to run a successful business.

"Hey, baby! I saw the show. I'm so proud of you. Call me when you're unbusy, xoxo!"

The text made me feel so good. There is nothing more joyous than true love. She had turned from a mere classmate into a loyal and trusting companion that helped keep me on track. Her love instilled an unwavering confidence in me that kept me focused and goal-oriented. She was like a boxing trainer who would coach me in my corner between rounds of a major fight. The last text message was from an unknown number.

"Hey, Mr. Stashi! Just wondering if we were still on for 2nite? I have big, big plans that I want to discuss with you. – Porsha"

Whoo! That text made me smile even harder. I didn't know if I was more interested in what she had hidden for me behind door number three or just excited I was exchanging text messages with one of the most influential women in America. Decisions, decisions. It was 6:05pm now, and our meeting hour was quickly approaching. What should I do? Well, for one, I shouldn't text Chloe back just yet. To do so would unleash a slew of more text messages and callbacks that I didn't have time for just yet. Two, I shouldn't jeopardize my business. Porsha had an offer for me that I had to take seriously. After all, she had unknowingly been on my side from the start. She begged the publisher time and time again to make me a guest on her show. I couldn't even begin to fathom the network and contacts that she could connect me with. I had to see for myself what she had in store for me. I could go there, strictly delve into business matters, then bounce. If she tried to get frisky, I would get skittish and leave immediately, simple as that. I couldn't cheat on Chloe. Plus, I didn't want to cross that line with Porsha. Business and pleasure should never mix— ever. I responded to Porsha via text.

"Hey! I just hopped out of the shower, and I'm getting ready now. What's the address again?"

The only way to succeed is to take risks. Decisions, decisions.

Chapter 50

The sound of the soft, rich classical music filled the lobby of the Downtown Palm Tree Plaza Hotel. There was a roaring fireplace surrounded by elegant furniture. The beautiful and cordial furnishings screamed luxury. From the abstract wall art to the complex woven rugs, every decoration was immaculate. This hotel made my hotel look like it was the projects. I took a seat on one of the comfortable chairs before texting Porsha that I had arrived. While awaiting her response, I sat back and watched the affluent checking in and out of the hotel. Some pulled up in limousines, while others were in exotic six-figure foreign cars. The majority of the people were older with modest but expensive jewelry. There were so many fur coats, pearls, and Rolexes that I felt out of place. I almost felt like I didn't belong with this class of people. It was only some odd years ago when I was renting textbooks and eating Ramen noodles with Chloe. Somewhere along the road. I had elevated to a higher level of grandeur. Sitting in this wealthy hotel waiting on a text from Porsha Gottfrey was the confirmation.

Vvv. Vvvv. My phone vibrated from an incoming text.

'I'm running a little behind. Sorry to keep you waiting. Can you come up to room 4703? I am almost ready.'

I had to grow accustomed to the celebrity lifestyle. I don't know why but it seemed like the famous took great pride in being fashionably late. I used to think it was an accident or pure coincidence, but now I know it's just a gimmick to make a flashy entrance. I didn't want to get used to it, but I knew I had to if I wanted to keep rubbing shoulders with the affluent. I walked over to the hotel clerk's desk since you needed a keycard just to access the elevator.

"Excuse me. I'm trying to go up to room 4703, Ms. Gottfrey." I disguised her name, so I wouldn't raise any red flags.

"Ahhh, yes, Mr. Stashi I presume…. She just called for you. Oh, Jeffrey!" he yelled at one of the bellhops walking behind me. I guess there was no secrecy needed for our rendezvous. Maybe this was strictly business.

"Can you please escort Mr. Stashi to room 4703? Thank you." I nodded my head in appreciation and followed behind Jeffrey. We entered the elevator and made idle small talk.

"That's cool," he said, pointing to my Hoverfoot. I smiled in acknowledgment. He questioned what my occupation was and I semi-lied by telling him I was a student. It was only partly a lie because I was no longer enrolled in any school, but it was partly the truth too because I was a student of life. I just didn't like revealing my identity because I didn't like being treated differently. When I got off the elevator, I tipped him a couple of bucks. I didn't do it because he was nice. I did it because he complimented the Hoverfoot. Compliments are like cash. He pointed in the direction of the room.

"Down the hall and on the right." I nodded again in appreciation as the elevator doors closed behind me. As I approached the door, I could hear the radio playing in her room. I knocked loudly so she could hear me over the music. I heard the volume lower as she called out from afar.

"Come in" I gulped. For just meeting her today, she trusted me immensely to enter her presidential suite while she was still getting ready. I felt privileged. I entered her room and closed the door behind me.

"It's meee—Randy," I called out announcing my presence.

"Hey, Randy! I'll be out in a second. Have a seat on the couch. There's wine on the counter. Help yourself, if you like." There's nothing like the feeling of being a welcomed guest. All the pressure and nervousness leading up to this moment suddenly subsided. At first, I walked over to the massive windows. The view was breathtaking! I was forty-seven floors in the air, and I could see the whole amazing city and more from where I stood. When you look down and see all of the major highways and landmarks, then it really does make it feel like you're on top of the world. I sauntered over to the counter and poured a glass of twenty-year-old Moet. I didn't know the exact price, but I could tell you had to save your pennies for this. It tasted delicious. It was sweet and bubbly with a light bite of alcohol. I sat down on the couch and powered on the flat screen. The TV channel preview station was on as I leafed through various women's fashion magazines that were spread out on the coffee table. I got to page twenty of Trendsetter magazine and saw Porsha Gottfrey on an advertisement for The Window. Wow. She really was a luminary. Just think, little old me was now sitting in her luxurious hotel room sipping wine on her couch, chilling. I know my mama is proud of me.

"Hey Stashi, I'm ready."

"ACCKKK!" When she emerged from her room, I choked and spewed out the wine that I was in the middle of sipping. It was bad. I snorted it out through my nostrils and mouth at the same time. While I thought she would be disgusted, she laughed at my reaction.

"I was thinking about going out tonight, but it's always a hassle with the fans and pictures. So, I thought, why not stay in tonight? Especially since we have the best view in the city." I was still trying to swallow the wine that I had semi-regurgitated. My oh my, she was stunning! She was wearing a fishnet thong where the satin fabric was the only part not see through covering her camel toe. Her busty round tiddies looked like plump grapefruits that were covered in matching turquoise satin. Her robe was barely on her shoulders. She fluttered her eyes while she slowly staggered toward me. She licked her lips at me while I sat there mesmerized and paralyzed. I felt helpless. I couldn't move. I couldn't speak. You would've thought the drink had been spiked if you had seen my motionless reaction. She opened my legs with both of her hands and sat her warm, soft cheeks on my thighs. She felt good. She smelled even better. She happened to be wearing my favorite perfume—Romance. Her hair was still damp and smelled like fresh sweet soap from a hot shower. I felt like a fly that had just got stuck in a spider web. I was hypnotized into her trance. I had to break away. Focus, Randy.

"Did you lock the door?" she questioned. I could barely even concentrate.

"Umm yeah, but ugh, I thought this meeting would be about…"

"Shhh, shhh, shhh…" She put one finger to her lips.

"As a talk show host, sometimes I get tired of talking. Tonight, let's let our bodies do the talking.…"

She pulled down the left side of her bra and revealed her luscious breast. She eased her pointy cold nipple into my face and into my mouth. Her flesh tasted so good. I kissed her nipple and sucked on it gently. She began to let out a soft moan as I took my tongue and moved it in a circular motion around her sweet spot. I began to feel my heart beat quicker as my dick began to bulge through my pants. Gradually, she began to move her hand from my knee cap to my third leg growing along my thigh. I pulled down the other side of her bra and began to suck on her other tiddy just as hard. On the way over here, I thought of a million ways to resist and elude her advances if I ended up in this situation. Now, as I sat in this extravagant room overlooking the city with my breast in my mouth, I couldn't resist. It felt so gratifying having her accept me in this fashion. Truthfully, I kind of wanted her too. I used to watch her on TV

163

and dream about her. Now she was half-naked in my lap. I had to have her, to conquer her, to make her feel me. I was the new up and coming hotshot with a point to prove. I had to make her submit, make her feel my pain, as well as my pleasure. Make her scream my name until her throat became sore. Make her unable to walk straight. Make her remember the day that she met Randy Stashi, forever. She was right. This was strictly business. I had a duty to fulfill. I had to give it to her thoroughly to prove that I was on her level and that she needed me, that I was on a winning streak because I was a winner destined for greatness.

"C'mon!" She grabbed my hand and walked backward toward the bedroom, as I kissed her passionately. I lifted her up by her butt as she wrapped her legs around my waist. The Hoverfoot was enabling me to move like I had no disability. I knew that I would need to take it off to remove my pants.

Muah...Muah... The sounds of kissing, slurping, licking, and drooling were the only sounds aside from the deep breathing, and the R&B coming from the radio. I opened the door and then threw her on the bed forcefully.

"Hee hee hee," she giggled playfully.

"I like it rough, Randy. Can you please give it to me rough, daddy?" OH, MY GAWD. This woman knew what to say and what to push to get me going. By now my stick was bulging through my slacks. If she wants it rough, then rough is what she gets. I leaned over, grabbed her head by her hair and drug her to the edge of the bed. She sucked air through her teeth letting off a slight hissing sound in displeasure. It was sexy. I started unzipping my pants, and by now my erect dick had flopped out.

"No hands!" I demanded, as I took both of my index fingers and pried her mouth open by her teeth. Then I shoved my manhood into her mouth and down her throat as I heard her simultaneously choke and gasp for air. Her gag reflex made her bite down with her teeth softly on my pipe. I slapped her in the face.

"Don't bite! You understand?" She looked up at me with a mouthful and nodded yes. I then grabbed a fistful of her hair on both sides and began slowly stroking my meat down her throat.

"Ahhh!" I let out a sigh of immense pleasure as I leaned my head back and looked at the ceiling. There was nothing like the feeling of hearing her slurping while she wrapped her warm wet tongue around my peter. Her mouth was so juicy. Her eyes started to water as her head was bobbing. I could tell she was enjoying every second of it by the way she clenched my butt cheeks. I removed myself from her jaws, drooled on her tongue, then jammed it back into her mouth. Tonight, my inner freak was on another level. I had to give her a porn star performance. I released my grip from her hair and began to rub her robust booty. They felt like smooth, soft pillows. I began to rub my fingers through her lace-front thong. She was wetter than a soaked sponge. Her thong was damp from being so aroused.

"Someone is ready for me."

"Mmm Hmm" Her response was muffled because my hard tip was blocking her airway. I curled my finger back and forth in her vagina feeling for her g-spot. She began to moan louder and louder. I then curled my finger in front of her face slowly.

"Bring that kitty here...." She rotated her body around until her legs dangled off the bed. I slid her thong down her legs and off her feet. Her pubic hair was shaved in a small triangular patch. I really wasn't the eating type, especially the first time around. However, this situation was different. This was the one and only Porsha Gottfrey. I wanted to taste her juices so bad. I wanted to taste her ambition. I wanted to taste her success. Her box looked like a succulent piece of meat. Her clit was bulging out at the top. I started with the tip of my tongue, and licked her down, then up slowly. She was juicier than a plump peach. She tasted so good to me.

"Oooh! Ooooh!" She let out loud moans of pleasure as she clenched the edge of the bed and the back of my head. I licked her clit clockwise until I felt her body tighten up.

"Ooohh Oooh! Don't stop!" She was submitting. I moved my tongue faster and faster until I heard her shrieking and coming at the same time.

"DON'T STOP! I'M COMING!" I felt her juices drip into my mouth. I sucked her dry then stood up and looked at her. She was smiling with excitement and satisfaction.

"Do you have a condom?" I asked. The Boy Scout motto is be prepared, and I disappointingly disobeyed that slogan tonight. She nodded her head no.

"Are you clean?" she asked. I nodded my head yes. She examined my face hard.

"So, you have no STDs?" she asked me again. "Don't lie to me...."

"No, I don't."

"Well then, you don't need one."

"You're clean?" I kind of already knew the answer, but I had to confirm.

"Of course, plus I'm on birth control...."

"Yeah, right. I've heard that before."

"I have no reason to lie to you, Randy. I'm not going to jeopardize my career over sex." I looked at her deep into her eyes to see if she was fibbing. Normally, I wouldn't trust something like this, but she did have a lot more to lose than I did.

"I want you inside of me—right—now. I want to feel you!" At that instant, I lost it. I lost total control of my body, lost control of my actions, lost control of the moment, lost control of my brain. I held both of her ankles straight up in the air with one hand. I took my other hand and began rubbing my erect rod up and down her juicy clit. She thought I was teasing her, but I was spreading her juices all on my tip before I eased it in.

"Stick it in, daddy!" I heard her moan. It flopped toward the bottom of her vagina and disappeared as it penetrated smoothly inside. She exhaled a deep breath, and I began stroking in and out of her, gradually picking up speed.

"What's my name?"

"Oooh...Ooooh!"

"What's my name?"

"Randy... Oooh...Stashi..." She gasped. This was unbelievable. I was really stroking Porsha Gottfrey while she called out my name. She felt so warm and wet while I was rocking back and forth inside of her.

"Oooh, Porsha! Oooh, Porsha! Oooooh.... You got some great box Porsha! Who's is this?"

"It's yours Randy. All yours babe...."

"Why?"

"Because you deserve it!" I slapped her in the face again.

"No! It's because I earned it!" I started stroking her faster and faster as her knees wrapped around my neck tighter.

"AHGGG! AAAAAGHH!" She shrieked.

"Rough!... Me!... Up!....Good!... Daddy! I've been a bad girl!" She was gasping in between every word she uttered. Her dirty talk was exciting me even more.

"Awww... awww... I'm *about* to *come*! Where do you *want* it?"

"In my mouth, please! I want to *taste* you!" That was all I needed to hear. This was way too much for me to handle. I started feeling that tingling sensation. I exited her and pinned her down with my arms as I climbed on top of her chest. Two thick milky squirts landed on her forehead and in her hair, barely missing her eyes. I directed my hard pipe in her mouth draining the remainder of my nut in her mouth. She choked at first but eventually swallowed it all.

"Mmmm... Did I get all of it?" A sigh of relief came over me. I was panting and dripping sweat all over her curvaceous body.

"You missed some...." I pointed to the spot on her cheek.

"She pushed it with her thumb into her mouth, and then licked her fingers. I rolled over and laid right next to her. Both of our hearts were still beating loud and rapidly as we stared at the ceiling.

"Wow! You're better in real life than in my fantasies." I was shocked at her revelation that she fantasized about me. It was kind of strange, but a turn on at the same time.

"Wanna go another round?" she asked softly.

"Rowr, easy tiger!"

She laughed when I said that.

"Wow! That's the second time I've heard that today!"

Chapter 51

We sipped some more wine and relaxed for a little bit before we engaged in another round, and another round, and another round. Each time was slower and more passionate than the time before. Each time started in a different room, on a different piece of furniture, in a different position. One time, I had her sprawled out on the kitchen counter almost knocking over and breaking the expensive bottle of wine. Another time, she rode me while I laid on the plush polar bear rug. One round kind of scared me. I had her leaning over the glass railing on the balcony, forty-seven floors up in the sky overlooking the beautiful city. When we had finally satisfied each other into exhaustion, we laid in each other's arms. Time flew by in flagrante delicto. It had only been mere hours before when I had felt out of place at this majestic hotel among the highly successful. Now, as I laid naked in Porsha's arms, watching the nighttime skyline through glass wall windows, I felt like I belonged there. I felt like I had earned and deserved it. I still had a long way to go, but this was blatant confirmation that I was making progress. I started drifting into a light sleep when she nudged me awake.

"Hey babe, let's go get something to eat. I'm starving." I was kind of glad she woke me up. I hated spending the night at other people's houses. It feels like the whole morning starts off wrong and all day you're trying to play catch-up.

"Downstairs. I hear the croissants are to die for."

"Mmm. That doesn't sound too healthy." I started relocating my garments. Her room was in shambles. Lamps knocked over, wall art hung crookedly, sheets, pillows, and clothes were littered all over the floor. We had turned this pristine penthouse into a playpen.

"Can I wear your shirt?" She held up my undershirt. It said 'Get Stashi' in big letters across the front. It was part of the publisher's merchandise package when you ordered the deluxe version of the book. I glared at her to confirm her seriousness.

"What? I want to get Stashi too!" I chuckled. "Sure, you can wear it." Giving a woman your clothes after fornication meant that you would probably never see them again. I put on my button down and slacks while she put on my shirt, pajama bottoms, and some sandals.

"You ready?" She waited by the front door. I made my way toward the front examining the room to make sure I wasn't leaving anything.

"You got everything?"

"Yeah," I said uncertainly. My mind was so discombobulated. I didn't even care. As long as I had my wallet and my phone, I was good. Everything else was replaceable.

"C'mon then." She held the door open as I walked backward taking one last look at the suite.

"We destroyed your room, annihilated it completely, like savages."

She giggled at my observation.

"Don't worry, that's what room service is for." I looked up at the ceiling. No cameras. Good. I hugged her and kissed her in the elevator one last time. I knew the rules. In public, we had to keep it platonic. I had to admit it though, she did look amazing in my get Stashi shirt. We sat in a booth. I was trying to sit on the opposite side, but she insisted I sit on her side because she was cold.

"You've never banged a superstar before, have you?" she asked. I laughed at her cockiness.

"I was about to ask you the same thing." I shot back wittingly. She stopped smiling.

"No...really. I wanted to be your first. Now you can scratch it off your bucket list." Even though I laughed, she kind of had a point. Knocking the boots with Porsha was no small feat. But I wasn't a nobody either.

"Soooo...how many copies of The Stashi Life book, have you sold?" I still didn't know how I felt about revealing such private information. It's ironic how you can have no problem getting naked with a stranger, but be totally tight-lipped about other subjects, especially financial ones. Either way, I knew telling Porsha would be more beneficial than detrimental.

"Not sure... Maybe two to three million. I don't keep up with it. I just cash the checks."

Her nonchalant giggle indicated that she was not impressed.

169

"How about your latest invention, the Hoverfoot?"

"None yet. They go on sale in a matter of weeks. We showcased it early just to unveil it on your show."

"Ohhh." Once again, she seemed unimpressed by my response. She looked at me and then gazed onward as if she was brainstorming.

"What are you thinking, Porshy Porsh?"

"I'm thinking that those numbers are satisfying for a newcomer, but aren't good enough to put you on top and keep you there."

"How many of these t-shirts have you sold?"

"Not enough, I guess." I didn't like it when my accomplishments were belittled. She could tell by the deflated energy in my voice that I was getting offended.

"The only reason why I'm asking you this is because I want to help you. Your book has rocked my world with its insightful perspectives, and the least I can do is help your masterpiece elevate to a global household level." My heart began to beat faster.

"So how do you plan on helping me?"

"Well, I'm *personally* going to call your publisher on Monday. I need a printed advertisement, and two thirty-second commercials. I want the printed advertisement in every magazine and news publication that I'm in, and I want the commercials to air during The Window's commercial breaks."

"Wow…" My excitement was revving up.

"Next, I'm going to need the same for the Hoverfoot 3000. You're going to be a household name by the time I'm done with you." I started laughing with joy when I heard the word household.

"Wow. I hugged her. "Thank you, Porsha. Thank you." I was so grateful for her help. I couldn't contain my gratitude in the slightest.

"What's your agent's name again?"

"Dana Sanchez"

"Well, I'll be giving Dana Sanchez a call first thing Monday morning.

Please forewarn her."

"I will; I will." I hugged her again. This time it was passionate, and slow. It almost felt like a massage. Just then, out of the corner of my eye, I saw a waitress walk by with her camera phone out. I stopped the hug abruptly and turned toward her.

"Umm… Excuse me! Yoo-hoo!" The waitress turned and looked at me while sliding her phone into her apron. "Did you just take a picture of us?" I knew what I saw, and that was absolutely the last thing that I needed, someone putting me and Porsha's escapades on front street.

"No, sir. I was just texting my babysitter." I squinted my eyes, examining her face for the slightest flinch or flutter, meaning that she was lying. She held her expression staunchly then looked over at Porsha.

"OH, EM GEE! Porsha Gottfrey! Of all people! Right Here! Right Now! Oh, my Gawd! I have to get a picture now."

"Now's not the best time," Porsha answered reluctantly.

"Please! I watch your show every day! It's The Window…." She proceeded to sing the theme song off-key but on beat. It was more amusing watching Porsha squirm to the cacophonous noise the waitress was making than her actual singing. Porsha smiled painfully. The way the waitress butchered that song, and you could tell that she was annoyed.

"I really appreciate you watching the show but please no pictures. We're eating a private meal, and I look a hot mess." You could see the waitress go from elated to disappointed in a fraction of a second.

"I'll tell you what though."

The waitress looked up to hear the glimmer of hope.

"Write down your name and phone number, and I'll get you some free backstage passes to the live taping of our next show."

"Are you serious?"

"As a heart attack." The waitress quickly took out a scratch sheet of paper and jotted her info down.

"Thank you! Thank you, Porsha!"

"No! Thank you for watching the show. I appreciate your support." They shook hands, and she left. I was still perplexed as to whether she took our picture or not. No one holds a phone that awkwardly without filming something.

"I really think she took our picture," I whispered quietly to Porsha. Porsha finished taking a sip of her hot cocoa before she responded.

"She said she didn't, and I believe her. Quit being paranoid, big Stashi." Maybe she was right. Maybe I was acting a little skittish.

"Who cares, babe? Finish your food." I looked at her and took a deep breath. I polished off my plate, and we finished our discussion. The early morning sun began peering through the glass sliding doors of the hotel's front entrance. It was late, or early rather. I had gotten too comfortable. It was time to go.

"I got to go."

"Aww…" she muttered reluctantly. "You can't stay just a little bit longer?" As tempting as it was to go one more round as the sun rose, I politely declined.

"I wish I could, babe." We hugged one last time and parted our respective ways. I caught a cab back to my hotel room. When I entered the room, it was almost 7:00am. Twelve hours had seemed like twelve minutes. Once again, time flies when you're in flagrante delicto. I laid down to go to sleep. After five minutes I realized that was pointless. I was still amped up from last night's festivities. Still on edge from the wild yet phenomenal sex from mere hours ago. My blood was still pulsating at the thought of how I had my idol sweating butt naked on a kitchen counter screaming out my name and begging for more. I reached for my phone and noticed it was still on silent from my encounter with Porsha. Twenty-three missed calls and eight missed text messages. All from…guess who?

Chloe…

Oh boy. I had to make up something, and it had to be good. Think Randy, think. Every possible alibi I thought up sounded ludicrous. I knew my life and well-being hinged on the answer I gave her. Whew! This was too much pressure for me. I needed a professional opinion for something this serious. I put back on my shoe & hoverfoot and walked next door.

Knock! Knock!

"It's me, Randy...." A minute or two passed, and then I heard the deadbolt clank. The door slowly creaked open, and a disgruntled Dr. Tracz appeared in his boxers with his glasses sitting crookedly on his nose. You could tell he had an amazing night.

"I'm sorry, but I need to smoke something to calm my nerves. You'll never believe what happened to me.... You got any weed left?"

"You got something to roll it up with?" I slowly pulled the box of joint papers out of my pocket.

"That's my boy! Keep it down, okay? The ladies are still sleeping. It was a never-ending saga last night." I walked in the room. At first glance bras, panties, and high heels were disheveled everywhere. Cocaine residue and a mound of weed were left on the granite countertop. I wouldn't have expected anything less from Dr. Tracz. He shut the door slowly behind me.

"Roll it up!" His room looked like the morning after on a college reality show. That's when it hit me that I didn't want my business on front street. That's when I decided not to mention a word about me and Porsha, not just to Dr. Tracz...but to anyone.

Chapter 52

Time. Time is a dictator. Time is the judge. Time is the enemy. If a child isn't potty trained by the age of eight, then people assume that the child is slow because it has taken too much time to master that craft. On the opposite end of the spectrum, if a child can read complex novels by age two then they are deemed a prodigy because they have learned a technique supposedly before their time. Companies are compared and contrasted based on the results they produce but, more importantly, the time it takes to produce those results. If someone does something wrong in the legal system and is convicted, the judge in some instances charges them money, but in most cases, charges them time. The reasoning behind the important significance of time can easily be summed up, as we are all human beings. As of right now, there is no cure or supplement that prevents aging. All humans have an expected lifespan of one hundred years give or take some. After a while, the body begins to fall apart, organs stop functioning, and sometimes disease sets in. If we could all live forever, then time would mean nothing. However, since our time is limited, we feel limited. That is why we cherish every second, every day, every year as valuable and something that cannot be taken for granted.

I woke up in a groggy stupor. The time was 2:30pm. *Damn*! Just my luck! My departure flight is scheduled to leave at 3:45. This is not good. I couldn't afford timewise to stay another day. I had a deadline of when I had to be back home that I had to abide by. As I slowly got up, I had no choice but to direct my animosity toward room service. Why didn't they give me a wake-up call? Those slick bastards must've wanted me to oversleep and book the room for another day. The game is dirty. I buckled on my Hoverfoot, brushed my teeth, and started gathering all of my belongings. I didn't mean to sleep so late, but I was exhausted both physically and mentally; physically because of my previous night of intense, vigorous sex with Porsha; mentally, because I had stayed up until mid-morning, talking, drinking, and smoking with Dr. Tracz. I stuffed the remainder of my loose personal items into my duffle bag before darting out of the front door. I took one last look at the room. Did I leave anything? Keys, check. Wallet, check. Phone charger? Umm no. It was still plugged in behind the nightstand. I had spent a small fortune in replacing chargers. Luckily, this time it wouldn't be more money flushed down the toilet. I exited the room again and walked hurriedly next door.

Knock! Knock!

Dr. Tracz answered the door lethargically. I could see the girls in the background squirming on the bed half-naked. The room had a light haze of weed smoke.

"Get ready, doctor! We're running late for our flight!" He looked at me dumbfounded.

"No, my boy! You're running late for your flight!" I originally hated when he called me boy. I found it condescending to my age and intelligence. However, after learning I was like the son he never had, I accepted the tag as more like a compliment. Plus, he wasn't even from this country, so I doubted he knew any better.

"Correction! We were on the same flight, but I canceled mine this morning."

"You can do that?"

"Yeah, silly, if you checked trip cancellation insurance for an extra forty dollars." *Whoops!* I vividly recall not checking the box in an attempt to cut costs.

"Why didn't you tell me that old *man?*"

"Do you want me to tell you when to take a bath and piss too? I'm not your mama."

"Ughhh!" I let out a sigh of grief.

"Why do you need an extra day anyway? We have work to do!" Dr. Tracz was always a fun and relaxing travel companion who always seemed to ease the tension.

"Your turn, doctor." Teresa came up from behind him, topless, reaching out to hand him a lit joint. It was at that precise moment, I became inundated with jealousy.

"Not now. Go back to the bed. We're talking." Teresa suddenly noticed me in the doorway.

"Hey Randy, we missed you last night." I lowered my head with a little bit of regret. Her naked breasts were staring at me with regret too.

"Sorry, Teresa. I'm the one who missed out."

175

She giggled lightly.

"Go back in the room now, darling." Dr. Tracz slapped her on her thigh playfully signaling her to leave. All I saw was her backside jiggling and bouncing until she turned the corner. I bit my lips and closed my eyes at the beautiful nudity I had just witnessed.

"You didn't want to hang out with us yesterday, remember?" Dr. Tracz reminded me in a matter-of-fact tone.

"I did. I was just engaging in business affairs." I snickered dryly at the pun.

"Anyways, before I was rudely interrupted, I can't catch the plane today. The girls are taking me sightseeing." He was smiling with anticipation at the thought alone. "Plus, at my age, I could really use the exercise. He started to do pelvic thrusts like he was humping the air. What a funny guy. The mere thought that this old man was alive, kicking, and sexing as much as he was, was admirable as well as humorous. I laughed at him.

"Don't you have a flight to catch?" he asked. While I was lost in the moment momentarily, I snapped back instantly into reality. Time was a merciless dictator.

"You're right." I shook his hand and gave him a hug. "Thanks again. We achieved a big, big breakthrough yesterday. Get back into town tomorrow, please. We have a lot more work to do." He looked at me sternly.

"Yes, Dad."

"I'm not your dad. I'm your boss. Take care."

"See you later Stashi." I waved goodbye as I made my way to the elevator. He slowly disappeared and closed the door. I rushed out of the hotel and got in the first yellow cab that stopped.

"Airport, please! Quick! Fast! And in a hurry!" It was 2:53pm. I still needed to talk to Chloe to confirm if she was still picking me up from the airport.

"Do you have a car charger for a smartphone?"

"Car charger...yes. Smartphone... no. I use an iPhone." Welp, that wasn't going to work. Hopefully, I could juice it up for a couple of minutes in the airport concourse before the flight departed. My mind was in a million different places at once. I was still elated about our Hoverfoot being the topic of the most popular talk show on television. I was also thinking about newfound stardom, and how I would have to carry myself more professionally from now on. I was also thinking about Porsha's naked and curvaceous body, and how I had her sweating and screaming for more. I smiled with satisfaction at the thought. It's funny how quick sex is, but the memories can last a lifetime.

"We're here!" The cab driver's promulgation awoke me from my daze. I paid the fare and tipped him generously before running into the terminal. The digital clock on his car radio read 3:18pm. Before all of this, I had worked for years in the service industry. I knew the deal with tips. A good tip goes a long way while a bad one will get you ignored next time. I'm a firm believer in karma. The airport was packed, but I got through it with no trouble. One of the agents actually recognized me from The Window and helped me speed through the process. I got my boarding pass and boarded the flight with six minutes to spare—success. I was panting hard from the last-minute rush of catching this plane. I politely asked the flight attendant if there was a place on board where I could charge my phone. She pointed down by my feet. There were two power outlets. Success again. Thank God, I didn't forget my charger in the room

"Be warned, though. They power off while we are in flight."

"Perfect." Five minutes was all I needed. I turned on the phone and waited for my notifications to pop up. Four text messages and two voicemails. Judging by her text message written in all caps, she was pissed. Porsha sent me a text as well, but that would have to wait. I typed furiously as the flight attendant announced procedures and protocols over the intercom. My time was running out.

"Hey, babe! Sorry 4 the delay, phone died. R u still picking me up frm airport? Flight lands at 7:15pm. C ya soon! Smooches!" I hit send and then powered off the phone to preserve the little juice it had left. Done. Hopefully, she wouldn't be mad at my negligence. Hopefully, she would understand that I was handling intense business these past couple of days. I leaned my chair back with a sigh of relief that I didn't miss my flight. It was an expensive flight. I mean yeah, I had the funds to book another, but who likes throwing away money. I sure didn't. I spent it like I was still poor. I closed my eyes and drifted off into a deep sleep. I was completely drained. I had a weird dream that Dr. Tracz and I were superheroes; flying through clouds, beating up villains, and rescuing damsels in distress. It was entertaining, exciting, and rewarding all at once.

***

"Please fasten your seatbelts as we get ready to land!" I awoke to the flight attendant barking over the intercom, sorely disappointed that my dream wasn't real, at least not the flying part. I gathered my thoughts as we jostled on the runway. I anxiously powered on my phone with the hopes that my girlfriend would've confirmed picking me up from the airport. Even after my night of infidelity, I missed her immensely. There was a huge difference. I was infatuated with Porsha, but I was in love with Chloe. I wanted to see her smile, see her laugh, and answer all of her questions about the trip (except for that one part) while holding hands with her on the ride home. I waited for the text response to pop up, and after I read it, I held my head down ruefully. Sadly, I realized that there would be none of that. The text read:

'DON'T HEY BABE ME! I WAS WORRIED SICK ABOUT YOU ALL NIGHT! CATCH A CAB HOME BUSTER!' There was no sugarcoating it. Chloe was still pissed off at my shenanigans. Well, that didn't go according to plan. Great. Just great. She judged me on the time it took to respond to her missed calls and texts. In this case, time was definitely my enemy. At this point, I had no choice but to resort to plan B. I walked out of the airport terminal feeling defeated, wondering if I should even go home.

"TAXI!"

Chapter 53

Tug of war was always a fascinating and entertaining game to me growing up. Who knew that such a simplistic game could be so fun. All that was required was a rope and a couple of riled up individuals. While it is hard to predict the future winner before the game starts, after it commences the victor becomes apparent pretty quickly. The game always pans out the same too. One side would get tired, lose traction, and gets pulled to the other side. Who's ever side has more strength and stamina, wins. In life, many times you are the rope. Your friends are influences, and your conscience are things that try to pull you to their side. I can see why people change their lifestyles many times throughout their life. They get influenced by something greater that sways them over. As I was riding home, all alone, listening to foreign music, smelling the cab driver's pungent incense, I realized that I was engaging in a very dangerous game of tug of war. On one end was Chloe. On the other end was Porsha. One was ready and willing to risk her name and neck for the future expansion of our business. The other wouldn't even come pick me up from the airport. I mean, I guess Chloe did have a good reason to be annoyed, but not to the point to leave me stranded at the airport. No bueno. I know she was trying to teach me a lesson, but I wasn't impressed with her pettiness. My phone was dead again. Surprise, surprise.

"Do you have a smartphone charger?" I asked the driver.

"Sure do." Success. He unplugged his phone and passed me the plug. I inserted it into the port and watched the device come back to life. There was nothing like the suspense of anticipating notifications from a previously dead phone. Beep, beep. A new text message from Chloe was the first thing that popped up.

"Heat up your own *freakin'* dinner! There're leftovers in the fridge."

Well, my night is getting better and better.

I pushed the other thoughts aside and decided to finally check Porsha's text. Maybe she could brighten up my mood.

'Hey, cutie! Just thinking about our amazing night! Txt me when your flight lands, so I know you made it there safe. Hugs and Smooches… -Porsha'

I smiled. I felt a surge of energy transfer from the phone to inside of me.

I wanted to text her how I truly felt, but I had to resist. For one, I had to keep business and pleasure separate. Two, I had to downplay our intimacy to keep the chase alive. It was just a little tidbit of the game that I had learned.

'Hey, I just made it back. Thanks for the remarkable evening. We'll catch up later this week to discuss the marketing process. :-)'

I sent it, then deleted the thread. I never hid my phone from Chloe, and I wasn't about to start now. My stomach growled on the way home, but I was too tired to go through the hassle of getting food. I just wanted to be home. I was still tired from the anxiety of being on the show as well as the previous night's activities. Pizza sounded like heaven. I'd probably call for a large with crispy pepperoni and diced onions. I could hardly wait. I awoke from my food fantasy right in front of my house. I tipped the driver and hauled my luggage out of the taxi. I just hoped Chloe would be over her pissy fit. I unlocked the front door not knowing what to expect.

"RAAANDY?" Chloe called out verifying if it was me or an intruder.

"It's me. I'm home."

"I'm in the bathroom. Heat up whatever is in the fridge, jerk!" Well, I guess I could throw my hopes for her in a good mood out the window. She obviously wasn't over her fit of rage yet. I heard her calling from the back of our bedroom, which was a good indication that I would probably sleep in the front part of the house tonight. Plan A was to avoid confrontation at all costs. "Errrwhrerrrerrr." I look down. That was the sound of my stomach crying out for help. The endless supply of airplane peanuts and cranberry juice did nothing for my hunger. I sat my duffle bags next to the front door, unsure if I was spending the night or I would need it again for a motel. Even though I could feel her distress in the air, I loved returning home. There was a certain peaceful vibe that the house gave off that soothed the pressure from work. I don't know if it was the scents, decor, or furniture, but as soon as you step in the house, you felt a relaxing vibe. We moved back to my hometown after college. I made my way to the refrigerator ready to ransack anything edible. I opened the fridge with my girlfriend's last command echoing in the back of my head. "Heat up whatever is in the fridge, jerrrrk!" Whoo. Harsh. I guess I should've come with a better story like I got mugged or was in a near fatal car accident. At least then I could've gotten some sympathy out of the deal. The top row had an old bowl of spaghetti that had been there before I left. I popped the lid open. Woof. The sour odor burned the inside of my nostrils. I tossed it in the trash. Leftover Peppers. Salads in Saran wrap. A half-eaten sub sandwich. Why oh why didn't I check the box for trip cancellation insurance like my partner? I could've been sightseeing right now with Dr. Tracz, Tonya, Teresa, and Tina. Aaarrgh. Don't be so hard on yourself, Randy. Unlike Dr. Tracz, you're in a beautiful relationship with a beautiful girl. Plus, someone has to run the company. Dr. Tracz already proved that he was incapable of completing a project by himself once. If I didn't want to fall into his rut, I couldn't practice his habits. 'You made the responsible decision,' I convinced myself. I knew overtime hours were inevitable and mandatory preceding our Hoverfoot 3000 launch. After rummaging through the fridge, I found nothing appealing. I guess pizza delivery it is.

"Honey, there's nothing in the fridge!"

I used the lightest, politest, and sweetest tone possible when addressing her for two reasons. One, never fight fire with fire. And two, you have to always kill people with kindness.

"Of course there's nothing in there, Einstein." Her voice was now at a normal volume, which meant she was in the same room and she was probably staring at me ducked behind the door. I grabbed the plate of leftover Peppers. Time was up. I could no longer hide from the monster. I closed the door and looked in the direction I heard her voice coming from. I jumped back at the sight of her. My jaw dropped to the floor when I saw her. I dropped the box of leftover peppers on the ground. If looks could kill, I would've been a dead man. She was stunning. She had on her dark red lipstick covering her juicy lips. She had curly hair that seemed to float on her shoulders. A shiny pearl necklace sat right in between her full, perky breasts. She was wearing a dress that started at her chest, slimmed at her waist, and expanded at her hips that were wide enough to grab as a handle for her body. Wow, she caught me off guard. Sweet Mother Teresa, surprise, surprise!

"Aye carumba!" I yelled with exuberance.

"Get ready Mr. Stashi. I'm taking you out tonight!"

"AH-HOOGA! Yes, ma'am!" Now, I suddenly remembered why I loved this girl. Just a couple of minutes ago, I was confused and also proud of the way that I had swayed the love of such a prolific woman such as Porsha. Now, as Chloe stood there radiantly, I gulped with a guilty feeling of remorse. I realized that I could never be disloyal again and betray her love. In the end, it

181

would always backfire because she was priceless to me. No one in their right mind would ever do what she had done for me. I think I was spared this time—or maybe I wasn't. I mean, I am a firm believer in karma. In the end, though, I guess I am glad I didn't check the flight insurance box.

Chapter 54

Things aren't always what they seem to be. As humans, our experiences serve as vivid, in-depth reminders of principles that we have learned when dealing with that subject. Since someone has already had that experience once, they might handle it differently or similarly depending on the results they received the first time. For example, I had an older friend who had a wife who never worked. All she did was spend, spend, spend, with no concept of the actual value of a dollar. Whether it was small shopping sprees, vacations, or plastic surgery, she had to have it. Even though he was a moderately successful businessman, he grew tired of being milked and filed for divorce. It was then when she turned avaricious and demanded every material thing they owned due to the fact it was acquired while they were married. Her greed was unexplainable because she never earned a dollar nor received a check from any employer or investments. He realized way too late that she didn't really love him; she loved his bank account. Fast forward the story to many years later when he was ready to remarry. He approached the situation much differently. He had one requirement for his new potential lover, and that was, she had to be working before they even started dating. Last time I checked they're still together and he's still happy. He learned from the fiasco from his prior marriage what to do differently. Since our experiences serve as learning lessons, we identify and judge almost immediately, so we don't waste time trying to discover something we already know. It cheats our understanding, however, because there is an exception to every rule. For example, when two gorgeous girls walk past you on South Beach and you wonder if one of them is holding the key to your life's happiness. So, you nervously stop them to strike up a conversation just to find out that they're giving blowjobs for fifty dollars. Things aren't always what they seem to be. Or this one time, when a dude pulled up in his brand new shiny Challenger on rims and deafening bass. I started asking him twenty questions about his ride, slightly envious of his lifestyle. He answered the questions slow and melancholic. It was only at the end of the conversation when he revealed that earlier that week he had lost a trial and had to turn himself in for a long prison sentence. Suddenly I didn't want his car anymore. Things aren't always what they seem to be. As I overlooked the beautiful city from my big office at Stashi Labs, I could see people on the streets below, looking like busy little ants. My office was lavish with modern furnishings, sparkling glass, and reflective wood floors. Outside my office, you could hear our gorgeous secretary answering the phone in a sexy, seductive tone. You might've thought you had mistakenly called a midnight sex hotline by her voice. In another office, nearby, we had our marketing manager Charlie who handled our media and public relations. Then we had a separate more secure sector for the science wing. This division was headed by the legendary Dr. Tracz, with his subordinates in their respective offices. I couldn't remember all of the scientists' names that he brought on board because some were seasonal and most of them I rarely saw. They were either locked away in the test facility engineering something new or hidden behind a large computer screen. It was actually none of my business. Dr. Tracz kept them all on track. At a glance, Stashi Labs would've seemed like the ideal modern-day multi-hundred-million-dollar corporation that was running as smooth as butter. However, things aren't always what they seem to be.

I would've still been running this business out of my mama's garage had it not been for the generous government grants, angel investors, and fundraising rounds that we had been awarded due to the curiosity of our technology. We were an unlisted company, with an unlisted phone number. We operated invisibly to protect and keep our work under wraps. Stashi Labs looked impeccable, but it had become a very costly ship to run. It didn't matter how profitable my book was. I wasn't prepared to throw down any more of my personal money into the vacuum called Stashi Labs. I'm glad I didn't have to. My theory was business should be self-sufficient and attract outside funding. Outside of that, Porsha Gottfrey began running a very aggressive television and print campaign for my book and our baby, the Hoverfoot. Because of that, book sales had blossomed to ten figures. It really is mind boggling when you think of how many people there are in this world. What's even crazier is, even though our wants are different, our needs are astonishingly similar. The source of all of my troubles was solely centered around the launch of our invention. This release was slated to be next week as advertised, but our overseas manufacturing was in complete shambles. I didn't understand how could they drop the ball so late in the game. I mean, I'm *furious!* They underquoted us both the cost per unit and the time it takes to produce them. Our phone lines were blowing up all day and all night, with people anticipating and impatient for its release. That would be great news except for the fact that the only ones we had were on my foot and the faux replica one that we used for office decor.

"What do you *mean* they won't be ready by next week? Guna, we've already launched a very expensive marketing campaign. We cannot take another second longer than we're supposed to. The world is waiting on us." Guna was our overseas production manager. He was one of the good guys. He was direct, honest and multilingual. I especially liked him because he had strong ties to India where production for our product was significantly cheaper.

"Randy, bear with me my friend. When you originally placed this order, you had quoted me a very low number of units. Now, you come to me demanding the same time quote but have increased our workload over here by 10,000%. Think about it from my end. We are humans, not robots." I really couldn't blame him; he was stating facts. Porsha's efforts were a huge reason for our need for increased production.

"You're lying to me!" I could feel myself getting very, very frustrated. His excuses were starting to anger me. "Machines are making this product. It's not like grandma is over there knitting *socks!*" I could see the spit flying out of my mouth. I wanted to cease business with him, if these were the results.

"I know that, Randy, but we still have to run a quality assurance test on each individual model to ensure that the product has no defects. That alone takes twenty minutes per unit. To be quite honest, we're talking well into next month."

"ARRRGHHH!" When he said that, I wanted to throw the phone across the room. This was not the news that I was expecting. I felt like breaking something expensive.

"Randy…I have some unfortunate news as well…"

"Maan, I thought you were already giving me the bad news. What is it *now* Guna? Gaahdamn! Spill the beans already!" I usually wasn't this livid, but today was going to hell in a handbasket. The epiphany of all this bad news in such a short time span was hard to stomach.

"Well, umm Randy. One of the machines that manufactures your product went down early this morning. The mechanic assured us that it can be fixed quickly, but the part won't be in until next week at the earliest." I slammed the phone down.

"Dammit!" I grumbled quietly. I could feel my blood rushing and my heart pounding. I put both of my elbows on my desk and started massaging my temples. Calm down, Randy. Calm down, Randy. There are bigger problems in the world. Calm down. God grant me the serenity to accept the things that I cannot change. I walked across the room to get a cup of cold water out of the aqua dispenser. I could still hear Guna's voice echoing through the phone receiver in an otherwise quiet room.

"Randy… Hello…? Are you there? Hellooo…?" Gathering myself after twenty seconds, I picked the phone back up.

"I'm here; I'm back. You know what, Guna? When we first began working on this project, you worked wonders for me. Now that we've reached the final stages, your performance has sunk below par. I'm thinking that this isn't going to work for the long term. I'm going to need a new manufacturer." I could hear him gasp at my dagger-like words. Everything suddenly got very, very quiet.

"Nooo, nooo.…"

"Yesss, yesss, you've underquoted me both costs and time, and the problems on your end keep popping up. We're are running a global business over here, Guna, not a neighborhood lemonade stand!"

"Nooo.… We've come too far, Randy, to quit. The problems that I am bringing up can be remedied. It's just going to take slightly longer than expected."

"Slightly? We're talking a month at the least!" I was fuming.

"True, but think about this. Let's say you do get a new manufacturer. You're going to have to go through the process of re-explaining the design, wait on a testable prototype, then once it's confirmed you still have to wait on production. On top of that, there's still no guarantee that it will work the way that you want it. This could take months, if not a year. It will be a catastrophic decision on your part." Sigh. I breathed in deeply. I soaked in what he just said. Sadly, he was one hundred percent correct. I had too much riding on this release to risk delaying it by months or a year.

"Don't you like the prototypes that we have made for you?" I looked down at the beta model Hoverfoot that I was wearing on my foot. I had to smile slightly. It was everything that I had hoped for. It was everything that I had dreamed of. It was everything that I had prayed for. It single-handedly made me forget my handicap and made me feel regular again. Sure, it needed to be charged every couple of days, but that was not too much of an inconvenience compared to life without it.

"Well, I must admit, I do like what you have made for me, Guna. I guess you do have a good point. I really can't risk the time. Just keep me updated, and please…please…hurry the hell up!" I could hear him chuckle a sigh of relief on the other end. He knew he had dodged a bullet. He was mere seconds away from losing this very lucrative contract.

"Yes, sir! I'll give you an update later this week, Mr. Stashi."

"Please… And Guna?"

"Yes.…"

"I know I sound frustrated and angry, but from the bottom of my heart. Thank you!"

"You're welcome, Randy."

Click. I walked over to the window and looked at the clouds long and hard. Even though it was daytime the only thing that was missing was a blimp saying, "The World is Yours."

Ring ring ring. The office phone rang loud and dull. I picked it up on the last ring.

"Stashi Labs, this is Randy."

"Hey, Randy!" I recognized the voice instantly. It made me feel relieved, almost like a kid again.

"Hey, Mommy! How are you?" I hated when she called my business line simply because she had my more personal cell phone number.

"Good. Why aren't you picking up your cell phone, honey?" I guess she had tried. The blame was on me.

"I didn't hear it. I've been on the phone all day."

"Is everything all right?"

"No. Everything is going haywire."

"Well, just keep working, honey. If anybody can handle it, it's you." Her confidence in me was always re-energizing.

"Randy, I've got to tell you something."

This couldn't be good. I've learned over the years that people warned you before they told you something ominous. I exhaled a long sigh.

"You too...? What is it?"

"Randy, I got a letter here for you, saying you must cease and desist print of your book The Stashi Life."

"On what grounds?" I raised my voice. Today just kept getting better and better.

"It doesn't say."

"Who's it from? I'll give the company a call."

"It doesn't say that either. No company name, no phone number, no email or return address."

"Whaaat?"

"Yes, Randy. It's almost like it's anonymous. I don't understand."

"I don't understand it either."

"Question Randy, did you ever take your father's name out of that book?"

"Ughh." I paused to rub the top of my nose in between my eyes with my thumb and my index finger.

"I tried to convince the publisher to revise it, but it was too late. We were over five million copies sold on every TV station and bookstore nationwide."

"Randy, *WHY?!* I told you before you even got that book printed I didn't want Dylan's *freakin'* name in it!" I know it was taking every ounce of restraint for her to not cuss me out right now.

"I'm sorry, Mom," I replied in a disappointed voice. I knew I had let her down.

"Shut up! It's too late for sorry. You promised me years ago. Gave me your word, son. And you just ignored my wishes and then lied to me about it. The nerve of you to just lie and betray me." I knew that there was nothing I could do or say to mend the situation. I disappointed her, and I couldn't be mad at her animosity towards me.

"I'm sorry, Mommy. I'll call them and tell them to revise it first thing tomorrow morning."

"It's too late, Randy!" She assumed we couldn't correct it or I was just talking.

"Too many people know now. What's done is done."

"So, what do you want me to do, Mom? You're giving me no options."

"This letter says to stop printing them."

"Ha!" I scoffed at the thought. "I can't do that, Mom, no way, no how! You want me to stop printing millions of copies because of one anonymous letter?" I could hear her get quiet and sniffle into the phone.

"Randy, I'm scared. No, I'm terrified!"

"Don't be, Mom. Everything's going to be all right."

"No, no! You don't understand Randy…. This, this letter was written in BLOOD! It's in dry, brown *blood*." The word "blood" echoed loudly in my head. I gasped at the combination of shock and confusion. Five million copies in print and counting. You would have thought everyone loved The Stashi Life but, then again, things aren't always what they seem to be.

Chapter 55

There's no place like home. You can travel the seven countries, sail across the five oceans and still never feel a feeling similar to it. It has a certain distinct smell to it. As soon as you step into the house, thousands of memories flash into your head instantly. Any new renovations stand out because you remember how the place looked originally. It makes you smile because you remember the good times. Even if there were bad times, the good times overshadow them. You feel absolutely safe. It's like an impenetrable base that no one can corrupt. Even though it was a less than pleasant experience the last time I stayed here, it felt good to be actually walking through my old front door again, a place where my favorite foods were cooked, and my mother's voice was the ruler of the domain, a place filled with love, joy, and happiness, but this time it was different. One look at my mother's face, and it felt really weird, like it was no longer safe, like our safe haven had been violated and vandalized.

"Where are the rubber gloves?" I asked. I felt angry and powerless at the same time. I felt angry because someone had the audacity to target this to my mother instead of me, powerless because I had no clue of who did this.

"They're under the sink. Why do you need them?" my mother asked inquisitively.

"I need to see the envelope and the letter." I grabbed the gloves and strapped them on. I felt like a detective. I had watched enough Forensic File episodes to understand that one mistake from our intimidator could potentially reveal their identity. They had written it in blood. Hopefully, we could use it to single out the perpetrator. My mom brought the letter over from the table.

"No, no!" I stammered. "Put it back on the table and don't touch it anymore unless you have gloves on." I wanted to preserve the integrity of the letter and envelope and not smear our fingerprints all over it before police had arrived. I really wanted to know who was responsible for this. I picked up the envelope first. It had no return address but a stamp on it. It looked like the post office mailed it but the ink stamp over the postage looked unprofessional. I hoped it was real because we could track it all the way down to the area it was sent from. However, if it wasn't, then that would mean this had just escalated to a whole new level. That would mean they know where my mom lives and dropped it off personally. Not good.

"Have you called the police yet?"

"Yeah, I called them right before you got here. They're on their way," she replied.

"They're taking their sweet time," I mumbled discontentedly as I pulled the letter out. I unfolded it slowly and read it.

"To Randy,

Please cease and desist your book The Stashi Life, or else it will cost you more than you can ever earn."

The note was written in cursive. The dried blood was a dark brown and dripped sloppily down some of the letters. Either this was a cruel prank or a very, very unhappy fanatic.

"Who do you think could have written it?" my mom asked as she peered at the note over my shoulder. I didn't answer. I started thinking about any and every enemy I had, dating all the way back to elementary school. My mind was drawing blanks. Who did this?

Knock, knock!

"That's probably the police," my mom guessed.

"Have a seat. I'll get it," I responded cautiously. I walked over to the door and looked through the peephole. It was two officers. One was fat and short, the other one taller and skinny. I opened the door quickly. I was relieved that they were there but disappointed by their response time.

"Hi! I'm Officer Brown, and this is Officer Ragans with the police department. We received a call about a threatening letter."

"Finally..." I murmured. I stepped to the side and let them in.

"So, tell us what's going on...."

My mother explained the whole story of how and when she received the letter. The officers started piecing the events together on the police report when he suddenly had an epiphany.

"Ohhh, you're the dude that was on The Window with Porsha Gottfrey. What's your last name again?" The one thing I started to despise about being well-known is people claim they know you, without really knowing anything about you.

"Stashi," I answered.

"Yeah, that's it.... Stashi! Hey, Brown! This is the dude I was telling you about not too long ago! The one that wrote the book, and invented a flying foot!" Officer Ragan's eyes got really big, and a smile slowly appeared across his face.

"AWWWW... You're him. OH, EM GEE...my wife is a huge fan!" He walked over and began shaking my hand. "Wait until she hears about this. Wowee!" I suddenly became confused emotionally. I didn't know whether to be happy, sad, or angry. I was partly happy because they had seen and appreciated my life's work. I was partly sad because my mother's fear had initially stemmed from something I was responsible for. I was also partly angry because I didn't think these bozos were taking this situation seriously.

"You're wearing the..." Ragans looked down at my foot as though he hadn't noticed it before. "He's wearing the flying footy thing RIGHT NOW!" He and Brown started chuckling.

"Can I try it on?" Brown asked. Wow! Now, I was officially getting annoyed.

"I would let you, but I'm afraid it's not going to support your weight. No worries, the Hoverfoot comes out next year for extra extra plus-size people." I said slickly. Brown stuck his tongue in his cheek with distaste at the sound of my revelation.

"Guys, I really need you to help me out here. We have a serious situation on our hands. We can chit-chat about the small stuff after the threats stop." Both of them suddenly sobered up with graveness.

"Okay, so do you have any clue about who would send this to you? Any unfound competition, rivals, enemies?" Ragans asked.

"No, no one I can think of just yet."

"Hmm..." he mumbled as he continued writing. "Well, keep your eyes and ears open for anything suspicious or anything you can think of that you haven't already told us." Brown was still scanning the house looking for anything out of place.

"Your case number is S-2408HOU." He wrote it down on a piece of his notepad and tore it off for us.

"Well, we'll keep this on file, log in these fingerprints, and send it to the lab to do a cross check on the blood, to see if anything pops up in our database."

"How long could this take?" I was clueless and curious.

"Anywhere from six months to a year. But even getting the results won't really help. It would just narrow it down to thousands of people in the country with that blood. Only then it would just be among prior offenders. To be honest, the chances are slimmer than dental floss."

"But there still is a chance!" Ragans chimed in.

Did these knuckleheads think this was a game? I was disgusted. They then proceeded to put the envelope and the letter in a plastic evidence bag.

"If you have any questions, updates, or information, do not hesitate to call us," Brown declared as he passed his card to me.

"Thank you, officers," my mother announced her gratitude. Her eyes were red and watery as she clutched on a crumpled Kleenex. I stood up and escorted them to the door to let them out.

"Thanks again y'all," I said if I was genuinely thankful for their visit.

"You're welcome. We're just doing our job." Ragans said as he walked out. Brown followed right behind him and then turned around abruptly. He looked like he had something on his mind.

"Hey, umm Randy, man my wife is one of your biggest fans. I was wondering if it's not too much to ask, do you mind if I can get your autograph for her? She'll never believe that I ran into you today." He jammed a pen and paper into my personal space. This was unbelievable. I put on a fake smile. "Be nice to your fans Randy. They're the ones who support you," I thought as I grabbed the pen and notepad.

"Who do I make it out to?"

"Martha."

"To Martha," I mumbled as I scribbled. "Stay blessed and stay Stashi, sincerely…Randy Stashi." I passed it back to him, and he looked at my writing in disbelief.

193

"She's gonna have a heart attack when she hears about this! Thanks, Mr. Stashi!"

"Well, break it to her slowly, so she doesn't die, okay? Y'all have a great day!"

I waved at them and then returned inside, closing the door behind me.

"What was all that about?" my mother questioned.

"Nothing major, just giving them a little more info." I walked up to her trying to make sense of what just happened. For some reason, I felt less safe after the police left than before they came.

"I don't like them."

"Like who, sweetie?"

"The officers who just left. I don't feel like they can help us." She just looked at me in anticipation of where this conversation was going.

"Then what do you propose we do?"

"I think you should move, Mommy."

"Well, son, that is not happening!"

"C'mon, Mom, I have money now. I can get you a bigger house, something overlooking a landmark, a chance to get away from this nonsense."

"No Randy, I'm not moving. I've lived in this house for over twenty-five years. This is my home. This is where I raised you and where I'll raise my grandkids. So that's out of the question!" I looked at her as if I was pleading non-verbally. She had her arms crossed and a stern expression on her face. I could tell she wasn't budging on the subject. I was in no mood to combat her stubbornness. I sighed in defeat.

"Look, I'm going to call the alarm people tomorrow to have a state-of-the-art security system installed."

"That would be good," she stammered.

"Yeah, it will give you a piece of mind." I suddenly thought about something else that would give her peace of mind. I walked outside to my trunk and pulled out a small box. I brought it back in and set it on the kitchen table.

"What's that, Randy?" I opened it up. It had a shimmery sparkle to it. It was brand spanking new and still had the fresh out of the factory scent.

"It's a Beretta nine millimeter." I loaded the clip with bullets and jammed it into the gun. Click clack.

"Oh, my Gawd…" my mom gasped. The house became very quiet.

"I didn't want it to come to this, but you might need it. This is it on safety. This is how you take it off of safety." I clicked it.

"Randy, I don't, don't…" She shook her head no.

"Take it!" I shoved it at her. If there's an intruder in this house, you shoot them until they stop moving. You hear me?" She slowly nodded her head yes. "Grab. Click. Squeeze." I demonstrated what each verb meant without pulling the trigger. "Grab the gun, click the safety off, and then squeeze the trigger. Keep it close to where you sleep, okay?" She nodded her head again, gradually understanding that having this was a necessity.

"I'm not trying to scare you but there are some crazy people in this world, Mommy. You're going to have to protect yourself, okay?"

"Okay." She grabbed the gun and moved it around getting accustomed to how it felt.

"I love you, Mommy, and I don't want anything to happen to you."

Remember, grab, click, and squeeze, okay?" She looked at me deep in my eyes as she put the gun back on the table. She walked closer to me and hugged me. I could hear her sniffle, and she began to cry on my shoulder. I squeezed her tighter.

"I love you, Son."

"I love you too, Mommy." She began to rub my back up and down as if massaging it. I felt a little bit of relief. There's nothing more comforting than a mother's touch. "Everything's going to be all right, Mommy. Everything's going to be all right."

I didn't know if this was the truth or not but I had to speak it into existence. I was hoping that this was just a senseless, cruel prank, and it would all go away. Deep down inside, I was kind of glad that she had declined my offer to move.

195

This house had always made me nostalgic, and I wasn't ready to give it up just yet. Plus, you know what they say, *there's no place like home.*

Chapter 56

The greatest revenge is success. So many times in life, we get the short end of the stick. The anger and energy still surge through my body, and my mind is suddenly consumed with evil thoughts and actions when I think about that fateful night. I wish I had some leads or suspects so I could cause the hurt and the pain that they caused me. The nightmares don't come as frequent as they used to, but I still wake up in cold sweats, gasping for air, awakening from the loud crack of the gunshot. I remember buying a pistol and waiting on the day if they ever returned. If I ever caught up with them, I knew I would torture them slowly and painfully. I wanted to make the misery last as long as possible. I always go into a deep dark evil trance and start to smile with satisfaction to what I would do if the tables were turned. Then I awaken from my daydream feeling guilty that I'm not grateful that I survived. I really could've been dead. That's when I realize that whatever I can do to hurt them would be short-lived. Not only that, there's a slight chance I could be caught and spend a good chunk of my life behind bars. I often gauged if it would be worth it, getting even. Hell yeah, it would be worth it! Just on the strength that they must pay, but then I think about my mom, crying her poor little heart out, unable to hold me again behind walls. My friends that I could no longer go out with or share a drink with. The woman I could never share my love with or have kids, and even if I did, I wouldn't be able to raise them. Or even the things I've seen now. I was a guest on the Porsha Gottfrey show and co-inventor of the Hoverfoot for the greater good of mankind. Yeah, if I would have gotten my revenge the violent way I once wanted to, but it would've been so short-lived that I would have been unable to savor it thoroughly. However, nowadays, being Randy Stashi has become a dream come true. No matter how you put it or think about it, the greatest revenge is success.

I was in the bookstore sitting at a table accompanied by a latte with a double shot of espresso in it. Today, I would definitely need all the energy I could get. Dana was behind me putting the finishing decorative touches on our pop-up shop display. There was a fellow employee manning the register beside me. I was surrounded by towers of The Stashi Life novel all around me. Not only that, but there were about ten boxes in the back ready to be brought out when all of the supplies diminished.

"Today's the big day! Are you ready?" Dana asked.

I looked at the line. It started at the front entrance and wrapped all the way around the building. It was filled with all walks of life, short, fat, tall, skinny, black, white, Asian, Latino, kids, and elderly. You name it, they were there. The table was filled with plenty of ballpoint pens. I just hoped that my arm would fall off. I didn't know how I was going to last writing all of these signatures, but where there's a will there's a way. I was planning on a lot of people showing up, but this amount was unreal. I could have never imagined this in a lifetime. Ever since my appearance on The Window and the aggressive TV marketing campaign, I guess things had kicked up a notch. I looked at all of the people and beginning to comprehend the daunting task that I had ahead of me, I gulped a loud swallow of nervousness.

"Yeah, I'm ready," I answered Dana.

"I'm so happy for you, Randy. The doors are about to open in two minutes. Let me know if you need anything, okay?"

"Like what?"

"Like water, food…"

"A wrist." I cut her off. She burst out laughing. I didn't hear the joke.

"No worries, Randy. Just take your time and be respectful. Remember, some of these people traveled hundreds of miles just to wait in line and meet you." I squinted my eyes and looked at her with a half smile. She was right. It was a blessing to have such a huge turnout for little old me.

"Opening the doors! Another employee walked toward the front door and unlocked it."

"Here we go, Randy. Get ready!"

"Let's get Stashi!" I answered back.

The doors opened, but they were more like floodgates. People bum rushed the table. Others were peeking over shoulders, and some were even yelling and waving at me just to get my attention. I just waved back and smiled.

"Let's make a single file line, people!" One of the employees barked. The fan's pandemonium was transferring to me, and I started feeling high, a life high, like I was invincible, almost like I was the president. Many already had a copy of The Stashi Life in their hands and just wanted an autograph. Others came with t-shirts or empty-handed with intentions of purchasing the book and merchandise. I was happy but sad at the same time. Happy because all of these people, and sad because my dad wasn't here to see it. I had to make an announcement.

"Hey everybody, my name is Randy Stashi and I'm delighted and grateful for everyone's time today. Thank you. I'm glad everyone here can see the positivity in this book, and my only hope is you use it to benefit and increase your own well-being and others too. Share it with as many people as you can! Well, I've done enough talking, it's time to read some of the greatest literature ever created! So without further ado, I present to you, THE STASHI LIFE! ENJOY!" Applause filled the bookstore.

"Oh my God! I can't believe it's really you!" It was a group of these young teenage girls, all of them with braces and screeching voices.

"You better believe it.…"

"ARGHH!" they screamed. "Can you sign our book?"

"Sure. Who do you want me to make it out to?"

"To Amanda, Cassandra, and Anna of the glee girls." I slowly mumble each word as I scribble it down.

"Can we get a picture?"

They came around the table, and we posed while another bystander held the camera.

"Get Stashi on three."

"One… Two… Three… Snap!"

They hugged me, and I turned my attention to the next supporter. I saw Dana look at me less than pleased.

"Keep it to a minimum, Randy. There're a lot of people waiting."

"I can't help it," I grumbled back before the next person was within earshot. I smiled until my face hurt, took the pictures like it was a photo shoot, and signed every item of memorabilia like I was a hall of famer. After all of this time, I was finally beginning to see the end of the line. A guy with red eyes walked up looking high out of his mind and vaguely familiar. I couldn't pinpoint where I knew him from, but he looked very familiar.

"Yo Randyyyyy!"

"Hey there buddy," I said skeptically.

"Yo..." he looked at my face from different angles to help me recognize him, but I was still clueless.

"Yo..." I responded, still confused about what was really going on.

"Yo! You really don't remember me, man?"

"Well, now that I think about it, you do look kinda familiar," I answered rubbing my chin. I lied because I wanted to get this game of guess who over with.

"Quincy Sterling. FVU. We worked on that monstrous project together as seniors. You really forgot about me, man?"

"Woooow..." I said finally realizing who it was. "After all of these years, it's good to see you, man. How you been? Thank God that project is over."

"Tell me about it. Look at you, man! I heard your ad on the radio. I was like, I know that guy!"

"Ha ha," I chuckled. "Yeah, just little old me."

"More like big old you. You're everywhere nowadays!"

"Lord knows I try. What have you been up to nowadays. You live here now?"

"Yeah, I moved here after graduation. I'm an architect for Campbell and Sanders. You seen our latest project?"

"No. What is it?"

"Horizontal condos."

"Oh! That upside-down pyramid in Midtown? I saw one article on it not too long ago."

"Ha ha, so you have heard of it! Yep. That's me right there, the first building ever with a diagonal elevator. It's pretty freakin' cool!"

"What?"

"The elevator contours to the shape of the building. I have to show it to you one day when you have the time. It will knock your socks off."

"Wowwww!" I was astonished by his accomplishments. It didn't sound safe, but it did sound like the future.

"Do you always make weird, I mean different, structures?" He laughed at my slip up.

"I mean I tried to, but what's the point of building a building that's going to look like everyone else's."

"I gotta admit, that's quite impressive, Quincy. Who knew you had it in you this whole time?" Quincy chuckled again and got closer to my ear so he could whisper.

"I'll take that as a compliment." He leaned back and raised his voice again. "I'm going to be launching my own firm soon. It's going to be called something spectacular."

"Ok, well I can help you brainstorm some spectacular ideas for the actual name since you're not there yet."

"No. That's the name. Something Spectacular."

"Ahem." Dana cleared her throat loudly behind me reminding me of my time constraints. "Do you have a card? Maybe we can do lunch soon?" He reached into his pocket and handed it to me.

"Yeah, it would be good to catch up with you. You still with what's her face?"

"Chloe?"

"Yeah, that's her!"

"Yeah, we're still riding the wave."

"Keep her dude. She's was so hot!" I smiled with pride.

"I will. And I'll catch up with you later, Quincy."

"It was good seeing you again, pal. Stay Stashi."

"I'll try," I answered. We shook hands, and he bumped into the table clumsily while walking away. "Damn, that boy gets high!" I thought to myself. Signature, signature, picture, smile, wave, compliment, signature. It was almost over. Hallelujah. I couldn't believe that I had actually considered stopping the print of this book due to that threatening letter. No doubt that I was seriously concerned for my mother's safety, but I couldn't let one bad clown stop the circus, especially after today's event. The world wanted the book. The world needed the book. This crowd was a testament to that. I was down to the last couple of supporters when a lady with a small boy walked through. She had on a straw sun hat with a big brim and a tight bright, flowery sundress. I didn't know who she was until she looked up and I could see her eyes under the brim. The little boy was holding her hand gently like a son would.

"Hey." She smiled at me.

"Heeey!" I irresistibly smiled back. It had almost been a decade since I'd last seen her. I couldn't help myself. All of those feelings of our young pure, innocent love still surged through me. I felt like a kid again.

"You remember me?"

"How could I ever forget you? It was my ex-lover, my ex-partner, my ex-girlfriend, Tracy.

"I didn't think I'd ever see you again," I said. She was smiling. I glanced nonchalantly at her fingers. To my surprise, no rings on. She wasn't married, or, at least she wasn't showing it.

"Me either," I said barely moving my mouth. We gazed into each other's eyes and paused after every word. It was like we were shy, too afraid to reveal our true feelings for each other.

"Look at you now." She pointed at the whole display station. You have really made a name for yourself!"

"Why thank you. It's been a long journey to get here, to say the least."

"I'm so proud of you!"

The antsy young boy what now tugging on her arm with anxiousness.

"Who is this little guy?" I asked, questioning their relationship.

"This little guy is my son, Troy. Troy, say hi to Mr. Stashi."

"Hi to Mr. Stashi," croaked out the kid in an adorable voice.

"Ha ha." It was so adorable. I had to laugh. "Hey, Troy!" He looked just like his mother. God, she made beautiful kids. I suddenly felt hurt that it wasn't mine.

"With all of this going for you, I'm sure you're happily married with kids by now."

"Me…? No way. I've been too busy."

Her eyes lit up. For what reason I don't know. I suddenly remembered how much I loved her, how much I used to play and joke around with her and plan our future together. I wanted everything to be normal and happy again like it was before the incident. Then suddenly something hit me. I remembered how she left me in the cold at my weakest point, how when I was hurt and paralyzed, she left me for dead, like a wounded animal disowned for its imperfections. I suddenly began to feel hate, distaste, and disappointment rev up my body. My mouth began to taste bitter as I mentally relived the pain.

"Do you want to go out for lunch sometime?" She fluttered her eyes at me as she asked.

"I would like to…"

"Well, how about this Thurs—"

"But I'm incredibly busy with my new invention." I straddled my leg to the side of the chair and slammed my foot on the table showing her the Hoverfoot.

"Ohhh…" she said shockingly, put off by my rejection.

"Well, how about dinner?"

"That sounds good.…"

"Maybe my place, my cooking skills have—"

"But I'll still be busy with the book tour, Tracy. It's a full-time job being famous."

"Ohhh…" she said flatly. She was starting to understand that I was less ecstatic than she was about getting together than she was. She took out a piece of paper and wrote her number on it.

"Well, just in case you have second thoughts, Randy, feel free to give me a ring. I still think about you and things have changed a lot for me. I'd love to catch up one of these days." She slid the paper to me and held my hand while rubbing it gently. I could smell her indulging perfume. It was my favorite— Romance. She's the reason why it became my favorite. I was lonely for a long time after she left me.

"I'll take it, but to be honest, my girlfriend would try and kill me if we met up. I try to stay faithful to those who are faithful to me." I narrowed my eyes when I looked into hers. I could tell that last sentence stung. I could see her heart fall out of her chest and plop on the ground after I said it. Karma *always* comes back around.

"Feel free to hit me up on Facebook though, Tracy Trace. I can add you as a fan." She scowled her face, but then forced a smug smile while shaking her head in disgust.

"You're a moron! Good luck with your book! Let's go, Troy!"

"Hey, lady! Have some respect for the man!" The next person in line blurted out.

"Ughh!" she said one more time before storming out the front entrance. The customer who spoke up smacked his lips.

"What a loser…" he mumbled.

"Can't win them all." I laughed, slightly satisfied.

"Who was that?" Dana asked with concern.

"Just an old friend.… Just an old friend."

"Oh! Well, keep it positive. Everyone is watching."

"I gotta keep it Stashi!" I nodded in agreement. After Tracy abandoned me years ago, it took a looong time to get over that girl. I had trust issues with others and developed insecurities about my handicap. It took years and courage to finally socialize again and feel normal, to feel confident. I didn't know if I was ever going to be able to satisfy a woman because of the mental state and manner that she left me in. Now, after all these years, to have her come witness my success, to have her wait in line to come to see me, then to watch her beg desperately to go out on a date with me, to actually see her crawling back to rekindle that flame that we once shared and to finally, put my foot down and tell her no. That moment was priceless. Telling her no just gave me the ultimate satisfaction. Just to see that regret in her eyes, after all these years, there was nothing sweeter than that moment right there. The moment where I was victorious, and she was miserable, asking for forgiveness and mercy, the moment when the tables had finally turned, and adversaries asked for mercy. That's why you should always treat people with respect because anyone's financial position can change at any given moment. That's why they say my friend, the greatest revenge is success.

Chapter 57

Life is all about learning. You have to learn how society works, learn how people work, but more importantly, learn how yourself works. That's why they say, the older you get, the wiser you become. You learn from the people around you who have possibly gained or lost a fortune. You learn about people who died, so you don't become a victim of the same circumstances. You also learn about your own abilities and capabilities. You never know you can bench press 400 pounds until the day you bench press 400 pounds. Learning sometimes crushes the imagination or assumptions because it is disproven with cold hard facts. Imagination can also challenge principles and concepts if they've been uncontested previously. Someone got tired of horses and built a car. Someone got tired of cars and built a plane. You just have to remember to challenge yourself to learn something new daily. Especially if you have to have a deep passion for that subject. That's why some people run around in circles all their life scared to try something new, scared to learn outside of their comfort zone. Scared to elevate. Then there are others always pushing the envelope with new technologies, ideas, and medicines. You have some people who love to learn because it's a way of revealing the truth, a way of uncovering a myth. A way of solving a problem. Others would rather be satisfied by the idea that ignorance is bliss. Ignorance is bliss only because you're left in the dark stumbling around peacefully while others have flashlights and are ransacking the room for all of its hidden treasure. I think that the most profound thing about learning is that there are only two ways to do it. You either learn the easy way or the hard way. The easy way is easy. It just means someone else tells you and you accept it as true. "Look both ways before you cross the street."

"Dark clouds means it's likely to rain."

"Never spend all your money."

What's easy about this is the time it takes to learn to reap the benefits. It literally takes only seconds to comprehend the principle before you can apply use to the rule. That's because it comes from someone else's experiences and beliefs. The hard way is completely different. There is no one guiding you with useful tips or advice and the hard way is comprised solely of your own experiences and hypothesis. For example, if someone refuses to learn the easy way of looking both ways before you cross the street, then they're forced to learn the hard way, which would probably involve a car running over them at a swift speed. After they get out of the hospital and nurse their injuries for weeks, they approach another crosswalk. Since they don't want to experience that ordeal again, they look both ways before they cross the street. With new challenges and uncontested circumstances, however, sometimes the only way to learn is the hard way because there is no alternative. The first man on the moon had to learn the hard way. Every man after that had the convenience of learning the easy way. While the easy way can be instantaneous, the hard way can take days, weeks, or even years. The only difference is that with the easy way you assume facts and the hard way you know for sure. The fallacy though is that you can't learn the hard way every time. Someone who does would be decades behind people that learn the easy way. In the race against time, this is nowhere near efficient or effective, and most of the time the journey is agonizing. On the other hand, however, someone can't learn the easy way every time because they'll uncover no new discoveries or unknown truths. At the end of the day, one must pick their battles wisely when it comes to what can be assumed as true and what needs to be challenged, put simply, the easy way or the hard way. You have to learn both ways. The intricate, delicate balance is what makes some people's lives prolific and others' lives meaningless. All of the principles in this book were handed down to me by my father. He learned the hard way, and I learned the easy way.

"It's here! It's finally here!" I gawked in awe at the delivery people bringing endless cardboard boxes and stacking them on our warehouse shelves. Dr. Tracz was standing beside me just as speechless as I was. His glasses were hanging off the tip of his nose. He hugged me tightly with one arm as we stood side by side.

"We did it, my boy. WE DID IT!" Years in the making and the dream had finally come to life. I looked at him with a look of disbelief. You talk and talk about something for so long, sometimes that's all it seems. It's not until it's glistening in its box, staring at you, surrounded by Styrofoam kernels and bubble wrap. It's like writing something down on your Christmas list, and you wake up one morning, and it's sitting right there under the tree ready to be opened.

"Yes, we did, Dr. Tracz! The day has finally come when the world will feel the pleasure of our treasure."

"Ha ha ha ha!" Dr. Tracz was overcome with giddiness. It didn't resemble a laugh but more like an expression of happiness.

207

"Set the boxes over there, from bottom to top gentlemen," I instructed the carriers. I had just acquired this warehouse not too far from our office. It was spacious, modern, secure, and most importantly, low-key. I made Charlie the interim facilities manager, who was in charge of the shipping operation until I could find someone else I trusted. This operation was growing at an exponential rate. I had to have people in place that recognized the vision and wanted to protect our integrity. It seemed like there were infinity boxes. As soon as one truck finished, another truck would pull up with another wall of boxes. Pretty soon, the drivers were sweating profusely through their brown uniforms. I had to admit, Guna really came through for us. It took him a month longer than the initial time he had quoted us, but I couldn't be mad. This is life, and sometimes things *don't* go according to plan, and sometimes unforeseeable events really do occur. Either way, I was impressed with the finished results and ecstatic about the overall quality of the Hoverfoot. The extended waiting time only fueled the public's desire to have it even more. Soon enough, the Hoverfoot would be a worldwide household name.

"Where's Charlie?" Dr. Tracz prodded.

"He'll be here later today to track inventory and start shipping."

"He should be here now!" Dr. Tracz scolded.

"Easy, easy… He's closing some major marketing campaigns, so all of the inventory will be depleted in a fraction of the time. Remember, every victory requires a strategy."

"You're working him like a dog, aren't you?" I scowled at Dr. Tracz. I didn't like his assessment of my delegations.

"Well, he doesn't get paid like a dog. That's for sure. Besides, it's only temporary until I hire more hands in here. I need people I can trust."

"You need to handle that asap! This is our baby, Randy. Putting that much on one person, will surely break their back."

"Great observation," I noted, "…but you should have your hands full with your own realm of this business without delving into these matters. Rest assured, it will be taken care of, doctor. No worries." He smiled smugly, unenthusiastic about how I handled his concerns.

"Rowrrr," my stomach growled. I had been so excited with anticipation of this delivery that I had forgotten to eat. Dr. Tracz looked at me confused as to whether that noise was a burp or a fart.

"Say excuse me."

"That was my stomach, dummy." He shook his head in disgust not believing me.

"After they finish, you want to do lunch?"

"You buying?"

"Ha ha." It amazed me that even after shelling out Dr. Tracz a hefty salary, he still wasted no opportunity to put an expense on my tab.

"Yeah, I got you," I answered hesitantly.

"Yippie!" he said sarcastically.

"We have to be quick though. We still have to get ready for the shindig this afternoon."

"What shindig?"

"You know, the press conference?"

"What press conference?" Now I was officially starting to get annoyed by his obliviousness.

"Damn man, do you check *any* of the emails that I freakin' send you?"

"Uhmm…occasionally. You send them so frequently that they seem to lose importance." I looked at him and nodded my head unsatisfied.

"Well, I'm sorry to annoy you, but this email was important! Believe it or not but we're actually finalists for the worldwide Hovel Peace Prize!" Dr. Tracz' eyes suddenly lit up.

"You serious?" I was astonished and appalled that he was just now hearing the news.

"Oh my God! You really haven't been reading these emails?" I exhaled a sigh of grief.

"Well, if you quit sending so gahddamn many, I might have a chance to." I looked away. It's always tough working with a genius. Why? Simply because they think they know everything. Just then a courier waved his hand toward me to get my attention. He was drenched in sweat from his neck to the top of his shorts.

"That's all of it, Mr. Stashi!"

"Thanks for all of your help." I walked over and shook his hand with a fifty-dollar bill in it. He looked down at his hand when he felt the folded piece of paper.

"Take your crew out for lunch. Ya'll earned it."

He shook my hand again, even firmer with appreciation.

"Will do, sir."

***

I let Dr. Tracz pick where he wanted to eat. He chose Papa Moe's Seafood kitchen. He loved it there. I hated it. It wasn't because they didn't have good food. It was more so the fact that I was just allergic to seafood.

"So, we did it, Dr. Tracz. This project is almost officially behind us! We made history."

"Yes, we did! Let's toast." We both held up our wine glass. I usually didn't drink until after the sun went down, but today was different. Today, was special."

"To the history that we have made, and to the history we have yet to make. Toast!" Clank! We touched glasses and took a sip. I took a small one while the doctor chugged it like it was the antidote.

"Drink slow, doctor. I need you coherent for the press conference."

"Unlike you though, I have the tolerance of a man! You have the tolerance of a junior varsity cheerleader!" I laughed nearly spewing out all of my drink.

"Now that, was funny." He ordered the halibut piccata with seared shrimp, and I ordered the grilled chicken with mashed potatoes. I liked to keep it simple.

"If I wasn't a doctor, I would've tried my hand at stand up."

"It might have worked."

"Yeah, I could've been on multi-million-dollar tours with supermodels, but instead I'm stuck with *you*."

"Don't blame me for your poor life choices."

"You don't realize how grateful you should be to even breathe in my presence." I just looked at him with a serious look on my face. The nerve of this guy. He was so outlandish, it was kind of humorous.

"So now that we've put this one away, what's next?"

"Dammit Randy, can we enjoy our drink first! Maybe bask in the glory of this success for just *one* second?"

"So, you think we should frolic around, hold our heads high for another year, prance and party before returning to work just to realize our competition has used our ingenuity and time against us and triumphed valiantly and ousted us out of our own market. Bionic technology is becoming the new trend in medicine. Is that what you want?"

"If I said yes, would you be mad?"

"You're not going to say yes because then you would be selling yourself short. We're on a hot streak right now, doctor. We have the momentum behind us and the world watching us. We have to keep pushing."

"I must say, my boy…I truly admire your ambition."

"So, don't keep me in suspense." I took another sip of my pinot grigio. "What's next?" I whispered with a smile. Dr. Tracz began pouring himself a full glass.

"Dr. Armin brought this to me about a month ago."

"Who's Dr. Armin?"

"Damn, Randy! You get mad because I don't check your millions of emails, but you don't even know who's been working in your office and on your payroll for the past six months." He shook his head side to side discontentedly.

"Well, for one, you fire those doctors and engineers as quick as you hire them. Two, the government grants pay for them, and three, that's your job. You are the head scientist, not me. That's why you get paid the big bucks. Anyways, go on."

"Anyways, before I was rudely interrupted, Dr. Armin had brought this to me a month ago, and I think that it's brilliant."

"Go on, spit it out."

"Basically, he found a way to merge the Hoverfoot technology with other technologies effectively and economically." He had just struck a cord. Now he had my attention, my full undivided attention.

"Like what?"

"A plethora of things, the most fascinating thing though is cars."

"Whoaaa…" I had to let what he had just said resonate in the air.

"Do you know how much we would be helping out the world if we got rid of rubber tires?' I chuckled and nodded my head. I took the last drink of wine emptying out my glass. I put my hand up to give him a high five. He smiled in acceptance of my admiration. We clapped hands in midair. I was getting excited.

"So you're talking about something like a hover mobile. No, a *hovercar*!"

"Exactly!"

"See, that's what I'm talking about Dr. Tracz! That's exactly what I'm talking about. Always being on the cusp of technology. WHOO!" I stood up and nearly knocked over the table. Dr. Tracz stabilized it with his hands.

"Randy, sit down!" Our waitress suddenly appeared at our table with piping hot plates of food in her hands.

"Who had the halibut piccata?"

"He did," I answered quickly. I wanted that plate nowhere near me. I sat down still jittery from the news. The wine was starting to kick in. She sat the grilled chicken in front of me. The doctor looked at me disgustedly like a parent displeased with their child.

"Please forgive my antics. I'm just excited."

"You're acting like an immature football jock."

"…Who's headed to the Super Bowl," I finished. "Let's eat and then let's make more history!"

"Uhmm, excuse me." He flagged over a waiter. "Can we get another bottle of—"

"Nooo! We'll celebrate after the conference." I looked at the waiter who was confused at who he should listen to.

"Some more water will be fine." I insisted. He walked away. "Let's stay professional, business then pleasure." He sighed and then started cutting up his fish. I looked at my watch—2:00pm. Time was flying.

"Hurry up! The conference starts in two hours. We can't be late." I still needed a hot shower and to practice my speech. Dr. Tracz ate his food dismally. My guess was, he was still upset about the wine.

"You're taking me to the strip club later." I chuckled. I'm worried about the fate of our company, and he's worried about some punani.

"We'll see." He looked as though that answer would suffice. I felt his pain. He was a young rambunctious rock star trapped in a sixty-year-old's body. He was also, not to mention, the braniac behind this entire operation. I hated playing parent, but I had to keep him alive, not just for me, but for the world's sake. Without him this operation would come to a screeching halt. And there was no way in hell that I was going to let that happen.

"Check please!" I yelled.

Chapter 58

"No more questions or comments! *Pleeease!*" I made my way through the barricade of reporters and news' cameras while ushering Dr. Tracz to the car. "Don't say a *word!*" I grumbled low enough for only Dr. Tracz to hear. Our chauffeur opened the door for us as we hustled inside of the Bentley. I was freaking pissed! The press conference we had just attended was semi-successful. Successful because we announced our new book, the release of the Hoverfoot, and our promise to continue to revolutionize the world. That was the good part. The reason why I said semi was because of Dr. Tracz's antics. He acted like a complete fool in front of the cameras and, more importantly, the world. He just disgraced our brand. We both sat in the car speechless—I, too angry to speak, and him probably in a drunken stupor not realizing the damage to our PR that he had just caused.

"That went well…" he mumbled lowly as he gazed out the window. I was fuming. As I looked at him, he was only making me angrier. He took out his flask and began drinking as we pulled off. Aww *helll nawww!*

"You can't be serious right now!" He looked over at me in the midst of chugging his drink and nodded a slight yes. I could feel the fury surge through my body. I rolled down the window, snatched his flask, and jettisoned it from the car. Now he could see I was serious. He suddenly glared at me with menacing eyes. This was the first time since lunch that he actually looked like he cared.

"What's your problem Randy?"

"What's *my problem*, Dr. Tracz?! Do you have any *friggin'* clue why I'm so pissed off right now?"

"Yeah, because you're a miserable prick ready for any mishap to get your panties in a *bunch!*"

"And you're a reckless addict that acts like a spoiled child."

"Well, I do have a baby face." He started to slowly stroke his chin. I was too hot to be amused. I took off my sunglasses.

"Look me in my eyes!" I waited for our eyes to lock in. "You just *embarrassed us* out there! Me, yourself, everything we worked so hard for, our brand."

214

"How?" He looked at me with a blank expression as if he didn't know what I was talking about.

"How? What do you mean how? Maybe by saying to the reporter, "Hey tits! Do you want to be a part of our next experiment?" Do you know how demeaning that sounded? Let's just hope and *pray* that she doesn't try to sue us for something *dumb*!"

"It wasn't my fault I could barely concentrate on her questions with her breasts waving at me like that!"

"That was on national television! *Possibly* even worldwide television!"

"Well, then I guess I made her famous!"

"And you just made us infamous! I can't believe what just happened! That frickin' quick!" I slammed my fist hard against the door. The driver stopped the car thinking we had been hit. "Keep going!" I shouted from the backseat. "That was me." I turned my attention back to Dr. Tracz. "Is vagina all you think about?"

"Well, besides helping craft the world's most innovative inventions for you...umm, yeah." I nodded my head in disgust and then stared out my window. Years worth of work, just to taint our image in seconds.

"You are *UN-believable*!... You're an addict in more ways than one. You know that?"

"No, I'm not.... I've just been liberated since my divorce. I am a philanderer."

"No.... You've got issues!"

"Clearly, which reminds me, are we still going to the strip club tonight? I know a girl who dances there with curves that'll make your eyes pop out of their sockets and bounce on the ground."

"Not me! Especially, not tonight! After what you just did?! Ha! You have fun, grandpa! I'm in a sour mood."

"Oh well. I'm not going to argue with you. I guess that means more for me!"

"Driver, stop!" I looked over at Dr. Tracz. It took every ounce of energy in my body to resist the urge to sock him right on the nose. I unbuckled my seatbelt and got out of the car.

"See you later. I'm walking home!" I needed to cool down because I was two seconds away from strangling that old geezer, possibly even killing him. The Bentley slowly pulled away, and I saw the window roll down as Dr. Tracz's head popped out.

"JUST REMEMBER! Before you say I *RUINED* everything, you wouldn't even be able to *walk home* if it wasn't for *meee*!

"REMEMBER THAT!"

I couldn't lie. He did have a point.

Chapter 59

"Hey babe, muah!" It was always rejuvenating coming to a peaceful home and a kiss from a lovely woman who missed your presence.

"My oh my, you look nice today." My girlfriend became a little lost professionally after college. She had worked at a couple of big firms but lost interest because of the cutthroat ethics and demanding hours in corporate America. She eventually got her license and became a real estate agent. While she only made a couple of minor deals since her inception, she loved seeing houses. It was something that she said had always fascinated her as a child, I guess because she never had a big house or even a house for that matter. I had always encouraged her in her career every step of the way. She was smart, sexy, and ambitious. She just didn't know what direction to take it in until recently.

"How was your press conference?" she asked as I started to take off my suit and loosen my tie. I growled like a vicious dog ready to attack.

"*Grrr...*" She laughed at my reaction.

"It couldn't have been that bad."

"It was a complete fiasco, thanks to the one and only...Dr. Tracz."

"Oh boy..." Chloe had grown familiar with some of the stories of Dr. Tracz's antics. "What'd he do this time?"

"He was just being Dr. Tracz as usual," I answered as I made my way to the refrigerator.

"That could mean an array of things...."

"Don't worry, honey. I'm sure it'll be on the 10:00 o'clock local news. Matter of fact, I can guaran*tee*, that it'll be on the news."

"Oh boy, I got to see this."

I sighed heavily. Did he really just embarrass us in front of the whole world? I needed to stop worrying. Whatever is going to happen is going to happen. Maybe a delicious meal would make me feel better.

"What's for dinner?"

"I would cook you something, but I'm tired baby...."

"Oh, really. How tired?" I gave her a hug and clenched a good portion of her left cheek in my palm. She giggled.

"Babe... I've been showing houses all day, a lot of leads and no sales," she said full of fatigue. "Honestly, I think some of my clients just want a lap dance and a blow job." I laughed at her frustration. "I'd bet you'd sell a lot more if you offered that with the purchase." She slapped me playfully on the chest.

"I know I'd buy from you, honey."

"Staaph!"

"I'm just kidding...."

"I know, but you know what would help me?" I paused for a second before answering. Her full attention was on me.

"What?"

"I would probably sell more houses if I had your last name." I looked at her with a smirk on my face.

"What's that supposed to mean?"

"Exactly what I said. If my name was Chloe Stashi, people would associate me with you and know that they're buying greatness." Uh oh. I knew exactly what she was hinting at, something I wasn't trying to think about—marriage.

"You couldn't handle being a Stashi, the lights, the attention, the mean and nasty tabloids, and the hate mail. I'm glad things are how they are right now. No one can bring you any harm or trouble on behalf of me. That's just not fair."

"Sounds like a load of crap to me."

"Chloe, I'm serious as a heart attack. No one can attack you because they can't associate us together. Think about it." She nodded slowly and turned away as if displeased with my response. She then said over her shoulder vindictively.

"But yeah, no cooking, tonight. Sorry."

"No worries, I wanted pizza anyway."

***

After some great pizza and some even greater sex, I was exhausted. I was in the bathroom taking a hot relaxing shower. It had gotten to the point that I wasn't even washing anymore. I was just letting the pressurized hot water massage my body. My mind was a million miles away from everything, away from the troubles, the challenges, my handicap, and my reality. I just closed my eyes and felt like I was in another world. It was like an out-of-body experience. I was extremely content with my life, but sometimes it was extremely demanding, and I felt like some people were way too dependent on me. Just then, the bathroom door burst open.

"Baby! Hurry up! It's on!" Back to reality.

"What's on?" I called out. She had already left, leaving my question unanswered. I hopped out the shower grabbed my towel and hopped to the bedroom still soaking wet. Chloe was staring at the TV with her eyes wide open when I had entered the room.

"What's on?" I still had no clue what was going on.

"Shut up!" She put one finger over her mouth and pressed the volume up with the remote. I hobbled over to get a closer view of what was going on. I heard the anchorman's familiar voice from channel eleven.

"And in other news, author slash entrepreneur Randi Stashi held a press conference today to announce the release of his revolutionary invention the Hoverfoot as well as announce the sequel to his global bestseller, *The Stashi Life*" The anchorwoman resumed the story where her partner had left off.

"The highlight today though wasn't Randy Stashi or his announcements but rather his lively doctor, Dr. Tracz. Let's take a look at a clip of the drama that unfolded today." The news suddenly cut instantly to the footage of the press conference where Dr. Tracz was pointing drunkenly to someone in the front row.

"Hey, Tits! You can be a part of tonight's experimentation. We got technology you've never seen before!"

"Oh my God!" Chloe gasped. Then someone blurted from the front row.

"Hey, knock it off, BLEEP-HOLE!" Dr. Tracz turned his head toward the heckler and replied.

"I don't *need* the Hoverfoot to *hover* my foot up your *bleep!*" Then the TV cut back to the news anchors who were making strained faces to refrain from laughing. Yep, that confirmed it. We were now the laughingstock of the world.

"Quite a circus Stashi is running over there." The newswoman coughed.

"When we come back, we'll investigate whether some of our mandatory drug sentencing laws are used to line pockets of the wealthy at private prisons. That and more on—"

Chloe shut off the television.

"Wow. You really weren't kidding," she snickered still astonished by what she had just witnessed. I exhaled slowly.

"That alcohol turns him into a monster."

"Why did you let him answer questions?"

"I didn't. He just butted in." Chloe was laughing at me. I felt ashamed. There's nothing more humbling than being laughed at. She could see I was annoyed.

"He made a mockery of us today, babe, a complete joke." I was still standing there, half-naked, dripping wet, and unimpressed.

"There, there, baby. It's not that bad." Chloe started walking toward me smiling. I just sucked my teeth and nodded my head.

"Look on the bright side. If it goes viral then you'll get even more views which might actually be a good thing, babe. There's no such thing as bad publicity." That was honestly the first positive thing I had heard since our catastrophe. It sounded plausible. Maybe she was right. Maybe there was still light at the end of the tunnel.

"I sure hope so, sweetie. I sure hope so."

Meanwhile…

Seven minutes earlier in a lavish house in another part of the world, another organization was becoming very agitated.

Ring. Ring.

It had been quiet these past couple of weeks for the Garbageman. He was the leader of their division of the organization. He had been notoriously nicknamed the Garbageman because he was responsible for all of the firm's dirty work. He mostly delegated the lesser tasks to his other cohorts, but ultimately, he was the one in charge, the one who reported the results. It had been relatively quiet these past couple of weeks. No one had been misbehaving, so he had seized the opportunity to take a mini-vacation to Europe. His position made him a very rich man, but not rich enough to quit. Either way, he knew he couldn't quit. He knew way too much, and he had pledged his life to the organization. To quit would mean his days were numbered. He would probably be killed as a safety precaution not to divulge the organization's secrets and maintain their code that had been intact for centuries. There was no way out. Betrayal meant death. He knew his life was expendable if he quit working for them. However, while he was the Garbageman, he lived like a king. He was the organization's best-kept secret. Anything he wanted was only a phone call away. On the same note, everything they needed done had to be handled skillfully, stealthily, and dutifully by him. He loved the challenge. He loved the thrill. He loved feeling important. It was a delicate and fragile balance, however. He had enough money to raise eyebrows, but his job required him to be invisible. As he laid in his rented mansion under a different alias, his cell phone began to ring. He looked at the display. It was his boss. He waited until the third ring to pick it up.

"Hello?"

"Hello Garbageman, alert your boys right now. Put the TV on channel eleven. You have to see this immediately."

Click. Call ended. Any call from the boss was beyond extremely important, almost a life or death matter. That's the reason he wore his cell phone around like an ankle bracelet. Ignoring the boss for too long for sure was a death wish. It seems like the world is big, but truthfully there was only so many places you could run. Only so many places you could hide. The organization was everywhere. Nothing was out of reach. What was even more alarming was you didn't know who was involved. It could be your own mother. You never knew for sure. You could only speculate. Everyone was sworn to secrecy. Everyone was disconnected. No one knew everything, but everyone knew too much.

"ROUND UP!" The other two men sprinted full speed down the stairs. They knew that "round up" was the assembling battle cry that sprang them into action.

"The boss called. He wants us to watch this!" The Garbageman powered on the sixty-inch flat screen that hung off the living room wall and clicked to channel eleven. Everyone's eyes were focused on the screen, not knowing what to expect.

"And in other news, author slash entrepreneur Randi Stashi held a press conference today to announce the release of his…." They continued watching the clip of the disastrous yet amusing highlights of the meeting.

"I don't *need* the Hoverfoot to *hover* my foot up your *bleep*!" They continued to watch until it had cut to commercial.

"Did you see those bumbling idiots?" the Garbageman questioned.

"What a joke!" One of the others added, "What was the point of watching that?"

"I'm about to find out," the Garbageman answered. He motioned his hands for them to leave the room, and they filed out.

Ring. Ring.

"I just saw it, boss. What a bunch of idiots."

"Maybe they look like clowns on television, but they're far from idiots." The Garbageman was all ears.

"He's getting powerful, too powerful. Pretty soon we won't be able to stop him."

"What's the issue, boss?"

"You don't see what issue is…? He's undermining everything this organization stands for. The wrong people get the wrong power, and they will *upset* our system that we have in place, our whole hierarchy, our whole heritage, the whole distribution of wealth. We are at the top of the food chain for a reason. If guppies start eating the shark food, then what do the sharks eat?"

"I understand."

"You said that last time. I thought you were going to stop him from printing any more books."

"We tried. We sent him a warning."

"A warning? You tried? I don't know if you heard or not but, he announced the sequel to his book today! Your warning has obviously meant *nothing* to him! His first book is becoming a worldwide phenomenon. We cannot let him make another book."

"So, what do you want us to do?"

"Stop him from making the second book at all cost...or else…"

"Or else what?"

"Or else we're going to make a book about you. Only you won't be alive to read it." Click.

The instructions were made very clear to the Garbageman. He assembled his cohorts, and they began planning. The deadline wasn't immediate, but time was of the essence.

Chapter 60

Human relationships are peculiar and unpredictable. Sometimes, in grade school, there might be someone who gives you funny looks and doesn't say much. It might seem like the outsider treatment, but in actuality, they have a secret crush, just like Helga in the Hey Arnold cartoon or, sometimes, how someone can have a sworn enemy, have an altercation with them, and then they become best friends. Many times, someone even thinks they have found their soulmate, just for it to end in a nasty near fatal divorce. It's hard to tell how certain relationships will grow because people are always getting smarter as long as they learn something new everyday. People change their ways based on knowledge. Therefore, no one is the same as they were yesterday. With that being said, it is almost mandatory that one must end relations as cordially as possible. One can never predict the future progress of someone else, or the point in time where they might cross paths again. Sometimes, correspondence will end on sour terms, and later someone hits the jackpot. No one ever remembers what exactly is said but everyone remembers how they felt. It's crazy how the cycle of life works. One has to care for their kids because one day they'll probably be returning the favor. Even though it is fun to fill up a glass bottle with alcohol, jam it with cloth, light it, throw it at people you don't like and say F you forever. One should never burn bridges—never ever. The reason is because you never know when you might need to cross that bridge again. You never know if you might need that person again.

So here I was crossing the bridge I never thought I'd cross again, eating lunch with my old colleague, Quincy Sterling. I never thought too much about Quincy. He was a pot enthusiast, who always asked spaced out questions that often lead nowhere. Randy remembered how sometimes he would forget the topic they were discussing in mid-conversation. His eyes were always red, and you could smell him from a mile away. Either way, I never offended him or criticized him, because he never offended or criticized me. It was simple as that. He never disrespected me, so why would I disrespect him? I guess all of his spaced out thinking finally led him into the right career path as an architect.

"I've never heard of this place before," Quincy noted as he looked around observing. One thing about handling businesses of our caliber is I know all of the exclusive spots in town.

"Yes, Elmyra's is a hidden gem. Great food."

"So, I see. What do you recommend?"

"I love their chicken Philly."

"Oooh. That does sound pretty good."

"Yeah. If you can't find anything else you like, I recommend it."

"I'm not really in a sandwich mood though. Let me look...." It's funny how offsetting it is when someone asks for a suggestion then rejects it.

"So how have you been since FVU?" I asked.

"Working like a Hebrew slave man, but it's finally starting to pay off."

"I'm proud of you. The horizontal condo is quite an achievement, the world's first diagonal elevator you were telling me."

"That's only the beginning Randy. You should see what we're working on next...."

"Like what?" He had my full attention. His ideas were unpredictable.

"Think spheres."

"Ohhh," I said nodding my head in agreement. I had no clue what Quincy was talking about, but I just nodded my head like I did. I don't know what he was smoking on these days, but then I'm thinking it couldn't be too hard because he did manage to keep his job. I guess he wasn't picking up the hint to keep elaborating on his spheres comment.

"Have you heard from anyone back at FVU?" I had to break the awkward silence.

"Yeah. I keep up with them sorta kinda via Facebook." He took a sip of his iced tea.

"Really. Like who?" I really didn't care. Everyone had their own flourishing lives and families. It had been a while.

"Well, our old group members. Do you remember Mariam Slater?"

"How could I forget the most organized person that I had ever met in my life. Can you say obsessive compulsive?"

"Yeah, her. She's head accountant at some big firm, but I don't think she likes it too much."

"Why do you say that?"

"Because she's always complaining about it on Facebook. She's making good money though."

"Money isn't everything," I revealed.

"Hey, gentlemen! Hey, Mr. Stashi." It was our waitress, Colleen. I always sat in her section because, surprisingly, she was the only waitress who could remember my order by heart. I never needed a menu for this place. Making someone feel important is priceless.

"Same as usual?"

"Yes." I nodded.

"No peppers, no mushrooms, diced raw onions, light mayo, and extra cheese." She remembered it like it was her last name.

"Like always."

"Mmm…that does sound delicious," Quincy imagined. "Let me have the same thing, but you can put the peppers on mine." Quincy changed his mind about my advice. He was cool with me. Colleen began to grab the menus.

"Coming right up." She took about three steps away from our table and then turned around.

"Oh, and I saw you on TV the other day. My oh my, you and that doctor sure are funny." She was giggling after she said it. After she could see I wasn't amused she continued walking away. My life's work wasn't intended to make people laugh. Did I look like a comedian?

"Damn, I missed it. Is it on YouTube?" Quincy asked.

"No. I don't think so," I answered hastily so he wouldn't bother searching for it. It was too late though. He was already on his smartphone doing his research.

"You know, everything you do nowadays is big news, Stashi…."

"Tell me about it," I replied dully. He was going to see it regardless.

"Here it goes right here.... Wow, quite impressive. Over fifteen million views."

"Wow, fifteen?" I had to admit, even I was impressed by the popularity of that clip. Within seconds, Quincy was laughing hysterically. "Ha ha ha!" Quincy was gasping for breath, and his eyes began to water. I thought he was being a little excessive. "Look, they even made a remix song, Hover my Foot up yo' Ass!" Quincy was making a lot of unnecessary commotion. I was starting to become annoyed when he started dancing. Maybe it was because he couldn't dance or our neighboring guests began staring at us. "Your partner is hilarious!"

"Only in doses. You done?" Quincy could tell I wasn't amused. I had to switch the gears from this nonsense. Something clicked in my head. "Anyways, you think Mariam hates her job, eh?"

"Only if she's being honest on social media."

"Well, give her a ring for me. I might have a job opening for her." We are definitely short-staffed right now, especially in the organization department.

"Will do." Quincy, answered, I was always thinking about advancing and expansion. Bringing up our old colleagues reminded me of another person.

"You still talk to Evelyn?"

"Maaan, I don't talk to any of these people, Randy. I went to school with them just like you did, worked on a project with them, just like you did, and lost contact with them, just like you did. They just pop up on my newsfeed when I'm on social media every so often." Randy realized he had struck a nerve.

"My bad. Let me rephrase. Do you happen to know what she's been up to nowadays?"

"Well, she was an environmentalist, but now judging by what she promotes, she's trying her hand at fashion."

"Really? Are her clothes any good?"

"Ahhh, it's all right. It's mainly for women. The logo is kind of bland. It's like a flower or trefoil."

"Interesting, very interesting. I was actually thinking about starting a line ourselves. The Stashi novel merchandise has been doing really well."

"Oh really? What's your logo going to be?"

"I was thinking something like a pig."

"A pig? Pigs are disgusting.... They eat their own turds for Christ's sakes."

"That is true, not to mention very foul, but I was thinking more in terms of a piggy bank. You know, like the challenge to acquire wealth."

"Ohhhhhhhh…" The epiphany had hit Quincy like a sack of bricks. "I mean, I guess it could work. You've been on a hot streak at everything so far. Why not try it out."

"Thanks." Colleen came back to refill our drinks.

"Food will be up in two minutes." Quincy nodded with a smile.

"You heard about Dylan Chazzy?"

"No. What about him?"

"He's head civil engineer in Orlando, Florida. He took it to that group project to the next level for real."

"What does he do exactly?"

"Make sure the city functions properly, from highways to roads, to pipelines. He's a one-stop shop."

"Well, Dylan was always a leader and hard worker. You remember that pep speech he gave us when everyone was ready to burn down the project? No real shocker there."

I was impressed with the news of all of our colleagues continuing their success.

"That's good to hear. Usually, at our age, everyone is fat and pregnant or strung out on hard drugs."

"Well, it hasn't happened yet, but keep your fingers crossed."

"For you…and for you." Colleen placed our lunch in front of us. It smelled delicious. I prayed before I stuffed my face with an oversized first bite.

Too tasty. The food was scrumptious. I reached for a napkin. Quincy wiped his mouth with both hands. He was speechless too.

"You know what the cause for today's luncheon is?" I asked between bites.

"To catch up as old friends and reminisce about the good 'ole days."

"Not quite Quincy. Even though I like you, not quite. I'm actually looking to move into a new building."

"Well, where's your building now?" Quincy questioned.

"In the heart of downtown."

"I don't like it."

"Why? That sounds like a dream." I took another sip of my water to wash down my food. I leaned in closer to him and lowered my tone.

"It's too busy downtown. Too many sets of eyes. We have some top-secret projects that we're working on in the near future, and we cannot afford to jeopardize the secrecy or integrity of our work." Quincy's eyes began to light up.

"Oooh… it sounds revolutionary. So why do you need me?"

"I need you for one simple reason. I like the way you push the creative envelope with your architecture. I want you to build me something on the outskirts of the city, preferably the north side."

"Mmm…" He was soaking it all in. "How soon?"

"Start drawing up the blueprints asap. I want it to look shabby on the outside, and something from the future on the inside. It's going to be our little bat cave." The way I imagined it made me smile. It made me feel at peace.

"I like the sound of this already. I can't wait to get started. Just a little heads up, Randy. I'm not cheap."

"Quincy, just for the record. I'm not cheap either.…" Quincy nodded and smiled, then extended his hand. "Happy to be on board with the Stashi Team!"

"Glad you can join us!" We finished our food as the meeting slowly came to a close.

"So, Randy, what exactly has Chloe been up to? Is she working for you too?"

"Naw. She's actually a realtor wheelin' and dealin' properties."

"Oh really? I could probably use her help."

"Naw, she's only residential. Sorry, Quince...."

"I actually was thinking about the residential end of my-"

"Sorry Quince, she's already booked up..."

He stopped smiling. I had to keep it professional. We finished up and surprisingly, Quincy paid the bill. He was probably just trying to butter me up for the deal.

Great tactic.

Chapter 61

"So Stashi… That's a pretty cool name. Where does is it derive from?" Years ago, when I stayed at my mom's house, I was a sad insecure recluse, scared to face the world outside, scared to overcome challenges, scared to look at myself in the mirror. I didn't know how to overcome my physical disabilities. Pretty soon, however, I made a breakthrough. I stopped caring about the wrong things. The real me was on the inside. Who cares if I walk, jump, or run again? Who cares if you reject me? Would you really give me a chance to listen to what I have to say? This nonchalant attitude helped build the confidence to achieve my goals. Now I was in a room with a reporter/editor for GQD magazine. We had just finished an intense photo shoot where they had named me as one of this year's top sexiest businessman alive. I didn't really want to do the interview because it made me look shallow. However, GQD had an enormous fan base, so it was an opportunity for us to influence some potential advocates. Remember, even bad publicity can still be good publicity. It's actually the lack of publicity that is the most damaging. Now, I was at a table with Rachel Rawlings, playing twenty questions that would later be transcribed and plastered on every newsstand and media outlet imaginable because I was this month's cover story.

"Not too sure. It does sound kinda German though?"

"Yeah, it does. Do you think you might have some German blood in you?"

"Possibly, but I think my mom named me that for different reasons."

"Like what?"

"Well, she told me when I was born, my eyes sparkled like jewelry. I looked valuable, no, priceless. Like anything priceless, you would stash it away for safe keeping."

"That's a beautiful explanation for your moniker."

"Thank you. I don't know if it's the truth or not, but it sounded good when she said it." Rachel laughed.

"This issue is going to put you in the hearts of women everywhere. Do you have anything to say to them?"

"Sorry ladies, I really am, but I'm taken."

"Awww…" Rachel groaned. I don't know if she was being dramatic for the interview or she had other hopes. "You married?"

"Not yet, but I know she's the one. She's been with me from the start before any of this."

Rachel's eyes gleamed at my happiness. I could tell she was excited for me.

"I know she must feel special. Like she hit the Lotto, huh?"

"Honestly, Rachel, I feel like I hit the Lotto." As corny and cliché as it sounded, it was the truth. What on earth would possess a beautiful college girl like her at the time to be with a wreck like me? Even after all of these years, I still had no explanation for that.

"Well, let's switch gears for a second. Your business partner, Dr. Tracz, he's a real hoot, isn't he?"

"He's something. Sometimes, he plays the parent, and I play the child, but most of the times its vice versa. He keeps life fun. You should always have someone close to you that's light hearted. Now, ladies, if you're looking for love, Dr. Tracz is the most eligible and amusing bachelor on the planet!"

"Wow, that was quite a shoutout."

"No worries. He'll owe me for it later."

"How did you meet him? There's quite an age gap between the two of you."

Well, he was in a deep dark place after his divorce, and he didn't want to do anything, anything at all. Most people would've chalked him up as a lost cause, but I could relate to his depression because I had experienced it years earlier. I felt like if I could pick him up in spirit, then this might have a shot at working. Millions upon millions of dollars later, here we are. I love that guy. He's shown me so much."

"That's amazing because you look like you wanted to kill him at the infamous press conference."

"Ha ha… Looks can be deceiving, but at times I do though," I said nonchalantly. She blurted out a laugh. She interviewed me for about twenty more minutes until I cut her off. As much as I enjoyed the break from the office, I had to get back. I had an incredible amount of work to do.

"Hey, Randy!" My secretary Marsha greeted me after I arrived. Usually, she would fill me in on anything I had missed while I was gone. "How was GQD?"

"Tiring, to say the least."

"You must be pretty excited though to make this year's sexiest businessman list."

"I don't see what all the fuss is about. I've looked this way for years. Just another day for me."

"Oh…" Marsha's voice trailed off. Her enthusiasm changed when she heard my modesty.

"I'm still the same person, Marsha. We can't let the tomfoolery distract us from our mission."

"I understand."

"Did you forget about your interview?"

"Interview, interview…" I couldn't recall what she was referring to. "Refresh my memory Marsha. What interview?"

"Your job interview with Mariam Slater. She's been waiting for you for over an hour. I can reschedule it if you like?"

"Aww Shazam!" I forgot all about Mariam. I flew her in for a preliminary meeting to see if she liked the organization, and was interested in the opportunity. This would be a drastic change to her current lifestyle and residence, so I had to make sure she was sure about it. Quite frankly, I needed her help. We were expanding, and I liked the idea of hiring her over a complete stranger. We had already worked together before, so we knew each others boundaries.

"Where is she?" I asked Marsha.

"Conference room number two."

I set down my blazer in my office and proceeded to enter the conference room. She was wearing a navy-blue blouse, a pearl necklace, with high heels. She had her head on the wall and eyes closed. She was snoring very loudly. Normally, if this was their first impression, I would have been appalled by this unprofessional slumber, but I really couldn't be because I actually knew her. She had a tenacious work ethic. She was probably exhausted from her flight. Plus, I was the one who was an hour late, not her. I was already inside the room, but I reentered with a loud knock to wake her up. Her head flew forward, startled by my entrance. She wiped her mouth with the back of her hand to clean up the drool from her face. She looked embarrassed.

"Well, hello there Mariam. What a pleasure it is to see you again." She stood up and shook my hand.

"Well, it's a pleasure to be here, Mr. Stashi. I like what you've done with the place." I smiled and motioned her to have a seat while I pulled out a chair for her. She looked at her watch. I could tell she was calculating how late I was for our appointment.

"Sorry, I'm late." I apologized as if I was reading her mind. "My interview took waaaay longer than expected."

"Who was it for…if you don't mind me asking?"

"GDQ…." Her eyes widened with interest.

"Really?"

"Yeah, just a little article. They ranked me in this year's top ten sexiest businessmen." She smiled and grabbed my hand with both of hers.

"Congratulations. You've been on a roll these days."

"I've been blessed."

"When can I read it?"

"They'll have an abridged online version later this week, but the full article will be on newsstands next month."

"That's crazy…. I'm happy for you!" Good 'ole Mariam, years earlier she would have denounced me as sloppy and dumb in college. Now, sitting at our grand office, high in the sky, she had garnered a new respect for me. It's funny how the table turns sometimes. The tables always turn.

"I brought you in here today because we are looking for someone of your stature. We are expanding at an exponential rate and desperately trying to keep up. I have a question for you. What was your last job like?"

"It was cool. The pay was nice, and I had my own parking spot." I looked at her seriously. She just gazed at me like she was trying to stick to her last statement. Something didn't sound right though. If parking spots are what she mentioned, then there must not have been too many highlights. I looked deep into her eyes.

"Mariam…you can be honest with me." She let out a deep breath and looked away.

"Well…honestly…I really didn't like it. It was boring. Always a rat race slash competition to get to the next position, always on the verge of getting fired, I just didn't feel appreciated." I could see her eyes beginning to water.

"It's okay, Mariam. That happens in a lot of big firms."

"I was even on the fence about working here, but after I seen a clip of that press conference with you and your doctor, I was inspired. It looks like y'all have a lot of fun. Not only that, but you're changing the world!" I was shocked. That was the second time today that I was reminded about that press conference. Both reminders were positive. It was ironic how something I felt so negative about was actually being well received. Word had already traveled fast, but with the advent of social media, now it was cracking sound barriers.

"You know why I want to hire you?" She looked confused as if she couldn't pinpoint my reasoning.

"No. Why?"

"Because your organizational skills really kept our group project on track back at FVU. That's something that always stuck out to me." Her eyes fluttered nervously as she smiled shyly. You could tell she was blushing on the inside.

"Thanks, Randy. I guess I get it from my mom. She's the true definition of OCD."

"Well thank her for inheriting it. It's exactly what this company is missing."

"When do you want me to start?"

"Today," I said hastily.

"Now, you know that's impossible. I still have to pack and, not to mention, move across the country."

"I'm just kidding. I know that's too soon. Let's just say two weeks from today. In the meantime, I'll fax you over the disclosure and arbitration agreement. Sound good?"

"Sounds perfect." I extended my hand for her to shake. Instead of shaking it, she jumped up and gave me a hug. "Thank you so much, Randy! Thank you! Thank you!" She grabbed her briefcase and practically skipped out of the office.

Well, that went well I thought to myself. I stood there for a second to think what was next on my agenda. GDQ...check. Mariam...check. That's when I drew a blank. I really needed to go back to my office to refresh my memory. I don't know why but forgetting things has become more frequent than remembering for me these days. Before I could even leave the conference room, Dr. Tracz barged in with a newspaper folded under one arm and spilling coffee from his mug with the other. I couldn't smell any alcohol on him, so that was a good thing. He rushed in and closed the door behind him with his foot.

"You dirty dog you!"

"What?" I answered. I wasn't up for Tracz's shenanigans right now.

"You heard me you dirty *dog!*" He put down his mug of coffee and put up his open palm to give me a high five. It wasn't a slap back on my end but more like a soft touch because I didn't know what I was being congratulated for.

"I still have no idea about what you are talking about." That's when he slammed down the newspaper on the desk. The front page happened to be facing up. I gasped.

"You never told me you boned Porsha Gottfrey, you lucky bastard!"

"Wooow!" I was still in a stupefied state as I slowly picked up the paper. The title read: "MULTI-MILLION-DOLLAR TYCOON AND WORLD-FAMOUS TALK SHOW HOST FIND LOVE!" The picture was one of me and Porsha cuddled up eating when we were in the diner post-intercourse. I had one arm around her, and she was wearing my "Get Stashi" shirt. I should've known that grimy waitress who had walked by at our breakfast wasn't just texting. I was speechless, but just then, my instincts kicked in. They told me to do one thing, and one thing only. Deny, deny, and deny.

"So, that's how we've been getting all of this free publicity on her show?

Ha ha. Quite impressive my boy." I had tuned Dr. Tracz out. I was still scanning the article looking for any flaws that I could point out in my defense.

"Star Entertainment?" I murmured. "What are you doing reading the tabloids?" I demanded.

"Looks real to me...."

"Are you serious? This is the most fictional magazine in the city. Look at this article. Justin Weaver has sex change to become lesbian. Oh, wait.... Let me guess. You believe that too?" Dr. Tracz glanced at the paper, scanning the titles of the other articles not knowing what was true anymore.

"No no.... This picture looks real, and you definitely disappeared for hours with no explanation that night."

"Now, Dr. Tracz, you know as well as I know how good these clowns have gotten with Photoshop. They can make anything look real nowadays." Dr. Tracz looked at me for a second to see if I was lying. When I didn't flinch is when he actually began to soak it in. He actually got disheartened.

"Sorry Randy for giving you credit for my assumptions. I should've known you didn't have enough game to knock boots with Porsha."

"Don't be sorry. Just don't spread rumors that aren't true. It could be damaging to us and the credibility of this company." Dr. Tracz nodded yes slowly and then exited the room with his head hanging low. As for me, my heart was beating through my damn chest as I gazed on the table at the article. I dodged the bullet this time by the bare skin of my teeth, but the truth would eventually come out. How long could I silence the lambs? Even worse, how long until Chloe would find out? This was not supposed to happen. I wanted to kill that sneaky waitress who snapped that picture.

Whyyyyyyyyy!

Chapter 62

'Anything is possible. And any dream or goal in life can be accomplished. It all starts with a thought. Thoughts are more powerful than they seem. They can transform moods, habits, and ultimately behavior. You could be having a great day, then start thinking about your puppy that you lost when you were younger and suddenly feel heartbroken, or vice versa. You could be devastated nothing is going right, and then feel happy that at least you're still alive. Thoughts are so random and sporadic that it's mandatory to write it down. Priorities are always changing, and it's too easy to get swallowed up in the daily grind. It's too easy to forget the task at hand. That's why writing things down is mandatory. It's an accurate way to measure progress and benchmarks. It also shows if the results are feasible in the allotted time frame. This is so crucial when evaluating efficiency. The last key is the most important but underrated technique of them all. People always overlook how important it is to speak it into existence. No one is a mind reader, and it might sound unrealistic when you write it down. However, the people who hold the keys to your locks will never know you need the keys unless you tell them. Plus, when you say it, it starts to sound natural, like it's your destiny or fate. What's even crazier is once people know your objectives they will either help you accomplish them or stay out of your way. So, if you're trying to accomplish a goal, think it, write it, then say it. (Get off your a** and make it happen!)'

I put down the book amazed at what I had just read. Years later, The Stashi Life is still fascinating to me. I could see the power of this book and why it was so highly praised by the public. Some parts of that book were so good it felt like I didn't even write it. I put the book down, gazed out my office window, and started daydreaming. Whenever I read something profound, I would sit for a second and let it resonate. This was partly the reason I was sitting at my desk after hours on a Friday afternoon. The other part was that I was too scared to go home. Hopefully, Chloe didn't read the tabloids. Even if she did, I hoped she didn't believe them. Yeah, right. This is the latest that I think I've ever stayed on a Friday at the office.

Knock! Knock!

Marsha my secretary peeked her head in with her purse under her arm.

"Are you okay?" Even Marsha could sense that something was wrong with me.

"Yeah, I'm fine. Just thinking."

"Are you sure, Mr. Stashi? It's Friday and after 5:00pm. This is very unlike you." My secretary knew my tendencies all too well.

"I'm sure. I'll be leaving shortly. You leaving?"

"Yes, sir. Time to start my weekend. Tonight is ladies night!" She was smiling from ear to ear.

"Well, have fun and be safe!"

"I will. You look like you might need a night out too, Mr. Stashi. Don't forget, stress can kill you!"

"I'm sure I'll be fine. Take care." She waved and then closed my door. I exhaled a sigh. I could hear the building's janitor at the other end of the hallway vacuuming. Maybe Marsha was right. Maybe a night out on the town would do me some good, especially a night out with Chloe. I had been working so hard these past couple of weeks that I had barely been paying any attention to her. I gathered my things and headed out of the office.

"Ciao!" I yelled out as I waved to the janitor. She smiled at me and waved back, never missing a beat with her vacuum. I called around on the way home to see what would be exciting to go to. A mini performance at Club Roxy—perfect.

"Ah yes. I'd like to reserve a table tonight, under Randy Stashi." After I had secured the table, I called my partner in crime—Dr. Tracz. He thought it was the best idea he's heard in years.

"Show up whenever you like. I got us a table."

"I can't wait, my boy."

"And doctor…"

"Yes…?"

"Please don't bring up that tabloid nonsense *ever* again, capeesh?"

"Capeesh."

I walked in the door with a bouquet full of roses. She was in the living room watching TV. Her feet were on the ottoman with a glass of wine in her hand. She looked tired.

"Chloe!" She looked over at me as I took off my shoes. Her eyes seemed to light up when she saw the roses. She started to get up. "Don't move! Don't move!" I commanded. She looked too comfortable to disrupt her relaxed state. I walked into the den and handed her the flowers. She smelled wonderful as usual.

"Just expressing my love for you!" I pecked her on the cheek.

"Awww…" she moaned. "That's so sweet!"

"Watcha watching?" I couldn't tell what program was on TV. It was on a commercial break.

"Oh, nothing much… Just this week's reruns of the Window. *Porsha's* a great host!" I looked her in her eyes, and then broke eye contact with her. Red alert! Red alert! Aww here we go, she's hinting at something.

"Yeah. She is something else.…" Was she testing me right now? Oh boy, just play it cool, Randy. Play. It. Cool. Just then, a commercial for Hoverfoot popped on the screen.

"Having trouble walking?" I was impressed, to say the least, about how frequently our ad ran. She was really fulfilling her end of the bargain by helping us with an aggressive marketing campaign.

"You sure do have a lot of commercials on her breaks," Chloe noted. "This is the third one I've seen."

"She really likes our products, babe. What can I say?" Chloe stared at me like she wasn't satisfied with that answer. Likes our products? C'mon Randy. You could've thought of something else better than that. Change the subject quickly.

"You feel like going out tonight?"

"Not really, babe. I'm tired. I've been showing houses all day to no avail."

"Aww… I'm sorry to hear that." My voice started to crescendo, "Because I just rented a booth for the Jay-z and Beyonce concert tonight!"

"No way!"

"Yes, way!"

"Ahhhh!" Chloe jumped up and started high stepping on the couch.

"It's a quarter till seven so hurry and dress nicely. We'll leave at 8:00pm." We traded positions. She went upstairs, and I plopped down on the couch. She always took an eternity to get ready. I only needed about twenty minutes.

"Wow!" I said when I looked at her outfit. She never ceased to amaze me. She was wearing a scarlet red dress that was slightly transparent. She had on matching bra and panties that covered everything that you weren't supposed to see. I could suddenly feel me growing rock hard.

"On second thought, let's stay at home," I said in my deep sexy voice. I started chomping my teeth like I was going to literally eat her. Chloe giggled.

"Umm nooo. I want to see Jay-z and Beyonce…."

"Rowr! You don't want to see me?"

"I'm going to see you while I'm watching them. Don't be such an attention whore, baby. It's not attractive."

"Wow…. Sooo, everyone wants to see and meet Randy Stashi except for his beloved girlfriend?"

"That's not true. They're just late to the party." She grinned. "Now let's go before we're late to the party!"

"Lead the way, madame."

We entered our garage. It looked more like an exotic European showroom than a garage.

"We have three options, babe. The Lamborghini, the Bentley, or the Aston Martin. I'll let you pick."

"Lambo."

"I was thinking the same thing. But what if I get too drunk to drive?"

"We'll call a tow truck." I shrugged my shoulders. It made plenty of sense to me.

Vroom! Vroom!

We cranked it up, reversed out of the driveway, and we were off.

Chapter 63

"So, what's gotten into you today?"

"Nothing much. I just feel like I've been neglecting you." I cut into my medium-well filet mignon with a tinge of pink. Just how I liked it. "Plus, I hired someone new to take the pressure off of Charlie. We've been growing faster than expected."

"That's a good thing. Your company as a whole has been overworked lately." She took a bite of her shrimp. God, seafood makes me cringe.

"Plus, we're celebrating because I got interviewed today."

"Really...? By who?" She took a sip of her wine. Her crimson lipstick stained the brim.

"By GDQ. Apparently, they think I'm this year's sexiest businessman. Go figure... Little 'ole me."

"You're kidding."

"No, I'm not."

"Ahhh!" Chloe let off a high-pitched trill that had guests at neighboring tables glancing in our direction. I hand signaled for her to lower her voice

"That's great, baby! Look at you! Wow... I mean wow. I'm speechless. Every day with you seems to get more and more exciting. She poured the bottle of wine until her glass was to the brim. She did the same with mine and then stood up on her chair. She grabbed her fork and tapped it loudly against the glass. The room went slowly from noisy chatter to silence. My crazy girlfriend had managed to get the attention of everyone in the spot.

"Ahem!" She cleared her throat dramatically. I was clueless about what she was doing. Hopefully, this wasn't another Dr. Tracz's moment for me. Alcohol seems to boost one's courage.

"Chloe! What are you doing? Sit down!" I said as loudly I could while barely moving my mouth. She was definitely cut off from drinking for the rest of the night.

"I don't want to interrupt anyone's meal," she continued. "But I need your help congratulating my wonderful, magnificent, one of a kind boyfriend, Randy Stashi! Earlier today he was awarded sexiest businessman by GDQ. I'm so proud of him, and I want everyone to know that he is the best part of my life."

"Awwww…" You could hear the soft sympathy cries from the other guests. She held up her glass.

"Cheers!" I held up mine and tapped it against hers. Applause filled the room.

"Congratulations." "Go Stashi," and "She's hot!" were some of the random cheers from the room. I was embarrassed at how she had put me on the spot, but I was also pretty proud about how she acknowledged my accomplishments. It made me feel special and appreciated. She sat back down, and I looked at her with a smirk on my face.

"You know, you didn't have to do that." She shook her head with a smile.

"Yes, I did. No one ever tells you how wonderful you are." I smiled bashfully. We sipped our wine and finished eating.

***

We valeted the Lamborghini and were ushered inside by a huge bouncer to our booth. Dr. Tracz was already there with two young women sipping something pink. My guess would've been vodka and cranberry. My other guess was that it was probably on my tab.

"Uh *ohhh*! We got a special guest in the house! Randy Stashi is here!" The DJ's voice boomed over the sound system as they put the spotlight on me. I put my hand up and waved. I felt important. We stepped into the booth where we were met with a warm introduction from Dr. Tracz.

"Heyyy therrrre my boy!" I extended my hand, but he gave me a rough one-armed hug around my neck. For a second, the choke had me gasping for air. "I want you to meet my lovely friends, Roxy and Ruby."

"Hi!" I waved.

"This is one of the top ten businessmen in America, Randy Stashi!" He announced.

"Hi Randy," Roxy said extending her hand. "Such a pleasure to finally meet you."

"Hey cutie…" said Ruby, licking her lips. I always found it ironic how Dr. Tracz always linked up with girls who had similar names. Not just once or twice, but every time. Where did he find these girls? I wanted to give him the benefit of the doubt and say he probably met them at the bar, club, or maybe the pool hall. But the way they dressed, it definitely screamed Backpage. I turned back around to see Dr. Tracz practically drooling as he eyed Chloe up and down.

"Sorry for being rude," I cut in, "This is my beautiful lady, Chloe. Chloe, this is the one of a kind, Dr. Tracz." He grabbed her hand and kissed it slowly.

"You taste like a princess. I've heard so many heavenly things about you." Chloe giggled and looked at me.

"He's gooooood.…"

"Well, honey, he's had time to practice. He was born in the 1800s!" I laughed dramatically at my own joke. The remark was a little insensitive, but I didn't like being out-schmoozed.

"Would you like a drink, Chloe?" Dr. Tracz asked.

"Sure, I would." I escorted her over to where Roxy and Ruby were sitting. I sat down relaxed. This was the first second of relief that I had felt in my whole high-strung day. I'm listening to great music while sitting next to my sexy girlfriend, and having a toast with my business partner. This ended up being a great idea! I made a mental note to thank Marsha on Monday for the suggestion. The wine from dinner already had me giddy, and these first gulps of vodka were taking it to the next level. After a couple of songs, Dr. Tracz was getting alternating lap dances from Roxy and Ruby while he was snapping his fingers with his head back. Chloe looked over at him and laughed.

"He sure knows how to enjoy life."

"Everyday is an adventure with him." I rubbed her bare shoulder and whispered into her ear. "We can't let them have all the fun though.…" Chloe leaned in and gave me a kiss, slowly and seductively.

"I'm not.…" She pried my legs open and sat on my lap. She started rubbing her smooth, soft behind on my bulge. I could feel it growing slowly against my thigh. I gripped my hands around her hips, and slowly moved them up, cupping her juicy breasts. Her hair was in my face as I started nibbling on her ear. God, she felt so good. Sitting there with her on top of me, I closed my eyes. I felt like I was in another world. Just then the DJ's voice boomed over the club.

"UH OH! Jay-z and Beyonce bringing out all the stars tonight! Porsha Gottfrey is in the building!" The name sobered me up instantly. Wooow! I was in complete disbelief. I quickly said a silent mental prayer. "Please God, I know you hear me in heaven right now and I'm begging you with all my heart. Please don't let Posha's section be anywhere next to mine. Amen." Chloe was still dancing on me, unmindful of my panic. I looked over at Dr. Tracz, who was staring at me with the same ghastly expression. The bouncer cleared a path while a small line followed behind him. Leading the line were a bunch of people I didn't recognize, and then trailing behind in slow motion, was her. She was glowing radiantly as she usually did. Her hair was up, and she was wearing an emerald necklace that sparkled every time the light hit it. Her hand was on the arm of a short dude in a flamboyant button down. Where were they headed? That was the only question on my mind. I watched her moves like I was a linebacker. I spun my head to the right, anticipating their direction. Just my luck, there was an empty section with a note on the table that read 'Reserved.' Aww, maaan. I hope this section wasn't assigned to her. Satan, I rebuke you! Please don't come over here! It was hard to keep my composure. The more I mentally pleaded, the more she and her entourage were getting closer to where we were. Chloe leaned her head back; her mouth was next to my ear.

"Oh my God! It's Porsha Gottfrey!" Chloe was oozing with excitement, while I was a little less than thrilled, really, the opposite of thrilled. Suspense— stressed—worried, maybe one of those words. They kept moseying toward us until they were directly in front of our area. Porsha glanced over to her right, and we made eye contact, literally locked eyes for what seemed like hours. She smiled, and I tried to wave as nonchalantly as possible. She was then pulled away by her escort. Hopefully (and I really was hopeful), everyone would respect the boundary lines tonight. Chloe turned around confused about my lack of excitement for her arrival. My smile was actually getting faker by the second. I didn't know if I should greet her, nonchalantly wave or ignore her.

"Heeey..." I waved to Porsha. It had to look weak on my part. I knew I had to play it cool. The bouncer removed the velvet rope in the section to the right of us. Low and behold, their entourage filed into the section one by one. Aww sugar! Isn't this great!? I didn't know how I was going to pull this one off. Out of all the nights I picked to go out, I picked tonight, with Chloe. Out of all the cities she could've flown to, she picked this one. Out of all the clubs in the city, we picked this one. This is the one that took the cake; out of all the sections in this grandiose club, we had sections right next to each other. I was either really really lucky or really really unlucky. I looked at Dr. Tracz who looked at me and started coughing in his fist to conceal his laughter. 'Laugh it up old man,' I thought. I hope you don't choke on something because I ain't going to help you.

"She's way taller in person," Chloe noted while gawking at her section.

"Yeah, she is.…" I agreed. I needed to keep the convo about Porsha as minimal as possible. Of course, I still remember those long legs flailing wildly in the air. The music changed, and I began to chug a strong drink. I already knew that this was going to be a long night. Hopefully this liquor would make it go by faster. After ten minutes, Dr. Tracz was dancing uncontrollably. The liquor was beginning to take its toll on him, and he was in full effect.

"I need to use the bathroom," I whispered to Chloe. When I walked by Dr. Tracz, he leaned over and whispered in my ear.

"I knew you *hit* Porsha." Before I could even respond to him, he was back dancing. I staggered into the restroom, finally feeling some relief knowing that it was much safer in here than out there.

"Just play it off, Randy. We are both here with our respective dates. No lines are going to be crossed. Anything we had in the past was pure coincidence and will never happen again." It did sound good when I said it to myself quietly in the mirror. I splashed some water on my face and then proceeded back to the section. When I came back, the unthinkable was happening. Porsha was leaning over her adjacent railing talking to Chloe. This was not good. I hope they could hold their liquor because alcohol always seemed to bring out the truth.

"Oh, heeey, Porsha! What a surprise you're here!" We gave each other a friendly hug. She looked at Chloe and then looked at me.

"Why didn't you introduce me to your lovely girlfriend?" She squinted her eyes and looked at me. Shots fired. Shots *fired*!

"I wanted to let you get settled into your section first. There's no need to ambush you." Porsha looked at me smugly as if she was unamused. "Babe, this is the most electrifying host in show biz, Porsha Gottfrey. And Porsha, this is my beloved girlfriend, Chloe." They shook hands.

"It's a pleasure to meet you. I was just watching "The Window" before we got here."

"No really. It's a pleasure to finally meet you, the woman behind the one and only Randy Stashi." Chloe looked flattered. "Come over to this section, I have some people that I would like you to meet. And bring Dr. Tracz too." I motioned for Dr. Tracz and friends, and we walked out of our section into hers. Porsha introduced me to the bald-headed guy she was holding hands with. "Meet my boyfriend, Carl Eubanks." I shook his hand with a sigh of relief. Whoo! She brought her boyfriend, I brought my girlfriend. Relief. Who knew she had a boyfriend? I guess everyone was going to be respectful.

"Pleasure to meet you, Carl. I'm Randy Stashi."

"Oh, I *know* who you are. You're everywhere! It's a real honor to finally meet you."

"Thanks. I know you have to be a man of class and stature to swoop up a queen like Porsha. What exactly do you do?" I asked. I really was uninterested, but I had to keep the bland conversation going. The more me and him talked, the less me and Porsha had to. I just didn't want this to get awkward.

"Celebrity services, from security to vehicles to venues. We make sure you're safe." He popped open his business card holder from his back pocket and handed me a single card. I looked at it. The words were spinning slowly. I was already on that level. I put the card in my inside chest blazer pocket.

"The industry needs people like you." I complimented.

"I know. That's what I'm here for, and that's how I met Porsha."

"She's amazing. You know you have a real trophy in your hands."

"I know." We both laughed and returned to our partners. The concert was awesome, a lot of fire and a lot of lights. We danced. We drank. We partied the night away. As it was coming to a close, Porsha made her exit first. I shook her hand.

"Thanks for all your help," I said, "You've worked miracles for us." She pecked me on both cheeks and gave me a hug.

"I know," she said, "Give me a ring this week. Maybe we can do business over lunch while I'm in town."

"Sure thing. Nice meeting you, Carl."

"You too, Randy. Call us if you need us." Porsha waved at the doctor.

"See you, Dr. Tracz." She shook her finger at him. "Don't drive tonight, okay?" He laughed drunkenly.

"Yes, ma'am!" Their entourage left, and I felt Chloe grab my hand.

"What a wonderful lady!"

"Yes, she is. Yes she is…. You ready to go, babe?"

"Yes, mister sexy businessman."

"I'll call the tow truck," I wrapped my arm around her neck as we began to make our way out of the section. I looked over my shoulder. Dr. Tracz was being carried by his ladies. A female head was under each of his armpits.

"See you Monday, doctor!" He picked his head up slowly and opened up his eyes.

"See… You…. Monday… My boy…" He said it slow and painfully. I staggered out of there as well, feeling like I had just lost a fight. I had narrowly escaped death tonight. Next time, I might not be so lucky. One good thing did come from this though. I vowed at that moment to never do anything again that might jeopardize my beautiful relationship with the love of my life, Chloe. Never ever *ever* again! That could've went south quick!

Chapter 64

"You look like shit!" Marsha arrived after me this morning. I didn't expect her to notice so easily, but Friday night's extravaganza had drained me. My body ached from dancing and even with the Hoverfoot on. My brain had just stopped throbbing from this weekend's overwhelming hangover. My voice was still as raspy as a chronic cigarette smoker from all of the yelling. I did feel less than stellar, but I think the part that hurt the worst was the epiphany that I was getting older. It used to be Friday night three times a week at FVU. My oh my, how times have changed.

"Well, good morning to you too Marsha!"

"Sorry if that came out wrong," she apologized.

"I'm going to stop taking your advice if you're just going to criticize me about it afterward." She squinted her eyes and nodded her head.

"Oh! I'm…flattered! The almighty Randy Stashi actually took my advice? And what advice was that?"

"Well… I was planning to have a peaceful weekend, maybe watch the sunset, and read a novel. But no… Someone was like turn up! Any guess who that was?" She smiled with her mouth wide open emitting a slow laugh.

"I have no earthly idea.…"

"Well, whoever it was, I just want to thank them. I hadn't had that much fun in a while."

"Well, in that case, you're welcome."

"Ten seconds ago, I thought you didn't know who it was."

I smiled. "I think I might have a clue."

"Hmm…" She was standing in the doorway of my office.

"Well, maybe you have some more great advice." I motioned for her to come closer to my desk. "Come here." She walked behind my desk, and I pulled up the email that I had just received from Evelyn. I began scrolling through the pictures.

"What's this?" Marsha asked curiously.

"Preliminary designs for a new clothing line I was thinking about starting. You like it?" She pushed her glasses toward her eyes and leaned closer to the computer screen.

"Wait.… Scroll back up." I scrolled back up, and after eight long seconds, she finally answered, "Hold on… It's a pig?"

"Umm yeah… What's wrong with pigs?"

"Well, they're filthy and disgusting. I mean they eat their own feces when given the chance. Are these women's clothes?"

"Well, I mean, they're for everybody."

"Ohhhh… I mean, I don't know, Randy. What if a woman is insecure about her weight? What makes you think she would want to wear something with a fat pig on it?" And that was a perspective that I had personally never thought of. In one little question, she had crushed my hopes and dreams.

"So, if this was in the mall you wouldn't buy it?"

"I don't know.… I mean he does look kinda cool with the sunglasses on." If I couldn't get my own paid secretary to like it, then I seriously doubted this plane would make it off the runway. I slumped back in my leather office chair disappointed that this new opinion of my project sounded like the previous ones.

"Is that all you wanted to know?"

"Yes. You can leave now." I said flatly. She walked slowly toward the door, opened it and turned around.

"Don't listen to me though, I'm not good with stuff like this. You've gotten this far by trusting your gut; plus, you're *hot* right now! Everything you touch seems to turn into gold!" I began to nod my head smiling with renewed energy. "And last thing. ANYTHING is better than what Dr. Tracz wears!" She chuckled and closed the door. I must admit Dr. Tracz did have some pretty tacky outfits. Ahhh why not? You have to throw the bait out there first before you pack up the tackle box.

Knock knock!

"Come in.…" Marsha poked her head through.

"Porsha called and said she wants to do lunch before she skips town Thursday."

"I'll get back to her. Thanks, Marsha."

"I think she likes you…" Marsha whispered excitedly.

"Thank you, Marsha." She got the hint from the tone in my voice that I wasn't trying to entertain her opinion. She closed the door lightly. Being wanted by someone of Porsha's status was the confirmation that I was doing something right. Every time I saw her I had to fight the temptation because I already had a woman that I didn't want to lose. I knew that accepting her lunch invitation was like playing Russian roulette. I had to resist her invitation at all costs. She caught me weak once, and I could never let it happen again.

Knock knock!

Before I could answer, Dr. Tracz opened the door and barged in.

"Hey! Hey, doctor! You have to wait for me to respond before you just plow through here. I could have been in here jacking off to some good Internet porn." He chuckled.

"You've got to get you some more action."

"I can't. I'm practically married."

"Well, don't marry her if she's already got you choking the chicken. Mark my words; it'll get even worse down the line. Just a little advice from someone who's been there done that."

"Ahhh…" I let off a sigh.

"Have you seen the sales yet?" He turned his laptop to face me. It was a visual graph of our first month's sales projections versus our actual sales for the Hoverfoot. Once I saw the commas my jaw dropped.

"Is this real?"

"Do lesbians love vagina?" I stared at him, unamused. "Randy, these numbers actually put us on another plateau. They're going to list us in the Forbes next to Bill Gates and Steve Jobs, under greatest innovators of all time! Ben Franklin! Thomas Edison! Randy Stashi! Me! Ha ha, my boy! We're going down in history!" My mouth was still gaping open. Dr. Tracz wasn't lying or exaggerating. Forget knocking the ball out of the park. We knocked it out of the city! I could feel myself getting lightheaded. Dr. Tracz snapped his fingers in front of my face.

"Well, say something, Randy!"

"I put up one finger, rotated my chair to the side and doubled over.

"Breathe BOY! BREATHE! DON'T DIE! WE HAVE TO SPEND THIS MONEY!" I desperately started gasping for oxygen. It took a long minute for me to regain my composure.

"This is *BANANAS!*" I exclaimed. "How?"

"The marketing strategy was pure genius, Randy! The press conference went viral! Not to mention, Porsha has been showing our commercials nonstop on her show! And we're on their affiliated radio stations! Whatever you did to her, keep doing it!" I looked over at Dr. Tracz. I knew exactly what he was talking about. As much as I wanted to ignore and resist Porsha's advances, her incredible efforts played a key factor in our success. I just didn't want to risk putting myself in a compromising situation, but I had to thank her. I had no choice but to go to lunch with her. I had to just so she wouldn't pull the plug on our business relationship. It was the least I could do. Yet, it was the most I could do. Damn, mixing business with pleasure was nothing but a very, very slippery slope.

Chapter 65

His cup of noodles was piping hot when it came out of the microwave. It was accompanied by a sandwich and a small bag of chips, if that's what you would call it. He squeezed out a dab of mayo on the bread, rubbed both pieces together, then clapped it on three thin slices of lunch meat. When he took a bite of the warm, sloppy sandwich, it reminded him of how bad he wanted this mission to be over with already. All of this cheap junk food and takeout was beginning to take a toll on him. It was slightly odd because he actually liked feeling grimy and nasty before he did anything malicious. It made it easier. They were staked out in a dingy motel room, watching flat screens and computer monitors for their cue. Jacoby was in charge of the visual feed transmitting directly from a disguised cable van. Putnam was relief for whenever Jacoby got tired. Their motel was not too far from their target either, Randy Stashi's mother's house. The Garbageman scooped a sporkful of noodles out of the noodle cup. He wasn't in a good mood.

"How much longer are we going to be stuck in this chicken coop?" Putnam asked in a thick Russian accent. He lit up a Marlboro. He really didn't like the taste, but they didn't sell his beloved Russian cigarettes in the states.

"We'll be here until hell freezes over if we have to. We have a job to do!" The Garbageman took another bite of his mediocre lunch.

"The temperature is beginning to drop in hell already!" Putnam complained.

"Well, it shouldn't be too much longer then, should it?" Putnam rolled his eyes and took another drag of his cigarette. Jacoby was on the bed looking at the latest issue of Maxim magazine holding it horizontally.

"Oooof!" He sighed while closing his eyes. "I'd like to wax her. Who is this?" he murmured to himself. "Baby J, the things daddy would do to you." He flipped the page slowly while smiling. The Garbageman looked over at him disgustedly. "Whaaat? You should see Baby J. Look!" He stretched out his arms to hand the Garbageman the magazine. The Garbageman looked interested like he was about to grab it but instead slapped it wildly out Jacoby's hands. Jacoby held up his arms with his mouth open in a disappointed surprise.

"I don't give a rat's ass about Baby J!" The Garbageman turned back around and looked at the monitor scowling. "I can't wait until hell freezes over too! It shouldn't be too much longer, Putnam."

Vvvv. Vvvv. The Garbageman's phone vibrated in his pocket. He pulled it out. It was the boss. He grimaced as he pushed the answer button. He already knew what this call was about.

"Hello?"

"How's progress coming?"

"We're still waiting on him. No sign of him yet."

"He doesn't live there?"

"No. But his mom does. It should only be a matter of time before he pops back up. They're pretty close to each other."

"You think that's good enough? You've been over there for almost a week dammit!" The Garbageman took a deep breath before answering.

"I understand, but this is the only address we have listed for him. Plus, it's low security. Randy probably has surveillance cameras and security guards up the wazzoo at his residence. We won't blow our cover with our plan. This is our best option."

"This is starting to take too long, Garbageman.... He announced in his online GDQ interview that he's already begun groundwork on the sequel to the book. That book must never see the light of day!"

"I understand boss, but—"

"No, you don't *UNDERSTAND*! Don't say you understand when you don't understand the gravity of this situation! If Randy is taking his sweet time to go visit his mother, then you go over there, apply pressure and make him visit his damn mama! Do you understand?" The Garbageman paused. He hated being spoken to like a child.

"Yes boss, I understand. We'll give it another week. He's liable to pop up at any second."

"No... You'll give it a couple more days. My patience is wearing thin."

"All right boss, we'll make sure tha—" Click. The boss had hung up the phone midsentence. He looked at the phone menacingly with flared nostrils and wrinkles on his forehead.

"What did the boss say?" Jacoby asked. The Garbageman turned his head slowly both ways until his neck began to make a cracking noise.

"He said hell is starting to freeze over...."

Chapter 66

Friday 9:48am

Life is rich with variation. There are so many different types of people, races, and cultures, that classifying anyone into groups would be erroneous as well as an injustice. However, the human race can be boiled down into three types of people. The difference between these three types is how they interpret a sixteen-ounce glass filled with only eight ounces of water. A pessimist is going to look at the glass and say it's half empty. They're going to question why they always get the half empty glass. They probably get so disgusted by their bad luck that they might not even drink it or scrunch up their face like it's spoiled milk if, in fact, they do end up gulping it down.

Then you have the optimist, the person who is always happy go lucky. They'll observe that the glass is half full and be grateful that at least they got this much. The only motivating factor of their happiness is their imagination that it could have been worse. They could've gotten no glass, or it could've had dirty water in it. These types of people are a blessing to be around because they never complain. It's almost fictional though because it's just a manipulation of reality. No matter how bad the situation is, they will always look at the bright side.

The last type of person is the one everyone should strive to be. The opportunist. They're going to look at the glass and ask how can we get more? The opportunist is always thinking outside of the box and on their toes. They're grateful but never satisfied. They understand that there are no boundaries, and always an exception to the rule, like I before E, except after C. The only way to appreciate and see everything that the world has to offer is to become an opportunist. Opportunities to help yourself as well as help others, will only lead to more opportunities and good karma. I was a traumatized pessimist after that nearly fatal incident, who grew into an optimist when I went back to school. Now, as I looked out of the huge windows of my lush office in the heart of downtown, it couldn't be ignored that I had evolved into an opportunist. Maybe I learned it. Maybe I inherited the genes from my parents. I gazed out the window in deep thought, grateful, but not satisfied. This world holds a little over seven billion people, but they can all be boiled down into three types: the pessimist, the optimist, and the opportunist.

Knock! Knock!

I always made it a habit to wait a second before answering just to make a note of my frame of mind before I would be presented with distracting issues.

"Come in!" The door was opened quickly by Dr. Tracz holding a manila envelope in his hand. He closed it without looking and hurriedly walked to my desk. "Whoa... You knocked?" I said surprisingly.

"Only because I don't want to see you stroking your meat! That imagery would haunt me to my grave."

"I'm glad I can put fear in your heart." Dr. Tracz folded his arms with a smirk on his face.

"Anyways Stash, we're in big trouble!"

"Whose husband did you piss off?"

"I didn't piss off any—"

"Did you get busted for drugs?"

"Not even. You know I've slowed down on th—"

"Well, then lemme guess. You were involved in an undercover back page sting?"

"DAMMIT RANDY. WILL YOU SHUT YOUR TRAP FOR TWO SECONDS?" I had always known Dr. Tracz to be a loose cannon, so whenever he alerted me of trouble, I had always assumed it had been caused by his illicit tendencies. "This came in the mail earlier this week." He slammed the manila envelope on my desk with enough force to blow the loose papers off. I looked at the papers float like feathers down to the ground.

"That was uncalled for." I murmured as I picked up the envelope. The return address was from Washington DC. "This is from the big boys?"

"Open it." Dr. Tracz sighed as he began pacing from one end of my office to the other. I whispered mumbles as I read the highlights of the letter.

"Dear Stashi Labs, blah blah blah, we've been funding your research and technology blah blah blah. Please, you've been delinquent on your payments. We are charging you late penalty plus interest. The new amount owed is... whoa whoa WHOA!" My eyes became as big as golf balls when I read the number they were trying to extort from us. "Hell nawww!" I exclaimed.

"Oh, keep reading. It gets better," Dr. Tracz noted unamused.

"In addition to the monies owed, we also need all potential technologies developed at Stashi Lab's, or else we will forfeit all past patents and ban all future patents. You have fourteen days to respond from the date of this letter before our agents will be sent to your facilities to investigate and possibly seize assets. If you have any questions or concerns blah blah…!" I slowly lowered the letter and exhaled a breath so long that I could feel my stomach muscles tighten up.

"This is some bullshit!"

"No. More like dinosaur shit!"

"So, let me get this straight. They want us to fork over this outrageous sum of money and give up all of our intelligence and designs of our past and future inventions?"

"Ding! Ding! Ding! What does he win, Johnny?" I ignored Dr. Tracz' sarcasm and focused on possible solutions.

"Let's just lie to them! We can give them some bogus research to cover up the real research. Hopefully, that will suffice."

"I already thought of that. You must not have looked at the other pages." I sifted through the pages and gasped for oxygen. There was all of our research, diagrams, and experiments to some of our most guarded projects. They had our implementation of the Hoverfoot on cars, our organic age reversal discovery, and vitamins that cracked our ever-so-demanding sleep cycle, etc. Some of these theories and developments had never seen the light of day. Some of it even I hadn't seen yet. But here it was, detailed in my face.

"I've never even seen some of this before. This is mind-blowing!" I exclaimed.

"What can I say? You put seven world-class scientists in a room together with nothing to do, and they might alter humankind."

"Next question. How did they get these blueprints? You mailed them in?"

"Mailed this in? You must be off your effin rocker. This is S-12 classified. It doesn't leave the laboratory, nor can it be spoken about outside of those laboratory doors. Everyone knows our consequences for divulging information."

"Then we have a mole in our camp," I resolved.

"Highly unlikely my boy. Any word of this jeopardizes any of our own scientists' claim to the intellectual property as well as a claim to the profits. That's not logical or rewarding on our end."

"Then, how do you explain how they got this?" I was baffled.

"My guess is we've been hacked," Dr. Tracz replied.

"How? We're password protected on a closed network."

"Where did the computers come from?"

"The government grant. They sent in state-of-the-art desktops and..." My voice trailed off. Suddenly, this was all starting to make sense.

"Bingo!" exclaimed Dr. Tracz. We had just solved the mystery.

"We've been hacked because we've been working on their computers." I slapped my palm on my forehead and began to rub my eyes. "How could I be so stupid?" Dr. Tracz shook his head with disgust. "This is a serious breach of privacy. I'm going to get some lawyers on this. This can't be legal. In the meantime, transfer all of the files, and burn those computers to ashes."

"Okay...."

"You stay working on what needs to be worked on. I'm going to fix this."

"We're going to need computers in that case, ones that don't monitor when I blow my nose or scratch my crack." I looked at the calendar. It was Friday. "You'll have them by the beginning of next week." Dr. Tracz began to walk to the door.

"Oh, and doctor, don't mention this to no one! Not a scientist, not a soul, until we figure this whole thing out."

"Agreed." He opened the door and slammed it when he exited. Normally, I would have been agitated by his slam, but I could understand his frustration too. Some people weren't smart enough to think of their own ideas, so they just flexed their muscle and stole it from the real geniuses.

Where is the money and the patents almost sounded like...

Where the hell is the cash and stash at?

This sounded all too familiar. It sounded like the same question the thieves that had shot me asked. The last question that I had heard, before my life had changed forever.

I sat back on the desk and tried to cool down. I needed a drink—bad. Vvvv Vvvv. My cell phone was vibrating. I looked down at it. It was my mom. I didn't feel like talking to her, not at this moment at least. Then I remembered how much she comforted me whenever I got upset. I hit answer on the last ring.

"Heeey!" I said with exaggerated enthusiasm.

"Hey, my beautiful son, you don't sound so good." No matter how hard I tried to conceal my genuine emotion, my mom could always detect how I was feeling. It was like a sixth sense.

"Just another day at the office. Nothing major Mom." I shifted my concerns to her.

"How are you?"

"I'm doing good. I was just thinking about you."

"How thoughtful. You always know how to make me smile."

"I was just checking on you, making sure everything was all right over there."

"Everything is peachy. Are you okay? You need money?"

"No, I'm still living off of what you gave me last month."

"That's good. Well, let me know if you need any more."

"You know, money doesn't solve everything," she said in a matter-of-fact tone.

"I know, Mom." I hated when she lectured me about things that I had already heard from her a million times.

"I see more of your money than I see of you." I rolled my eyes. As harsh a comment as that was, it did have some truth to it.

261

"I'm sorry, Mom. Things have been helter-skelter around here lately with the new launch and expansion."

"I know, but a man should never neglect his family, ever, especially your mother. You only have one." I was riding shotgun on this guilt trip. I had no choice but to pull out the white flag. I sighed.

"How about this? How about I stop over for dinner tonight? Just me and you."

"Really? That would make my day, Randy! I could even cook your favorite, wings and blue cheese or steak and garlic potatoes. My mouth began to salivate as I thought about her delicious cooking.

"Sounds amazing! I'll be over around sevenish…."

"Early seven or late seven? Your timing is always a little off."

"Ha ha. More early or middle than late."

"Okay baby. Bring your appetite. I love you."

"Can't wait to see you, Mommy. I love you too."

"Remember son. Family is everything. We're all we got. Muah." Click. I was smiling. What was I thinking before she called? Oh yeah. That nonsense with Dr. Tracz. I was kind of glad I picked up the phone. My mom always made me feel better no matter how troubled I was. She brought me back to a comfortable state of mind that felt light-years away. I began to walk toward the window and get lost in a daydream. As soon as I began to wonder…

Knock Knock!

Gahdamn! I couldn't even get a second to scratch my nuts.

"Yeaaahssss!" I yelled annoyed. I should've made my door a revolving one. Marsha poked her head through the door.

"Sorry to disturb you again Mr. Stashi, but Porsha Gottfrey left another message for you. She said her flight got switched and it's her last day in town. Are you going to do lunch?"

"Ahhh." I let out a deep slow sigh. The look on my face must've screamed hell no.

"Can I say something?"

"Shoot."

"I think you're acting like a jerk. I don't know why you're blowing her off. She has the hottest talk show in America. She's cute. And she always airs your commercials, which might I add, has contributed greatly to the company's success. If she wants thirty minutes of your time, I think she deserves it." I nodded my head slowly as acceptance soaked in. I hated when other people made more sense than I did.

"I'll set something up."

"You never know. It could be worth your while Mr. Stashi."

"Thank you." She closed the door. Marsha did have a point though. I was acting a little ungrateful toward Porsha, especially given everything she had done for us. She really was a key factor in our recent success. Knock! Knock!

"WHAAAT?" Now I was officially annoyed. Marsha poked her head again through the door.

"Sorry again, Mr. Stashi...."

"You're not sorry..."

"Actually not really, I mean you are paying me to relay messages, aren't you?" I guess she did have a point.

"Ok. Spit it out already! What is it?"

"Evelyn called. She said the first samples of the clothing line are finished."

"Woow, it hasn't even been a week."

"Yeah I know. And I must say, they definitely look better than the first pictures I saw. I might actually wear them now."

"Really?"

"Yes, really. I think she might taste than you." I narrowed my eyes at her. "I mean only in the fashion designer department though."

"Thanks, that will be all Marsh!" To be honest, that was actually the first bit of good news that I had heard all day. I looked at my watch—11:23am, not even lunchtime yet. I'd deal with Evelyn later. Right now, I had to figure out what to do with Porsha. Opportunists never pass up opportunities.

Chapter 67

Friday 11:30am

Sometimes, you have to listen to other people, not because they know more than you, but because God talks to you through them. Once again, Marshy-Marsh gave me some great advice. Porsha had not arrived yet, but I was already on my second Belvedere and orange juice. What could I say? It was Friday. Pretty soon my troubles would be drifting away.

"It's pretty rude to start without me," a familiar female's voice whispered into my ear. An aroma of berries and cinnamon invaded my nostrils. I smiled as I turned my head.

"Hey, beautiful…" I responded. We gave each other a tight hug, and she sat down across from me. She was wearing a tight purple dress with a belt snug around her midsection. Her buttocks jiggled lovely with every move she made. "I got worried. You kept me waiting."

"Don't even start with me, Mister I-don't-return-calls-anymore." I rolled my eyes. I felt guilty because her accusations were semi-accurate.

"This week has been nothing short of hellacious. Please, Queen Gottfrey, forgive me!" She smiled. Barely.

"Well… I guess I can spare your head. One of the country's sexiest businessmen does need to stay intact."

"Ohhh… Well, thank you for your divine mercy, your highness!" She nodded her head slowly. The waitress walked over to our table and interrupted our gibberish.

"Hi! My name is Skye!" Her eyes suddenly lit up when she saw Porsha. "Oh my God! It's you! It's REALLY you!" She extended her hand. "I watch your show almost every day after I pick my kids up!" Porsha smiled. I put my forehead in my palm. I didn't know how she did it, but she had fanatics everywhere.

"Thank you, for your support. Wait until you see next week's episode. We're bringing all the highlights from this year's Jubilee Fashion Expo in New York."

"You're so beautiful, Porsha. You really are an inspiration to women around the world!"

"Oh, stop it! You're making me blush!"

"That makes two of us. You mind if I get a selfie?" Skye asked. Porsha took a deep, deep breath. You could tell she was slightly annoyed. I tapped her foot under the table and nodded yes to remind her not to disappoint her fans.

"Sure. Why not?" Skye was already adjusting her phone into camera mode.

"Cheeeeese" They froze in an awkward pose together for mere seconds. It looked like someone had hit a real-life pause button. After their picture, Skye turned to Porsha.

"What would you like to drink?" Porsha looked over at my glass.

"That looks tasty. What are you drinking?"

"A screwdriver." She looked at me unamused. I guess she thought it was just juice.

"I'll have the same thing." I laughed lightly. Maybe we were both having one of those days.

"Coming up.... I'll bring you water as well...." Skye practically skipped away, still excited from her selfie. Porsha leaned in closer to me.

"Refresh my memory. What exactly is in a screwdriver again?"

"All the vitamins and nutrients that you need to complete a day filled with turmoil!"

"Ha ha. It hasn't been that long of a day, has it? It's only lunchtime." I raised my eyebrows and nodded a slow and painful yes. "Well...tell me about it."

"Actually I'm really trying to get amnesia right now. And you're not helping—at all."

"Well then, there has to be something good that has happened to you today."

"Naw...not that I recall."

"I must admit that doesn't sound very Stashi-like Mister gung-ho-for-positivity." I guess she did have a point. I was supposed to be the ambassador for optimism, and I was pouting like an unsatisfied spoiled eight-year-old.

"Oh yeah. Oh yeah… I almost forgot. They just finished the samples for our clothing line."

"You're starting a clothing line. What's it called?"

"Take a guess."

"Flashy Stashi."

"Ha ha. I like that." I pointed my finger at her. "You're witty."

"What? I was right?" Skye put her glass on the end of the table.

"Your screwdriver."

"Thanks."

"No. You were wrong." I corrected, "But I like that name…. It's just Stashi though." She took a sip out of her drink and started smacking her lips to identify the flavor.

"It's either rum and orange juice or vodka and orange juice. You know I drink wine, not liquor."

"Whatever…"

"So, it's just Stashi. I liked the Get Stashi shirt you gave me."

"You mean the one you stole."

"No. The shirt you owe me as repayment for your relentless TV time. You have to give to get. You know that. It's in your book"

"You know sometimes, I wish you didn't know my book so well…."

"It's so funny using it against you." I pulled up the proofs on my phone and showed it to her. "Ohhh…" I guess it was a little different than she imagined.

"It's a pretty sharp looking pig, ain't it?"

"Ahhh… I guess it could grow on me."

267

"People are going to love it. It stands for piggy banks."

"Ha ha ha" She clapped her hands together.

"Now that's witty."

"It's bold," I reinforced.

"I like it."

"I knew you would."

"How much progress has been made?"

"The first samples were completed this morning," I revealed.

"You weren't playing. This really is brand new!"

"I honestly wasn't even supposed to show this to you. You don't have proper clearance."

"Ooooh…" She leaned back. "Well, excuse me."

"This is strictly area fifty-one we're discussing." I put one finger over my mouth. "I'll fax you the nondisclosure agreement today."

"Are you serious?"

"Maybe." She examined my poker face. I held a stern look for a couple of seconds and then broke off into a smile.

"You play too much," she responded. "Anyways…you know the Jubilee is in New York this weekend."

"I heard you mention it to Skye. What exactly is the Jubilee?"

"You've never heard about the Jubilee?"

"Umm no. Are you going to tell me or make me look it up on my phone?"

"I guess you really do exist in your closed off Stashi-world. Look, it's *ONLY* the biggest fashion show in the world. All of the globe's top name brands and models will be there showcasing their latest collections. Wow. I'm surprised you've never heard of it. Most of the hottest models walking the earth are usually there."

"I write books and make inventions. You're the one who's the social butterfly."

"True. Well…usually, to enter a new clothing line from a new designer this late in the game would be impossible, but I might have some connections to get Stashi on the list if you think you can have some samples ready for the show." My eyes lit up like a Christmas tree.

"Porsha…" I paused and gazed deep into her eyes.

"What…?"

"I'm always ready." She chuckled when I said that.

"I should've known."

"You know why?"

"Why?"

"Because I hate having to get ready." She laughed louder this time. I don't know why though. It wasn't a joke.

"Definitely good to know Mr. Stashi. And check this out, I might be able to get some of the girls to model it on the runway for you."

"Wow." This was sounding better and better every second. Thank God I took Marsha's advice again. "Like who?" I questioned curiously.

"Like Baby J…"

"Like the REAL BABY J? No way…"

"I'm guessing you never heard of her."

"Who hasn't heard of Simoniqué Gopoulous, the petite goddess who has graced the cover of every magazine from here to Pluto."

"You know Pluto doesn't exist anymore, right?"

"Oh yeaaah…I keep forgetting. But you know what I mean" In reality, that was my first time hearing about Pluto was gone. I had to look that one up later.

"Anyway, she's a good friend of mine, and she owes me a favor. If you need me to, I could give her the word." I climbed out of the booth, walked over and hugged Porsha so tight that she lifted out of her seat. I spun her around in circles with a firm grip on her. By now, the whole restaurant had their eyes on us. "Put me down, Stashi!" she muttered as loudly but as quietly as she could. I wanted to but I couldn't. She was like an angel to me. Some people held out their phones. I noticed but didn't even care. I sat her back down. We were both a little disoriented from spinning around in circles. I leaned back into my seat, winded but smiling.

"No more screwdrivers for you." She started fixing her disheveled hair.

"What do I have to do?"

"Well, I fly in tomorrow morning. Just make sure you're there at the venue with your clothes no later than 3:00pm Eastern."

"Sounds like a plan. Whoo!" I shook my finger at Porsha. "I don't know why I like you, but I'm glad I do."

"Good, 'cause I need you to help me pack my clothes at the hotel after this luncheon...." She fluttered her eyes and smiled at me. Abort abort. You go up there Randy, and you'll definitely be packing something. Like her stuff in. And she looks good today. No, Randy. Think about Chloe. Chloe held me down, even when my shadow dipped.

"Umm, I'd actually *love* to help you pack, but I can't today. I have to handle a lot of last-minute affairs before this weekend, plus, get these samples coordinated for tomorrow." She looked disappointed.

"Ohhh, I see. Sounds like a load of rubbish."

"What?! I know you're not going disrespect my grind, babe. Especially with this ordeal being tomorrow, I really don't have a second to waste. But let's make a deal. I'll take a raincheck and help you pack up after our ordeal in New York." She smiled a little. "Deal?"

"Deal," she confirmed. I pulled out my money clip and dropped a fifty on the table.

"We didn't even get to eat, Randy!" I pecked her on the cheek and talked to her while walking backward.

"No time to eat, beautiful. WE'VE GOT TO GET STASHI!" She smiled even wider. "See you in New York!" I turned around and exited the building. It was so, so hard resisting her advances. She was so tantalizing. Whoo! That was a close one! I think that's why I darted out of there so quick. I've learned to always remove yourself from situations where your self-restraint might falter.

Next time, I might not be so lucky.

Chapter 68

Friday 3:03pm

Meanwhile, they pulled up to the address with the plan. The Garbageman and Jacoby got out of the undercover vehicle. It resembled something like a police vehicle with the steel frame and the red and blue lights behind the grill, Putnam's objective was to transport their surveillance van into an inconspicuous location as well as their current transport. The plan was simple: Lure Randy there, then make sure he understood not to release his book under any circumstances. They had to try strike a little fear in him. Hopefully, it didn't get messy. But if it did…then they knew how to clean it up. They were no strangers to the heartless underworld. They had no real ties to society, no emotions, and no mercy. They got closer to the front door.

Ding! Dong!

Randy's mother was just about to head out on a grocery store run to pick up the much-needed supplies for her highly anticipated grandiose dinner with her son when the doorbell rang. She looked through the peephole. It was two men wearing sunglasses in a FBI windbreaker jackets holding up badges.

"FBI!" the Garbageman yelled.

"What do y'all want?" she yelled from behind the door. The Garbageman had already prepared this answer a million times in his head.

"We've got a lead on the dangerous threats that you have been receiving in the mail. We almost have the case closed, but we need your help in identifying the lead suspects." It sounded logical enough to her. She opened the door but kept the screen door locked. She glanced over at her security keypad, ready to hit it just in case.

"Seems a little extreme that they would send FBI agents over here," she noted. "Ma'am, with all due respect, those idiots at the police station couldn't solve a Scooby Doo mystery. They always end up calling the higher ups, which is us. We bring the expert personnel, the forensics, the nationwide database of prior felons into play, not to mention these suspects span several jurisdictions. Please, Ms. Stashi, this is a matter of personal safety. Your life might be at risk." Ms. Stashi gasped and put her hand over her mouth. She suddenly felt terrified but relieved that they were there to help comfort and console her.

"Well, thank you so much fellas. I've been on pins and needles ever since I received this letter…" The Garbageman's eyes began to light up as Ms. Stashi fiddled with the screen door latch and clicked it unlocked. He looked over at Jacoby with satisfaction before he proceeded to enter. Jacoby closed both doors behind them. Ms. Stashi walked toward the dining room table with her back facing her new guests.

"Have a seat, gentlemen. I'm so glad you cracked this case. I've been worried about it ever since I got the letter.…" The Garbageman and Jacoby followed closely behind her. He pulled out the handkerchief doused with chloroform.

"Quick question, Ms. Stashi…" the Garbageman said very slowly.

"Yes…?" she said without looking.

"When is your punk son Randy dropping by?" Ms. Stashi turned around and gasped. No. Way. Her eyes shot open with terror. She realized that she had just made a *horrible* mistake.

But it was too late…

She was too shocked to even scream.

Chapter 69

Friday 5:16pm

"And remember, you must make up your own mind about how much you should give. Don't give reluctantly, or in response to pressure. For God only loves the person who gives cheerfully. And God will generously provide all you need. 2 Corinthians Chapter 9 Verse 7. And that message was brought in part to you by Sprucewood Baptist Church. Come this Sunday. Service starts at 8:00 and 10:00am. See you there.... And now back to our Friday rush hour mix on 103.9. We're going to kick it off with 2pac, Me against the World, Let's Go!" Even though I loved that song, I lowered the volume and let the commercial I had just heard resonate. Hmm, God loves a cheerful giver. Maybe there's some truth to that. I thought about how Bill Gates thrived, and Steve Jobs succumbed to one of the rarest forms of cancer that not even wealth could cure. One gave to charity, and the other gave very little to charity at all. I started to think about how I could fulfill my duty to the less fortunate or youth. I should start a foundation perhaps. Life's been way too good to me recently for me not to share the wealth. Rush hour traffic was pure anarchy today, and that left me with plenty of time for my mind to wander. I yawned. All of this starting and stopping was mentally and physically draining.

I came in through the garage door ready to kick back and relax. I wasn't even sure if I was still up for the dinner that I had promised my mom. As soon as I walked in, I jumped back startled by Chloe's ear-shattering shrieking.

"HEEEEY!" I froze up. Was I in trouble? Was this a war cry or a death warning? Did she find out about that tabloid article? It was crazy how many questions you could think of in the blink of an eye. My mouth was gaping open, and my heart began racing. Chloe started running full speed at me. She didn't have any weapons in her hand, so that was a good thing. I put up my fist defending my head as I braced myself for impact.

"Raaaaandyyyyyy!" she shouted, not even slowing down in the slightest. She jumped in the air and wrapped her arms and legs around me, nearly knocking me to the ground. We fell back against the wall and she began kissing me rapidly all over my face and neck.

"Baby! Baby!"

"What!? What's got into you?" I was borderline being raped right now. I

274

was still transitioning from defense mode.

"I sold it, baby! I sold that house. He was going to say no!" Her frantic story was interrupted with sporadic kisses. "But I convinced him. Four bedrooms, three bathrooms, I did it. I *FINALLY* freakin' did it." I began laughing at her excitement. I was happy for her achievement. I knew it had been stressing her out, so I was glad to see her happy.

"Wow. That's great baby. See I told you, you could do it!"

"Yes, you did! You said be patient, and that's what I did. I love you!" She jumped off me. I could feel her sticky lipstick on the exterior layer of my skin. I kicked off my shoes, and she led me to the couch.

"Chinese is on the way, your favorite too, sweet and sour chicken!" Chloe's energy made adrenaline surge through my body. I could feel her excitement. It made me happy that she was happy. She grabbed a brown paper bag from the kitchen and brought it to me. She took two bottles out of it.

"I got Hennessey for you and Patron for me."

"I'll take Patron too...." I said remembering my lunch with Porsha. I never liked to mix light and dark liquors, a sure concoction for puking your stomach out. I felt at ease, sinking into the soft Italian leather couch. I had dodged Porsha's advances and felt good about it. Chloe made margaritas and brought them over.

"So how was your day?"

"Nowhere near as exciting as yours. We had some technical difficulties with our computers, and have to sort out some financial issues."

"Awww..." Chloe sympathized. "That doesn't sound too good."

"Cataclysmic disaster is more like the adjective I would use to describe it, but don't remind me about it please."

"Nothing good happened on a Friday, babe?" I shook my head no until I thought about the Jubilee in New York.

"Oh yeah, our new clothing line got selected to be showcased in New York tomorrow."

"Wow, that's amazing. But umm... When did you start a clothing line?"

"This week," I replied.

"And they selected you that quickly?"

"Yeah... Crazy ain't it?" I took a quick sip from the cup. She gave me a look of disbelief as if something wasn't adding up. If I left out the details about Porsha, then technically I wasn't lying. Chloe shook her head in slow acceptance.

"Well...you have been on a hot streak lately...."

"Ayyy... What can I say?" I did not want to open that can of worms.

"You know what else good happened to you today?"

"No, what?" She grabbed my glass out of my hand and placed it on the table. She leaned over and whispered in my ear while licking it.

"THIS!" I tingled at the tickling sensation. She rubbed her hands on my knee and then slowly moved upward until she got to my crotch. I exhaled slowly and leaned my head back. She unbuckled my belt, unfastened my slacks, and unzipped my zipper. She tried to pull down my pants, and I helped her by lifting up slightly in the seat. She pulled out my semi-limp dick and began to kiss it. I reached down her shirt and put my hand in her bra, I began to massage her pointy nipples. I felt her wet warm tongue spiral slowly around the top of my stick. I let out a moan. Damn, this felt awesome. The only sounds that could be heard in the room were me exhaling and her sucking with gobs of spit, which sounded like someone smacking on bubble gum. While she was leaning over me with her head in my lap, I gently massaged her soft, bouncy booty. I then slid my hand under her skirt and felt her luscious thighs. I stuck my fingers between her legs. I could feel her damp walls begin to drip as I pulled my curled fingers in and out of her. My pipe was sticking straight up as she bobbed her head up and down, up and down. I patted her head and brushed her hair out of her face as she kept sucking. Ohhh, I needed to feel her now. I wanted to be in her. I leaned over, grabbed her by her waist, and sat her in my lap. She wrapped her arms around my neck and lifted her bottom. I pulled her skirt up to her waist and her bright panties to the side. I spread out her butt cheeks and started licking her from behind. She was so wet. After a couple of minutes of eating her, I leaned back, and slowly eased her on my dick.

"Ohhhhhh..." she exclaimed relaxingly as she slid down my pipe. She began to move her body slowly like a snake as she moved up and down, with her head back on my shoulder, breathing loudly in my ear. I spun her around slowly so that she was facing me. I pulled her top down to her waist and her bra too. I began to suck delicately on her nipple as she moaned louder and louder. I pulled both of her tiddies together and began licking both of her nipples at the same time. Gawd, she tasted so good. While my dick was still inside of her, I spun her back around. She readjusted her legs so they were inside of mine and her feet were touching the ground. She leaned over and resumed bouncing in my lap.

"Touch them toes, baby…" I yelled to her. She reached down and grabbed her ankles. All you could hear was us panting and the clapping of her bare cheeks bouncing on my thighs. Inside of her was so warm and creamy. I spanked her on both cheeks until she screamed.

"Yesss!" I suddenly felt the tingling sensation as my scrotum tightened.

"I'm almost there! Almost *THERE!*" She lifted her beautiful, robust booty off my lap and got on her knees. She opened her mouth and stuck out her tongue as my pipe spewed gushes of thick milky cream all over her face.

"Yes, baby!" she mumbled with her eyes closed. It got all over her face, and some of it dripped slowly on her bare tiddies. She opened her eyes and moved her tongue around the exterior of her mouth cleaning up the mess.

"Whoo-wee mamasita!" She smiled mischievously. Then we both laughed. After we both cleaned up, she made us another round of margaritas. She laid her head in my lap as I petted her hair softly. "Tequila makes you wild babe."

"Tequila makes everyone wild!" Chloe responded halfway laughing.

"Let's watch a movie…"

"Suurreee…" I replied, knowing that if she picked the movie I'd probably be asleep in the first 30 minutes. "What time is it?" I asked.

"Nine uh….nine eighteen," she said glancing at the analog clock. That's when my prior obligations hit me like a brick.

"Damn!"

"What's wrong baby?" Chloe rose up from my lap.

"I was supposed to have dinner with my mom! Damn I forgot!"

"Mama Stashi? At what time?"

"Sevenish, aww man! I don't even wanna go over there now! Hell, she'll be pissed!"

"You should go over there if she cooked for you." My mom and Chloe were pretty close to each other. They could talk well into their next lifetime if I let them. I started weighing my alternatives.

"By the time I get over there and come back, it will be 1:00am. I can't do that. I have a looong day tomorrow."

"What are you doing tomorrow?"

"Remember? The fashion show I told you about, it's in New York, tomorrow." Which reminded me that I still had to charge my Hoverfoot tonight.

"Wait. You're going to New York tomorrow?" Her tone of voice did a complete one eighty.

"Yeah, babe. I told you that earlier," I said as sweetly as possible.

"No you didn't. You said the *clothing line* was going to be in the show tomorrow. You never mentioned anything about *you* going to be there."

"Wellll… I have to be there to make sure everything runs smoothly, meet a couple of people, take a couple of pictures, politics as usual. You know I'm the boss right?"

"Wellll… Can I come? Please please! Pleeease!" I thought about how that might be a distraction. I mean this really wasn't a vacation, this was work. Plus, with Porsha there, everything would be awkward. Point blank, it would not be a smart move on my part. I mean NBA players don't have their ladies setting pick and rolls on the court while they're playing a game. There's a time and a place for everything.

"Not this time, babe. It's strictly business—in and out. I'll be home Sunday."

"Aww man, you never let me do anything fun with you."

"What are you talking about?" My voice raised a couple of pitches. "Seven days ago. Remember? Jay-z. Beyonce. Wild concert." Chloe sucked her teeth realizing that she wasn't going to win this argument. I looked at the clock again. I smacked my lips again. "It's too late to get to my mom's house now." Chloe looked directly at the television. I knew she didn't care whatever I did now. I could tell she was displeased about not being able to come. I plopped down on the couch and gave her a kiss on the cheek in an attempt to butter her up. "Hey, babe, we still have tonight. Instead of going to my mom's, I'm going to stay home with you, make us some more margaritas, and cuddle to hopefully a good movie with you." Her eyes lit up at the thought. She looked at me and smiled.

"Okay!" She marched into the kitchen. "But look, if you aren't going to go to your mom's, then you should at least text her, so she doesn't stay up and worry about you. She doesn't deserve that."

"Yeah, you're right." I pulled out my phone. No missed calls or texts. She probably had already expected me to cancel and wasn't worried. She would've texted me by now, if she was really worried about me coming. I began to text her my apologies.

'Sorry mommy, I couldn't make it out 2 u 2nite, have to leave early in the am. Can we reschedule? I'll make it up 2 u, I promise. I love you.'

Chapter 70

Saturday 12:13am

Ms. Stashi had just regained consciousness, and her vision was coming back into focus. She had just woken up from a horrible nightmare and fallen asleep in the chair. She tried to move, but she couldn't. Her legs and arms were bound by rope to the chair. When she tried to speak, all that came out were muffled sounds. She had been gagged with a handkerchief. When she realized that this wasn't a hellish nightmare, but in fact real life, she started squealing like a pig. It alerted Garbageman, and he walked over with a disgusted look on his face. He scrutinized her in her terrified state and began to speak slowly.

"Listen to me very, very closely. If you scream, I'll kill you." He pulled a knife out of his pocket and rubbed the side firmly against her neck. If he applied any more pressure, he would've drawn blood.

"Do you understand?" Tears began to stream down Ms. Stashi's face as she slowly nodded yes. She was beyond terrified. He reached his hands behind the back of her head and untied the rope securing the handkerchief that was stuffed in her mouth. She coughed it out.

"I thought Randy was supposed to be here tonight."

"He was.... I don't know why he didn't sh—"

"You liar!" The Garbageman slapped her so hard that spit flew out of her mouth. It sounded like a clap of thunder. She started sobbing uncontrollably as blood filled her mouth and dripped on her blouse. He stuffed the cloth back in her mouth and retied the rope around her head. "We'll try again tomorrow, Ms. Stashi." He pulled back out the chloroform handkerchief and put it back over her face. She drifted back into unconsciousness. Putnam called down to the Garbageman from the top of the stairs.

"I found the safe, boss. It was in the wall in the guest room. Ask her what the combination is." He looked at Putnam and then slowly turned back to a slumped over Ms. Stashi.

"We'll ask her tomorrow. She's already resting for the night." The Garbageman was starting to get very frustrated.

"You're making this waaay harder than it needs to be, Randy," he murmured to himself.

Chapter 71

Saturday 2:41pm

I awoke to the plane bouncing on the runway. I woke up groggily as the flight attendant announced over the intercom joyously, "Welcome to New York City!" The Big Apple, I thought to myself. Time to see what all the fuss was about. This was the first time I had ever been to the Big Apple, even though I had seen the New Year's ball drop in Times Square countless times on television. I began to get antsy. I knew I would be mingling with some of the industry's top socialites. Not only that, but the world-class model Baby J would possibly be modeling the new Stashi clothing line. My smile broadened with anticipation. I shuffled off the plane through the terminal. I looked at some of the restaurants on the side that I had passed, and the thought alone could've made me barf. Chloe had made me a breakfast feast earlier that was fit for a king; crispy bacon, syrupy pancakes, and tasty boiled eggs. What more could I ask for? I think she did it because I was leaving and needed to remind me how great she was. She didn't state it, but subliminally, it made sense. I powered on my phone. I was so used to it always vibrating that sometimes I wish I could just throw it in the trash. I held it out over the trashcan just contemplating the idea. Yes. Freedom. I lowered the phone slowly. Hell naw, I resolved coming back to my senses. How else am I going to correspond with Porsha for the show?

Vvvv. Vvvv.

It vibrated for thirty seconds while all of my new notifications posted— four text messages and one voicemail: one text and voicemail from Chloe, one text each from Porsha and the hotel, and one text from my mom. All of them were expected except the one from my mom. I was in no rush to read it either. I still kind of felt guilty and ashamed for ditching our dinner plans, and I knew she was going to condemn me for it. I read the one from Porsha first. She gave me the address to the convention center and her hotel address in case I couldn't find one. It was a very enticing offer because I knew she was staring at the city from a height that would make anyone acrophobic. But I knew I couldn't go there for two reasons. One, she might put me under her alluring trance. Reason number two was because the samples were being shipped to my hotel. I was still amazed at how packages could travel from the west coast to the east coast in a day, but I guess everything has a price. Chloe's text advised me to take pictures and reminded me of our love. Chloe had become even more entertaining to me these past couple of weeks. I laughed when I thought about how she tackled me yesterday when she sold her house. She's so goofy. She always found a way to take my mind off my problems and had always supported me blindly in every endeavor. I'm such a different person now than when I was that entering freshman at FVU. The main reason was because of Chloe. We rarely fought, and if we did, we never stayed mad at each other for longer than twelve hours. She really made me complete.

"Mommy look! He's flying!" I smiled at the little child pointing at me.

It was always a spectacle walking through the airport with the brand-new Hoverfoot 3000. I had made sure it was fully charged for this weekend's festivities. I was a walking testimonial as well as a real-life demonstrator for the product. When I got out the terminal, I held up my hand and waited for a cab for ten long minutes. It was only when I darted in front of a cab that it stopped, and my heart was racing, anticipating a collision when it didn't slow down at first. The taxi came to a screeching halt. The driver rolled down the window.

"I almost hit'chu *fool*! Get in!" I threw my luggage on the back seat and hopped in. "You're going to get yourself run over doing that out here. Where you from?"

"Texas."

"Figures. I could tell you're not from these parts. Don't get killed out here in the Big Apple!"

"That's the last thing I'm trying to do," I mumbled blandly. I passed my smartphone to him. "Look, have you ever heard of this place?"

"I've worked this job for twenty years. Quite frankly, I know where everything is at."

"That's reassuring." I could finally relax a little. I checked the last remaining text message from my mom. It was written a little weird.

"Hey son, you coming over today=)" It struck me as weird because she never used emojis. Hell, she barely even knew how to use a smartphone, but who knows? Maybe she was learning. Older people always find it fun trying to keep up with the times. I began to reply to her text.

"Sorry about last night, Mom. I got tired. I'm in NY rite now 4 the jubilee.

283

I'll have to take a raincheck til l8r this week. I luv u, mommy. Take care."

I hit send and then leaned back in the seat while closing my eyes. I was enjoying every second of peace in the back of this taxi. I was in a new city on a big night, ready to handle business and have fun. I didn't have a worry in the world.

Chapter 72

Saturday 7:23pm

"Three, six, forty-three."

Ms. Stashi stammered as she told Garbageman the code. The Garbageman originally had no intention of keeping Ms. Stashi captive so long. It was supposed to be a quick job. Lure Randy, thwart the book and escape. However, due to Randy's aloofness, this weekend had evolved into a brutal hostage operation. The Garbageman wanted to just threaten Randy about his mother, but then he would alert authorities, so that wouldn't work. Hopefully Randy would come home soon, if he didn't this would probably turn into a kidnap operation. They had made her a sandwich and snacks out of the ingredients in the fridge. They had allowed her to use the restroom while Jacoby stood in attendance. She was beginning to realize that they had no intention of killing her, although her son might be a different story. Her original plan had consisted of wriggling free and pressing the alarm keypad. All she needed to press was one button. That almost stood a chance until she realized they ducktaped the whole keypad shut. Penetrating that layer wouldn't be a quick task. Ms. Stashi had to think of something clever, but as of this moment, she had nothing, not to mention, they were just about to unlock her secret safe.

"Three, six, forty-three!" the Garbageman called upstairs to Putnam. He looked back at Ms. Stashi and grimaced. "This better be the correct combination." The Garbageman grabbed the barrel of the gun indicating that if it wasn't, he was prepared to pistol whip her with the handle. The sadistic Garbageman thoroughly enjoyed being ruthless.

"There's no money in there!" Ms. Stashi exclaimed. The Garbageman scoffed at her declaration.

"You think we're petty thieves, don't you?" Ms. Stashi squinted her eyes afraid to answer the question. "You think we're here to rob you of your petty cash and jewelry?" Ms. Stashi nodded her head hesitantly. The Garbageman started laughing and then slowly became enraged. "We don't give a drop of piss about your money!" The Garbageman pulled his hand back to slap her, and Ms. Stashi flinched with the anticipation of the impact. The Garbageman stopped, sparing her this time. He knelt down right in front of her so that they were at eye level.

"This is way bigger than the little money you have." He paused and looked at his fingernails before making eye contact with her again. "Randy is starting to toy with *our* money. He's trying to upset the balance, but he's only upsetting us." Tears started trickling down Ms. Stashi's face as she began to whimper. The Garbageman reached over and wiped Ms. Stashi's tears with his thumb.

"Randy is very special to you, isn't he?" Ms. Stashi shook her head reluctantly. "Yes. We know." He patted her on the cheek repeatedly, increasing his force as he stood back up. Putnam reappeared at the top of the stairs with the contents of the safe in his hands.

"We got some birth certificates, a photo album, a wedding ring, a couple of grand and a shoebox." The Garbageman motioned for him to come down the stairs. He stood akimbo and looked back at Ms. Stashi.

"I thought you said that there was no money in there?"

"Just take it and leave!" Ms. Stashi begged.

The Garbageman leaned over and whispered in her ear. "We're going to take it all right. But we're not going anywhere…" Putnam spread the items on the table and then began to reach for the cash. The Garbageman grabbed his wrist tightly before he could touch it.

"Don't I pay you enough already?" the Garbageman asked. Putnam frowned and snatched his arm back. The Garbageman began to focus on something else. He lifted the lid on the shoebox and pulled out an old, dusty videotape. It read 'World-class Wealth featuring Stewart Milde and Dylan Mladenka.' The Garbageman was about to smash it on the ground, when Ms. Stashi yelled, "PLEASE! Don't *break* it! Please!" she pleaded. "That's the only memory that I have left of Randy's father, and Randy uses it to write his books." The Garbageman began to smile, then he looked over at Putnam. Ms. Stashi gazed at them perplexed. The Garbageman slowly nodded as he glanced back at Ms. Stashi.

"Ahhh… Randy's father. I've heard stories about him. Pretty cool guy wouldn't you say?"

"I knew y'all had something to do with this! You killed him!"

"Hahaha…" The Garbageman chuckled at her sinisterly. "No I didn't kill him. And even if I did, you think I would tell you?"

"BASTARD!"

"ENOUGH!" The Garbagemen reached for his gun tucked in his pants. Ms. Stashi clenched her teeth together.

"Does Randy have any copies of this?" The Garbageman raised his hand with his palm open, to let her know he was only a couple of seconds away from slapping the truth out of her.

"No!" she screamed. "That's the only one left! Please take anything else but *that!*" The Garbageman stared at her face to examine her authenticity.

"Can we watch it before we destroy it?" Putnam asked curiously.

"Sure. Why not?" The Garbageman smiled as he stuffed Ms. Stashi's mouth with the cloth and retied the rope. Ms. Stashi didn't know if she had said the right thing or the wrong thing, but by gauging their interest level in that videotape, she knew that that was one of their primary objectives. One thing she couldn't gauge though, was if they were going to let her live. She wasn't about to let them make that decision for her. She closed her eyes and began to pray. After she said "Amen," she just sat there with her eyes closed. Sure enough, a brilliant plan began to hatch inside her head.

Everyone watched as the videotape began to play.

Chapter 73

Saturday 10:10pm

By the end of the show, my hands were bright red from the excessive applause. I was surrounded by the socialites, trendsetters, and tastemakers of the fashion world. I always treated everyone as equal humans, but it was hard not to be humbled by the stature of some of these individuals. It felt like I was walking on eggshells because I didn't know who I was talking to, or how receptive they would be to my personality. I just got this money. All of this was still somewhat foreign to me. Luckily, I had my intermediary there, Porsha Gottfrey. She was always polite enough to brief me on who a stranger was or formally introduce them to me. It was all very engrossing because you never knew who you were going to meet next. After the show, we proceeded backstage courtesy of Porsha's credentials. She had informed me that we had more people to meet. Politics as usual. I kind of felt like the a foreign ambassador because even though I knew no one, there was nothing off-limits or inaccessible. When we passed by groups of people, their eyes lit up when they recognized Porsha (and a few eyes when they saw me, not trying to sound cocky or anything). We stopped, and she knocked on a random dressing room door backstage.

"Who is it?"

"It's Porsha...."

"One minute!" Porsha smiled at me while we waited for the door to open.

"Who is it?" I mouthed to Porsha inaudibly while pointing my thumb at the locked door.

"You'll see..." she whispered back. The suspense made me bubble.

"Tell..." Before I could utter the word "me" the door clicked open. Out popped Baby J's head.

"Porsha?"

"AWWW!" They shrieked and screamed and started hugging each other. Juicy body parts were jiggling everywhere. This seemed like a fantasy or a mirage. It was just too good to be true. Porsha stopped and drew her attention toward me.

"Simoniqué, I have someone speacial that I want you to meet." Baby J fixed her gaze toward me. In the blink of an eye, I had suddenly forgotten who I was, where I was, or what I was doing. Her beauty was mesmerizing. I think I was just enamored by the fact that I had never seen her in person.

"This is Randy Stashi," Porsha continued, "the creator of the clothing line that you modeled for tonight." She extended her hand. "And Randy, this is the world-renowned, Baby J." I was still dreaming and biting my lip when Baby J raised her extended hand a little higher for me to notice it. Wake up, Randy! This is real life! I grabbed her hand and lightly kissed it. I was pulling a move out of the old Dr. Tracz handbook.

"What a pleasure.… I mean, such a pleasure…to finally meet you." Baby J started blushing and then covered her mouth with her hand to conceal her giggles.

"He is cute," she mumbled to Porsha.

"Well duhhh.… He's actually won the GDQ for this year's sexiest businessman in the world!"

"I try," I interjected.

"You looked great out there, girl!" Porsha told Baby J. "You never disappoint."

"Stop!" she said nonchalantly. "I was just doing my job. By the way, I loooove the pig. You thought of that?" she asked.

"Well, I can't take all of the credit. My counsel is amazing."

"That logo is sheer genius!" she complimented.

"I appreciate it. That means everything coming from you." We both chuckled, and they got back to their girl talk. I had gotten lost in the fantasy when I was tapped on the shoulder.

"Randy Stashi?" I turned and looked. It was a pudgy man with thick glasses and short hair.

"That's what they call me," I responded.

"Dante Bivers, buying agent for Gracy's. Pleasure to meet you." We shook hands firmly. "I thought that I was going to have to wait until Monday to contact you, but low and behold, you're right here."

"Actually, I was going to miss this occasion, but I managed a last-minute flight."

"Well, I'm glad you made it. I saw a couple of world-class models strutting in your modish garments elegantly, and I have a question for you."

"Ask away."

"Why haven't I seen this before? We've been looking for something bold and remarkable such as this. How long has Stashi the Pig been out?" I started laughing, startled by his investigation.

"Well, we've been working on it for quite some time now," which was the truth. "We've just been waiting for the perfect occasion like the Jubilee to unveil it to the world, Mr. Bivers." He clapped his hands with excitement.

"What a brilliant strategy, Mr. Stashi, if I do say so myself. I have a proposition for you that you might be interested in."

"I'm listening," I replied curiously.

"Well, Gracy's is located in every big mall, in every major city from Maine to California, over 300 to be exact. Not to mention we are top ten in online sales worldwide. Being that I'm the buying agent for Gracy's, I think your brand would do well in our stores. How about we give Stashi the Pig a six-month run to see how it fares against the competition?" I began to blink rapidly. Then my heart started thumping louder than a jackhammer. Then, everything became mute. I think I'm about to faint. I can feel myself getting lightheaded. Snap out of it, Randy! Mr. Bivers stared at me in awe, confused at what I was doing.

"Is that a yes, Mr. Stashi, or do you need more time to think about it?" I bear hugged him energetically lifting his feet off the ground.

"Hell yes! MISTER BIVERS, HELL YES!" He started laughing frantically until I set him back down.

"I didn't expect that reaction, but I thought that'd be the answer. Do we have a deal?" He extended his hand back out. I shook it stronger and firmer than I did the first time.

"Deal!" I exclaimed. I slid him my business card, and he slid it inside of his breast pocket.

"I'll call you Monday to work out the particulars."

"Sounds wonderful." He walked away, and when I was out of eyesight, I started doing my touchdown dance. Porsha walked up and halted my celebration.

"What was all that about?

"Guess who's clothing line is about to be in every Gracy's store nationwide? She looked at me and examined my face. She lit up with elation.

"OH, MY GOD! That's wonderful, Randy!" She gave me a firm hug. I could feel her nice supple breasts against my chest. I pushed her back so I could look into her eyes.

"And it's all thanks to you, Porsha. Thank you." She hugged me again.

"You're welcome, Randy. You've earned it." I pulled her away again.

"I want you to know that I couldn't have done any of this without you." She smirked.

"Well, I guess you owe me dinner then." I let out a victorious chuckle.

"I guess I do."

She grabbed my wrist and whispered, "Let's go!" We began toward the exit. I pointed with my thumb to the now closed dressing room.

"Baby J didn't want to come?" Porsha looked at me and narrowed her eyes.

"Why? So, you could drool on her some more?" I wiped my mouth with the back of my hand.

"I wasn't drooling."

"Yes, you were, like a fat kid at a candy factory. Let's go!" I continued walking. I was ecstatic. I couldn't wait to tell my mom the wonderful news. Soon, she would be able to buy our brand at all of her favorite clothing stores. It felt like everyone was finally working with me. Everyone was onboard with the Stashi team.

Everyone wanted to see us succeed.

Chapter 74

Saturday 10:54pm

They watched the tape and kept it. All of her other belongings were returned. Ms. Stashi awoke to a house rumbling with loud snoring. Perfect, she thought. She was still gagged and tied up. The knots used were nearly impossible to break free from. They had barricaded the front door with furniture. They also used gloves the entire weekend, never making the mistake of leaving a fingerprint. She concluded that they had done this before. These guys were professionals. They had no emotion tied into this. She was expendable. When she realized this, she started panicking. She just needed to get upstairs, she thought. The gun Randy gave her was disguised underneath a pillow on her bed. All she had to do was grab the gun, click off the safety and squeeze, just like Randy had taught her. She squirmed even more anxiously now, pulling the rope in an attempt to wriggle free. Sadly though, after an hour she had made no progress. She started concocting another plan. The two subordinates were passed out in the den, while the head honcho was asleep five feet away facing her. She started tapping her foot to get the boss' attention. At first low, and then she started to gradually get louder when he wasn't waking up. It was only when she started humming that he sprung up nearly falling out of his chair. He scrutinized her as she fluttered her eyes. She nodded her head backward to beckon him to come closer. The Garbageman didn't know what she had wanted, but as the weekend progressed, he had become less malicious as she had become more cooperative. He ungagged her and put one finger over his mouth.

"What do you want?"

"It's not what I want..." Ms. Stashi said. "It's what do you want?" The Garbageman rubbed his chin contemplating if he could be candid about his demands. Before he could even think of an answer, she responded,

"I know what you want." The Garbageman began to polish his teeth with his tongue.

"I'm listening."

"You want to have me, the mother of such a powerful, influential person. You want to know what it feels like to be inside of me, making me beg you for

293

mercy, giving you the pleasure and satisfaction of being able to say that for the rest of your life!" Ms. Stashi was very attractive in her heyday, but even at the age of fifty she still had it going on. She still had a great figure due to her rigorous exercise and dieting, and only a couple of wrinkles on her face. She looked about twenty years younger than what she really was. The Garbageman began to envisage this cougar naked. He started to become aroused by her slow, sexual tone of voice, not to mention, this remarkable feat ahead of him. Having sex with the powerful Randy Stashi's mother would be something he could gloat about to his grave. Grab. Click. Squeeze. The Garbageman was kind of skeptical as he pondered. Something didn't sound right.

"As you very well may know, I'm a widow," Stashi whispered. "I haven't been with someone for so long. I'm beginning to forget what the sexual sensation feels like. I mean, I'm sure someone as dangerous and domineering as you could command me in a way that would mutually satisfy our desires. I'll make Randy do whatever you say. Just be nice and… gentle, with me." She nodded her head to the den where Jacoby and Putnam were sleeping peacefully. "No one would ever have to know." The Garbageman started rubbing his dick.

"You're a kinky little slut, aren't you?" She nodded her head.

"You ain't seen nothing yet."

"You aren't trying to bamboozle me, are you?"

"It's three against one. Y'all are bigger and stronger than me. Y'all have already ransacked the house and cut the phone lines. I'm powerless. Plus, I can give you something else."

"Really…?" The Garbageman licked his lips. "Like what?" Ms. Stashi's eyes narrowed.

"Like, what you came here for, that videotape and dissertations of Randy's father. Without them, Randy can't write his books." Now the Garbageman was at full attention. She had sparked his curiosity.

"Now, that doesn't sound too bright on your part. Why would you do a thing like that?"

"I had already begged and pleaded with Randy not to write the book—the first one. I knew the trouble it would stir up. If I give you the last remnants of his father, then he can't write the sequel. I give it to you, and you leave this family alone *forever*. For me, it would actually be a blessing. Those belongings have brought me nothing but painful memories and experiences." This had totally caught the Garbageman by surprise. She was actually on his side.

"I see." He laughed quietly.

"Let's go upstairs," she said as she winked. The Garbageman smiled and walked over to untie her. Grab. Click. Squeeze.

First, he untied her ankles and began massaging her calves up to her knees, and then her thighs. Ms. Stashi fought with every nerve in her body not to cringe at his touch. She had to appear stimulated by his advances, or her plan wasn't going to work. She hissed air through her teeth when he started groping her breasts.

"Wait until we get upstairs," she mumbled quietly. He could barely contain his excitement. He moved to the back of her chair hastily and quickly untied her. He grabbed her firmly by the arm to get up. Her plan was working.

"No funny business sweetheart." He lifted up his shirt. Ms. Stashi glanced down and saw the handle of his revolver sticking out of his pants. She looked down and gazed back up at him smiling.

"You're not going to need that kind of magnum." He let off a soft chuckle.

"Lead the way, frisky." He patted her on her buttocks as she walked past him. Grab. Click. Squeeze. To pull this off, she had to be almost at the top of the stairs. She strutted slowly up the stairs, twisting her hips to entice the Garbageman even more. She was actually trying to buy as much time as possible. She had twelve steps to go. It's gotta be quick, she thought. If worse comes to worst, could she jump out the window? It was only two stories. Eight steps to go. She could possibly climb the fence to her neighbor's house. Hopefully, their dog wasn't outside tonight, or maybe that would be a good thing. The more noise, the better. Hopefully, they hadn't found the gun she had stashed under her pillow. Four steps to go. Why hadn't Randy come last night? He could've ended all of this and killed these savages. No, she thought. They would've killed him. This was the best way it could have happened. Everything happens for a reason. God makes no mistakes. I love my son with all of my heart and I'd rather it would be me who died instead of him, she reflected. Don't think like that, she thought. No one is going to die. Grab. Click. Squeeze. If anyone is going to die, these bastards are going to *die*. *Action!*

295

As Ms. Stashi's right foot was in midair to land the last step, she jutted her foot back with all of her might. The Garbageman was looking but defenseless. Her foot hit him square in the chest, and he fell back, reaching in midair for the banister. He wasn't able to grab ahold of it and stumbled back down the stairs rolling out of control as he descended. *Bum! Bam! Boom!* All you could hear was him bouncing down the stairs until you heard him plop on the hard floor. Ms. Stashi barged in her room, twisting the lock in the center of the doorknob simultaneously. She knew the flimsy lock wouldn't hold for long, but it would buy her the precious seconds that she needed to save her life. She slammed the door closed and locked it. She heard the Garbageman yell. "Get Her!"

Her heart began thumping out of her chest. She was drained and sore from being tied up in a chair all weekend, but the adrenaline had given her a sudden burst of energy. At a quick glance, her room was completely trashed. The clothes, drawers and papers scattered everywhere had made the room a complete disaster. She dove across the bed and began feeling the underside of the pillows. Grab, click, squeeze was all she could think about. She heard the pairs of feet stomping louder and louder up the stairs. She knew she was running out of time. Not this pillow, not this pillow, or this one.

"Pleease be here!" she yelled out in frustration. "Maybe it fell out," she thought. She lifted up the draping sheet to look under the bed. Not there either. Then she heard doorknob wiggle back and forth. "They're going to get me," she thought. "Where was the freakin' gun?"

Thump!

They were kicking at the door. She began to feel in between the mattress and the headboard. For two feet, all she felt was cushion against wood. Then she felt the cold hard metal.

"YESSS!" she rejoiced. She grabbed the handle, pulling it from it's tightly wedged position.

Baam!

The door flew open, and suddenly everything seemed to freeze in slow motion. She turned her body around to face her bedroom door. She grabbed the gun and pointed it at the entrance. One of them straddled in and had his gun pointed in her direction. She *clicked* the safety off. He took another step closer toward her. She squeezed.

Pow!

The sound was deafening.

Chapter 75

Saturday 11:02pm

It was cold in New York. However, cold to me was anything below seventy-five degrees. Anything below that fell into the category of chilly, blizzard or tundra. It felt good sitting in front of the faux fireplace. The view was overlooking Times Square, and I had the heater set to toasty. I relaxed on the couch, full from tonight's extravagant dinner of spicy greasy mexican food. I suddenly felt a sharp pain in my chest. I rubbed my pectorals and assumed it was heartburn. Pretty soon, I knew I would have to transition into a much healthier diet. I let out a long bellowing belch to try to relieve some gastric pressure.

"Excuse you!" Porsha turned her head around and looked at me in disgust. She waved her hand over her nose.

"That was those fajitas," I murmured. She smiled. She rested her head back in my lap, as I began to stroke her hair again slowly.

"Well, that just interrupted the serenity," she grumbled.

"Well, excuse meee…" I replied. "You should like that smell. It's like reliving those fajitas all over again."

"If I even look at a fajita, I'm liable to barf." She turned over and stuck out her tongue."Ehwwhh…" she groaned as she imitated puking in my lap.

"Do it if you want. I'm going to make you eat it," I admonished.

"No, you aren't."

"Yes, I would." I nodded. She examined my face to see if I was serious. After a second, she responded,

"That's rude and gross. You'd really make me eat it?"

"Yes, because it's really rude to barf in your guest's lap. You started it." She chuckled and repositioned her head so that she was looking up at me. I looked down at her. Everything felt relaxing as I began to stroke her neck. A few quiet moments went by as we looked into each other's eyes.

"Did you call your mom and inform her that the hottest clothing line in the world is about to be in Gracy's?" Ha ha. I laughed.

"I tried. She didn't pick up. It's probably past her bedtime," I resolved. There was a moment of silence after I said that.

"So, how are you adjusting to it?" She asked.

"Adjusting to what?" I specified.

"You know, adjusting to the fame. Everyone screaming your name and taking pictures. No privacy." I looked out the window and exhaled contemplating my answer. "I don't know. I mean I guess I'm slowly getting acclimated to it. They haven't found me dead in a hotel room yet, overdosed on hard drugs, so I guess I'm faring well." Porsha laughed lightly as I took a sip of wine. I gulped it down slowly before speaking.

"How are you adjusting to it?" I asked. She paused and then reluctantly began whispering,

"I don't know. I would say I'm fully adjusted, but I'm a lot better than when I first started."

"How so?" I asked.

"Whoo, gosh! When I first started receiving attention, I was a nervous wreck. People are always trying to slander your name in the news and in the tabloids. Your meal will always be interrupted by devotees. Don't try to use a public bathroom. They'll try to take pictures over the stall."

"Sounds like hell," I interjected.

"Hell nooo. Overwhelming is more so the word I would use."

"That's funny, because every time I see someone recognize you, it seems like you are fervently filled with joy." She giggled again.

"One day I just told myself that if I'm going to do this job and put my hours, passion, and life into this, then I'm going to have to accept all parts of this lifestyle. That's one thing about life. If people are going to break their neck to get a glimpse of you, then you're going to have to break your back to serve them. It's a balance. As soon as you stop breaking your back, they stop breaking their neck." I rubbed my chin as I let that soak in.

"That was eloquently put."

"Thanks." I didn't want to bring it up, but I had to.

"What about Carl? Doesn't he lighten your burden some?" She looked into my eyes and then looked away.

"Me and Carl, umm, how should I put this. Me and Carl are trying to rekindle it."

Ding. Ding. Ding. Now, this was getting juicy.

"What happened?" She had to pause before clarifying.

"You see, Carl was my high school sweetheart. I've known him since I was fourteen. Gawd, I loved him. Hell, we were both deeply in love until we went to college, I went to the best journalism school, and he went to a decent business school. We were still together, just long-distance lovers. I had decided to surprise him by visiting him one weekend, and my whole world turned upside down. He was thumping his classmates, sorority girls, cheerleaders, volleyball players. You name it, he was doing it. I guess the long distance made his libido rage into Hulk mode. I admit I was hurt, but he insisted that he made a mistake and we could reconcile. I believed him too. I tried to love him all over again and then I found out that one of his cheerleading side pieces popped up pregnant with his baby. That's when I officially had enough."

"Well, look at you now. I know he regrets it."

"Yeah, he does. He tells me that all the time, but he was also a factor in my success. After Carl, I stopped looking for love and boyfriends and dedicated all my energy and passion to perfecting my craft. Ten years later, I'm on every newsstand and hosting the biggest talk show in the country." She took a slow sip from her glass. "So, I guess I do have Carl to thank."

"Yeah. You would've been the one pregnant instead of that cheerleader and maybe would've dropped out."

"Who knows, that same girl ended up having a miscarriage. Carl was devastated."

"So, ya'll are back together now?"

"We're testing the waters. One thing I do appreciate is that he knew me before the fame. Nowadays, it seems like everyone just wants you for money or other things."

"Ain't that the truth," I agreed. We both laid still, enjoying the moment. It felt good talking to Porsha. Most of the time things happen so fast that you never have time to unwind and analyze life. I guess we both needed someone to talk to who would genuinely listen. It was therapeutic.

"So, who was that girl?" Porsha questioned breaking the silence.

"What girl?" I clarified.

"The girl at the party. Carla?…Candice?"

"You mean Chloe?"

"Yeah. She was so pretty. Was that someone special or just a nightly escort?" Now she was digging. I had decided that I was just going to keep it frank with her.

"That's my girlfriend."

"Aww… How long have y'all been together?"

"Since college…" Porsha looked at me with a stern gaze, realizing that I had cheated on her.

"I didn't know that you had someone special."

"How could you not know? I told you in front of a studio audience on nationwide television! Someone wasn't listening." Porsha looked away.

"Well, why did you have sex with me if you had her?" I let out a deep sigh.

"I don't know.… I guess you caught me at a weak moment. I've fantasized about you way before I ever met Chloe. It felt like it was a dream that finally came to fruition." She laughed while biting her finger. "When I went home after our first encounter, I realized that I had messed up."

"How so?"

"I mean, I really think that you and I are compatible on so many different levels, but I don't want to hurt Chloe—ever."

"Why do you love her so much?"

"I know you're looking at me with this thing on." I pointed down at my Hoverfoot. "You probably think I'm some rich genius entrepreneur who had

301

everything handed to him but once upon a time, I had nothing. I lost my leg, then my girlfriend and then became confined to a wheelchair. It was a very depressing and demoralizing time in my life. But one day, out of nowhere, this girl named Chloe Dorr wanted to study with me. She used to wheel me to class, cook for me, and even pay the rent when the money didn't add up correctly. She really pulled me out of that quicksand that I was drowning in. We've been through soooo much together, and truthfully, I don't think that I would've ever been able to pick the pieces back up if she hadn't been there." Suddenly, my thoughts had shifted to Chloe. I wondered what she was doing, what she was wearing and where she was. I suddenly felt guilty for sitting here in the wee hours of the morning stroking Porsha's hair. She turned her head and looked at me as if she was reading my mind.

"You're thinking about her right now, aren't you?" Caught red-handed. My mind had been magically read.

"Nooo…" I lied.

"Yes, you are. Don't lie. Y'all two really have a great love story." I was taken back by her openness. "I definitely did not know all of this." She shook her finger at me. "I knew you were too good to be true." I chuckled softly. "Well, I guess we're just going to have to be friends," she resolved.

"I'd love to be friends with you, Ms. Gottfrey." I leaned in to kiss her on her forehead. She closed four of her fingers and stuck out her pinky in my face.

"You got to pinky swear me, Randy." I looked at her and smiled.

"I'm listening."

"Pinky swear me that if anything ever unfortunate happens to y'all's relationship, you keep me in mind." I was astonished by what I was hearing. I stuck out my pinky to grab hers.

"I'll give you more than a shot, Porshy Porsch." I looked her in her eyes and wrapped my pinky and hers. "I pinky swear." She kissed my knuckles. I laid my head back and looked at the beautiful city view while the fireplace illuminated the room. It was so peaceful and quiet. Slowly but surely, we both dozed off on the plush couch.

Chapter 76

Monday 9:28am

"You look like shit.…"

"I appreciate th—"

"…That's been trampled on by a pack of wild oxen." I just shook my head with a half smirk on my face, pausing to see if he was finished.

"Thank—"

"That's been thrown into a mulcher and then lit on fire." This time I just put my one hand on my other fist and gazed at him in silence. After an eight second awkward silence, he replied,

"I'm done."

"I have to hand it to you. You're getting more and more witty with your descriptions. Do you practice before you step into my office or is it just an improvised freestyle?"

"I actually look at you first, and then the analogies begin to form effortlessly in my head." Dr. Tracz' humor could be "gasping for oxygen" funny at times or "throw a tomato at the stage" annoying at other times. This was definitely a tomato day for me.

"So why do I get a lovely visit from you this morning?" It was only Monday morning and way too early for him to already be in my office.

"Well, the wonderful geniuses in the science wing have nothing to work on because we trashed the compromised hacked computers last week. Would you like me to tell them to go home or would you like us to continue looking at each other with our thumbs up our asses on your dime? The choice is yours." I sighed, hissing through my teeth.

"Oh, yeah… They should be here this morning, no later than lunch. If they aren't here by then, ciao!"

"Hmm, so what should we do until then?"

"Umm, resume looking at each other with your thumbs up your asses I guess." I laughed. Dr. Tracz scoffed.

"I was thinking about hitting on the new girl. What's her name?" My face switched to apathetic mode.

"Mariam," I said glumly.

"Yeah, Mariam. She's kind of cute in a dorky, nerdy, do my homework kinda way."

"You like 'em all, don't you?"

"Life's too short to discriminate."

"You're right about that," I affirmed. "But no."

"No, what?"

"Don't try to flirt with her or schmooze her. She might not take a liking to your advances, and I desperately need her. Charlie has been working like a mule."

"Oh please! You know all the ladies love me!"

"That might be the case, grandpa, but the last thing we need is a sexual harassment lawsuit, or her to quit, understand?" Dr. Tracz rubbed his chin,

"I'm probably the thunder that she's been missing from her life," he mumbled.

"No. She's missing a great occupation, with a comfortable working environment, and benefits. Do you understand?" He took a sip of his coffee and nodded his head yes.

"So how were things this weekend?"

"Couldn't have had more positive results. Stashi the Pig, the clothing line, is about to be in Gracy's as well as their online worldwide website."

"That's funny. I didn't even know that we had a clothing line." I chuckled.

"Well now ya' do. I sent it in an email that you probably ignored."

"Probably," he confirmed. "But that's not what I was referring to. I was talking about Fortissimo's hottest new power couple, Randy Stashi and Porsha Gottfrey!"

"Na unnhh…" I denied in disbelief.

"Unh hunhh. Check their website." I logged onto their blog from my office computer before he could finish his sentence. I couldn't believe my name was on one of the side headlines.

"Awww…" I groaned. I clicked on their article and saw a collage of pictures. The latest were harmless ones of us sitting next to each other during this weekend's Jubilee. We kept it professional the whole weekend, so I knew I had nothing to worry about.

"So, how was it?" Dr. Tracz inquired.

"You know you're really going to have to quit reading those tabloids and blog sites. Their idiosyncrasies can be damaging to your health."

"I don't read them. My lady friends do. They just ask me to confirm the highlights."

"Hmm…" I responded dubiously.

"So, I'll ask you again. How was it?"

"How was what?" He put his arms out and began thrusting his hips back and forth.

"The goods! Maan! The GOODS!" He plopped down rudely on my desk.

"You know, sometimes, I think that I'm back in middle school when I'm conversing with you."

"You know as well as I do, you were a virgin until college, so questions like these would've never been asked…"

"Ha ha ha," I sarcastically blurted out.

"Tell me. I'm jealous. How was it?" I took a deep breath.

"There's nothing to be jealous about, doctor. We went to the show, got something to eat, and then fell asleep. There was no fornication or penetration of any sort." He stared at me for long seconds as if my answer didn't suffice.

"Not even a finger?"

"No maaan! Not even a finger. Believe it or not, we're just friends."

"*We're just friends*" he mocked in his high-pitched voice.

"You're so lame, Stashi," he muttered as he began walking toward the door.

"Somebody has to be, to counteract your antics." He opened the door, turned around, and pointed at me.

"Computers here by 12:00, or day off, capeesh?"

"Capeesh!" I confirmed. The door slowly closed as he exited. I nodded my head no slowly. What a character, I thought.

Back to business. I dialed Dante Bivers at Gracy's. We talked for about thirty minutes about how the procedure worked. We then exchanged emails for contractual purposes. Totally boring, yet, exciting at the same time. Boring because of all the paperwork, exciting because we were breaking new ground. Another notch on the belt. Another baby to raise. After that, I dialed Evelyn to inform her of the great news. She didn't believe me the whole time we were on the phone. She was having a hard time swallowing the gospel because of how quickly everything happened. She had been working on her personal clothing line for two years to no avail. With her help and my connections, it took a little over two weeks to solidify a nationwide deal. I replied nonchalantly, "Connections, my dear."

The numbers on the phone from Dante sounded so lucrative that I realized I would need a couple of full-time employees to manage the line. Evelyn was ecstatic at the opportunity to come on board with the Stashi team. She said it would take her a week to get moving. It seemed like every week we were adding something new to the puzzle. I was so busy on the phone that I had to ignore the other line several times. Luckily, Marsha would get it. I couldn't survive without my wonderful secretary. I became so swamped with my agenda that I missed lunch.

Knock! Knock!

"Come in!" I yelled. It was Mariam.

"Hey! What's going on?" She was smiling brightly with folders in her hand.

"Not a lot, Mr. Stashi. I just wanted to thank you for everything."

"Do you like it?"

"I love it. It's such a nice office, and everybody is so nice to me. I'm glad that you decided to employ me."

"How was orientation with Charlie?" She took a sigh.

"It's a lot of stuff, but I can handle it. Plus, it's exciting because it's a product that's actually benefiting mankind."

"Yes. I'm happy that you see the vision, and even happier for you to be on our team."

"Thank you. Quick question. How'd you come up with the Hoverfoot?"

"You're going to have to ask Dr. Tracz that question." She smiled when I said his name. I didn't know if it was a fake or real one. "Have you met him yet?" Hopefully, he didn't make the wrong impression.

"Yes, I have. Very charming…" She let off a slight chuckle. I had to hand it to Dr. Tracz, he definitely had a way with the ladies.

"Well, I'm glad you like everything, go home in a little while and get some rest, so you can be fresh for tomorrow. You're in training for now, no pressure."

"I will." She walked over, shook my hand and then scurried out the door. Shortly after that, Marsha buzzed me on the phone. It's a very busy, busy day, today.

"Umm, Mr. Stashi, you have some packages here. Something like computers?"

"Finally!" I exclaimed. "Call Dr. Tracz over here to come get them!"

"I would, but he left for the day. He said something like the tiddy bar was calling his name." I groaned a low exhale.

"Typical Dr. Tracz. Well, just point them to the science wing then, if you could, Marsha. Thanks." I looked at my phone. No missed calls or texts. "Oh, and by the way, has my mom called?" She looked down at her clipboard full of notes.

"Nope."

"Thanks," I responded with dismay. I knew she was probably still mad that I had skipped our dinner. Oh boy, I should give her some time to cool off before I surprise her with a gift. Hopefully, she would understand and forgive me. I mean, she had to. I was her only child. This did seem a little out of the ordinary though, because mad or not, *she always responded to my calls.*

Chapter 77

Tuesday 11:23am

"Do you have more money than Uncle Scrooge?" After confiding in Chloe my guilt of not engaging in charitable work, she made a suggestion. It was a pretty good one too, at least I thought it was at the time of discussion. She counseled me to give motivational speeches and priceless advice to young school children. So here I was, standing in front of an auditorium of third graders at my old school, Quail Alley Elementary. I still remember the impact of some of the speakers who spoke to us when I was their age. Reaching out and becoming involved in the community was something that felt rewarding to the soul. I never remembered being that short or looking that young when I was their age but who knows, the speakers who spoke to us probably said the same thing about our class. Now, as we entered our question and answer session. I began to question if I chose a mature enough grade level to lecture to.

"Well, I don't know how much money Uncle Scrooge has, but I doubt it…" The little boy with freckles began to reveal his estimates.

"Uncle Scrooge has so much money that he has a vault, with a pool of money that he dives and swims in. He spits out the money like *brbrbr*!" He made the sound of water spewing out of his mouth, and the crowd erupted hysterically with laughter. I smiled blandly before answering the childish curiosity.

"Well, in that case, Uncle Scrooge definitely has more money than I do! We don't even have a pool, much less one filled up with money."

"I knew it!" he yelled, and everyone laughed even more.

"Cute kids…" I muttered to the teachers on the side barely above my breath. "Next question." A thousand arms with shaking hands shot up simultaneously. I chose this little girl who looked to be more sophisticated among the dominion of rascals. "Girl in the blue shirt. What's your question?"

"Are you the new Jesus?" My hypothesis had been sadly disproven. More tomfoolery.

"No, I'm not the new Jesus," I confirmed. "Why would you say that?" The little girl pushed back closer to her eyes before speaking.

"Because we learned in Sunday School that Jesus could make the crippled walk again. Doesn't the hubberfeet do that?" There were only a couple of munchkins who laughed while the rest waited intently for my answer.

"That's a great deduction you've made," I started off. "…However, there's only, and will only be, one Jesus. Plus, when he healed people he didn't need silly little gadgets like this one," I pointed down at my Hoverfoot, "…to do it."

"Ohhh…" she said understandingly but disappointed.

"That was a great question though!" I added with enthusiasm to cheer her up a little. A teacher in the back held up her wrist and tapped it with her finger indicating that we were out of time. "We have time for only one more question, y'all." Everyone's hand popped up like before. All you could hear was little high-pitched voices shouting,

"Pick me! Pick meee!" I ended up choosing a chubby kid with a striped shirt. The only reason was because his face was turning red, and I didn't want to be held accountable if he hyperventilated.

"You, with the red hair in the stripes." I pointed. He put his hand down and started smiling a mischievous smile. It was at that moment I realized he was going to try to stir up trouble.

"Do you ever wrestle your girlfriend?" I was awestruck by his question, but I knew I had to set a role model example. These kids needed guidance through life's gauntlet.

"Violence is never the answer. Sometimes, we might disagree, but we never fight, wrestle or put our hands on each other in a hurtful way. Remember, anything can be resolved with conversation. Conversation rules the nation." Eloquently put, Randy. I smiled proudly. I was really transforming into a model citizen out here.

"Can you tell my parents that Mr. Stashi? Because every night after they put me to bed, they wrestle. My mom screams "Oooh oooh, Big Daddy" and my dad slaps her and makes her call him Papi Loco!" The munchkins howled with laughter, as my eyes widened thinking how I should respond to this silliness. Just then a teacher walked up to my side.

"All right class, now that's all the time that we have for today. Let's give

Mr. Stashi a big Quail Alley round of applause!" The acclamation filled the small auditorium as the students stood up and were slowly ushered out of the room. The teacher stayed behind as I packed up my briefcase.

"Thanks again for stopping by, Mr. Stashi."

"You're welcome. The pleasure was all mine. Colorful little group, you have there."

"Yes, they are. And you've seen only an hour of them, imagine having them for a whole year!" It looked like she was about to cry.

"... And that's why y'all are my heroes," I complimented in an attempt to cheer her up.

"I know you're trying to do something positive in the community, and I admire that, but next time, we'll shoot for a higher age range."

"Agreed. That's a great suggestion."

"Do you know the way back out?"

"Of course. Believe it or not, once upon a time, I used to go this school." She extended her hand.

"Well, thank you again for coming. Hopefully, we'll see you soon."

"Sooner than later," I replied while gently shaking her hand. I took the long way to the parking lot to take notice of all the renovations that had occurred since my enrollment. It's amazing the nostalgia that comes over you when you are walking through your alma mater. I put my stuff in the back seat and ripped the visitor sticker off my shirt. It was fun strolling down memory lane, but I did think that I would take the teacher's advice next time and aim at a more mature audience.

Vvvv. Vvvv.

My phone began to vibrate with an unknown number flashing across the display.

"Hello," I answered dubiously.

"Hello, is um this Randy Stashi, who lives at 8115 Canyon Meadows?" The man asked in a gruff concerned tone. I was still curious to how whoever this was got my cell number.

"Umm, I don't live there anymore. Who is this?"

"This is Detective Edwards with the police department. Was anyone living in the house or occupying the house this weekend?"

"Uhh yeah. My mom still lives there. Why? What's going on?"

"Could you please get down here, ASAP."

"Yeah, what's going on detective? You're making me nervous."

"Just get down here as soon as you can, please." Click. Call ended.

I hadn't heard from my mom since last week's botched dinner date. I began to pray to God for the best, but I had a strong premonition that the worst was yet to come. I revved up my Ferrari and sped out of the parking lot with my tires screeching.

Skrrrrrrtttttttt!

Chapter 78

Red light. Green light. Green light. Red light. I didn't know if I really wanted to stop or go. Part of me wanted to rush over at breakneck speeds to see why I had been called there. The other part of me didn't want to go at all. I didn't want to learn of any bad news or trauma that would trigger any unstable emotions. I said a quiet prayer begging God to let everything be all right. Let my mom be over there with open arms waiting to give me a hug. I didn't know how likely that was though. Only two facts were certain. One, I hadn't talked to my mom since Friday afternoon. And two, Detective Whatever-his-name-was, was calling, and not her. Not good. Think positive though, Randy. Think positive. Maybe this detective was her new boyfriend, and they called me over for a surprise engagement. Yeah, Randy. That's it. Mommy is getting remarried, and she's trying to fool me. As absurd as that explanation sounded, it was the only logical thing that I could come up with, the only reasoning that actually put my mind at ease. My mouth went agape as I pulled up to my childhood home. My bottom jaw suddenly weighed two tons. My lips began to quiver, and adrenaline started pulsating through my body. There were about seven cars there, parked in every direction, four standard police cars and three unmarked cars. Red and blue lights were flashing everywhere. No signs of any ambulances or coroner vans, so that was a good thing. I parked as close as I could and got out. One hand covered my open mouth as I was wide-eyed gasping for air. Yellow tape was everywhere. I ducked under it as I heard other officers try to stop me.

"Sir! You can't be here. Thi—" Everything went mute and slowed down. I felt angry, shocked, disappointed, hostile, defiant and spiteful instantly. I didn't know how to react.

"*Mom!*" I yelled. "*Mommy!*" I felt the officers' hands from all directions pushing me back and restraining me. I was looking at what was left of my old home. With the exception of a few struts still standing, everything had been burned to the ground. Charred rubble, wood and concrete plagued the scene. Everything was black and the odor was abominable. I could see over the charred heap of rubble directly into the backyard. All of the memories, pictures, belongings, that I had in place, gone forever. In the worst way possible, just destroyed and obliterated. I began to frantically scream at the top of my lungs.

"MOOOOOOOMMM! WHERE ARE YOU?" I knew that she made it

out safely. With the alarm, she had to. She was probably just on the side or in the backyard, in a place I couldn't see. "GET YOUR HANDS OFF OF ME MAN!" I slapped the hands away restraining me and broke free.

"Where is she? MOM! IT'S YOUR SON, RANDY! GET OUT HERE RIGHT NOW! I JUST GOT HERE!" I started walking to where the garage used to be, began picking up big chunks of wood. I could feel my eyes began to fill up with water.

"*Mom*!" I turned back around to the investigating police force who had now become a crowd of spectators. One of them came toward me while looking into my eyes.

"ANSWER ME! GAWDAMMIT! WHERE IS SHE?" He continued to walk slowly toward me nodding his head no. His dismal expression looked as sad as I felt. At that moment, that's when the worst nightmare, the most dreadful possibility, became a reality.

"NOOOO!" I screamed, "NOOO!" I began sobbing and yelling uncontrollably. The tears flowed out of my eyes like a waterfall. The officer embraced me with a firm hug. I closed my eyes and cried on his shoulder.

"I'm sorry, son," he began to explain. "She burned to death in the fire. Ironically, her phone was still intact. That's how we got your number."

"NOOOO!" I screamed even louder as I struggled to breathe. My throat had been clogged with mucus as I whimpered frantically. I began to feel lightheaded.

"Sit down, son," the officer ordered. "Deep breaths, deep breaths." I felt powerless. I was on an emotional roller coaster right now. It felt like a wrecking ball had plowed into my stomach. I was hot all over, still trying to assess the events, and figure out how my body was reacting. I was a nervous wreck. After gathering myself and taking slow sips of water, I stood back up. Another officer, who was bald on top but had hair on the sides, walked up to me. He had a folder in one hand and extended the other one to shake my hand. I kept my arms crossed. I didn't feel friendly, and I wasn't in the mood to socialize. He took the hint and placed his hand back on his hip.

"Are you Randy Stashi?"

"Yes."

"I'm Detective Edwards, head of this investigation. I can't even begin to fathom the pain that you're experiencing right now."

"Cut the sappiness, OKAY? I know you don't really mean it!" He took a deep breath and put his tongue in his cheek. "Just tell me what happened DETECTIVVVE!"

"Well, we had reports of a fire that occurred here early Sunday morning. Upon investigating the scene, we found a woman burned to death." I gasped as I heard the grisly details. "On the surface, it looks like a typical victim that fell asleep with something on the stove, simple open and shut case, but—"

"But what?" I interrupted, snarling at him.

"Let me finish Mr. Stashi, but in a more thorough investigation with fire experts, we suspect this house was susceptible to arson."

"Arson?"

"Yes, arson. This house burned down way too quickly for it to be an accident, not to mention your mother's condition."

"What do you mean her condition? I thought you said that she was burned to death."

"On the surface, yes. That's what it looks like. But in the coroner's preliminary corpse report, they found some other things that might suggest another cause of death."

"Like…" I was growing tired quickly of his withholding facts.

"Like the bullet wound in her chest. They found a thirty-eight slug in her left lung that barely scraped past her heart. I started shaking my head no in disbelief. He continued, "And they found her index finger chopped from the middle joint down."

"Nooo…. Nooo…." Imagining my mother's last moments made me cringe.

"That's why we're out here right now looking for more clues." I let what he had just explained soak in. I began to bite the inside of my cheek. It was so vile and disgusting that I began to feel queasy.

"Did you find anything else?"

"Yes. We found a safe. Luckily, it was fireproof. It was closed but unlocked when we got to it. A couple of thousand dollars, some jewelry, and a shoebox."

"Shoebox?" Something suddenly clicked. "Was there a videotape in that shoebox, or pictures, or notes?"

"Well, there were a couple of photos, but no videotape or notes in there."

"Are you sure?" I double checked to see if he was certain.

"I'm beyond sure. No tape and definitely no notes." I looked away from him, and back down at the burned down rubbish that I used to call home. I could feel my lips quiver as I started to break down again.

"And we just found this in your mailbox today." I turned back to the detective as he held out a paper in airtight plastic. It was written in blood similar to the mailed threat that my mom had received earlier this year. I stared down at it, as I felt uncontrollable rage begin to flow into my bloodstream. It read,

"I TOLD YOU THAT THIS WAS GOING TO COST YOU MORE THAN YOU COULD EVER EARN!" ~~TSL2~~

"We're still trying to figure out what TSL2 means, and why it's scratched out. Any clue?" I shrugged my shoulders.

"No clue." He looked into my eyes and then put the plastic bag back into his folder. He gripped my shoulder firmly with his palm.

"I have to get back to work. I'll have one of the officers give you our department's number in case you or we have any leads. Okay?" I looked at him in a daze. Half of me was here. The other half of me was lost in space.

"Okay." He patted me on the shoulder from the side.

"I'm sorry for your loss, son." I nodded. I just wanted to be left alone. I kneeled down and began crying my heart out. I wiped my face, but the tears kept flowing uncontrollably. I knew exactly what TSL2 meant. It was the acronym of my sequel's title. The Stashi Life 2. After about eight minutes, two familiar faces walked up to me. They were the officers from the first time we reported the mysterious letter, Officer Brown, and Officer Ragans.

"Hey, Mr. Stashi…" Officer Ragans began, "I'm in deep sorrow hearing about what happened."

"You aren't sorry scum. Because you could've stopped it! We told you about this months ago!"

"I know Randy, but there was nothing we could do about it." Ragans finished. "The blood had no match, and there were no fingerprints found." I bit down on the inside of my cheek with my teeth. I was beginning to get irate.

"If it's any consolation..." Brown smiled mid-sentence, "My wife loved the autograph." Did he just say what I think he said? I was trying to keep it cordial but after that remark, I suddenly flared up. I don't know what came over me, but that was the straw that broke the camel's back. Suddenly, Brown became the scapegoat for all of my aggression. I clenched my teeth so hard that I felt my jaws lock up. Everything slowed down to a screeching halt. I balled up my fists so tightly that I could feel my fingernails digging into my palms. I drew my arm back and thrust my fist forward with every ounce of power that I had in my body. The fury of my world landed on Officer Brown's chin. All I heard was the loud crack of his jawbone breaking away from his skull. His eyes rolled back into his head as his eyelids closed. He lost consciousness before his limp body even hit the ground. That's when a sea of uniforms came running toward me.

ZZZZ!

I felt the stinging sensation of 50,000 volts being conducted through my body from a taser. I locked up and my body went numb. Everything became mute again. I hit the ground on my side and rolled on my back. All I could do was look up and see the beautiful sky. I gazed in awe at the beauty of mother nature. Then, a bird flew above me in slow motion, blocking the sun momentarily. It was so graceful it seemed to just glide in the air. I would give up everything I had right now just so I could be that bird. Just to not have to check in with anybody and fly anywhere I please. I wanted to fly to where my mom was. I wanted to fly away from all of this pain and suffering.

That's when everything faded to black, and I lost consciousness.

317

Chapter 79

It felt good to be back at their lavish abode. They were back to their elegant amenities, dazzling flat screen televisions and luxurious imported furniture. Work sucked at times, but the compensation put them on another plateau. After missions, the Garbageman treated the crew to some of the best call girls that the city had to offer. Muffled moaning, groaning, and screaming could be heard all throughout the house. That was his way of showing gratitude for another mission complete. Their episodes were always intense and dramatic, so this was a way to alleviate their mind and help them forget. They only had two rules with the women. One was to never use real names, and two was to never collect phone numbers. Everyone had to remain invisible.

The Garbageman's company had just hopped out of the shower. She was a sexy chick with a funny accent by the name of Bella. She was drying her warm, wet, naked body off in the full-length mirror while the Garbageman watched from the bed. The room was filled with potent weed smoke and expensive perfume. He rarely smoked but would take a couple of tokes after sex to relax. Bella made her way over to him and crawled in the bed. She looked at the alarm clock on the dresser.

"You now have only thirty minutes left." She looked into his eyes, then turned over and reached into the ashtray for the half joint that remained.

"You're worried about the wrong things," he mumbled as he looked at the television playing music videos.

"Really?" Bella responded while flicking her lighter.

"Yes, really. Your only concern should be to make me happy. The happier I am, the more time that I might want to spend with you."

"Ha ha… I've heard that before," she scoffed. "Look, I don't make the rules. I just play the game." Bella looked at him and then blew smoke in his face.

Vvvv. Vvvv.

The Garbageman's phone buzzed in his jeans. He reached over and picked them up off the ground. It was the boss. He looked over at Bella while putting his finger over his mouth.

"Hello?" the Garbageman answered hoarsely.

"How did it go?" The Garbageman exited the bedroom while closing the door behind him.

"It went well."

"That's good to hear. Randy Stashi has been exterminated?"

"Well…not quite."

"Well, how did it go good if you didn't complete the objective?"

"Well, we did complete it. Kind of…"

"I don't like the phrase 'kind of.' Kind of sounds like a false truth, misleading dishonesty, an indicator of some grade A pasteurized and processed hogwash! Do go on though.…"

"Well, we have some good news and some bad news." The boss took a deep sigh and groaned on the phone.

"You're really starting to agitate me. You know that?"

"I'm sorry sir, but Stashi never showed up to the residence. We waited for him all weekend while we took his mother hostage."

"Is that the bad news?"

"Well, part of it. She briefly got away and managed to shoot Jacoby in the arm, but luckily her aim was off. We had no choice but to kill her and burn the house down."

"The bad part about that is you didn't get Mr. Stashi. I don't care if Jacoby's head got blown off! He's a big boy. He knows the risks. Now… What's the good news?"

"The good news is that we recovered a videotape and the transcripts of Stuart Milde's and Dylan Mladenka's seminars. We think they are the last copies of it. Without them, Stashi can't write another sentence!"

"Hmm… What makes you think those were the only copies left?"

"The way his mom desperately guarded them, they have to be the only ones." The boss paused for a second.

319

"My oh, my… That is good news. Make sure all of it is destroyed before anyone else can get their hands on it."

"Yes, boss."

"Quick question though. I know you're proposing that those were the last of the transcripts, but how do you know that Mr. Stashi didn't make copies of them beforehand?

"Because his mom said those were the only ones."

"If his mom said she was riding a unicorn to get to the Bob Marley and Elvis Presley concert, would you believe that too?" The Garbageman grimaced speechlessly.

"You see where I'm going with this, Bozo? The only way to stop Stashi one hundred percent from writing this book is to end his life. Do I make myself crystal clear?" The Garbageman exhaled a deep breath before answering.

"Yes, sir."

"So, quit jacking off, round up your clowns and finish the job. Is that clear?" The Garbageman sighed while nodding his head slowly.

"Yes, boss."

"Next time, no good news or bad news, no kind of, or any other nonsense you can conjure up. You better find him, or we're going to end you. Clear?"

"I understand boss, how mu—"

Click. The call ended.

"Arghhhhh!" the Garbageman yelled out of frustration. Now he had to go back and finish the job. He was pissed all the way off. He re-entered the bedroom, where Bella was watching TV. She glanced over at him as he made his way back to the bed.

"That must've been your wife. You know you only have twelve minutes left, right? Unless you want to pay for another hour."

The Garbageman had reached his limit with the harlot. He looked over at her haggardly, and said in a calm voice,

"Take your stuff and get the *hell* out."

"Really?" she questioned, gradually comprehending his sudden brashness. "Really?"

"Yeah," he confirmed, "…and leave the weed."

"You're a jackass!"

She began to scramble around the room for her clothes frantically. Within minutes, the Garbageman's enjoyable evening had completely turned upside down. He began to fixate on one thing and one thing only.

Randy Stashi.

Chapter 80

"If I move that, you're going to go there. If I move that, you're going to take that. But I can move there, and that's when this piece will move over." He kept flicking his index finger in the air. I don't know if he was visualizing the moves, trying to distract my concentration or really just trying to piss me off. I really didn't know how many days had passed. My arms felt like they were on fire at the sockets. I had protruding lumps on my head and cuts on my eyes, not to mention my memory had gotten really shoddy. They had confiscated my Hoverfoot, so I had regressed to crutches. I don't know if it was because of the electrifying taser that lit my life up or the thorough beatdown that I had immediately received after socking that idiot, Officer Brown. Either way, I was here now, separated from the dangers that possibly awaited me in the free world. I was caught in a crossfire of emotion, and I didn't know which side I was on. Part of me wanted to avenge my mother's death; another part of me was depressed she was gone. Hell, I couldn't even arrange a funeral or memorial service in here. I cried a couple of nights to sleep thinking about her. The shock and news of it all was still setting in. Another part of me was fearfully nervous that whoever was responsible for this wasn't done. I was an emotional wreck. My mental state wasn't stable enough for society or to even run my business properly. So here I was, in the county jail, in hideous navy blue garb playing another inmate named Callaway in chess. I hated being in jail, but at least I felt safe in here. My injuries plus my 5:00 o'clock shadow helped me disguise my real identity, that combined with my temporary name change to Russell and a funky attitude. If anyone asked if I was Randy Stashi, I'd readily remind them that I wish it was me. The real Randy Stashi would've had enough to get out of jail already.

"Can you move already? I'm turning older than Methuselah over here...."

"Hold on, Russell!" He started flicking his fingers to stretch them. He moved his bishop and killed my pawn on the frontline. "CHEEEECK-MATEEE!" He started laughing and smiling as he said it. I put my chin on my fist still evaluating if it was an authentic checkmate or did he just have me in check. Yep, he had me.

"Gotcha again!" he gloated. "What's that, like three times now?" I looked at him disgustedly. I hated losing. I honestly was the word for word definition of a sore loser. "Hey, come check this out!" He called over his fellow jail buddies so he could relish in his moment of victory a little longer. I didn't like losing, but what was even worse was being ridiculed.

"Good game," I muttered then I knocked over all of the pieces.

"Awww, you mad, Russell?" He chuckled even more. "You wanna play again? The fourth time is the real charm!"

"Maybe later," I grumbled while getting up from the table.

"What happened?" the dude named Sayvon asked while walking up.

"Another opponent crumbles to the mighty Callaway. That's what happened!"

"I got next!"

"Play Gino," Callaway responded. "I'm tired."

"Aww, don't act like that." The conversation decreased in volume as I walked away. I needed to call somebody. I had completely cut off correspondence to everyone in the free world until I figured out what I was going to do. I had been in here a week, maybe two weeks tops. My charges were pretty serious. I was being charged with battery on a law enforcement officer and resisting arrest. The jail guards in here weren't too fond of me either when they heard my charges. I knew that I had to get out of here, but was that really the best move for me? I didn't know if there were people looking for me or Chloe. The best thing I could do was stay under the radar until I had everything sorted out. Now, I was officially tired of staying under the radar. I had to make that call. Cowards hide while the brave face their fears. I picked up the phone and dialed the number that I knew by heart. Luckily, the cash I had in my wallet when I was arrested transferred into my commissary. Thank God, because I rarely kept cash on me.

"Your call is being connected. Please hold...." Four seconds of silence passed before the computer operator's voice returned. "Thank you for using Jail Talk...."

"Hello."

"Hey babe, it's me, Randy!"

"Don't hey babe me *JERK*!" This definitely wasn't the warm, sweet welcome I was expecting. I think she might've heard me wrong or I had the wrong number.

"Chloe?"

"Yeah, this is your girlfriend, Chloe Dorr, or did you forget you even had a girlfriend when you were wining and dining the country with that ho Porsha Gottfrey?" Oh boy. My worst nightmare had officially made its way into reality. Rule one of being caught is denial. Deny, deny, deny. Take it to your grave if you have to. Watching marathons of the First 48 had taught me that.

"Porsha who?" I realized too late that that wasn't the brightest question.

"Oh, so you want to play this game with me right now, RIGHT NOW? Well, I'll hang up this phone right now too! How about you CALL HER!"

"Baby, baby, calm down!"

"I do calm down, regain my composure, and then I wander on the Internet, and what do I see? More pictures of you and Porsha GOTDAMN Gottfrey! Do you know *how* this *feels*?"

"Baby, it was just business. Calm down...."

"You have your *frickin'* hand around her waist while you're looking into her eyes! Business my ass! It's like I don't even exist. Don't forget who was wheeling you around when you were choking down Ramen noodles!" There is always that one thing that someone can say that will trigger someone's berserk mode. Strangers don't know what it is because it can only come from someone who knows you truly and dearly. Chloe, whether inadvertently or not, had just struck that nerve.

"You think I give a damn about Porsha Gottfrey right NOW? My mom was murdered! I'm in deep, deep trouble with these charges! That lady is the last thing on my mind right now!" Porsha was light years away from this whole fiasco.

"Baby, I know you're hurting right now, but my mother was just shot up and burned, and it was by no means an accident. I need your full cooperation now, and we'll deal with the other nonsense later. You're the only one who can help me, okay?" It seemed like eons before she responded.

"I'm listening...."

"Okay, first and foremost, I need you to lay low right now. Return all of the cars back to the dealer. Just sell them back for whatever you can get."

"What?"

"Baby don't argue with me! Look, make sure you're writing all of this down. I'm doing this to protect both you and me! You remember that one day you mentioned you would sell more houses with my last name?"

"Umm…yeah."

"Well, just be grateful that you don't have my last name right now! That's probably the only reason why you're still alive right now."

"DEAR GAWD!"

"I'm serious as a heart attack right now. You gotta move. Put all of your belongings into storage and move discreetly and quickly. You understand?"

"RANDY! You're scaring me!"

"Well, welcome to my world *sweetie*!" I said sarcastically. "Ok, the next thing I need you to do is find a business card for me. Do you remember that blazer that I wore to the concert that night?"

"The Beyonce and Jay-z concert?"

"Bingo! Look inside the inside pocket, and it should be there. His name is Carl. Oh, you mean Porsha's boyfriend?"

"Yeah, him." She sighed discontentedly. "I need you to tell him to find me a lawyer that will get me off these charges and a bodyguard to escort me off these premises. Someone's after me. This incident was no accident. I also need you to bail me out on a random day. Not in the daytime though, at night, preferably late. I need to throw off whoever is after me. Got it?"

"I think so."

"Read me back the list."

"Return cars. Move to a discreet location. Get you a lawyer. Get a bodyguard. Bail you out randomly."

"Good. Chloe, please handle this ASAP."

"I'm terrified, Randy. Who do you think wants you killed?"

"I don't know, but these guys are professionals and ruthless. I need you to be strong right now. Make sure you change your number too. I'll figure out a way to get in touch with you."

"Okay."

"And one more thing, Chloe."

"*What?*"

"I love you...."

"You're making this very hard on me, Randy."

"I know, and I'm sorry, but this will all be over soon. I promise." She began to sniffle into the phone.

"I love you too."

Click.

Someone who's there for you when you're down and out is *priceless*. Never take them for granted.

Chapter 81

Patience is a virtue required for success. It's crazy how quickly you think something will take off, only to have it never leave the runway until years later. Let's take Coca-Cola for example. The first year they only sold twenty-some-odd bottles of soda. Can you imagine the disappointment the makers felt when no one wanted to buy it? Another example is Red Bull the energy drink. Taste testers repeatedly compared his drink to the likes of urine. That didn't stop it from becoming the most popular energy drink in the world. Patience is a test of your commitment and confidence because after a while most logical people would pack it up and try something new.

Patience was something that the Garbageman was running out of. He had been waiting for eight days straight and was starting to grow weary of this tedious assignment. He and the gang would take shifts in different cars, staking out the county jail. He thought someone of Randy's stature would've bonded out by now due to the strenuous conditions under which the inmates live, but he was wrong. Randy Stashi's booking report showed no updates of being bonded out, even though his bail amount was chump change. Why was he still in there? That was the million-dollar question that the Garbageman and his cohorts had no answer for. The only thing that they could come up with was that he was still shaken up from his mom's graphic murder. She wasn't supposed to die, especially in the manner that she did. But in this business, nothing was unexpected. When things went south, he had learned it was best to just torch everything. Not only that but he had cut off her finger and wrote the last note in her blood. No trace, no case. Everyone in the SUV was sound asleep when the bright flashing lights suddenly pulled up behind him. The pudgy cop got out and shined his flashlight into the car. It was only when he heard the car door slam that the Garbageman jolted to attention. But, it was too late! The cop tapped on the window with his pistol. Even though the Garbageman was a fearless seasoned killer, the police still made him nervous. It wasn't the fact they had a badge and gun. It was the fact that they could take his freedom away forever. He would rather die in a shootout than to be caged up like an animal for the rest of his life. His henchmen felt the same way.

Putnam reached for the gun while the Garbageman nodded his head nonchalantly. The police officer tapped on the tinted window with his pistol again. He had a strong country accent. The Garbageman rolled down his window as the officer shined the flashlight in his face.

"Well, well boys. What in Sam Tarheel, do you think you're doing here tonight?"

"Just waiting for my daw-ter to get out of here. We just bonded her out, awfficer." The Garbageman watched enough John Wayne westerns to emulate his thick country accent. He always practiced his vernacular in public to disguise his true identity. it never raised any red flags.

"Just bonded her out, huh? You got a license and registration, sir?"

"Yes sir, I shure do." The Garbageman began to panic mentally. His falsified documents were left back at the hotel, and he couldn't remember the assumed name or id number. He had to buy some time to think. *Thump! Thump! Thump!* His heart felt like it was beating out of his chest. He looked back over at Putnam and grimaced. Sure, putting a bullet into the cop's head would unquestionably hinder their mission, but it would buy them time to get away, and switch cars and plates. He reached over to the glove compartment and clicked it open. Click! Whoosh! The officer had cocked the hammer back and aimed it at Garbageman in the blink of an eye! Thump! Thump! *Thump!* His heart was beating louder and louder. He leaned back with his hands up.

"Whoa there, officer! A little trigger happy today, aren't we?" The cop had a mean unflinching look in his eyes.

"There could be a grenade in your glove compartment sir."

"That's some brash logic you're using. You're really going to shoot someone that's innocent?"

"I'm just doing my job, sir. You can proceed." The Garbageman had honestly had enough. He was ready to splatter this pig's brain all over the street.

"Can I reach back in there, officer?" Thump! Thump! *Thump!* He looked back at Jacoby, who looked ready for action. The Garbageman winked at him to give him the signal. He reached back over to the passenger's side glove box. *Thump! Thump! Thump!* Just as Jacoby was leaning toward his piece, the officer's staticy shoulder radio blared loudly interrupting the silence.

"Requesting units for back up! Requesting units for backup; 211 in progress at 2470 West Pensacola. I repeat, 211 in progress."

The officer started shaking as if he was undecided what to do.

"You're going to let the real criminals get away..." The Garbageman mumbled. The cop slowly put his gun away, and then darted back toward his patrol car. The Garbageman's whole body slumped back into the seat instantly, relieved that the probable didn't unfold. The same cop pulled up beside him and rolled down his window.

"I spared y'all tonight! Next time, you won't be so lucky!" The Garbageman saluted him as he did a three-point turn and peeled off.

"You're a real douchebag!" he muttered to himself. The Garbageman was no stranger to danger, but that was definitely a close call. He could hear Jacoby and Putnam chuckle with relief as well. They didn't take it for granted that they had been spared that night. He put the car in drive and exited the parking lot immediately. Everyone rode in deafening silence with their hearts still racing from the suspenseful encounter with the police. There was only one thing though that was still on everyone's mind.

How were they going to get to Randy Stashi now?

Chapter 82

"Dearly beloved, we are gathered here today to celebrate the life of a person who was truly special to all of us. We're here to rejoice in her accolades and accomplishments, but also to reflect on our own individual lives. We each realize that our time is coming, for this life is only a temporary home before we are brought into our permanent home. That is why it is so important not to count the days but to make the days count." The streams started rolling down my eyes as I stared emotionless at the casket about to be lowered into the ground. Alterity is the correct word. It means feeling alien to the conscious self. That is exactly what I had felt at this moment, like I was a spectator watching a horrible, heartbreaking movie that I just could not take my eyes off of. She was gone. Just like that, bye bye. All of the memories that we had ever shared could now only be told by me.

"Do you want to end up like your father, dead?" Flashbacks of my mother's voice and warnings still haunted me. She saw this whole thing coming before anyone did, and I had ignored her. "Putting his name anywhere is like playing with fire in a gasoline flood!" she revealed to me one time. Damn! Not only was I miserable about it being my fault; I was angry about the vicious manner in which she had passed. I felt regret because I had inadvertently missed my meeting with her. It wouldn't have gone down like this. I wasn't there for her in her time of need. It felt like I had killed her. I finally had more money than I could ever dream of, but what does that matter if all of your loved ones are dead? It was hard to ignore her voice. Her blatant warning just played back over and over again in my head. She would've still been here if it wasn't for me.

"Well, you're tearing it down, Randy! You're going to tear what's left of this family down!" I was stupid, naive and selfish. No one knew what was really going on, except for me and the bastards who did this! I had tuned out her whole ceremony and was just thinking to myself a billion quadrillion things. Her body was so burned, I was contemplating cremating her, but ended up having a closed casket. I communicated with the spectators clandestinely about the funeral arrangements, and we held it in private. I couldn't risk or compromise the location for the safety of others. My mother's sister was there, Mavabeth, and I invited a couple of employees from the company. I didn't want them in my private life, but I really needed to see some familiar faces to help return back to a state of normalcy. I hadn't been to the office since the chaotic seminar with the third graders. I knew everyone was worried in my absence, but my hope was that everyone was continuing to handle business unbothered. I had been riding around in bulletproof cars, surrounded by bodyguards since my jail release. As the casket began to be lowered into the ground, I wiped my eyes slowly coming back into reality.

"In Jesus' name, we ask, and we pray. Amen!" The preacher concluded the prayer. Chloe was sobbing harder than I was, as we slowly got up and watched the last remnants of my mother at the bottom of a dark, dirt hole. We began to mill out to our cars. Chauncey, our bodyguard, led the way. I gave Mavabeth a hug and a kiss and invited her over for dinner later. In times of mourning, there's nothing like being surrounded by family so you can reminisce about the good times. I looked back and thanked everyone for coming and their support. It had been incredibly difficult because she was the only parent that I ever had, the only parent that I ever knew. I had informed them that I would be back at the office soon. Everyone clapped at that. I almost made it back to the SUV when I heard a familiar voice.

"Hey there! My boy!" I almost burst into laughter. I signaled Chloe to go ahead. His comforting voice always eased any kind of tension. I looked over at him.

"How are you doing?" I asked.

"It's not about me, my boy. How are *you* holding up? It seems like you haven't been in the office in years...."

"It's been three weeks more or less. How's the office been running?"

"Smooth."

"Oh boy! Smooth coming from you means it's turned into a fully functional brothel."

"Ha ha!" he chortled. "I'm glad you think so highly of me, Mr. Stashi."

"C'mon Dr. Tracz. Don't act like I don't know how you get down. Give me an update man."

"Well, your clothing line, which is headed by Evelyn, is picking up nationwide attention. Mariam has been taking care of the Hoverfoot operation and your book sales. Everything has been going smoothly to my knowledge.

OH! And they're getting antsy for the sequel too, The Stashi Life 2. Dana's been blowing us up!" I had to interrupt him.

"I don't think there is going to be a Stashi Life 2. I don't know. I'm just like really having a hard time with all of this. My mind is a million miles away right now…"

"Are you drunk?" I froze and looked at him stone-faced.

"No."

"Well, have you been drinking? Or are you high, right now?" He didn't know my reasoning, so my decision obviously made no sense to him.

"No." I reiterated.

"Well, you must be snorting something then because you have the hottest book in the world right now! You'd be a fool not to write a sequel."

"I am a fool, a lucky fool," I said blandly. I wasn't quite ready to spook him with my conspiracy theories surrounding this whole mess. "I'll talk to you soon, Dr. Tracz." I hopped in the SUV. He began knocking on the window. Chauncey nearly snapped his neck with his gun drawn to see who was knocking on the window.

"Roll it down," I commanded politely.

"We have bigger issues to deal with Randy. I almost forgot."

"Bigger issues like what?" I asked while putting my sunglasses back on.

"Remember our friends from DC?" Awww… I exhaled heavily. I just remembered the eminent threat. They wanted us to fork over our documents. I hadn't even given the issue proper thought to even reach a decision.

"What do you suppose we do?" I wanted to hear a different perspective on the matter.

"We have only two options."

"What are they?"

"We can pull our pants down, bend over and pray they use lube, orrr…" He paused and looked at me.

"Or what?" I wasn't in the mood for Dr. Tracz's usual antics.

"Or we can fight for what's right. What do you think?"

"I'm a fighter, so you know what I'mma say."

"Well, let's get back to work then. Shall we?"

"Sounds good to me." I shook his hand, and then we pulled off as my window rolled back up.

My team needed me. It was time to get back to business. Time to get back to changing the world. All I could think about though, was my mommy. My eyes began to water up behind my sunglasses.

Chapter 83

This was definitely a climatic and chaotic point in my life. I was trying to keep it together, but it was hard. My mother's mysterious death had left me with a void that couldn't be filled. I definitely tried to fill it though, with vodka, Hennessey, weed smoke, and rocks of shiny cocaine. I knew drugs and liquor weren't the answer, but I was at a point where I really didn't care about anything, anymore. This was the best and the only way I knew how to cope, by just traveling somewhere else mentally. It was a little past 11:00 o'clock when I lit my third joint in a row, chasing it with Hennessey and cranberry. Between puffs, I would do bumps of coke to jolt me back to life with energy. A bump wasn't enough anymore though. I needed lines, fat lines. I chopped it into fine granules with my credit card. I examined how much I had left in the powdered sandwich bag. Not good, barely enough to last me until tomorrow.

As much as I didn't want to believe it, a dangerous habit was starting to form. I had stayed cloistered in our new apartment and didn't want to face the outside, partly because I didn't know who was waiting for me on the outside. Another reason was because everything luxurious that we had acquired was gone. It's very humbling when you have to downsize. It wasn't for financial reasons why e had regressed back to quiet middle-class lifeIt was a safety issue. I placed the phone on the table and began texting with one hand while alternating the joint and the cup with the other.

"I need more. Where do you want to meet?" I texted the dealer. I know I had pushed him in this game because he was only a user, just like me. But he knew where to get it, and was very sympathetic to my needs, especially 'cause of the position I was in. I awaited his reply and began to roll up a hundred-dollar bill about to snort a fat one. I only got to the middle of the line when Chloe entered the room.

"RANDY! HAVE YOU LOST YOUR MIND?!" She could tolerate the weed smoke even though she didn't like it, but she *hated* when I did blow. She said I got too hyper on it, and she knew how addictive and destructive it could be. I felt the powder rush from my nose to my brain. The euphoric feeling was like no other. I had to lean back in the chair to enjoy it.

"*Maybe…*" I grumbled. Even though I was rich, these drugs were way too expensive to just let someone come in and blow my high, especially because I was almost out. She had both of her hands on her hips.

"Look at you!"

"How? There's no mirror over here." She walked over to me closer and raised her voice even more.

"It's not enough to just drink and smoke, huh? Now you need to snort coke! What's next, shooting heroin? Bath salts?" I looked at her with my eyes halfway open. I really wasn't in the lecture listening mood.

"I'm an emotional wreck right now, baby! Just leave me alone."

"Noo! You're just wrecking your *own* life. You think that this right here is going to solve your problems? Staying in the house getting high all day?"

"Well…you know what's not going to solve my problems? You yelling at ME!"

"You're turning into an addict. Is that what you want, to die of a heart attack overdosing, to let all of these people out here that believe in you down?"

"If I die, at least I'll be with my mom."

"AND LEAVE ALL OF US BEHIND YOU SELFISH BUM?!" I could tell I had struck a nerve. She pushed me back into the chair and then grabbed my bag of goodies—both girls, the white girl and Mary Jane. I leaned forward, now I could feel myself getting pissed off

"Wait! What do you *think* you're doing?" My eyes grew wide. She hopped over to the restroom where she yelled out,

"PROTECTING YOU FROM KILLING YOURSELF!"

"AWW HELL NAW!" I got up to stop her, but I could already hear the toilet flushing. I got to the bathroom just in time to see the last of my baggies swirl around the toilet bowl.

"YOU WENCH!" I grabbed Chloe by her throat and squeezing until I heard her gag. "WHY WOULD YOU THROW MY BAG AWAY, YOU CUNT?!" She tried to answer, but all that came out was her gasping for breath. Her face began to turn colors.

"RA—RANDY LEH ME GO RA— PLEASE!" she squeaked out. I pushed her back. She tripped over the toilet and fell into the tub. I could see the damage I had inflicted on her by the look on her face. She looked terrified with her hands up protecting her face. She immediately burst into tears.

"You're turning into a monster, Randy! I don't even know who you are anymore!" I turned away from her and looked at myself in the mirror. She had a point. Even I barely recognized myself. I had bags under my eyes that drooped down to the latitude of my nose. My unkempt hair hadn't been groomed in a month. I looked like a poor, scary madman. I looked back at Chloe crying uncontrollably in the tub. She was still shaken up by being choked. The old me would've consoled her, hugged her and apologized for my barbaric antics. However, I felt no remorse. She had mercilessly flushed my narcotics down the toilet, and my sympathy was flushed right along with it. I suddenly didn't want to be at home anymore. I rarely traveled without my full-time bodyguard, Chauncey, but tonight I was going to make an exception. Why? Because I didn't *care* anymore! About *anything*! I grabbed my phone and my leather jacket to combat the chilly night air. I had just received the perfect text message too.

'Headed there now. Hw long r u gonna b?'

'I'm OMW' I texted back.

"I'll be back *later*!" I called out angrily to the bathroom not caring if she heard me or not—not caring who was out there—not caring if I came back or not. I grabbed my pistol.

My high was officially gone and the only thing on my mind was trying to get it back…

Chapter 84

Tolerable is defined as capable of being endured. It is what defines us as a person. For example, some people can endure tragedy after tragedy, and they don't let it stop them while others commit suicide over a petty incident. After tolerating so much, the body builds up a tolerance. It's how people increase their max bench press weight or improve their running time. It can also backfire though. If you overexert more than you can tolerate, your body will break down, or you can overdose. I didn't know where I stood with this addiction, but I knew I had crossed that line. I knew that I was building up a tolerance. I knew that messing with hard drugs was bound to backfire, but I didn't care. I wanted to feel numb, so I wouldn't have to think about everything that was consuming my mind right now. At this exact moment in time, overdosing wasn't scary to me. Being sober was.

"Yo, where you at?"

"On the backside, dark blue Charger." My dealer made good enough money that he was always switching out cars. I never knew what he was going to pull up in. He was living that life. We met up at Colorado's, a fancy strip club cabaret with an illuminated outdoor sign that should've been on the Las Vegas strip. I circled around to make sure no one was tailing me, pulled up next to him and parked. I got out of my car and into his passenger side.

"You look like sh—"

"Don't start with me tonight! I'm not in the mood for it at all."

"Okay.... Sheesh, I was going to say something nice." I looked at him disgustedly. I just wasn't in the right frame of mind for playing.

"Sorry for calling you so late."

"The night is just getting started, my boy." I let out a small sigh of relief. Dr. Tracz always knew how to ease the tension. "I want you to know that I'm just doing this to help you out, Randy. I'm a user just like you, not a dealer. I just know you don't know where to get the real good stuff."

"Yeah, well, I appreciate it. I've definitely been needing this to stay up and alert."

"Yadda yadda, Stash. You want my opinion?"

337

"Not really."

"Well, I'm going to give it to you anyway."

"I knew you would blabbermouth. What is it?"

"I think you're becoming paranoid. I don't think anyone is out to get you. I think you—"

"WHAT?! I can't even believe I'm hearing this right now! My mom mysteriously gets shot and burned. Her finger was cut off, and there was a note in the mailbox!"

"Note in the mailbox? I never heard about that," Dr. Tracz said surprisingly.

"Yeah, a note in the mailbox with the title of the book sequel crossed out. Someone is waiting on me, man. I just don't know who they are or where they're at!" I was practically yelling at him before I looked away and began to rub my eyelids. I was emotionally exhausted. "Aww man, awww maaan." I was trying to hold back the tears, but every time I reflected on the horrific details of her murder, I became sentimental. I just didn't want to imagine the pain she went through in her eleventh hour. Dr. Tracz lightly put his hand on my shoulder.

"Are you all right, my boy?"

"I don't know. I mean I'm trying to be all right, but I'm at a tough place in my life right now. I miss my mom, the government is trying to confiscate all of our intellectual property, I'm out on bond for assault and battery on a law enforcement officer, and me and Chloe are on the rocks. I pushed her into the tub before I came here. That's why I had to leave, to calm down. I'm trying to hold it together, man! I'M REALLY TRYING, DOCTOR!" The tears and the truth oozed out of me. I was a desperate man on the brink of breaking down. I didn't even realize how much I had on my plate until I had itemized the list for Dr. Tracz.

"There, there now." Dr. Tracz reached over and hugged me. "You sound exactly how I was when Penelope left me." He was right. I remember that time vividly. Dr. Tracz was on the verge of self-destruction when I had met him for the first time back in college. "You're going to have to work these problems out one by one. That's the only way that this is going to blow over. What is the lawyer saying about your case?"

"It's still pending, but they're talking about a possible prison sentence. I broke that rookie's jaw."

"Ohhh kay" Dr. Tracz let off a slight chuckle.

"Next problem. You and Chloe. Lemme guess. She found out about Porsha, didn't she?"

"Affirmative," I confirmed.

"Is she still with you?" I nodded my head yes.

"You better count your blessings, Stashi. She might be the one if she's still riding with you." I took into account what he was saying. It did have some truth to it. Our argument at hand was over something dumb like flushing drugs down the toilet. I couldn't be mad at her. She just wanted me to stop.

"And what happened to your fancy car? When you pulled up, I thought I was about to get robbed."

"That's good then. You would never expect me to be in that. I have to stay incognito until we can find out who is responsible for these threats."

"Ohhhh, I see," Dr. Tracz replied rubbing his chin. "You thought any more about what we're going to do with our research for the government?"

"Nope. Why? Have they sent any more requests? I know that deadline is coming up."

"It already passed, Stash. I took the liberty of getting us a thirty-day extension while you were handling family issues. I think I have a plan for them."

"Really? What is it?"

"Let's just pay 'em, get 'em off our back, dead the projects as junk research, move far, far away and pick up right where we left off."

"Paying them is a lot of money though. A helluva *lot* of money."

"It's not even a fraction though of what we'll make off these new cans of worms we have. Plus, I'm sure they have payment plans."

"Hmm" I began to think. "Pass me the bag." He handed me the chalky bag. I crushed it down and dipped my key in it. I scooped up a small bump and inhaled it with my right nostril. I could smell that sharp, pungent glue-like cocaine stench. I could feel my blood begin to rush and the high take over my mind. Damn, this stuff was good, way better than last time. I leaned back with satisfaction. "Oh, boyyy!"

"You like it, eh?"

"The plan for the company or the coke?"

"Ha ha. Either one." I looked at him and smiled.

"I like 'em both. The plan and the coke is A one. See, I knew that I kept you around for something." I looked up and saw a girl walking with three-inch heels, a duffle bag and the body of a goddess.

"DAYUM!" I exclaimed. I looked at Dr. Tracz. His eyes were fixated on the same thing. I heard his seatbelt unbuckle.

"Wanna go in?" I provoked.

"I thought you'd never ask, my boy." We turned off the car and followed in right behind her.

"You mind if I spend the night at your house?"

"You can if you don't mind hearing women screaming for mercy all night." I chuckled. I was already starting to feel better. I didn't know if it was the coke or the jokes.

"You coming to work Monday?" Going to work seemed like a place that was planets away from where I was right now.

"I'm thinking about it."

"It's a no-brainer. Everyone misses you, my boy. Everyone."

"I know. The wait will be over soon."

Chapter 85

"Well, where is HE DAMMIT?" The boss was growing furious at their perpetual mission.

"I don't know," the Garbageman answered. "We've been staking out his office building for almost two weeks to no avail."

"Well, is he coming back?"

"I don't see why not."

"Ha… Ha… You don't see why not. What about his residence? Any activity there?"

"No boss. Just a for rent sign in front of it. I think they moved while he was in jail."

"My oh, my… This story just keeps getting better and better, doesn't it?"

"Not really boss."

"I know, you imbecile. Why didn't you get him when he was released from jail? That should've been a simple and quick stakeout. Tail him and knock him off when the time was right! Huh? What was so hard about that?"

"Well, umm, we had some interference. The nosy trigger-happy police at the jail almost shot us when we couldn't show our ID."

"It seems like I can't get you bozos to do anything right! Am I really going to have to fly out there and put a bullet in him my *damn* self?" The Garbageman wanted to say yes, but he knew that getting smart with the boss was a request for suicide.

"No sir!"

"Well, find him then, idiot!"

"We will. He's liable to slip up somewhere. We'll catch him when he does, boss. I guarantee it."

"Arrrrghhhh!"

Usually, the boss was impressed and content with the Garbageman's results, but this, however, was draining the life from him. The Garbageman could sense it and became fixated on Randy Stashi paying for it in cold blood. His name and reputation depended on this mission.

Their lives depended on it too.

Chapter 86

"The Lord is my shepherd I shall now want, He maketh me lie down in green pastures…" I was reciting Psalms 23 as I washed my face in the office building's first-floor bathroom. It was my first day back to work in what seemed like an eternity. I had Chauncey drop me off and escort me from the underground parking lot entrance. Few knew about it. I walked in so disguised, I was unrecognizable to anyone who knew me. I was wearing a wig under a brimmed hat, sunglasses, a trench coat and a scarf that covered my mouth and neck. I almost looked as if I was about to go on a shooting spree. People looked alarmed, but that was better than being recognized. I didn't know who was watching. I was washing my face trying to shake and rinse off the booze and the drugs. Sadly, it wasn't working. Dr. Tracz was about to have a field day with his introductory analogies. My eyes were bloodshot. Under them were big, puffy bags. My nose was running too. I don't know if it was because of the cold weather or the cocaine usage. I was somewhere between hungover and tipsy. Today really was different. I really did look like shit. My mother made me memorize Psalms 23 when I was little for some odd reason. She told me to recite it whenever I was afraid, worrisome or feeling defeated. Right now, it felt like a combination of all three. It did give me some peace of mind though.

"As I walk through the valley of the shadow of death, I shall fear NO EVIL! Thy rod! Thy staff! They comfort me! Thou preparest a table before me in front of mine enemies.…" I finished drying off my face with a rough brown paper towel, and then leaned my head back to drop Clear Eyes in both of my pupils. I put my trench coat back on and began to walk out.

"Surely, goodness and mercy shall follow me all the days of my life! And I shall dwell in the house of the Lord forever!… Amen." I was grateful for having to memorize that as a child. I looked up at the ceiling. I knew who was responsible. It came in handy on days like today. I pressed the up button and hopped on the elevator.

I didn't know what to expect on my unexpected return. I really wanted to see the office hustling and bustling as if my absence went unnoticed. I wanted it to look like the stock exchange floor on a Friday morning: people on the phone yelling at the top of their lungs, waving papers, running on high emotions, but enjoying the thrill of business. I wanted to see if my company could run without me. Everyone assured me things were going all right at the funeral, but you know how people are. They'll tell you what you want to hear. When I walked in the door of Stashi Enterprises, my worse nightmare had been confirmed. The opposite of everything that I wanted to happen happened. There wasn't an employee insight, no Marsha, no Dr. Tracz, no Mariam, no Evelyn. Ahhhh. What a disgrace. I felt ashamed to have believed in these people. My employees were trying to sucker me while I was away. Get paid for a full-time work week without even showing up. I guess since I was on vacation everyone else decided they were on vacation. An old proverb once said, "Lazy people are a pain to their employer. They are like smoke in the eyes or vinegar that sets teeth on edge." They were a pain all right, billows and billows of smoke in my eyes too. Damn, where is the trust and loyalty? Now, I began to wonder how many days, out of my time away, did they really take off. I could feel my anger coming to a slow boil. This is how businesses collapse. So disappointed in these people.

Ring, ring, ring!

The office phone at Marsha's desk had come to life. I rushed over to answer it.

"Stashi enterprises. This is Randy."

"Hello, it's Dante Bivers with Gracy's. Man oh, man! Your work ethic impresses me every time. You even pick up your own phone calls!"

"Thanks," I responded, not knowing if it was a true compliment or a backhanded one.

"Just calling to let you know that Stashi has been flying off the shelves! The public has been gobbling it up like hotcakes on a Sunday morning."

"You serious?"

"Beyond serious! We've blown right through your introductory order. We're going to another order twice that size while winter is in full swing."

"Wow. This is a blessing! I'll get on the phone with our supplier and relay the message. Send me an email whenever you can."

"I sure will, Mr. Stashi. It's a pleasure doing business with you."

"Honestly, Dante, I can assure you the pleasure is all mine."

"I had a feeling you were going to say that."

"I have to. As long as you keep cutting the check, what else can I say? Take care."

"You too." I hung up the phone.

"Yes! Yes!" I shouted with joy. Now, a tougher mission would be to locate Evelyn. Maan, my employees were sorry as hell. I opened the door to my office, and jumped back when I saw people in the dark shadows! Where was my gun? Where was Chauncey?! THEY WERE IN HERE! RIGHT NOW! I froze up!

"Surrrrr-PRRRRRRRISSSEEE!" The lights came on, and everyone screamed! The surprise left me breathless. I clutched my heart. I thought I was having a heart attack! It was all of the employees huddled together with Marsha in front holding a candlelit welcome back cake.

"AHHH!" I screamed back while still holding my chest. They literally knocked the wind out of my lungs. I was panting heavily with my belongings scattered all over the floor.

"We gotcha good, Mr. Stashi!" Marsha said while walking toward me.

"I got it on camera!" Mariam said excitedly while giggling. I lowered my head in shame while smiling.

"Yeah, y'all got me good." I finally piped out. "YOU'RE ALL FIRED!" Everyone burst into laughter. I didn't know if I was serious or not.

"Welcome back, Stashi Stash!" Evelyn yelled.

"How did y'all know that I was returning today?" I said in bewilderment.

"Dr. Tracz told us. He came up with the plan and everything."

"Gotcha good, my boy!" I started clapping and laughing.

"Well executed, y'all, very well executed. But you almost threw me into shock. Don't do that again." The room exploded with laughter again.

"Good to see you again," said Charlie. "Now cut the cake. I'm starving!" So, we had a little luncheon in my office while everyone took turns updating me on their realm of the business. I had dreaded coming back to work this whole time, but surprisingly the energy was comforting and replenishing. The hardest part about doing something isn't doing it. It's thinking about doing it!

Dr. Tracz began to pass out the champagne glasses. I was awestruck at his audaciousness. I was thinking that he was taking the celebration a little too far. I mean, we still had business to conduct today. He popped the cork on the bottle and began filling everyone's glasses halfway.

"What are you doing?" I interrupted.

"Shh. Shhh…" he chided me. He handed me a glass, then topped it to the brim with champagne. I was all for the drinking, but I didn't want to set a bad example in front of our employees. Before you know it, the employees would come into work sipping and ready to party. Dr. Tracz emptied the bottle into everyone's glass. Then he tapped his fork against his own glass.

"AHEM! AHEM! Ladies and gentlemen, I'd like to propose a toast." Everyone's banter slowly stopped as the room quieted down. "To the man, the myth and the legend, Randy Stashi! My dear friend, my boss, my partner and the…LATEST RECIPIENT OF THE HOVELL PEACE PRIZE! May the world keep rewarding you for all the sacrifices and contributions you have made so far and let's keep pushing for greatness! Cheers!" We all yelled "Cheers" back and clanked glasses.

"Congratulations" was the repeated response that everyone kept giving me. I pulled Dr. Tracz aside. I know he wanted to keep the company morale up, but I hated when people jinxed the outcome because they jumped the gun.

"You're going to jinx our chances, idiot. Why would you announce we won when you know we've only been nominated?"

"…Well, because nominations are over! Idiot! You actually won! I mean, WE actually WON!" I examined his face carefully to see if he was lying. It took a second to process what he just said.

"AGHHHHH!" I yelled while hugging him.

""Yep my boy, the annual banquet is this Friday, dress fancy."

"HA HA," I laughed giddy with excitement. "UN-FREAKIN-BELIEVABLE!"

And to think, I wasn't going to come into work today. At times like this I used to call that special person. I'm sorry mommy.

Chapter 87

"If I was a multi-million-dollar entrepreneur, where would I be?" The Garbageman was awaiting his breakfast at an old-fashioned diner with his henchmen, Jacoby and Putnam. It was outside the city limits and low-key, meaning no cameras. The Garbageman hated cameras. This mission had evolved into a labyrinth with all roads leading to dead ends. The Garbageman knew his time was dwindling, but there was nothing he could do about it. Randy Stashi was nowhere to be found. He wasn't at work. He had changed residences. Their operation had come to a screeching halt. Now, they were in the diner attempting to orchestrate a new modus operandi.

"If I was a multi-million-dollar entrepreneur, I'd be in Italy, in a quaint Tuscan villa in a part of Venice, growing grapes and tasting wine," Jacoby rambled. The Garbageman looked at him with narrow eyes.

"You know. Sometimes I pray…" he started, "that you say something thought provoking, that something profound will leave your lips, and then you open your mouth, and all hope is thrown out the window. And that just proves that praying, religion, God, it's all just a large slab of bologna in a complicated plot to extort ten percent from the weak minded." Putnam's face was buried behind the daily newspaper.

"Oooh, that's pretty harsh."

"What…the part about it being bologna?"

"No… The part about Jacoby not saying anything thought provoking. I mean, he isn't a complete nincompoop."

"Thanks, Putnam."

"But bossman does have a point. You should really reduce the amount of time your mouth is open unless you're eating." Jacoby focused his glance straightforward. He didn't like how they were ganging up on him.

"Well, answer your *own* damn questions *then*!" he replied glumly.

"Food's here guys!" Their waitress was an old woman named Dorothy. She was waaay past the normal waiting age and grimaced every time she had to bend down

"French toast." Jacoby raised his hand.

"Boiled eggs and waffles." the Garbageman nodded his head. And by process of elimination, she passed Putnam his food. "Let me know if you need anything else." They resumed their conversation without acknowledging her. Dorothy flashed them a dirty look as she walked away.

"Where would I be? Where would I be?" the Garbageman pondered aloud. "On the beach. No, 'cause I have business affairs to tend to," he replied, answering his own question. "Putnam, do you mind putting down that freakin' paper!"

"No, I can't…" he muttered quietly while turning the newspaper page, "…because unlike you mongrels, I have to keep abreast with the world." The Garbageman inhaled and exhaled slowly realizing he was going to have to figure this one out on his own.

"If we don't find Randy Stashi, you're going to get shot in *the breast*!" Jacoby started snickering. The Garbageman banged his hand on the table causing all of the restaurant patrons to suddenly glance at their table.

"THIS isn't a laughing matter!" He paused while he sprinkled salt and pepper on his eggs. "Isn't he with that talk show host, what's her face?"

"Porsha Gottfrey," Jacoby answered.

"Yeah, that's her. Maybe he's with her in California."

"I highly doubt it," Putnam declared while cutting into his pancakes. "She's too busy for him to just be loafing around her house. Plus, this is where he makes his money at. I doubt he'll just walk away from everything he's built so quickly, especially if it's lucrative."

"Good point," replied Jacoby. The Garbageman looked at Jacoby with solemn eyes. "Whaaat…?" Jacoby frowned trying to break the tension.

"Nothing." The Garbageman said disgustedly. "So, we're all in agreement that he hasn't left the city?" Jacoby nodded while Putnam kept reading.

"Dammit, answer me, Putnam!"

"I'm reading right now. Answer your *own* bloody questions!"

"Hmph! Well, if he's in the city and he's not in the office, we might have to take one of his co-workers hostage."

"We did that already, remember? It got very messy last time, and we still didn't get him. I reeeally don't wanna go through that again."

"Well, golly Jacoby, you think we're in the home and gardening business?"

"No."

"What about the baking muffins business?"

"No."

"What about th—"

"Look, all I'm saying is that we have specific targets. We should minimize bystander casualties as much as possible. Unnecessary bloodshed. Not good for business."

"Aha!" Putnam exclaimed.

"What?" said the Garbageman looking concerned

"He did it." Putnam murmured, with his head still buried behind the newspaper.

"He did what?" said the Garbageman curiously.

"You said, Jacoby never says anything profound or thought provoking, and he just proved you wrong. We *should* reduce our recklessness. We're *professionals.*"

"See…" Jacoby confirmed gladly. The Garbageman banged his fist on the table angrily, arousing the restaurant's attention again.

"Y'all morons think this is a fun little game, don't you? I don't think I've made myself clear. Either he dies, or we die. He's worth three of us right now! And the boss is not happy with how long…this is *taking*!" He said it firmly but low enough for only them to hear.

"Bingo!" Putnam said staring harder at the paper.

"Bingo *what*?" the Garbageman answered.

"The mystery is solved. I know where he's going to be."

"Where?" He suddenly had the Garbageman's undivided attention. He leaned in even closer to Putnam. Putnam folded the paper and smacked it down right next to the Garbageman's plate. The Garbageman scooped it up and began skimming the headlines from top to bottom looking for the revelation Putnam was referring to. There it was, at the top of the local section. It read:

"THE HOVELL PEACE PRIZE AWARDS RANDY STASHI FOR HIS CONTRIBUTION TOWARD HUMANKIND."

Then under it, in smaller print, it read:

"This Friday at 7:00pm @ the Omni Hotel. The banquet starts at 6:00pm. Tickets $50. Formal attire required."

"You guys should really start reading more. Knowledge is power," he said it in a cocky tone before he took a prideful sip of his coffee. The Garbageman began to laugh.

"We got you now, Mr. Stashi. Ha ha." He grabbed the paper and began to scoot out of the booth.

"Let's go!" he announced. He reached into his pocket and flicked a twenty off of his money clip. Jacoby and Putman stuffed their faces before getting out of their side."

"You think that's enough plus tip?" Putnam questioned.

"Who cares?" the Garbageman said gruffly.

"The Bible says that the stingy will lose everything," Putnam added. The Garbageman screwed up his face and snarled at him.

"Well, for one, I don't read. And for two, I'm sure there's something in there about you can't take the money with you. You see how old she was? She doesn't have too much longer!"

Putnam shrugged his shoulders at the Garbageman.

"You're a real savage," he mumbled under his breath before he followed them out the door.

Chapter 88

"Hey honey, can you please hurry the fuzz up?" Being on time means everything. It shows that you can handle business, that you're responsible, but more importantly, that you value other people's time. So many times, when I've had to wait for someone, I start to question their reliability. It may seem petty in the regular world, but in the business world, it means everything.

"How do I look?" Chloe came out in an astonishing tight, bright pink dress. It started a little at the top of her juicy milky breasts. It draped all the way down to the floor and dragged behind her like she was royalty. She had on satin, shimmery white gloves and a matching pearl necklace that swooped between her chest. She had matching mascara painted on her eyelids, with curly hair that sat on her shoulders. She looked like a fantasy straight out of heaven.

"Wooow, Mami!"

"You like?"

"I mean… We can just stay home… I can give my speech on skype, technology is..."

"No! Ha ha," Chloe giggled. She cut me off.

"Alriiight, let's go!" I took her hand, and we walked outside. It felt good to use my Hoverfoot again. Chauncey was waiting outside an older black Maybach with the back door open. I wanted a cream colored one for the evening, but this was the only one they had that was bulletproof. I'll sacrifice style for safety each and every time. Chloe took a deep breath when she saw the car. Even though we had grown accustomed to foreign supercars, I'm sure she was stoked because this was the first luxury vehicle we had since we downsized. On the other hand, maybe she was scared.

"You're pulling out all the stops tonight, aren't you?"

"You know we gotta look good for the cameras, babe," I replied.

"Your chariot awaits you!" Chauncey announced as we approached the vehicle. I winked at him.

"How are you doing tonight, sir?" Even Chauncey looked dapper with his matching bow tie and cummerbund.

351

"Doing great. I'm kind of excited. Congratulations on winning, sir. That's a big accomplishment."

"Thank you. And this is only the beginning..."

"Well, it's definitely not the end," Chauncey responded.

Chloe hopped in the car and slid over. Then I followed suit. Chauncey slammed my door closed. When I looked up suddenly, there was a man I had never seen in my life! I was alarmed at once, and he must've sensed it instantly.

"Pleasure to meet you," he said while extending his hand. "I'm Al." I was still in bewilderment, but I shook his hand.

"Pleasure to meet you too. Sorry if I seemed a little uneasy. I just wasn't expecting you." He looked unamused. The driver side door opened and Chauncey jumped in.

"Sorry Randy. I forgot to tell you. I brought along another bodyguard for the event. Al, Mr. Stashi. Mr. Stashi, Al." Al put his hand up meagerly.

"It's going to be a lot of people there tonight, and we can't take any risks."

"You're right about that," I interjected.

"Al is a third-degree black belt in Shotokan, as well as an excellent marksman." Al looked at me and nodded his head grimly. Judging by his stoic face, I could tell he'd probably put a few people in the dirt with no remorse.

"Good call," I confirmed to Chauncey and then reached for my girlfriend's hands. We locked them together, and then pulled out of our generic apartment complex. We were on our way when I remembered about an important phone call that I had to make.

Ring. Ring. Voicemail. Damn, he didn't pick up. I started licking and sucking the front of my teeth. Chloe knew that I did that whenever I was dissatisfied about something as a way to calm down.

"What's wrong, baby?"

"Oh, nothing," I said trying to play it off. I'll call him back later.

"I know something's wrong, but I won't ask you again."

"Thank you." The radio was at a low volume, but I could still hear my song.

"Turn it up, Chauncey! This is my jam!" It was a classic—DMX "How's it going down?"

"Aww yeaah!" I said bobbing my head. "They don't make it like this anymore!" This was the *perfect* song to ride out to. When it was over, I reached in my pocket for the phone again.

Ring. Ring. The third ring was about to go to his voicemail, but then his voice came on.

"Hey, my boy!"

"What's up, partner? Where are you?"

"I'm on my way to the extravaganza. Where are you?" he questioned.

"Enroute as well. Look, I wanted to ask you about two things. Really not ask, but set some guidelines."

"Oh boy! Spit it out!" he gruffed in the phone.

"Well, first off, I want to thank you. We are here because of your ideas and efforts."

"Cut the crap. What is it?"

"Well, I know that they want you to speak for a second. But I am strongly refusing that action."

"What?"

"Look here, buddy. I already know what's going to happen. You're going to start drinking, turn into Mr. Hyde like always, start cussing people out and I'm not goi—"

"Randy, no!"

"No! Listen here. I'm not going for it tonight. Remember last time? It turned into a complete catastrophe."

"That wasn't my fault! She was dressed like a two-dollar wh—"

"No! It was your fault! Not tonight, doctor! You're not making a mockery of this company tonight! There are too many important people going to be there, and we have to raise more money for our developmental projects and pay our debts." I could sense he was getting irritated on the other end of the phone, but I had to set some house rules.

"Last time I checked, Mister Stashy Stash, I'm the reason why your press conference went viral worldwide. You think your boring ass press conference would've got millions of views without me?" He kinda had a point, but I didn't want to be the laughingstock of the country again. This was serious business.

"Maan, porn goes viral, but it ain't something that everyone respects. Remember the three p's"

"Yes, I remember your three dumb little p's. Practice, presentation, and professionalism."

"No one is going to give hundreds of millions of dollars to a company whose lead scientist is a reckless drunk. Remember that."

"Ahhh, wahn wahn wahn, I hear your babble."

"Thank you. And remember, I still love you."

"I wouldn't know based on how you treat me."

"Do your checks still clear?" He got quiet on the phone.

"Yep. That's what I thought. I still love you."

"Whatever you say, Mister I-got-a-stick-up-my-butt-and-I-don't-know-how-to-get-it-out. So, now that that's out the way, what was the second thing you were going to ask me about?"

"You gonna bring some stuff?" I asked without hesitation. I could feel Chloe's eyes staring at me.

"Party favors?" He started chuckling. "Ha ha ha. You're a bad man, Mr. Stashi."

"Ha ha. Yes, I am. I'll see you when I get there." Click. Call ended. I grabbed Chloe's hand again.

"Put the music back up, Chauncey! WHOO!" I yelled. "TONIGHT'S GOING TO BE A GREAT NIGHT!"

The whole Maybach erupted with laughter.

Chapter 89

"Nope, not him," Jacoby mumbled while looking through the binoculars. The Garbageman and his henchmen were posted inconspicuously in a tinted out SUV near the entrance of the Omni Hotel. They awaited the arrival of their guest of honor.

"You think he'll come through this entrance?" Putnam asked while taking slow drags of his cigarette.

"There are cameras and fans waiting in the front. He'll definitely be coming through this entrance," the Garbageman reassured.

"Nope. Not him," Jacoby stated again, as another formally dressed couple pulled up to the front.

"Please spare me the agonizing updates, Jacoby. Just let me know when you see him."

"Ten-four."

"Do you think it would be smarter to kill him after the ceremony?" Putnam asked. The Garbageman took a second to think about what he just said.

"So, what do you propose?"

"Well, I was thinking that we follow him, find out his residency, then attack on a different day."

"What? No way!" Jacoby scoffed while putting down his binoculars.

"What do you think is wrong with that plan, Jacoby?"

"Well, first off, we're going to have to stake him out even more. Then there's no guarantee that he's even home after this. He might get a hotel or even fly out after this occasion. Even if he does go home, how do we know that there isn't gated security there, that won't allow us in or blow our cover. That's a stupid plan."

"Jacoby does bring up some valid points."

"Plus…I'm getting tired of this mission. Let's just pop him in the head and be done with it."

"Yeah…I am tired of bossman breathing down my neck," the Garbageman gruffed.

"I think that we should really wait for a quieter opportunity, but… you're the boss." Putnam groaned.

"Yes, I am the boss," the Garbageman nodded. "Well, here's the plan. We'll let Randy give his pissy peace speech, accept his award and bask in the ambiance of his success. When he thinks everything is sweet and he pulls off into the sunset, we GUN HIM DOWN! This way, it resonates that anyone who tries too hard to defy the laws in place or upset our balance will not be tolerated. We clear?"

"Clear!" Jacoby and Putnam said in unison. Just then, a black older model Maybach pulled up. Jacoby pressed the binoculars to his face.

"Mmmm Hmm. Looks like the man of the hour has just arrived. And wow his date is hot!" The Garbageman laughed.

"More like the man in his *last* hour. Enjoy it while you can Mr. Stashi.

It'll all be over before you know it."

Chapter 90

The banquet was nothing short of royalty. I sat with Chloe at the long table facing the rest of the audience next to the podium. The food was phenomenal. It ranged from lasagna to succulent chicken, to delectable seafood (that I was allergic to). There had to be close to 2,000 people in attendance all dressed in formal garments. I'm not trying to brag, but it kind of made me feel important. I sipped slowly from glasses of tasty sweet wine while waiters refilled my cup and other attendees thanked me. The feast and treatment felt like it was intended for King Solomon himself.

"How do you like it, babe?" I muttered to Chloe in between bites.

"I wish every day could be like this," she whispered into my ear. "I'm so proud of you, Randy!" Then she snuck a kiss on my cheek. "There will be more where that came from later." Ha ha, I laughed with giddiness. I really did feel like a king that ruled over the region with my beautiful queen. I leaned in toward Dr. Tracz.

"How do you like it?" I asked Dr. Tracz. He started smiling ear to ear before he answered.

"I could kiss you—on the lips."

"Please don't," I answered. "And to think, you were going to throw that silly little Hoverfoot in the trash."

"Ha ha... Yes, you did save me, Randy. I would've never imagined the popularity of this in a million years."

"Hey... We kind of saved each other, doctor," I clarified.

"More wine?" The waitress asked.

"No thank you for me." I looked over and saw Dr. Tracz guzzling his glass. After he was done, he passed his glass to her.

"More please." I looked at him in astonishment.

"Just remember our talk, doc. You keep drinking, no speaking."

"You keep drinking, no speaking!" he repeated in a high-pitched voice.

"We need to take a bathroom break." He looked at me finally taking the hint.

"Oh okay…well, lead the way."

"Hey babe, we're going to the men's room to iron this speech out. Can you watch our drinks?"

"Sure, babe." I signaled for Chauncey to follow us. I got up and led the way to the less used restrooms in the back. Dr. Tracz was already swaying. I made a mental note to myself to cut him off when we got back to the table. After we entered the doors, Chauncey checked under each stall to see if he saw any feet dangling. Nope. The coast was clear. Chauncey proceeded to wait outside.

"You got it?" Dr. Tracz produced a small bag of powder from his inside jacket pocket.

"Voila!"

"You're a lifesaver!" I exclaimed and grabbed the bag from his hands. I went into the stall and began my recent ritual.

"You know, Randy," he began quietly, "you're really going to have to reduce your dependency on this stuff. You're moving at a dangerous rate. That's not good."

"Wooooow!" I said astonished. "Isn't that the pot calling the kettle black tonight?"

"Touché. I'm just saying Stashi, I started this habit when I was much older than you. You're not going to make it to the age I am if you keep it up." I dipped a house key in the bag, closed one nostril and inhaled with my eyes closed.

"Aaaaah…" I could feel the euphoric sensation rush to my brain. I put my head down to relax and soak up every ounce of the powder.

"You hear me, Stashi Stash?" I opened my eyes slowly and suddenly remembered exactly where I was.

"Yeah, I hear you doc. Now, I've got a question for *you*."

"Ask away…" I dipped my key into the bag of dust again.

"What are you going to say tonight for your portion of the acceptance speech?"

"I'm still thinking about it." I took another hit.

"Sounds like disaster is about to strike again."

"Quite the contrary, Randy. I always do my best work under pressure. Remember, pressure makes diamonds."

"Yeah, but don't forget, pressure also busts pipes." He laughed lightly. I closed up the Ziploc and put it back in my jacket pocket. I fiddled with the stall lock before opening the door.

"Now, I have a question for you," Dr. Tracz mumbled when I walked out of the stall.

"How does one receive a worldwide peace award while out on bond for beating up a cop?" I checked my face in the mirror to make sure that there was no visible residue of white powder around my nose.

"Life is ironic ain't it? FYI I didn't beat him up, it was one punch. And it had nothing to do with his badge."

"Can't control your temper, eh?"

"Can't control your liquor, eh?"

"Now, can we please get back to our celebration?"

"Lead the way *Mister* Peace Prize."

"Well Mister Peace Prize says you've had your last cup of wine until your speech, all right? After that, you can drink until you piss and vomit on yourself!"

"Gawd. You're such a party pooper."

Chapter 91

"Okay, so Jacoby, you're going to trail behind them in the other car. If they try to reverse or make a U-turn, *cut them off!*" The Garbageman was going over the final details of the hit.

"Putnam, you're going to drive this truck, and I'm going to sit right behind you." Putnam nodded his head to confirm.

"Put your walkie-talkie on channel eleven, and wait for my signal." Jacoby began fiddling with the gadget. The Garbageman looked closely at his digital watch.

"We have about an hour and ten minutes, gentleman. Let's get Stashi and be done with this!"

Everyone nodded their head in confirmation. The drizzle softly pitter pattered on the windshield as the storm began. The weather was only going to get worse.

The thunder would disguise the gunshots, and the rain would wash the blood from the streets.

"This is the perfect murder weather," The Garbageman thought. He was finally starting to get excited.

Chapter 92

I was jumping in the air fifty feet at a time taking bites of creamy strawberry cheesecake. Everything was blinding white. It seemed heavenly. Ugh! I don't know if I was awakened by the crack of thunder outside or Chloe's elbow digging into my ribs. She looked at me with wide eyes.

"Babe, you were snoring," she whispered sternly. No wonder these nominees didn't win a peace prize. They couldn't entertain a crying toddler. The last speaker was the most boring of all. His life's work revolved around making domesticated pets talk. I thought the whole reason people got pets is so that they *couldn't* talk. I don't know. He lost me with that one. Either way, I looked around, and no one noticed that I had dozed off. The coke must've been weak, or I just needed some more. My sleep cycle hadn't been the best lately. Anyway, if they said anything about me resting, my excuse would be, I have been working overtime to ensure peace and improve the human quality of life. I looked in Dr. Tracz' direction. At first glance it looked like he was staring down concentrating on his food. But once you saw his empty plate, you knew he was passed out too. At least I wasn't the only one unamused at this function. The last speaker finally wrapped up his speech. Thank God. The host made his way back to the microphone.

"In a world where dogs could talk, they could potentially save lives. They could warn us of intruders or fires in our homes. Man oh man, I can't wait until this concept is fully developed!" He looked around the crowd and then made eye contact with me. It was go time! "Well, ladies and gentlemen, it is with my greatest pleasure and honor…" The clapping and whistling erupted, filling the banquet hall with a range of loud noises. It suddenly became as loud as a football stadium. I couldn't help but smile from ear to ear.

"Hailing from FV University! Winner of GDQ's top sexiest businessman! Bestselling author and entrepreneur! …and inventor of the new world phenomenon, the Hoverfoot!" I began raising my hand and waving at everyone while I slowly stood up. The cheers gradually grew louder.

"Let's give a warm Hovell Peace Prize winning applause to Mr. Randy Stashi!"

"Whooo whooo whoo!" The audience was standing while clapping and whistling at the loudest volume that I had heard all evening. I made my way to the podium, putting extra emphasis on the shiny Hoverfoot 3000. I felt like everyone's favorite wrestler getting cheered on as I walked to the ring. All of those long days and hopeless nights, all of the struggling and strife, to finally be exalted by these people. The joy that I was feeling was indescribable. *Unexplainable.* I reached the podium and waited for the acclaim to settle down.

"Wow…" I said still astonished and soaking up the energy.

"Go Stashi!" someone yelled from the crowd.

"I just want to say that it's an honor and a blessing to be here! Thank You God!"

"Whooo!" More cheers. It felt more like a high school pep rally than a formal ceremony.

"It was a lot of long and lonely nights to get here, but we did it. I would like to dedicate this award to my mother. I remember when I was first told that I wouldn't be able to walk again and was depressed and suicidal, she told me not to give up on life. Her exact words were, 'walking isn't everything.' I really wish she could be here today." It took a lot to fight back the tears. Change thoughts, change thoughts. Happy times.

"Could we have a moment of silence for her please?" Even though I tried not to cry, I could feel the tears start to fill up my eyes as I thought about all of the invaluable moments that we shared. I bowed my head. After forty-five seconds of deafening silence, I raised my head back up. "I love you, Mommy." I took out my handkerchief and wiped my eyes. "Look, I'm not going to bore you today with my accolades and accomplishments. Everyone knows how to use Google. What I came to talk to you today about is hope. Life is very brutal. Sometimes, it can knock you down, knock you unconscious, take your legs away, take your mom away, almost take you away. But what life will never be able to take away from you is your hope. As long as you have hope, you will never give up. If you never give up then eventually, you'll make that breakthrough. Remember, energy and persistence conquers all. I believe that everyone in this room has a talent, a special trait, and a purpose for being on this planet. That's what we were put on the earth for, to share and contribute our talent with the masses. We have to reach deep within ourselves to pull it out of us no matter what obstacles might be staring us in the face. They're hailing me as one of the greatest minds of this millennium." I chuckled lightly. "It sounds awesome. Truthfully though, when they announce me, I feel like they're talking about someone else. Even though being one of the great minds sounds iconic, the simple truth of the matter is, I'm just another human being who hoped to walk again. Everyone can find a problem that they can personally solve or attempt to solve." I moved to the front of the podium so everyone could view me. "Look at what I solved! Look at me, *now!*" I started doing the robot with the shimmering Hoverfoot on, and the crowd burst into ear-shattering clapping and cheering. I walked over to the podium and waited for the praise to diminish. "My only hope is that Stashi Enterprises is around for centuries to *come!* And we stay a leader in innovation, healthcare, and ideologies that will not only help make the world a better place. But make a person a better person." The chants and screams peaked again as the audience became excited. "Before I leave this stage in a couple of seconds, I want you to remember one thing I told you, just because tomorrow is never promised. Always, I repeat, always *keep hope alive!* Thank you all for coming out tonight. Thank you all for this award. And we are going to continue to excel and set the standard here at Stashi Enterprises! This is only the beginning! Y'all have a great night and get home safe!" I waved again at all the applause and motioned for Dr. Tracz to take the podium. "And now the doctor behind the Hoverfoot, my partner, and fellow genius, Dr. Tracz!" I clapped until he was in handshaking distance, then I whispered into his ear.

"Keep it short and sweet, please."

"Gotcha." The backdraft of booze from his breath slapped me in the face. Not a good sign. I made my way slowly back to my seat while praying silently for the Lord to spare us from any embarrassment.

"Well, well, well...if I had known Randy was going to give that Oscar-winning speech, then I would've asked to go before him. It's nearly impossible to follow that." The attendees started laughing. "I'm going to try though. We are truly thankful and honored that this committee has recognized our strenuous efforts and has bestowed upon us this accolade. We. Are. The champions. My friend. And. We'll. Keep. On fighting. Until the end. No time. For losing." Chloe nudged me, as I put my head down.

"Isn't that the Mighty Ducks' song?" I grumbled in agreement with the shame of my association with the man speaking.

"Yep..."

Some of the people in the crowd began to laugh or look around to see if anyone else had picked up on the folly.

"Cause we. Are. The champions. Of the world!" Dr. Tracz began acting like he was playing a guitar, and was voicing the notes. After he was done, he took a bow and then proceeded to walk off the stage. The whole room sat there in awe and silence—or maybe it was just an awkward silence. I put my forehead in my palm. When he passed me, he clicked his teeth and winked at me.

"Short and sweet, boss!" It was at that precise moment I wanted to strangle him—very, very slowly. Breathe, Randy. Breathe, Randy. He's not worth the time. The host jumped back up to the stage still in shock, I guess about Dr. Tracz's soliloquy. The room got very quiet.

"Well, let's give it up one more time for our winners and guests of honor!" The crowd gradually started clapping, still trying to process what had just happened.

"Well, thanks for coming. This ceremony is almost over, but before we part ways, can we get a dance for Randy Stashi and his beautiful date?" Everyone applauded as we made our way to the dance floor. The lights dimmed, and they played something smooth and romantic out of the nineties. We slow-danced like we were in the eighth-grade prom. It was ironic but miraculous how the only reason I could dance was because of something I invented. Camera flashes were coming from every direction.

"I love you with all my heart," Chloe whispered passionately into my ear.

"I know you do," I whispered back. She slapped me lightly, on the shoulder playfully.

"You don't love me back?"

"Ha ha. I wouldn't be here if it wasn't for you, baby. Don't be silly."

"Aww…then say it."

"Chloe, you know I love you more than life itself!" I paused. This exact moment felt so magical that I wanted to freeze it. I wanted it to last forever. I wanted to feel like this all the time. "…And we might need to take our love to the next level pretty soon." She hugged me tighter when she heard this.

"CRAAAACK!" Just then a thunderclap so loud it could've been mistaken for an earthquake happening. The lights flickered briefly. Then the whole place went pitch black.

My heart began to race. Chauncey grabbed my shoulder. "Get down!" he barked at us.

It was officially time to go!

Chapter 93

It was a semi-frantic rush of people leaving the building. Al walked with us while Chauncey darted ahead to fetch the car from the valet. Everyone inside the building had the flashlight on their cell phone out in this now dark building. When we got outside, it was pouring down blankets of rain. We were huddled up and semi-hidden while we waited at the front entrance for our car to pull up. The evening had officially ended in madness.

"Great weather," I said to Al, to try to lighten the mood. He looked at me with a stern gaze, as he shook his head no.

"Duck down." He advised. I lowered my head. It was comforting how focused he was about protecting us.

"I'm so proud of you, baby!" Chloe whispered in my ear seductively. I pinched her on her cheek while biting my lip. She leaned back to stare at me, then returned closer to lick my ear.

"Please give it to me rough tonight, daddy." I became tickled with laughter about what I was hearing.

"I'mma tear you up when I get in the car," I whispered back. She began giggling.

"The car's here." Al waved to me as our black Maybach pulled up. Al opened the back door hurriedly as Chloe rushed in, and I followed.

"This weather is horrible," noted Chauncey from the driver's side. When the heavy door closed, the loud storm muted. I had to admit, it felt really comfortable and safe inside this Maybach.

"Where are we going?" he asked.

"Let's just find a lavish hotel downtown. I don't feel like going home tonight." Chauncey exhaled deeply when he heard my answer.

"Something wrong?"

"I don't think that driving around in this weather is a good idea, but you're the boss."

"Thanks, Chauncey, but a little water never hurt anyone. Can you turn up the radio, please?" The volume gradually got louder as a party song came on. I started bobbing my head. This was a groovy tune. I looked over, and both Chauncey and Al were bobbing their head to the beat.

"Yo, who's this on the radio?" I asked. Chauncey lowered the volume briefly enough to speak.

"Deuce Debonaire." He put the volume back up.

"Who?" I asked again uncertain if I had heard him correctly.

"It's a new artist named Deuce Debonaire. It's pretty good, eh?" I smiled as I listened to the punchlines.

"I kinda like it." He put it back up with one hand still on the steering wheel. I pulled Chloe's thighs closer to me, so she had her back on the seat.

"Hey, we're going to be busy back here, so don't look, okay?" I announced. Chauncey responded verbally. Al gave a head nod.

"Now, where were we?" I whispered in Chloe's ear.

"I forgot," she murmured back. I shoved my tongue into her mouth and began biting her bottom lip.

"Oh yeah. You said you wanted it rough."

"Give it to me," she begged. I pulled the top of her dress down as her beautiful, robust tiddies flopped out with pointed nipples.

"I'ma get started on you but first…" I fished around inside the jacket pocket for the little bag I had and the small straw I kept from the banquet.

"What are you doing?" Chloe asked curiously.

"Shhhh…" I said, putting my finger over my mouth. I opened the bag of coke and sprinkled some on her nipple. I then jammed the straw up my right nostril and sniffed it off her left tiddy. She started giggling. Chloe was so ticklish. I pinched my nose to make sure none of it fell out. When I opened my eyes, I smiled at her.

"You gotta be still when I'm doing that, baby." I chuckled "Now, I'm going to have to do it again.…"

"No!" she interjected. "It's my turn." I sat back up. What? I was startled by her request. Chloe had always condemned my drug use. Now, I guess that she was feeling good, she wanted to see what all the fuss was about.

"Look, if you're going to do this, you're going to have to sniff it off my dick." She looked at me in disbelief. I stared deep into her eyes. She could tell I was dead serious.

"Well, c'mon whip it out." She started reaching for my pant's buckle. I tingled at the moment that was unfolding.

"Yes, ma'am." I started undoing my pants and then stuck my now erect dick through the hole in my boxers.

"I just inhale it?" She asked.

"Sniff it hard through one nostril, so it goes up to your brain," I instructed. I held my dick at an even angle and sprinkled the crushed powder on it. "Put the straw in your nose, and inhale it until you see no dust left."

"You ready?" I asked. She nodded her head yes with the straw in her nose. "Go." I urged. I had to admit, I've done a lot of things in my life, but there is no high like the high of watching a girl sniff blow off your dick. I was suddenly turned on to the max times ten to the tenth power! She leaned her head back with her eyes closed and exhaled slowly. She didn't say anything for a couple of seconds, just soaking in the feeling.

"Wow!"

"What's up?"

"I kind of liked that," she said slowly. I grabbed the back of her hair, and I wrapped it around in a tight fist. I then pushed her head back in my lap.

"Lick it all off." She wrapped her warm wet mouth around the tip and began bobbing up and down on it. My eyes rolled back into my head. I let her suck on it for every bit of a minute before I pushed her back onto her seat with her legs into the air.

"Time to tear that kitty up." She began sucking on her fingers.

"Please." I spread her legs and moved her panties to the side. She was dripping wet. I stuck my finger inside of her and let off a quiet moan. I took out my finger and licked it slowly. Her juices tasted so good. I pulled her thighs closer to me and began to massage the tip of my pipe up and down her juicy walls.

"Stick it in," she begged. When I finally penetrated her wet flesh, she let out a louder moan. She felt so good. I began giving her a show with rough thrusts as I bent down and licked her breast.

"Stuff me, daddy," she said while grabbing the back of my head. I leaned back up and started thrusting inside of her more rapidly. Suddenly, I felt the car slowing down. I poked my head up and saw blue and red lights flashing on the window. Aww the police! Why *Now*?! I sprang up and began looking on the seat for the small bag of coke.

"What's up, Randy?" Chloe asked sensing something wasn't right. As soon as she saw the flashing lights, her facial expression changed. She started straightening up her dress and covering herself back up.

"What did y'all do?" I demanded angrily at Chauncey.

"Nothing Stashi. They came out of nowhere." We pulled over to the left on a one-way street. I looked over and a tinted SUV, with its driver side window down, was waving his flashlight at us, motioning to roll our window down. You could barely see anything. The rain was coming down too heavily.

"Roll down the window, Al," I instructed. Al rolled the window down a couple of inches.

"Yooo!" Al yelled. I think we all were a little annoyed by this peculiar traffic stop in the middle of a thunderstorm.

"Your taillight is o—" Before he could even finish, the window behind him rolled down, and bright flashes from a muzzle were all I saw.

TAT! TAT! TAT! TAAAAAT!

Chapter 94

Al's body jolted back and forth as he was struck with a barrage of bullets. I could hear them whizzing by my head in the car. I dove over to shield Chloe from the gunfire.

"ROLL UP THE WINDOW! ROLL UP THE FREAKING WINDOW!" I yelled at the top of my lungs. It seemed like it took an eternity for the window to roll up. I suddenly felt a sharp throbbing pain in my arm. I reached over and rubbed it—blood, and opened flesh. I had been hit!

"Arrrrghhh!" I shrieked. Chloe was screaming. The SUV darted in front of us about ten feet and cut us off.

"Ahhh…" Chauncey moaned. Judging by that sound, he didn't get lucky either. I looked straight ahead to where they were cutting us off.

"REVERSE! REVERSE!" I yelled at Chauncey. He slammed the gear into R and stomped on the gas pedal. I was looking through the back window to help guide us when I saw another similar SUV cutting us off from behind. Chauncey jammed the brakes. We jerked back.

"*WHOAA!* HOW MANY OF THEM IS IT?"

"MAN! GO! FORWARD!" I yelled at him with all the air left in my lungs through spit and mucus, when we had come to a complete stop.

"THEY'RE BLOCKING US UP FRONT!"

"RAM THEM OUTTA THE WAY! THIS THING IS LIKE A TANK!" Chauncey nodded frantically. I looked at the speedometer. Twenty to thirty miles per hour. I glanced over at Al, still in disbelief at his contorted body position. His head was leaned back as he lay motionless. I didn't want to accept it, but he was probably dead. We were at forty to fifty miles per hour as the engine revved louder. I focused back on us.

"Chloe, *BUCKLE UP!*" I grabbed her seatbelt and handed it to her, as I jumped back in my seat trying to get buckled in.

"It won't *buckle!*" Chloe screamed as she fiddled with it desperately trying to get it to click. "HELP!" she yelled. Sixty to seventy miles per hour. We were about sixty feet from the SUV, headed directly in its direction. TAT! TAT-

TAT! TAT! Gunfire began to hit the impenetrable windshield. I stopped fiddling with my seatbelt and grabbed Chloe's. I couldn't buckle it. *Damn*! The belt had locked up because of our velocity.

"Hang on, baby!" I warned as I laid down on the floor where her feet were and held my hand out to restrain her. It wasn't the brightest idea, but it was the quickest thing that I could think of.

"AHHHH!" She let out a blood curdling scream as we made impact.

Boooooom!

Our car spun out of control as the SUV in front of us flipped and began to roll. I bounced around the back seat like a pinball until our car stopped. My arm was burning. And my whole body started throbbing. Chloe had headbutted the back of Chauncey's headrest on impact, hard. Her body was contorted and not moving. Chauncey was slumped over in the front. I looked through the front windshield and saw the SUV flipped upside down. I then looked through the back window at a crooked angle. The SUV that had cut us off from behind was fast approaching. Its headlights seemed to get brighter as it got closer. I felt inside of Al's jacket for his gun. I unclipped it from the holster as I focused on the back window. The driver's side door of the SUV opened slowly. I could feel my heart beat out of my chest. My arm was throbbing with fire. He began walking over to our car in a very slow and steady manner like he was in a movie. All I could see through the darkness was his outline and a long black pipe. As he got closer to our car, I started to realize it wasn't a pipe he was holding.

My heart began to beat like a jackhammer.

Chapter 95

Jacoby got out of his SUV and started walking to the car where Stashi was. He had his assault rifle ready as he slowly walked toward the car. The car was facing forward at a slightly pointed angle with the driver side of the trunk closest to him. He began to smile devilishly for two reasons. One, because this mission was about to be over. And two, it would be all because of him. He would be able to take all the credit for this mission. The thought alone made him even more desperate.

"Let's hurry this up," he thought in the cold dark rain.

Chapter 96

I saw a man approaching closer. He was about fifteen yards away. "*Think quickly! Think quickly!*" I told myself.

"Get out of the car!" a voice inside my head whispered to me. The way the car was angled, he couldn't see the side with Al and me; only Chloe and Chauncey's side. I creeped out the door and crawled on the ground with my forearms and elbows. The rain was coming down in torrents. I sat, crouched behind the back tire.

Tat! Tat! Taaat! Tat!

Whoever the gunman was, was out here to kill. This was no accident at all. Thank God, the car was bulletproof. "*What should I do? What should I do?*" I looked under the car in his direction. All I saw were his feet. Perfect. No one wears bulletproof shoes. I aimed Al's gun at them and started returning the favor.

Pow! Pow!

I saw one leg off the ground, and the other hopping up and down. I think I hit him.

Pow! Pow!

Suddenly, I didn't see his feet anymore. That bastard must've hopped on the top of the car.

I opened the door and got back into the car.

Tat! Taaat! Tat!

I could hear the shots ricocheting off the roof of the car. I ducked down instinctively. I scurried over to Chloe's side, gently moving her out of the way. She was still out cold. That's when my blood began to boil, and I was ready to make these faggots pay. I could see the gunman hanging off the side of the car. I could only see the bottom half of him through the tinted window. "Perfect." I whispered to myself. I barely lowered Chloe's window, just enough to stick the gun barrel out at an upward angle. I pointed it right at his crotch.

Pow! Pow!

He dropped like a fly to the ground. He began squirming on the ground grabbing his dick.

"That's what you get," I thought. I lowered the window another inch so I could point the gun downward. I aimed for his head while he was shouting out in a foreign language. "It's over for you homie." I proclaimed.

Pow!

He jerked on impact and then stopped moving. Relief. I took a deep breath and slumped back in the seat. I panted heavily as my heart raced. One down, and for sure two to go, if not more. I exited the vehicle on Chloe's side and grabbed the assailant's weapon. I tucked Al's gun in my waist and began walking toward the SUV behind me. I wanted to make sure no one else was in there. I checked the front seat and back seat cautiously. No one else, the coast was clear. I began walking toward the overturned SUV. I drew the gun back up and began watching everything through the crosshairs. I was shooting anything that moved. The heavy rain obscured my vision. As I got closer, I saw the driver lying face down on the side of the street with his head fixed in an awkward position. His neck probably snapped when he was thrown out of the rolling SUV. Such a shame. He should've worn his seatbelt. I was still curious though if he was still alive or not. There was only one way to find out.

Tat! Tat! Tat!

His body bounced briefly off the ground as my rifle rounds hit him.

"You're dead now!" I murmured to myself gruffly.

Two down. One more to go.

375

Chapter 97

The Garbageman lay in the turned over SUV in extreme pain. He had a couple of broken bones as well as a cut-up face from the windshield's shards of glass.

"Putnam! Puuuut-Naaaam!" He called out in desperation. He looked around but saw no signs of his partner. The only possibility he could think of was he must've been thrown out of the vehicle. "The SUV rolled over at least five times," he remembered. "Why didn't Putnam press the gas?" he questioned disappointedly to himself.

Tat! Tat! Taat!

It was gunfire coming from close range. "WHERE IS MY GUN?" The Garbageman reacted frantically.

"Arrrghh!" he groaned in pain. He quickly scanned the interior of the SUV. Not in here, nor was Putnam's rifle. He then scanned beyond the car. Through the heavy rain, he saw his big firearm laying in the street about twelve feet away. He began to climb out of the shattered window opening on his arms and knees.

"*I got to get that gun, NOW!*" was the only thing on his mind. Only ten feet away. *Damn.* "*How could this mission go so sour?*" he thought as he climbed closer. Seven feet. Just then he spotted a man limping toward him hastily with a rifle drawn and his face covered. The Garbageman became excited. It had to be either Putnam or Jacoby bringing the good news, letting him know he had just finished Stashi off. The mission was finally complete. Stashi's dead, and it's time to go home.

"Putnam. Jacoby?" the Garbageman called out ecstatically. The man walked closer, the weapon unwavering.

"No.... No.... NO. No Putnam! And No gahdamn Jacoby! It's Stashi *BITCH!*"

The Garbageman's hopes suddenly did a freefall into an abyss as his head lowered into the water.

Chapter 98

I approached the last enemy still limping in excruciating pain. The hoverfoot was barely kicking out enough power. The impact from the car accident, plus being shot in the arm had taken a huge toll on me. The guy on the ground was calling out all of the names of his help. I made a mental note of the names before I had to politely inform him that there was no more help. He began to crawl faster on his hands and knees in the direction of his assault rifle. With my rifle pointed at him, I sidestepped between him and the gun, and then kicked it backward with my heel. The night sky turned bright with a white flash of lightning for a full two seconds.

Krah kruh!

The deafening clap of thunder startled me. I focused back on him through the crosshairs. Lord knows I wanted to pull the trigger so effiing bad, but I needed some answers first. I needed to know when or if this madness was really going to end with them.

"WHO ARE Y'ALL?" I screamed angrily through the tempest. He sank his head down in the pavement like he was trying to go to sleep. Oh, I got something to wake you up.

Tat! Taat!

I fired the gun at him, barely missing his body. I know he could hear the bullets ricocheting close to him. His head sprang back up instantly. He didn't think I was serious. His smile almost broke into a laugh, with his teeth covered in dark crimson blood.

"WHY! ARE! Y'ALL! TRYING TO KILL MEEE?" I yelled at him. The sheepish smile he had on his face turned into a look of serious concern.

"ORDERS ARE ORDERS, STASHI!" He yelled back. "YOU ARE TRYING TO UPSET OUR CHAIN! THE BALANCE!" I was confused, yet, infuriated at the same time. I repositioned the crosshairs, so they intersected right between his eyes.

"I SHOULD KILL YOU!" I warned. He looked up at me and laughed even harder.

"DON'T YOU GET IT? YOU FOOL! EVEN IF YOU DO KILL ME, WE'RE GOING TO KEEP COMING UNTIL YOU STOP SPREADING YOUR FILTH! YOU ARE SINGLE-HANDEDLY DESTROYING THE BALANCE! WE MUST REMAIN IN POWER AT ALL COSTS!" I began to hear sirens in the distant background. The man rolled over on his back and began looking into the sky.

"KILL ME, STASHI!" he begged. "I'M BETTER OFF DEAD!" He rolled back over on his stomach and began crawling toward me like a possessed zombie. He had a crazed look in his eyes like he was taken over by an inner demon. I wanted to kill him so bad, but I knew that the answers would stop. The possibility of doing a hundred years in prison might scare him enough to give up his counterparts. I backpedaled and turned to pick up his gun. The Hoverfoot was surprisingly still going in all of this rain. I turned back around to face him.

"NO SCUMBAG! I'M GOING TO LET YOU ROT IN PRISON FOR THE REST OF YOUR LIFE! YOU'RE GOING TO BE PRAYING FOR CHEESEBURGERS AND TO NOT GET BUTT RAPED BY THE CHAIN GANG EVERY DAY!" He put his head back down in defeat when I unveiled his probable future. The wail from the sirens was getting louder. I turned around and picked up his gun. I began backpedaling toward my car. I had to get back to Chloe. If she needed CPR, time was running out. I had to let the authorities deal with the last bastard.

"Stashiiiiiii!" he shrieked as soon as I turned around. I was still hopeful that he might be ready to reveal more information. I *really* wanted to know who was responsible for these attacks on me and my family.

"WHAAAAT?" I yelled back as I began to walk back towards him. He began to chuckle very slowly.

"YOUR MOTHER SAID SHE LOVES YOU! HA HA!" He kept laughing even harder than before. My blood began to rage as hot as lava. I could feel the fury pulsate through my body as I clenched my teeth.

"WELL IF YOU SEE HER, TELL HER I SAID I LOVE HER TOO!" His laughing came to an immediate halt when he saw me drop his rifle and pull mine back up to shooting position.

TAT! TAT! TAAAT!!

His body bounced up and down in the puddled streets as the bullets hit him. You could see his blood began to dye the water a deep crimson red under the streetlights. He laid there still, with that devilish smile frozen on his face. I stood there and closed my eyes. Everything suddenly became eerily quiet. I felt like I was going numb and deaf. It was probably from the gunfire.

"ARGHHHHH!" I shouted in agony. I was furious. Furious that I now knew who killed my mother. Furious that I couldn't restrain myself enough to not pull the trigger. Furious that I might never ever get the answers that I needed. "*AGHHHH!*" I screamed. Cop cars suddenly pulled up out of nowhere and skidded to a stop mere yards in front of me.

"FREEZE! PUT THE GUN DOWN!" they commanded over the cop car's PA system. I threw the gun down to the side and dropped to my knees. I interlocked my hands behind my head.

I screamed again angrily. My mouth was filled with blood, thick mucus and adrenaline. I was fuming and felt like crying at the same time. I had looked into the eyes of my mom's killers. I missed her so bad right now. I wished she could give me a hug right now, and tell me everything was going to be okay. For some reason, it didn't feel like everything was going to be okay though. For some reason, I have a feeling that this ordeal was far, far from over. I lowered my head in exhaustion.

"Please call an ambulance for the lady in the car! PLEASE OFFICER!" I begged.

Chapter 99

My name is Max Snyder. I am number #235189-15 under the witness protection program. I live in a mobile home in a trailer park somewhere in the northern Midwest. I feel nonexistent, scatterbrained, and unmotivated. It had been many months since the horrific, life-changing night of the Hovell Peace Prize. The aftermath of that incident was cataclysmic to me. One of the bodyguards died, while the other remained in critical condition. The woman that I purportedly loved was still in a coma. Her name had changed to Barbara McCrawton for protective reasons as well. She had been transported to a hospital closer to me where she had still not awakened. The doctors had asked me repeatedly if I wanted to pull the plug on her. They had advised me that there was little to no chance she would recover. My answer was always the same. No. To do that would be to give up on someone who never gave up on me. That's not fair.

Sometimes, I would stare in the mirror for hours trying to recognize who I was. I shaved my head bald. My scraggly beard added a good ten years to my appearance. The highlights of my day were drinking beer (which I never liked before), playing video games, and jacking off. My diet had regressed to hot dogs and peanut butter sandwiches. Whenever that ran out, I would cook noodles. If that was out, then I would hop in my dusty old school Ford pickup truck and drive way out to the gas station. It wasn't the grocery store, but it did do the trick. The only thing that kept me going was my dog, Chuck. I had contemplated suicide so many times, but the question that always stopped me was, who would feed Chuck? The life I had once lived was gone—galaxies away. I remembered bits and pieces of it but remembering it was far more painful than forgetting it. I looked at the dog's empty food bowl.

"What do you want to eat, Chuck?" It wasn't like he had much of a choice. It was either bagged dog food or nothing. I just talked to him to keep myself sane. It would get so lonely in this trailer. Sometimes, I had to speak to make sure I was still alive.

Knock! Knock! Knock!

My eyes widened at the thought of who it could be. Company was never expected, nor welcomed. I looked through the door's peephole. It was the neighbor's snot-nosed kid, Sammy. I opened the door wide enough to poke my head out. I wasn't in the mood. Plus, I was still in my daily attire of a stained, stretched tank top and boxers.

"Sorry to disturb you, Mr. Max, but my mom wanted to know if you had any salt? We're making chili tonight."

"Ughhh…" I groaned. He was interrupting my daily routine, but his mom had always been nice to me, so I had to cut him some slack. Besides, she always made sure I had a plate of the finished product.

"Hold on." I slammed the door and filled up a plastic bag with the last of my salt. Not much, but enough to get the job done. I opened the door back up and handed Sammy the salt.

"Thanks, Mr. Max!" he said excitedly. He started walking away when he turned around. "Oh yeah, my mom said you're invited to dinner if you want." The thought of playing twenty questions with Sammy's family sounded like torture. I would gladly take a togo plate though.

"I'll think about it!" I yelled before slamming the door. Hopefully, they would bring me a bowl, so I could reap the benefits without the headache. She wasn't the best cook, but I could use a break from all of the processed food I had been eating. The microwave was my chef. I filled Chuck's bowl and then went to the fridge to grab me a cold beer. I plopped down on the recliner, popped the top on the can, chugged an icy swig and grabbed the remote. It was cheap watery beer, but I made it work. It made me smile, it made me feel sleepy. I cut on the daily talk show trash. Today's episode was themed "I thought you were a woman." I was perplexed by how you wouldn't notice someone had balls, but then again, if the man only received fellatio, he might be able to be hoodwinked. But who knows? It might have all been fake. Ironically, I had became so busy, I never watched television. Now I had strangely addicted to this televised garbage. As trash as it was, it made me feel better about my own depressing life.

"How could you do this to me, Sheila?" The guy on TV looked devastated.

"So, you didn't know Sheila was a He-la?" The crowd erupted in laughter.

"Ha ha ha…" I even chuckled myself. That was a pretty funny question. Just then, I heard the sound of an engine pulling up. I paid it no mind because it could've been anyone in the trailer park community since our homes were so close together. I took the last swig of beer before crunching the can and throwing it somewhere near the trash can. I began to hear the footsteps of gravel crunching closer and closer toward my door. I suddenly became alert when they stopped.

Knock! Knock! Knock!

They were intense knocks. I grabbed my shotgun from under the sofa. I approached the door slowly. I looked the through the peephole but could barely recognize the person due to his baseball cap and reflective sunglasses.

"MAX?" he called out.

Click! Click!

I clicked the shotgun loudly to let whoever it was know that I was armed.

"Who is it?" He looked scared when he heard the loaded gun. He took off his hat and sunglasses.

"It's me!" I opened the door. It was a face I hadn't seen it felt like in decades.

"RANDY?" he exclaimed. His eyes and his smile lit up with elation. I looked at him glumly with a brazen face.

"Randy's dead." I murmured. His whole facial expression changed as he tried to make sense of what I had just said. He looked shocked, but at the same time examined my new, haggard appearance. I was trying hard to remember where I knew this guy from. A surge of vague past memories began to replay instantly in my head.

Mister. Ughhh. His name was on the tip of my tongue. Mister. Umm. No. More like doctor. Yeah, that's it.

Doctor Tracz.

But what in the world was he doing here? And how did he find me?

Chapter 100

"Wanna beer?"

I made my way to the fridge as I heard him fall back on my recliner. I didn't like the fact that he took my seat, but I guess I could sit on the counter.

"So, you're drinking beer now?" Dr. Tracz asked half surprised, half disgusted.

"So, I take it you don't want one," I inferred as I began to close the fridge door.

"No, no," he stammered. "I'll take one." I opened the door back up and grabbed another can.

"That's the spirit." I staggered toward him.

"Man, you look like…" I glared at him menacingly to let him know that I wasn't up for any games. He must've picked up on the vibe. "…like, you're doing good, especially since twenty minutes ago I finally got a visual confirmation that you were still on the face of this earth. That's crazy! The myth and the man are still alive."

"Thanks," I said glumly. "I'm trying." He began to do a 180-degree scan of my trailer. It was nothing short of a disaster. I had a waist-high mountain of empty beer cans in the kitchen. Used dishes and utensils spilled out of the sink, and there was a heap of dirty clothes laying next to my pullout bed. Not to mention the loud sound of flies buzzing by your ear or into a wall and a peculiar stench that I hadn't quite located the source of. Hell, I'll be the first to admit that I had given up on this dump.

"I like what you've done with the place," Dr. Tracz concluded while cracking open his beer.

"The maid got sick."

"You sure you didn't scare her away?" Dr. Tracz smiled meekly. I bit down on the inside of my right cheek. We just stared at each other for a minute. Our faces were frozen trying to remember the past while thinking of the next witty thing to say to break the tension. After moments of awkwardness, I just popped the question.

"So why are *you* here?" He took a painful swig of his beer.

"Welp, umm the police came by and told me that someone named Max Snyder wanted to see me...."

"Yeah, I did, but that was *months* ago when I first went into hiding. You're just now getting that message?" He took a deep breath before answering.

"No. I had gotten the message months ago, but to my recollection, I never knew a Max Snyder. So, truth be told, I thought it was a setup. Everyone at the office has been slightly paranoid, and on pins and needles since you mysteriously disappeared, Randy." I hadn't heard that name in forever.

"DON'T CALL ME RANDY!" I demanded in a way different tone.

"Well, whether you like it or not, that's your real name. I don't know what world you think you're in pal, but you need to snap out of this fantasy world!"

"RANDY IS DEAD!"

"How is he dead, when I am staring at him, right here, right now?" He glanced around my trailer again repugnantly.

"Look at this place man. You're living like a slob in this shoddy trailer park home." He held up the can, "drinking this nasty piss water. This isn't how millionaires are supposed to live." He had suddenly struck a nerve.

"You think I care for a *millisecond* about being millionaire! My mom's *dead*! My girlfriend is in a coma! AND THEY ARE STILL TRYING TO KILL ME.... Aarrghh! I don't want to be RANDY STASHI THE MOGUL ANYMORE!" I crumbled the beer can and threw it up against the wall. My eyes filled with tears as I thought about all that I had endured with the people closest to me hurt and the pain. I wiped my closed eyes with my fingers. Dr. Tracz' voice returned back to a soothing tone.

"Max...I have a real question for you. What *REALLY* happened that night after the award ceremony?" I leaned back against the wall and began to slump down until I was sitting on the floor. It took me a quiet moment as I tried to piece back together the events of that night. I had relived it in my nightmares so many times. I started describing my recollection of thoughts slowly.

"You really want to know?" I asked him to make sure.

"Yea, I do… When the lights blacked out, everything got fuzzy…"

"It was fuzzy because you had been drinking. We left and got about 10 minutes away when there were two black SUVs." I leaned my head back against the wall and stared at the ceiling as I recalled the description. "One of them imitated the police and tried to pull us over. When we rolled down the window, they opened fire." Dr. Tracz' jaw dropped as he listened intently. "We tried to get away, but they blocked us in, one in the front, and one in the back. We rammed the one in the front, and it flipped over. I got out and killed two of them instantly, but the third one…the third one is who I got to have a conversation with."

"What did he say?" Dr. Tracz questioned.

"He said, he didn't care if he died. He said more people were going to come and finish the job unless I stopped everything I was doing. Books, inventions, the whole entity."

"Ohhhh…" A low expression of understanding had come over Dr. Tracz. "I understand now. So that's why you went into hiding." I nodded my head slowly in agreement.

"What's the point of having success if it costs you everything that you ever loved?" A moment of stillness passed as Dr. Tracz peeked out the window.

"I've got to tell you something, Randy."

"Don't call me that!"

"I'm sorry—Max. They're trying to shut our company down."

"Who's they?"

"The same people from before, the government. They said we haven't relinquished our research or paid them their fees."

"Screw it! Let 'em shut it down. I don't care." Dr. Tracz exhaled with frustration.

"Is that how you feel about everything that we've built so far? All of the relentless hours of work that we put in, all of the people that depend on us, and you're ready to flush it down the toilet just like that?" He snapped his fingers when he said "that."

"I don't care, doctor. It doesn't make any bit of difference in my life." He glared at me with indignation.

"You selfish bastard, some people would sell their soul to be you and kill to have the gifts you have, and you're ready to sulk around for the rest of your life? Doesn't make any sense." I looked at him with narrow eyes.

"No one in their right mind would sell their soul to become Max Snyder." He shook his head no slowly in disbelief.

"You've lost it, my boy. You've really and truly lost it." I nodded my head yes as confirmation. "I'm sure whoever is chasing you Ran—, I mean Max, I'm sure that they would stop chasing you when they felt a sense of victory. I mean look at you. You're not even a tenth of the man that you used to be." Dr. Tracz began to put his hat back on his head. "You're pathetic, Max, just a solid waste of life." I smiled.

"I appreciate the compliment."

"And I don't appreciate how you've given up on everybody either. Our employees have families too. As a matter of fact, I don't think those supposed 'people' would even be chasing you anymore if they saw you like this."

"Yeah, they probably wouldn't be."

"You damn skippy they wouldn't be. Look, I'm going to do you a favor that will save your life."

"I'm listening...."

"I'm going to get you an interview with the world's most popular interviewer, so this madness can stop."

"Hmm… And who might that be?" I asked curiously. I always knew Dr. Tracz had a trick up his sleeve.

"Our old friend. The one and only...Porsha Gottfrey."

"No. Don't do that!" I pleaded

"I have to do it because I miss you and love you. You have to get your life back on track." I stood in the doorway to stop him from leaving.

"You think you're going to stop me? Ha!" I looked him in the eyes. It looked like he already had his mind set. He opened his arms and wrapped them around my body. He hugged me tightly, then he whispered, "I don't care what you say. You'll always be Randy Stashi to me. You're the greatest human being that I've ever met in my life and an inspiration to the world. You are the hope for the future."

His admiration had left me speechless. I didn't know what to say.

For the first time in a long time, I was really glad I wasn't dead.

Chapter 101

The old motel was dingy and reeked of cigarette smoke. I used to hate the smell of cigarette smoke, but now, it didn't bother me so much. The room was outdated, yet adequate for its intended use. The cameraman was setting up the lights and cameras while we were getting situated.

"You *sure* you didn't want to choose a different location?" said Porsha as she looked around in fear of roaches or disease popping out of the vents and windows.

"This is fine." I murmured. "It's not like I'm sleeping here." I had chosen this location for two reasons. Number one was I didn't want anyone to recognize this world-class socialite entering my trailer. A visit from her might blow my cover in the trailer park community. I had to keep this as low-key as possible. The second reason was… drumroll please… I didn't want Porsha to see my trailer. It was an unkempt filthy pigsty that only I had grown accustomed to. Truth be told, it looked kind of cozy when it was clean, but doing that required too much effort right now for me. I never realized how much Chloe kept the house together until now.

"It's quite a surprise seeing you. I still can't believe that I'm here with you, right now! It doesn't feel real."

"You're just yanking my chain, Porsha."

"No, I'm not. Believe it or not, a lot of people miss you, and have assumed something terrible has happened to you."

"Well, they're right. Something *terrible* has happened to me."

"Are you going to get into the juicy details during the interview?"

"Go to hell." Porsha smacked her lips and breathed heavily through her nostrils. I could tell she was getting agitated by my pissy attitude.

"What's your problem, Randy? I come allllll the way out here to who knows where we're in the *hell* at, risking our safety to help you recover from your fall from grace, and this is how you're talking to *ME*? I *reeeeally* don't have to be here, if you don't want me to." The cameraman stopped shuffling his things and stared directly at us. I could feel his pupils beaming at me, ready for an altercation to ensue.

"Wait, wait… You're trying to help *me*? No. You're trying to help yourself, and your show, to get better ratings by having the first exclusive interview with tech tycoon Randy Stashi, who mysteriously disappeared off the face of the earth, until now!"

"That's *not* true."

"Yes, it is true! You're just trying to use my misery to fuel your popularity and your ratings and have something to gossip about. You think I'm dumb?" Porsha turned her face up to me.

"Lookie here SNOBBY! It wasn't my freakin' idea to do this. I didn't want to come in the first place! You could've gotten abducted by aliens for all I care. The only reason why I am here…" I glanced away and down at the floor. I could hear the sincerity in her voice. "Look at me, Randy." I focused my gaze back on her. "…I repeat, the only *reason* I'm here is because your friend and partner, Dr. Tracz, begged me repeatedly for weeks on end. Man oh man that guy is persistent. Don't thank me. Thank him!" I could see she was being truthful. A good two minutes passed before I looked her back in the eyes. I kind of felt embarrassed.

"Well, if that's the case, I'm sorry for dragging you all the way out here. Interview over."

"*What?*" Porsha stammered.

"You heard me," I said gruffly. "Have a safe trip back to California. I'm out." I got up from the chair and made my way to the door.

"Stashi!" Porsha yelled behind me. I tuned her out. I had tried to make it work but low and behold, I was done. I really didn't even want to do this interview in the first place. All of this arguing had rubbed me the wrong way. "STASHI!" Porsha yelled out again. I could feel her footsteps thump closer toward me as I started fiddling with the deadbolts. Click. Click. I felt both her hands grab my wrist as she pulled me away from the door. I turned around and looked into her eyes. "Randy, if you don't want to do this interview because you think I'm doing it for my own personal gain or because Dr. Tracz had begged me to do it, that's fine. But think about this. What if Chloe pulls out of that coma? You gonna drag her back to your trailer in the desert and bologna sandwiches for the rest of your life? Huh? You can't hide forever, Randy. You need to do this for you. Do this for your family. Do this for the people after you. I know it's a longshot, but at least it's a chance. Then maybe they'll see what you've become and leave you alone. You're in bad shape right now. You're probably the least of their worries. But they need to see that!" I lowered my head and thought about the logic she had just explained. If and only if Chloe made it out of that coma would it all be worth it? She was right. I really didn't want to be cooped up eating sandwiches with a bunch of hillbillies for the rest of my life. I missed Chloe more than anyone or anything in this world. This was the very least I could do for her. I stood there silently, still weighing the pros and cons of going through with this. Porsha took my hand and kissed it softly.

"I know you can do this Randy, and I'm going to help you. Just think about Chloe." She continued to hold my hand as she led the way back to our chairs. As much as I didn't want to admit it, Porsha did make me feel comfortable. Almost like I was at home. "You ready to start filming, Joe?" she asked her cameraman.

"In about one minute…" he responded. He put on the stage lights, which damn near blinded me. She reached over and straightened out the collar of my shirt.

"Remember, Randy, you don't have to answer anything that you don't want to." I nodded my head in agreement. I was in a sudden daze. Being in front of these stage lights made me nostalgic. "Speak loudly and look at me, not the camera," she said refreshing my memory about the rules.

"Okay," I said in acknowledgment.

"Ready when you are," Joe called out. Porsha took a deep breath and fluttered her eyes in front of her pocket mirror. She put it away and then stared directly into the camera.

"Count me down," she instructed instinctively.

"Okay," Joe replied. "Three… two…one…"

"Hello, America! It's me, Porsha Gottfrey, and I'm coming to you today under different circumstances. I'm not here today as your usual host or spokesperson, but as a person that wants to help out a friend of mine. It's been months since his mysterious disappearance that left the whole world in shock. Today, I'm privileged to be right here, right now with one of the biggest minds and moguls of this millennium to catch up and get some answers. Mind you, this is his first interview where he will address anything he is comfortable with. Allow me to welcome my friend and special guest, Randy Stashi. Say hi to the world, Randy." I looked directly at the camera.

"Hi, world."

Aww, here we go again.

Chapter 102

"So here you are, the latest recipient of the world famous Hovell Peace Prize. I know you had to be excited and proud on your drive home, so proud that you never wanted to be seen again, which is hard to believe, unless…something else happened that night, something that we don't know about that fateful night in December." I took a deep breath and rubbed my eyes with my palms.

"Ohhh, Porsha, Porsha…" I responded in a low, slow tone. "I don't know what happened that night. It was like… It was like a scene from an action movie. I'm no Indiana Jones or James Bond. I'm just a regular guy. I blacked out mentally, and when I woke up, I realized that I wanted nothing more than to disappear. I had to go." Porsha stared at me intently with her chin resting on her face.

"So, you don't remember ANYTHING from that night?" I looked into her eyes. She kept digging but that night was a traumatic blur that needed to be left buried. I nodded my head no, as I stared at her with a blank expression.

"I don't," I replied firmly. Porsha didn't look satisfied with my answer, but took the hint and moved on.

"So, you're back now. What are your…"

"I'm NOT BACK now." I cut her off. "I'm STILL not all the way here. I've lost some of my most prized possessions, my loved ones. I'm still grieving, mourning and coping. I don't know how long the rehabilitation process is supposed to take, but I'm still depressed. I'm still fighting." Porsha nodded her head slowly empathizing with me.

"So, I see. Well, are there any future plans for Stashi Enterprises? I remembered you were gearing up for the sequel to your book The Stashi Life." I nodded my head no dramatically.

"No. There are no future plans for any books, products, inventions, or any of that. All I want to do is live in peace with my loved ones, and have my piece of mind. My focus has completely shifted. Things that once mattered don't mean anything to me anymore. All of the materialism is worthless. It doesn't make me happy. Being alive, seeing my loved ones alive, that's what makes me happy." Porsha sat still for a second soaking it all in.

"Well, I really want to thank you for sitting in and doing this interview with me today, Mr. Stashi. I know that this has been a tough ordeal for you."

"Extremely."

"Is there anything else that you'd like to say to the people before we sign off."

"Yeah. Thank you for all of your support and well wishing. And keep on smiling. Smile for people that can't smile, people like me." I waved the peace sign at the camera.

"Thank y'all…and cut." The cameraman clicked off the blinding lights and took off his headphones.

"Hang in there, Randy." Porsha looked sad. She got up from her chair, leaned over and hugged me. Her tender touch and sweet fragrance comforted me as I closed my eyes. She leaned back and stood straight up.

"Are we all done?" I asked impatiently.

"We sure are."

"Thanks, Porsha." I got up and began staggering toward the door with my cane in one hand.

"Oh Stashi, I almost forgot to tell you." I turned around slowly and looked at her. Mr. Foster has been trying to reach you forever about your pending battery case on that officer you punched." I exhaled heavily. I had completely forgotten all about that.

"Well, he contacted Carl, and it's some good news. The officer feels bad about what you've been through and wants to settle out of court."

"Everybody wants something. How much is he asking for?"

"$50,000." I scoffed at the audacity of this number.

"Well, look, tell him that I said, 'kick rocks.'" Porsha turned her face up.

"I'm not going to tell him that."

"Well, what are you going to tell him?"

"Randy, you broke his jaw. I mean, let's be real, he had to be hospitalized and had to take time off."

"Sooo…he shouldn't have been running his mouth when I was in mourning."

"I know. I know. But think about it though. Fifty grand is a small price to pay to avoid spending years in prison or decades of probation. Assaulting law enforcement doesn't blow over too well in this country. Remember that." I thought about what she had just said. She did have a good point.

"Think smart not with your heart, Stashi." She handed me her card. I looked at her and put it into my back pocket.

"I will," I announced.

I turned back around and headed out the door.

Chapter 103

"Hey Mister Max…after this, you wanna go play with snakes and find out which ones are poisonous?" Sammy smiled with a smile that only a mother could love. A combination of missing and chipped teeth left much to be explained. But hey, no one is perfect.

"HUT!" Sammy took off running. When he was about twenty-five yards away, I launched the football high in the air, to give him time to catch it before it landed. It hit him in the chest before his elbows clamped down on it securing it into place.

"*TOUCHDOOOWN!*" I yelled with all of the wind in my lungs. I was already exhausted from the physical aspect of playing catch football with the neighbor's kid. He ran back excitedly toward me.

"I don't do well with snakes Sammy, especially poisonous ones…."

"Awww. They're fun, Mr. Max. You just can't make them *maaaaad*." I had to hand it to him. The kid had big kahunas for playing fearlessly with dangerous exotic animals. He wasn't accepting no for an answer from me either.

"Maybe later," I answered, just to give him some hope.

"Okaaay," he answered unpleased. "…But you can't wait for too long. My cousin, Dirty, is coming to sleep over later."

"Dirty?" I repeated curiously. "Quick question. Why do they call him Dirty?"

"Because soap makes him sneeze unless it's the special kind."

"Oh Gawd." I tried not to laugh but a mental picture popped into my head. These kids out here were entertaining enough to be on reality television.

"I'll let you meet him when he gets here, Mr. Max." I don't know why Sammy called me by my name every time, but it was a constant reminder of what I had become. Just then, a brand-new Dodge Charger turned into the community with its lights on. I had never seen this car before, so I ran inside to grab my handgun.

"Get inside your house, Sammy, and lock the door!" I advised in a serious tone. When I was in the house, I closed and locked my door, and began peeking through the blinds. "Keep going. Keep going…" I mumbled under my breath as I hoped the Charger kept driving by my trailer. But it didn't keep going. It moved slower and slower, eventually coming to a halt within mere feet of my door. My heart began to race. Adrenaline rushed through my body. An unknown vehicle, parked in front of my house. I could sense danger was in the air. I already had the handgun, but I whipped out the shotgun for extra measure. Gently, I pulled down the blinds again with one finger. "Open up the door. Open up the door you bastard," I whispered to myself. If anyone came bringing trouble, I was ready to put them into the ground with just like I did their other friends. My hands and fingers began to tremble with anxiety. The car door opened slowly, and a man in a cowboy hat got out looking confused. He squinted at my door trying to read the address, and then looked at the neighbor's address for confirmation. I didn't recognize his face immediately, but I did recognize his movements. He always had a weird way of stretching his neck, like a linebacker before the snap. I opened the door.

"Chazz?" I yelled out. He smiled when he saw me standing at the top of the stairs. He looked slightly alarmed when he saw my weapons.

"RANDY?" he called out. I put one finger over my lips.

"Shhhh…" He began to chuckle.

"Maan, what in the *hell* are you doing all the way out here? This ain't BALLIN!" I began to laugh. Hearing his voice made me relax. I walked down the stairs and extended my hand. He met me in the middle and wrapped his around me giving me a tight hug.

"I missed you, playa."

"I missed you too." He backed up and looked me up and down, assessing how I had changed. He patted the back of his hand against my belly.

"Picking up some weight, I see."

"It's just beer weight. I could sweat it out if I wanted," I explained nonchalantly.

"Suuuuuurrrreeee." he responded unconvinced. We began to walk into my trailer.

"Want something to drink? Water? Beer? Juice?"

"I'll take a beer please."

"Same 'ole Chazz." We had only taken a couple of steps inside when it seemed like horror froze Chazz's face in disgust."

"What's wrong?" I asked obliviously.

"There's no way in hell you can be living like this." He put his shirt over his face.

"What's wrong?"

"WHAT IS THAT GOD AWFUL SMELL?" I sniffed the air loudly.

"Mmmm... I don't smell anything."

"Yo bro, I'm getting nauseous!" He scrambled back out of the house, coughing and wheezing. "Let's go somewhere else!" he called out between gasps. He bent over and started making loud vomiting noises.

"Where to?"

"A park, a lake, a stream, *anywhere* but in *there*!" I grabbed the twelve-pack and locked the door.

"You always did whine like a little two year old. Let's go!"

"Ahhh..." he grunted. "My eyes *still* are burning from that odor!"

We hopped in his car and drove off.

Chapter 104

"So, I see. Well, are there any future plans for Stashi Enterprises? I remembered you were gearing up for the sequel to your book The Stashi Life." The replay of the interview played on a huge flat screen in front of a room full of cabinet members and council advisors. The boss stood at the head of the long table. His back was turned to his cohorts as he rubbed his thick gray mustache and stared contently at the television.

"No. There are no future plans for any books, products, inventions or any of that. All I want to do is live in peace with my loved ones, and have piece of mind. My focus had completely shifted. Things that once mattered didn't mean anything to me anymore. All of the materialism was worthless. It didn't make me happy. Being alive, seeing my loved ones alive, that's what makes me happy." The boss clicked off the television screen and turned toward his audience of cohorts slow.

"Well, well…it looks as if our friend Stashi has had a change of heart after all." You could hear the tension release in the room as many people let off quiet grins and smiles. "Rest in peace to those who are no longer with us, but they did not die in vain. Even though they didn't complete the mission, we've accomplished the same result. We will keep this organization alive and thriving at all costs. Any interference will be annihilated." Just then, applause filled the room of the undisclosed location. Suddenly, a hand shot up from a stone-faced older woman.

"With all due respect, boss, what if this is just some little ploy conjured up to keep us off his back?" Upon hearing her question, the boss began pondering while gently rubbing his chin. He put the TV back on, rewound the interview and hit pause.

"Look at our subject!" he said while pointing to Stashi. "He's lost it. He's lost his hair, his health, his ambition, his M.O., and most importantly, his fans. He'll never have the power he once had to sway the majority. He even said it himself. He has nothing left to contribute to society. He's just going to wither away, living in the past of a memory he once was.…" Her hand shot up again in the room full of twelve people.

"… But shouldn't we just kill him, and get it over with?" The boss laid his palms flat on the table and leaned in.

"We could, but to relocate him again and pull off that mission would just be a waste of resources. We've accomplished our goal of knocking him off his high horse and thwarting his powerful influence. The people can no longer and won'trust him. He's weak. That interview was the proof. Plus, we have bigger fish to fry. Waaay bigger fish to fry." The boss laughed. "That sucker isn't even worth mentioning anymore compared to our new threats!" She nodded her head slowly as if she began to understand. "And now let's resume our meeting..." The boss smiled as he cracked his neck back and forth. The organization had fought so hard to be an unstoppable world force that no one could challenge. All threats would be decimated accordingly.

Another one bit the dust.

Chapter 105

I reached over and grabbed two beers from the twelve-pack. I tossed Chazz one and cracked open mine, taking a cold refreshing gulp from it. He and I stared at the sun as it began to settle behind the wide reflective lake. I picked up a rock while leaning on my cane, and skipped it across the water. It made gentle ripples disrupting the smooth surface. I looked at Chazz as he gazed deeply at the sun as if he was contemplating something that required intense thought.

"Whatcha thinking about?" I asked, interrupting the solitude that separated us. He took a slow swig of his beer before answering.

"I don't know. My brain is still frazzled from that stench inside your crib. Dear God, what was that?"

"Quit playing," I responded solemnly. He knew how to wear a joke out.

"No human should ever live in those conditions."

"You finished?" He began grunting heavily through his nose.

"I think it burned the inside of my nostrils." He started pinching and wiggling his nose from side to side.

"Yo, knock it off playa!"

"What? You asked me what I was thinking about." I sighed. Another long moment of silence passed as I skipped another rock on the lake. It bounced, one…two…three…an amazing four times. I still had skills from being a young Boy Scout.

"What are you thinking about, Randy?" Chazz asked. I took a deep breath of the serenity.

"How soothing nature is. How, if a rock moves fast enough and hits the water at the right angle it can skip along the water like it's concrete."

"Yep. It's only when it slows down that it falls in," he added. Chazz tilted his can all the way up to the sky draining the last drops of his beverage.

"You still doing taxes for the company?"

"As long as y'all keep paying me, I will."

"How we looking?"

"More prosperous than ever. You have some real trustworthy people holding down the fort in your absence."

"That's good to hear. I figured if they sabotaged their own farm, they couldn't reap the harvest."

"Your hypothesis held true. Toss me another beer." I reached down and pitched him one. "So, what's your plan, bro? You can't just live out here like a bum in the woods forever." I glared at the sun as if it had all the answers.

"I don't know man, really. Just stay alive, I guess." You could hear the snakes hiss in the trees as dusk approached.

"What's the point of staying alive, if you aren't going to do anything with your life?" One thing that I hated, but loved about Chazz was his dagger-like honesty. I said nothing. "You know when I first heard about your incident, I was sad. I thought you had died. But then I started piecing together that there was no body, no funeral or memorial, so it was always in the back of my mind that you were laying low somewhere."

"Why did you come out here? Wait. How'd you even know I was I here? I'm under a new alias sheltered by witness protection."

"Well, for one, I came out here because I saw how lifeless you looked on the interview. I mean, you looked borderline suicidal. And two, your friend Dr. Tracz insisted consistently to come out here to cheer you up."

"Wait. How does he even know that we know each other?"

"Don't you remember, bonehead? I'm the one who drove you to meet him when we were at FVU."

"Oh yeaaah…." I chuckled. "That part."

"You've got to get back on your feet man. Nobody's going to feel sorry for your situation, but you."

"Naw bro. I'm out of it. I don't want to do anything else." Chazz picked up a rock and flung it like he was attempting a buzzer beater Hail Mary. "So, you mean to tell me that all of the years and sweat that you've put into building this elaborate and grandiose company, you're just to walk away from it?"

401

"People change, man. Priorities change. I used to be so concerned about obtaining wealth, now my focus has shifted to solely surviving.

"This is sad, man. This doesn't even sound remotely like the Stashi I used to know. The Stashi that I used to know was a fighter, a motivated, driven leader always overcoming a challenge. You remember when we were kids and you wanted that PlayStation 2?"

"Yeah. Vaguely." I really didn't remember the story at all.

"Your mom wouldn't get it for you; so, you went door to door to everyone in the neighborhood and offered your carwashing and landscape services." Now that he mentioned it, I did remember. I remembered sweating so much when I came home my Mom asked me if I went swimming without a towel.

"Ha ha…. Good times."

"Or what about that time in high school when we played football, and coach Whitforde made you a lineman?"

"Oh yeah."

"You begged him every day to play running back, and even learned the plays as a running back before the coach gave in and finally said yes."

"Yeah, I did do that," I recalled smiling.

"And think about what your mom would say." I cut him off immediately.

"She's dead, man."

"I know she died, and I'm deeply sorry for your lost. She was almost like my mom too, ya know? But if she was still alive, do you think she would be impressed or proud of your newfound vagrant bummy lifestyle?" I grew silent. Mentioning my deceased mother would forever be a tender and touchy subject. I knew she was smiling down on me. Or was she? I just stood there quietly reflecting. "No. She wouldn't be happy Randy. She would want you to pick yourself back up and get back to changing the world like you're supposed to be. What's the point of living if you're not really living?" I exhaled heavily. Chazz was right like always. I had to pick myself up and keep fighting.

"You can do this, Randy. You're built for it. I know it in my heart. While others may cower, you have the courage of steel and a heart of gold." I nodded my head slowly back and forth feeling some sense of confidence.

"Maybe you're right bro." Chazz lifted himself up off the ground and dusted off his hands. He walked toward me and stuck out his fist.

"I know I'm right." He responded without hesitation. I looked at his extended hand and then his face.

"Thank you." I bumped my fist into his and then got closer and gave him a hug.

It was a quiet ride back to the trailer park. Sammy, his mom, and I'm guessing his cousin were sitting around a dim campfire. Chazz parked the car, and we just sat there, soaking everything in.

"You spending the night?"

"Hellll to the *naw*! That stench from your trailer has the potential to kill all of my remaining brain cells. I'm still slightly dizzy from the earlier tour."

"It's not that bad." I shrugged it off. Chazz's face grew very serious as he turned down the music.

"*Bro*! You *have* to clean this up! No *human* should live like that! Remember, cleanliness is next to Godliness.

"All right all right, I got you. So, I guess this is goodbye...."

"Naw man. It's more like a see you later."

"Cool." We hugged each other one more time. I exited his vehicle and waved as he drove off. Just then, Sammy and his other buddy came running up to me.

"Who was that, Mister Max?"

"Just an old friend."

"Oooh," he croaked, slowly understanding. "Hey Mister Max, this is my cousin, Dirty. Dirty, this is Mister Max." The little boy extended his hand open palm for a handshake. However, after quickly remembering his soap allergies, I extended my fist to give him a fist bump.

"Nice to meee—" I was in the middle of my sentence when his shirt caught my eye. There it was. A black Get Stashi t-shirt with the pig on it. I was smiling at the same time.

"Where did you get that shirt from?" I demanded.

"All of the kids wear it at my school, Mister Max. My mom ordered it online for me. They say it means get money!" He smiled while rubbing his thumbs against his middle and index fingers. I suddenly surged with excitement. I picked him up and started shaking him up and down. Sheer joy had my adrenaline pumping as I began to laugh hysterically.

"Get Stashi! Get Stashi! Get STAAA-SHI! HA HA!" I chanted loudly. Seeing that shirt teleported me back down memory lane. Dirty looked terrified as I manhandled him. I suddenly became motivated and inspired all over again. It was amazing that people were still excited about our work. All wasn't lost! The shaken up kid had a terrified look on his face as I placed him back on the ground carefully and hobbled back quickly inside of my trailer.

"For some reason, people go crazy over this shirt..." I overheard Dirty say to Sammy through my cracked window.

"I don't know what it is about it...."

Chapter 106

I started the day bright and early with renewed energy and spirits. This was the best that I had felt in it seemed like years. My first objective of the day was cleaning out my trailer. One thing that I had learned in life was the hardest part about doing something was thinking about it. The easiest thing about doing something was actually doing it. I separated my clothes into two piles. One pile was full of clothes that needed to be washed. The other pile was filled with clothes that needed to be destroyed. How could I allow myself to live like this for so long? After I cleaned up my "bedroom," I moved into the kitchen. One thing was for sure, it did smell like an uncleaned barn with farm animals. I threw all of the trash on the bed of my Ford pick up and emptied it at the nearest dumpster. When I came back, I showered and began to think of how I was going to get back on my feet. Well, first things were first. I would have to call off the dogs, meaning addressing the issue that Dr. Tracz had brought to my attention head on. I sat down and began to ponder an escape plan where we could all have our cake and eat it too. That's when it hit me. They were concerned with our growing influence and technology and wanted money. If we paid the money to get them out of our hair, we still needed a place where they couldn't disturb us, a place where we could test and develop our inventions away from the general population. Anything we built could be emulated and broadcasted unintentionally to the rest of the world. However, if we controlled the territory and manipulated regulations, we could protect ourselves from any invaders. I began to get excited as I plotted. We needed our own space where we could work and live in peace. I began to draw up the proposal to be sent to our headquarters. It looked good and sounded even better. I knew the agency would agree once they saw the amount of "leave us alone" money they would be receiving from us each year. I began to finalize the document when I heard a tapping at my door. I looked through the peephole. It was the landlord. He was chubby, with a scraggly beard and a thick mustache. He had on some dirty overalls with his chest hair protruding. I hated when he stopped by because it meant rent was due. I never kept track of what day it was. Hell, I didn't need to or want to.

Tap! Tap! Tap!

I opened the door slowly.

"Good day, Mr. Snyder...." When he began, I frowned. I wasn't in the mood for the pleasantries, and he could sense it. "I'm actually here for two reasons."

"I'm listening," I responded. "What's the first?"

"Well, as you very well may know, your rent is *late!*" he gruffed in his country twang.

"Oh yeah. About that..." I murmured seeming suddenly uninterested.

"I don't see why you always pay your rent late and make me drive out here to come get it. Do you even have a job?"

"Honestly..." I stated in a matter-of-fact tone. "I'm working on getting one, but the rent late isn't a question of money. It's more a question of effort. Why go through the hassle of having to travel into town, get a money order, get a stamp and then mail it, when I can get world class service and get it picked up right from my doorstep?" I could see he didn't find the humor.

"Well, if you're going to keep relying on home pickup service then I suggest that you find another place to live." I began to chuckle.

"You know, I was thinking that too. Do you think you could pass along a message?" He looked at me unentertained.

"Depends on the message."

"I looked up owns this land and come to find out, they own a huge amount of land out here."

"Go on."

"Well, could you tell your boss or the owner, that I'm interested in buying ten square miles of his land. We're looking to relocate." The landlord Billy chuckled in disbelief.

"That's over 3,000 acres fancy pants. That's in excess of nine figures. You got that kind of money?" I had looked at him with a stone-cold gaze while he was laughing. His chuckle came to a slow, quiet halt when he saw I was deadly serious.

"I got people, you just worry about relaying the message," I started looking nonchalantly at my fingernails, "...it's not about how much I have, it's about how much I can raise, Billy." Billy nodded his head slowly trying to analyze how serious I was about my proposition. He was in disbelief.

"Get to it! We need to move quickly!" I started laughing.

"Awwwright..." he mumbled slowly while staring me up and down as he walked backward. I was just about to shut the door when I had just remembered.

"Oh, and Billy..." I yelled. "What was that other thing you were going to tell me?" He turned back around when he opened the door to his suburban.

"Oh yeah, Mr. Snyder...the hospital has been trying to reach you. It's about a lady close to you."

"Who?" I asked curiously. I didn't want to jump to conclusions.

"*Barbara McCrawton.*"

It felt like my heart had stopped.

Chapter 107

I finished the proposal and stuffed it into a manila envelope. I was kind of confused about what speed I should move. Part of me wanted to rush at the speed of light to see the love of my life. The other part of me was lethargic, dreading the possibility that the hospital didn't call to deliver good news. I was hoping and praying for the best, but I was prepared for the worst. Before I visited the hospital, I made sure that I mailed the envelope to Dr. Tracz with specific instructions on how to correspond with this agency. I sat in the hospital parking lot, grooming myself in the rearview mirror as if I was preparing myself for a first date. It almost felt like one. I'll be the first to admit how nervous I was. I didn't even know if Chloe, I mean Barbara, would be able to recognize me with my newer less than stellar image. I straightened out my beard with my fingernails and sprayed on some cheap cologne.

"Welp! Let's do it!" I clapped and rubbed my hands together. I entered the hospital and was directed to the sixth floor, Barbara McCrawton. The nurse who was in the room treated me like a lesser priority when I revealed that I was just her boyfriend. I guess boyfriend doesn't wield the same influence as the title of husband or brother. It's almost like a make believe or wishy-washy claim. I vowed to myself at that instant that I would do something to change that when the time was right. I looked at her while she was sleeping and my pulse began to skyrocket. Even in the hospital with IV tubes coming out every which way, she was as beautiful as ever, as beautiful as I remembered. I became breathless as I grabbed her hand tenderly and began to slowly rub her forehead. I turned back around and called out to the nurse as she was halfway out the door.

"How is she doing, nurse?" She peeked her head back in the doorway with a gloomy expression on her face.

"The doctor will be in here shortly to explain her status," she said as her head disappeared and the door silently shut.

"Explain her status?" I repeated to myself quietly. My mind began to race as I began to think. What could this possibly mean? I started examining all of the monitors beside her. Beep. Beep. Well, she was breathing, and her heart was beating, so I eliminated that possibility from my head. But what if she was brain dead and we were just waiting on the word? The speculation alone was going to kill me. I resolved that the best thing to do was not think at all. I pulled up a chair and began to sing her some Michael Jackson. She always loved Michael Jackson.

"Gonna make a change, ugh...for once...."

I stopped singing when the door cracked open, and a lady with short gray hair, a stethoscope and a white lab coat walked in.

"Don't stop singing. I like that song," she insisted. I smirked halfway at her suggestion. "You must be her boyfriend, Max Snyder."

"In the flesh."

"I know you get this a lot, but you look a lot like Randy...." I nodded my head at the ground.

"Please doctor, if I had a dollar for every time I heard that I could move out of my trailer park." She grinned at my revelation and then focused back on her clipboard.

"We have desperately been trying to reach you, Mr. Snyder, Barbara has been..." I closed my eyes crossed my fingers. "...recovering wonderfully!"

"YES!" I stood up and gave the doctor a bear hug lifting her off the ground. Her face was red as I set her back on the ground.

"Oh, my!" she said straightening out her glasses. "I wasn't expecting that, but listen, her memory is very shoddy." I stopped smiling.

"Shoddy? What do you mean, shoddy?"

"I mean that after being in a coma for months, she doesn't remember too much, where she's from, what she's doing...."

"Does she remember me?" The doctor sucked air slowly through her teeth.

"There's a strong possibility that she doesn't." Her words knocked the air out of my lungs as I slowly began to feel a deep sadness. I walked over to her side.

"Baby, baby, baby...it's me..." I said as I began to hold her hands and stroke her hair again. As I looked at her lying helpless, I felt a tear roll down my cheek. The sharp, witty woman that had my heart might be gone forever.

"Is... Is, is this *permanent?*" I stammered as I felt the doctor's hand rest on the ball of my shoulder. My brain wasn't functioning properly.

"I've seen a multitude of cases where the patient recovers one hundred percent."

"So, it's temporary?" She inhaled through her teeth again.

"But I've also seen cases where memories have disappeared forever. All I can say is take it one step at a time. Be grateful she's alive, and reminisce with her as much as possible. Hopefully, she'll start clicking."

"How do I do that?" I asked eagerly.

"Pictures, aromas, anything that can be brought up slowly helps cure amnesia, *hopefully.*" I took a slow deep breath.

"When will she be awake?"

"At any time. She's probably just taking a light nap."

"If you have any more questions, ask the nurse, or call for me."

"Thanks, doc." She quietly exited the room as I sat there solemnly next to Barbara. I slowly began squeezing her hand gently to wake her up. She groaned at a low volume as her eyes began to flutter open. I figured I could use her real name since we were in private. "Chloe... Chloe... Wake up; it's me." I whispered to her. She took a deep breath and scrunched her face as if it hurt her to speak. Her mouth began to move, and her words came out slowly and painfully.

"Who's Chloe? And who are *you?*" I bowed my head in disbelief. She looked at me clueless like a complete stranger.

"If you don't tell me who you are, I'm going to call the nurse to make you *leave....*"

I bit down on the inside of my cheek while nodding my head no. *Despicable. This whole situation is despicable.*

Chapter 108

Even though she was alive, there was a different person in my girlfriend's body. Reminding Chloe of her past was a frustratingly, painstaking exercise. Everything we shared, gone, not to mention how difficult it was trying to get her to remember things that I was trying to forget. Her health was slowly progressing, and that's what rejuvenated my spirit about her situation. I didn't know to what extent she had deteriorated; so, I resolved that the best solution was to keep her under medical watch until her memory was back up to speed. But who knew how long that would be? I had become a tenant at the motel across the street. It wasn't extravagant in any sense either. It was more like the Bates Motel. I only preferred it for two reasons. It was quiet and low-key.

"Your name is Chloe Dorr. Don't you remember we went to FVU together?" It was tricky using her real name and her protection name.

"What's FVU?" I had grown way too tiresome of the tedious and monotonous process of questioning her day in and day out. It was frustrating, to say the least, having shared so many magical moments with your significant other, who happens not to remember a thing. Sad, sad story, but I guess it could've been worse. I vowed to stay by her side though. She was the closest thing that I had, to my past life. I bought a laptop so that we could watch all of our favorite movies together with the hopes that something would click. It was cool to wander online too and catch up on everything I had missed.

"Hey, Max!" she would exclaim as I entered her room for the day. Her greeting was so bittersweet, sweet because she was alive and her smile could light up the darkest of rooms, bitter because my name wasn't Max. I tried so hard to look like the old me in her room, but truth be told, I barely even recognized who I was staring at in the mirror. But something else began to consume my time.

I became curious about how a city thrives. Why were some cities booming and some cities ghost towns? I started revisiting theories and ideals that we explored for our graduation project at FVU. Cities thrive based on businesses that keep the currency in circulation. Imports hurt growth, especially if domestic substitute goods are available. Excessive taxes could also cripple an industry. I wanted to build something that was ahead of its time, a place that was conducive to innovation and invention, that could never be intruded on. I was still slightly paranoid after the way they muscled us at Stashi Enterprises.

411

We would have to be secluded from interference and protected from ridiculous tariffs. Stashi Enterprises was designed for the future. Its original inspiration came from a problem. As long as we continued to solve problems creatively through technology we would be the world's front runners. We could also thrive potentially by only doing business among ourselves, like empires used to. If our currency never leaks out of our circulation, our buying power could be tremendous. In the midst of mapping out the blueprints for this capitalistic utopia, I started to finally feel alive again. I could feel my brain sparking again like it had once upon a time.

One day, I had a crazy idea. Hell, at this point I was willing to try anything. I sprayed Chloe's old favorite perfume "Romance" all around the room. I stood still and took a deep whiff. A calming wave of nostalgia came over me as all of the fond memories of Chloe and me popped into my head. It felt amazing. It reminded me of so many places, especially my college years. No response from Chloe. I went back to my laptop. After my daily online routine of checking the news and my favorite blog sites, I stumbled into my old company email. Most of it was junk mail and spam, but there was one email that stood out in particular. It was a couple of weeks old from Dr. Tracz. I had become increasingly giddy and excited as I read it. It read:

"Dear Stash,

I don't know what exactly you wrote, but the government has accepted your proposal."

"AHHHH, YESSS! YESSS!" I exclaimed. "STASHI IS BACK! STASHI ENTERPRISES IS BACK!" I couldn't help myself. I was jumping up and down in the room like a lunatic. Chloe woke up alarmed. I looked at her and started apologizing for my behavior. She started sniffing the air and then looked at the room with a panicked look on her face. I instantly rushed to her side and began stroking her arm.

"It's all right, baby. It's me, Max." I whispered calmly. She looked at me confused while nodding her head no.

"Max...? Your name's not Max, baby..." She spoke very slowly and softly. "It's Randy Sta-" I shushed her immediately and kissed her lightly on the forehead and rang the buzzer for the nurse.

That was our cue. We had officially overstayed our welcome.

412

Chapter 109

They say that you never realize how much you miss something until it is gone. I never knew how much that woman named Chloe Dorr meant to me until she was almost taken from me. Now that she was back, I couldn't stop smiling. I couldn't stop singing. I couldn't stop staring at her. I always thought that Romeo was stupid for killing himself when he thought Juliet was gone. But it was only now that I could empathize with him. Chloe couldn't believe how my look had transformed or my lavish living conditions.

"Where are we?" she would ask.

"Somewhere safe," I would always respond. I had no intention to return to the city we called home, no intentions to reinsert myself into society, no intentions to be back in harm's way. My only hope was that Chloe didn't want to return either. That would be idiotic considering what we've both been through.

"So how long do you plan on living here or living like this?" she asked. I was slightly embarrassed but also appreciated that I was still above ground.

"As long as it takes. At least we're out of harm's way."

"We can't live our lives in fear, ya know?"

"Yeah, I do freaking know, but we can't live our lives in a casket either. I can't believe this is coming from you of all people! The woman who has just woke up from nearly a year-long coma is ready to forget everything that happened." She stopped talking and gave me a deathly stare. Usually, I found her seriousness was sexy. Today, however, was different.

"This is like jail. There's barely room to breathe. There's no room to stretch. Hell, this place is barely big enough to think in!"

"Shuush! Okay! I've heard enough. Think of it like this. You're on a country getaway. It won't last forever, but who knows when it will end. You're going to have to get used to it for the time being. Leaving this place is a death wish. Hell, you haven't even been going by your alias name, Barbara McCrawton."

"But I'm not Barbara McCrawton. I'm Chloe...."

413

"No! Out here you're Barbara McCrawton, no questions asked! This isn't optional, babe. These are mandatory precautions designed to keep us safe." Chloe looked at me and sat down defeated. She put her hands over her face and started crying.

"They're going to kill us, Randy. I know it. They're going to kill us."

"NO! THEY'RE NOT GOING TO KILL US! NO! THEY! AREN'T!" She was tearing up. As the tears were streaming down, she removed her hand and looked me square in the eye.

"WHY?"

"Because I have you, and with us together we're going to keep fighting. I think the threat is over, but I'm not sure."

"I don't know how long I can take this."

"You're going to have to take it as long I can take it."

"Why you say that?"

"Because there's this question that I should've asked you a long time ago, but I never did because I was afraid."

"Afraid?... Elaborate."

"Well, I was afraid of dragging you through the mud with me, but now that we're ducked off in a remote location with fictitious names, I know you can handle it."

"Well, I am a tough woman. I was the only girl among my brothers in my family."

"I know. And that's why I wanted to ask you this...."

"Ask me what?"

"Barbara, no, Chloe Dorr...I love you with all of my heart and soul. And I don't see myself trusting or building with another woman the way I've already built with you. Can we take the next step of life together? Can we continue this journey forever? Will you marry me?"

She turned her head sideways, and her eyelids began to flutter. Her eyes lit up, red and wet from the tears. She stopped sobbing momentarily.

"Are you serious, babe?"

Chapter 110

The ceremony wasn't anything too extravagant. Sammy's mom did most of the cooking; so, the wedding was set up in front of her trailer. The priest of the ceremony was a friend of Sammy's mom, so we actually got a discounted rate. Hey, I wasn't complaining. It wasn't too big either, mainly people from the trailer park. I had seen them around but never cared too much to pursue a conversation. Honestly, I think they were there just for the free food. I scanned the serene scenery while the preacher was talking, and I felt at peace. This felt right. As I looked at Chloe in her dress, I knew I had made the right decision. This occasion was long overdue.

"*Ahem!*" the preacher cleared his throat, I guess in an attempt to wake me up from my daydream. Everything felt like it was moving in slow motion. This was really happening.

"I *do!*" I said firmly. Chloe looked at me with a scolding look. I guess she wasn't feeling her fiancé daydreaming during the vows. It's all good. She knew how epic this was for me too.

"Now, you may kiss the bride," the preacher commanded.

I grabbed her face slowly and softly and looked into her eyes while balancing on my crutch.

"We did it," I whispered. She smiled so hard it moved my palms that I had placed on her cheek. I kissed her slowly and succulently. She tasted like sweet fruit. She smelled so warm and inviting. I realized that I had truly lucked out to be able to call this woman my wife. I was blessed to have a second chance. This was the official stamp so the world would finally know about my other half—or maybe let my other half know that she was my world. Yeah, it might put a damper on my female fanbase, but they're going to eventually accept it. Life is too short to waste any more time. I could hear the sparse clapping from our small audience cheering us on. I walked her to an open area.

"Hit it!" I signaled Sammy to start playing the music. It was one of our favorite songs, Whitney Houston, *I Wanna Dance with Somebody*. We stepped and tangoed our way through that whole song with smiles. I did the best I could since I was working off one crutch. Times like this made me miss my Hoverfoot. As I watched her dance fluidly, she looked different to me now. I guess it was because we had taken our love to the next level. She was actually my wife now. After the dance, we sat at the newlywed table and cut the cake. Everyone came by to congratulate us and get a piece. It was a red velvet layer cake cooked by Sammy's mom. She had really outdone herself with all of the food.

"Congratulations you two! I'm so happy for y'all!" Sammy's mom exclaimed as she passed by.

"Thanks!" acknowledged Chloe.

"I don't know *how* you whipped all of this up…" I pointed at the food. "…but it tastes like it's out of heaven!" I complimented.

"Y'all are so welcome. I really enjoyed watching your wedding. True love is a beautiful thing. Plus, it really gave something for all of us to do today. Sometimes, it gets a little boring around here."

"I know. I know," I remarked. She giggled.

"Well, I'll leave you lovebirds alone. Let me know if you need me to cook you anything else. Okay?"

"Gotcha!" I responded. She was such a sweet lady who really helped me out when Chloe wasn't around. A true friendship with someone of the opposite sex is priceless. We ate and mingled a little bit more when an unfamiliar gentleman walked up to our table. Danger was never a thought too far away for me. I moved my hand closer to my waist.

"Hiii! Mr. Snyder…."

"Yes…?" I said slow and cautiously. I don't know why I was at attention, but I was. Maybe it was because I had never seen him before, or maybe it was because he wasn't dressed or looked like the normal hillbillies that lived here.

"First off, congratulations on your wedding. Can I speak to you in private?" My suspicions were starting to become real.

"Umm… I'm not trying to be rude, but now's really not a good time…" I looked around, "…if you know what I mean."

"I totally understand, but I'm not here to waste your time, and I hope you're not here to waste mine." Now, he had put me into full alert mode.

"Huh?" I didn't know what he was talking about.

417

"Did you inquire about buying a vast amount of land in this area semi-recently?" I had to think about what he was saying. This conversation had just come out of the blue.

"Umm… Now that I think about it, yeah…."

"Well…I'm the owner, Rudy Tee." He extended his hand for a handshake. That gesture put me at ease a notch or two.

"Pleasure to meet you, Max Snyder." I had become a little annoyed at him interrupting our moment to discuss business. "Look, umm Mister Rudy Tee, now is not a good time for this…."

"I totally understand, but I want you to know something."

"And what's that?"

"I'm a very important person. I don't play games, and I don't waste time. I'm not trying to sell the plot of land you are asking about at all, not to anybody. But I'm all about growth and prosperity. I want to hear your plans for the land, and if I like it, I might just give it to you." I looked at him crazy. Give me all of those acres, that sounded way too good to be true, like a dream come true. I was astonished.

"You really might give me, Max Snyder, that vast amount of land depending on what I want to do with it?"

"No. I might give it to you because I am eager to see what you are going to do with it…." He leaned in closer so that he was practically whispering in my ear.

"*I know who you are, Mister Stashi…. I just realized it about five minutes ago.*"

Chapter 111

"You want to go another round?" Chloe looked at me with the facial expression that said, "Are you serious?" I just smiled.

"Let me get some water first. You're still a real *animal*. You know that?" She got up, and I watched her butt bounce on the way to the kitchen. We had been fornicating nonstop for a week now. Even though we didn't leave the city (or country rather) for our honeymoon, we didn't need to because we stayed locked up in the trailer. We could've easily gone away and done something on the high end, but we still had to remain low-key. Either way, we were both happy. We had already seen a lot of things, and after a super close brush with death, we appreciated life more than any type of empty luxury.

Our wedding gifts included a lot of cookware, but also a good amount of love toys. We were handcuffing, whipping, blindfolding and vibrating our passion for each other. Even though we had been having sex since college, this week had escalated to a whole new plateau of freakiness. It had gotten so intense that we had a "Do Not Disturb" sign unless you were bringing food. I just prayed and hoped I didn't impregnate her because it had gotten really wild, rough and messy. Eventually, I would have to wake up from this dream and figure everything out, but for the time being, ignorance was bliss.

"Can you grab me a water too, babe? And don't forget about Chuck either..." I yelled from the bed. He barked when I said his name. We had to stay hydrated. This was a never-ending exercise.

"Su—"

Knock! Knock!

"Ahhhhhhhhh..." I groaned. Chloe ran back toward the bedding area to grab some clothes. "Damn, babe, I should've taken you somewhere 'cause these country bumpkins don't understand the meaning of DO NOT DISTURB or HONEYMOON!" Chloe started picking up random articles of clothing, and I put back on my underwear and a shirt. "WHO IS IT?" I yelled.

Knock! Knock!

Now I was truly getting pissed off. The combination of loud banging and neglecting our "On our honeymoon" sign made my blood boil. No respect.

419

They give me no respect! I grabbed my shotgun from next to the door. I took it off safety and cocked it.

Chick chick!

I wanted to inform whoever was behind the door, that I wasn't in the mood for guests right now. I swung the door open and pointed it up. My jaw dropped to the ground like an anvil. I stumbled backward a little. I put down the gun and picked up one of my crutches. I came back to the doorstep and started moving down the steps toward the massive crowd. There were so many familiar faces. I just surveyed the scene from left to right. There were all my old colleagues Mariam, Dylan, Evelyn, and Quincy; my coworkers: Marsha, Dr. Armin, and Charlie; my childhood friend, Chazz; Rudy Tee, the landowner; Dana, my book agent; I even saw Porsha Gottfrey! There were a hundred more people that I didn't really recognize, but their faces looked familiar. In front of the pack was the one in command, the one and only, Dr. Tracz. He was standing there with open arms like he was waiting to give me a hug. The magnitude of this moment seemed unreal.

"What are all y'all DOING HERE?" I yelled loud enough so everyone in the trailer park heard it. I wasn't too excited about my old pals blowing my cover.

"We're here to help, MY BOY!" Dr. Tracz yelled with enthusiasm.

"Help WHAT?"

"Help you build a place where we can continue GREATNESS! WE CAN CONTINUE THE FUTURE!" Cheers and claps erupted from the crowd. Someone started the chanting.

"Staaa-SHEE, Staaa-SHEE, Staaa-SHEE!" They grew louder and louder. I sat there just soaking up the moment and the faces. It was like we were at a presidential rally. I looked back and saw Chloe in the doorway with her robe on, chanting and shaking her fist in sync with the crowd. I began to feel my energy level surge.

"Wait! Wait! HOLD THE PHONE ONE MINUTE! SHHHH" I put a finger to my lips to motion everyone to quiet down. "SHHH! Now look people! I'm really flattered that we've come together, and y'all have definitely made me feel like a king right now. But let's be real, we can't pull something like this off. What on God's green earth makes you think we have the resources!"

"NEVER USE THE WORD CAN'T, MISTER STASHI!" Mariam yelled. "Remember, you wrote that in your book!"

"Yeah!" Quincy interjected. "I really have ties with one of the biggest construction companies in the world. There's nothing in this world that we can't build!"

"YEAAAH!" Were the cheers from the crowd. It began to soak in, that these people were determined to make this a reality. These people were *my* people, who I had influenced and motivated positively at one point, over the course of my life. They were people ready for a change in their lives—or maybe they were just ready to change the world like I was. Perhaps they were fed up with selling themselves short.

"Look y'all, it all sounds wonderful, but let's be real, this could take years or EVEN DECADES! Y'all aren't ready to commit that kind of time or energy!"

"Yes, WE ARE!" someone yelled.

Someone started the chanting again.

"Yes! We! Are! Yes! We! Are!" I was floored. I started bobbing my head to the rhythm of the chanting.

"Y'all aren't ready to build the future and set the bar on improving the quality of life!"

"YES, WE AREEE! YESSS WE AREEE!" The chanting started back up. Everyone was riled up, yelling and screaming and clapping! I motioned for them to quiet down before I proceeded.

"Y'all aren't READY TO HELP ME BUILD STASHILAND!"

"WHOOOO!" The cheers and applause erupted like never before. The crowd was yelling at the top of their lungs. It felt like I was running for president. "YES, WE ARE! YES, WE ARE!" I waited for the chanting to cease, but it wasn't. It was just growing louder and louder. I took off the Get Stashi shirt that I was wearing and began to tie it around my crutch. Then I pulled off the rubber stopper at the bottom of the so it was only metal.

"WELL, DAMMIT!" I staked the crutch into the ground, and the shirt waved in the wind gracefully like a victory flag on a battlefield. "LET'S BUILD Stashiland THEN!"

"RAWWWWWR!" The shouting was so loud that it kind of knocked me off balance. I fell facedown on one knee. Dr. Tracz rushed to my aid. The crowd grew silent at my fall, anticipating the severity of my injury.

"Don't worry, my boy. I brought something for you." He took off his backpack and unzipped it. He pulled it out slowly and carefully. Something that I hadn't seen in ages. It sparkled when I laid eyes on its beautiful craftsmanship. One of my proudest life's work, ever, the Hoverfoot 3000. Dr. Tracz buckled it on for me and powered it on. It hummed to life. Dr. Tracz grabbed my arm and helped me back up. I bounced up and down adjusting to the gadget again. I looked down and started laughing. I began to walk fluidly again as I looked at the crowd revving up their chants and cheers again. Tears of joy began to stream down my face.

"WELL, LET'S GET STASHI THEN!"

"RAAAAWRRR! WHOOOO!"

"I DEPEND ON YOU, JUST LIKE YOU DEPEND ON ME! AND I WILL NEVER LET MY PEOPLE DOOOOOWN! WE CAN ALL WIN, IF WE JUST KEEP IT IN THIS CIRCLE! "

"WHOOOO!!"

Everyone ran up and started patting and hugging me. They hoisted me on their shoulders and began chanting "Stashi-Land" repeatedly while I bounced around in midair. I felt like I had won an election or threw the winning touchdown. I couldn't stop smiling, and I was struggling to catch my breath. It had taken so much blood, sweat, years and tears just to get to this point and surprisingly, our journey had only just begun.

This was only the beginning.

To be continued....

The Rise of The Stashi Empire

Acknowledgments

I have to acknowledge everyone who helped me mold and craft this amazing story. I want to thank God first and foremost for giving me everything I needed to create this magical body of work. The way some of these ideas and scenarios popped into my head could only be explained by a higher divine power. Next, I would like to thank Amazon.com for opening up a movie competition. It took less than 10 days to write the movie script, but it introduced so many unanswered questions. It birthed a motive to explain the backstory. The funny part is…the original movie script was never submitted. As awkward as it sounds, I also want to thank the Leon County. I never want to reflect or glorify a dark place like that, but if I hadn't done my little stint there this project would still be unfinished. The time in a place of confinement, restriction or despair can still be utilized to do amazing things. It takes focus, planning and a positive mental attitude to turn any situation around. I would also like to thank my angelic editors at WordSharp.net. I don't know how I found them, but I'm sooo thankful I did. After months of going back and forth with edits and rewrites, they have transformed this project from an ugly caterpillar into a graceful butterfly. Dotting i's and crossing t's is waaay easier said than done. The last person I want to thank is, you guessed it, ME. It might sound selfish but there was so many times I wanted to give up and didn't. I think the greatest disservice we can do in this lifetime is to not believe in ourselves wholeheartedly. Whenever the going gets rough, GET TOUGH! Thank you again for reading and please write a review online.

-DS III

About The Author

Del Simpers III is an entrepreneur from Mo. City, Texas. He is a graduate from Florida A & M University with a degree in Business Administration. His passion lies in creating inspirational music, visuals, and apparel. It took him over five years to write The Rise of the Stashi Empire. He currently resides in Houston where he is formulating the next addition in the Stashi saga.

Made in the USA
Coppell, TX
26 August 2023

20807653R10256